LOVE MISUNDERSTOOD

a novel by
Ailene Frances

This book is dedicated to all of the incurable
romantics in the world.

ONE

March 1799

She made her way down the darkened alley between build-ings that were constructed in such a way that the brilliant moon beams did not stand a chance of illuminating it. Her face laden with oversized spectacles distorting her vision and suffering from a mild case of night blindness, she did her best to steer clear of the multitude of hazardous obstacles cluttering the taxing and never ending journey to her destination.

Elizabeth wished she dared remove the cumbersome wire rimmed spectacles assaulting the bridge of her delicate nose and prominent cheekbones. Finding her way through the poorly lit streets in the dark haze of predawn London was difficult enough without being encumbered by blurred vision. They were not even her glasses. Her vision was perfect. She secretly snatched them from the estate overseer's desk just before departing to help with her disguise. Since the spindly old man kept a variety of vision assistance, from wire rimmed glasses to magnifying lenses, she doubted he would miss them.

The frame of the pair she hastily selected transformed her striking aristocratic beauty into what could only be described as common and mousy. With the hood of her unlined, coarsely wo-ven gray woolen cloak pulled low about her oval face and the oversized glasses there was little left exposed. She felt confident she would attract minimal attention from any curious onlookers she may encounter at this hour.

Elizabeth pulled her cloak tighter around her slender body, ignoring its rough assault on her tender flesh. Although the prickly fabric was not something she was accustomed to, she preferred enduring its rough touch to the bitter wind whipping through the abandoned alley. It felt abnormally cold for this time of year. Or, maybe it was not the weather. Maybe the weather was normal and she was colder than usual for another reason. Could it be from her fear of the being discovered before she was able to carry out her plans? Or, possibly her anticipation of what was to come?

Her pale yellow slippers, adorned with rows of multicolored beading blended to create a beautiful peacock, provided a flimsy walk. Their delicate constitution was certainly no match for the thick muck coating the final stretch of the dark, dank alley. Elizabeth heaved a sigh. She had almost maneuvered her way through the perilous debris permeating her path without a mishap. She was so near. Now, she would be presented to the good Doctor Jameson with the all too questionable and unpleasantly thick goo coating a great deal of her slippers.

She should have taken the time to steal a more serviceable pair of shoes from one of the servants. When secretly preparing her costume for her big escape, she completely forgot about her footwear. Not only were her slippers not serviceable, they were far too fashionable in comparison to the rest of her attire. Elizabeth shook her head. She was reduced to stealing. She hated thieves. It was a thief who caused the death of her mother and father.

Her eighth birthday had barely passed when the courier arrived with the horrific news that her parents were killed during a robbery while en-route to court. Nine years later, Elizabeth still recalled that fateful morning as if it was only yesterday.

The soft, orange glow of the rising sun was just climbing up from behind the tips of the tree lined hillside and silken droplets of morning dew blanketed the estate's garden when the courier's horse pranced into their courtyard. Only a few of the servants were up and about. The absence of activity accentuated the loud echo of his lathered horse's hooves on the cobblestone.

Already awake, she clearly heard the courier's heavy pounding against the solid oak entry door directly below her open window.

The messenger had foregone using the wrought iron eagle's head door knocker, not trusting it to be loud enough to alert the residence of his presence at such an early hour.

Her room was positioned in the center of the second floor directly above the great hall. Although she could easily hear the muffled chaos the news caused, she was unable to make out the actual words being spoken.

She assumed the sense of dread she felt was over leaving the warmth of her cozy bed before the revival of a fire in the hearth could transform the cold stone floors and horsehair plastered walls into the welcoming haven she knew and loved. She sunk deeper beneath the folds of her thick coverings and watched the mist from her breath dissipate into the air like little puff clouds. It would not be long before someone would be in to stoke up the fire-place and she could inquire about the courier's disrupting visit. He was probably sent by a neighboring lord or lady in need of her father's ministering, not realizing her parents were on their way to court.

When the door opened it was not a servant with a bucket of hot coals for her fire who entered, it was her governess, Isabelle. Her reluctance was apparent as she shared the shocking news that would change Elizabeth's life forever.

Elizabeth's family spent her early years living blissfully in the country, with her father traveling back and forth to court as summoned. Both he and her mother loved the peaceful beauty of country living. But, when King George's health noticeably started to fail, it was her father's duty, as the senior royal physician, to be available at all times; something that could not be accomplished unless they took up residence in the king's court.

Elizabeth had developed a nasty head cold after disobediently playing in the light rain of an evening and chilling her body to the bone. Her brother, Herald, caught it from Elizabeth almost immediately.

Aware the king would frown upon the family arriving at court with two sick children but unable to delay their trip long enough to allow the children to recover their health, her parents reluctantly left their little darlings with in the care of Isabelle. The children were to join their parents as soon as they were healthy enough to be presented at court. That never happened. Instead, they were whisked off to London to live with their mother's brother, Lord Cyrus Roberts.

A childless widow with minimal inclination toward warmth and expression where Elizabeth was concerned, Lord Roberts provided her with her basic needs minus affection and love.

Elizabeth looked at the starless sky. The only hint of illumination came from the tiny sliver of the moon as it prepared to change places with the rising sun. Soot and smoke shot relentlessly from London's multitude of chimneys of all shapes and sizes as they were fired up in preparation for the day's cooking.

She wished it was easier to see her surroundings. She would have at least liked to know more about the goo that clung to her appendages before she continued on. Better yet, she would have liked to find a means of cleaning it off.

She was so busy musing about the goo on her feet she didn't realize she reached her destination until the alley was at a sudden end. Looking as far into her surrounds as she could, she slipped from the alley and made her way up the front steps of a large, red brick townhouse.

Lifting the ornate, solid brass knocker from the thick walnut door was no easy feat. She used both hands to wrestle the heavy, formidable looking lion's head far enough away from its cradle to produce an adequate sound when she released it. When a small aperture in the door, no more than six inches wide and two inches high, slid open within seconds after dropping the brass knocker she found herself staring into squinting bloodshot eyes that hinted of the blue luster of a youth gone by.

"Declare yourself!" bellowed a strong, steady voice.

"'Tis Lady Elizabeth Nottingham, sir. I come to see Doctor Jameson," she replied far more confidently than she felt.

His gruff tone did nothing to soothe her already frazzled nerves. The silence seemed deafening while she waited, for what seemed like eternity, for the heavy door to slowly pull open.

"He is running behind, miss. I shall show you where to wait. Pray follow me and do not dawdle," the steward stated in an authoritative tone.

There was something oddly familiar about his tall, gangly features as well as the way he carried his narrow frame. She eyed him briefly before sliding through the small opening he allowed between the door and its frame before he was able to heave the thick wooden mass fully open.

Once inside she immediately noted how his house coat was unusually grand for a member of the staff, even if he was in a position of authority. She found him frightfully intimidating. He was an easy twelve inches taller than she, forcing Elizabeth to tilt her head back when she smiled up at him in an attempt to soften his demeanor. Perhaps a little warmth sent his way would melt away some of his gruffness.

"Kindly refrain from smiling at me in that fashion, miss. It shan't fetch the doctor any faster for you," he huffed. "Now, pick your feet up and make haste."

Elizabeth was not only shocked by his impudence in addressing her, but surprised by the perfect diction in which the man spoke. This was an unusual thing to find within a servant's class. She considered questioning him about his perfect diction and fine dress but the thought passed as quickly as it came when they simultaneously looked down at the mention of her feet.

A mixture of a loud cluck, a squeal of dismay, and a gasp of horror escaped his lips with such fervor as to wake the dead, "What? Where have you been? You cannot come in like that, miss! The master will be furious if I allow you to track in that... What is it?"

Elizabeth's agony over the condition of her slippers renewed as she lifted one foot and then the other. They were far worse than she imagined.

"I really cannot say," she replied. "'Twas quite dark in the alley."

"The alley? You traveled through the alley?" The old man made a loud 'humph'. "Well, whatever it is, pray remove it promptly."

He clapped his hands briskly and within seconds a slight,

young housemaid who looked to be about Elizabeth's age appeared carrying a thick rag.

Elizabeth assumed she must have been standing in the shadows. How else would she know I was in need of a cleaning rag?

As if reading her mind, the old man blurted out, "This is Sally. She carries that confounded rag with her wherever she goes. This is the first time it has come in so handy."

"I dare say," Sally exclaimed when her eyes settled on Elizabeth's slippers.

Elizabeth looked at Sally's weary expression and sighed. She thought how sad it was that the poor girl was summoned before her normal waking hour because of her dirty feet.

Being a woman who valued her sleep, the knowledge that she robbed the young housemaid of precious minutes of her much needed rest filled Elizabeth with remorse. Now the obviously overworked servant girl would probably be dragging around all day while she struggled to complete her duties. If only she had been more careful where she was stepping.

Trying to ease some of her guilt, Elizabeth smiled warmly at the tired looking wench. This resulted in the young woman blushing and looking away. The rose hue crawling up her cheeks brought out a hidden sparkle for the briefest moment before it slipped away into the abyss of her emotionless green eyes.

"What are you doing?" The old man roared. "Leave the wench to her business. I shall inform the doctor you have arrived." He glowered at Sally, "I trust you shall rectify this situation post haste."

"Yes, Master John," Sally timidly replied while she diligently scrubbed at the disgusting goo that clung stubbornly and threatening to destroy Elizabeth's expertly crafted, satin slippers. As she did so, the colorful beads in the pattern of peacocks fell loose and rolled across the meticulously scrubbed slate floor. "Oh, miss, I am so sorry. Your slippers are ruined for sure."

Elizabeth barely realized Sally's dilemma as she pondered the manner in which the servant addressed the steward. Master John? Surely a man servant, even the steward, would not be addressed in such a manner. Would he?

"Sally," Elizabeth's voice was barely audible. "Who was that man?"

"'Twas Master John, miss," Sally answered just as softly.

Sally stole a moment to steel closer look at Elizabeth. Young ladies rarely called upon the Jameson household, and certainly never without escort in the pre-dawn. Her clothing was that of a servant, but the steadiness of her violet, almond shaped eyes spoke of a woman who was sure of herself. Her skin glowed with health and her soft, supple hands had surely never seen a day's work. No, this young miss was no servant. Although for the life of her, Sally could not figure her out.

"What does he do here?" Elizabeth asked, oblivious to Sally's musing.

"Why miss, he's the steward, miss. He's in charge of the others in the house," Sally responded with obvious confusion.

"You called him master, did you not?" Elizabeth's tone was mildly impatient.

"Aye, I did that, miss," Sally replied.

"Why?" Elizabeth asked.

Sally looked dumbfounded.

"'Why, I don't rightly know, miss," Sally said in earnest. 'Tis the way I was told to address him since the time I first arrived. I never questioned it, miss."

"Why did he answer the door? The house has a footman, does it not?" Elizabeth continued.

"Aye, miss, several," Sally replied.

Although Sally answered the questions as were presented, it was clear she preferred to be allowed to just do her job.

"Then why..." Elizabeth shook her head. It was obvious the housemaid would be of no assistance in clarifying John's role. "I find this very strange, very strange indeed."

Sally kept her head bowed toward the floor to hide a smile. She found it humorous that a lady who arrived at her master's residence in the wee hours of the morning with her fancy slippers covered in some sort of disgusting goo, no escort, and dressed in a costume that obviously belonged to a woman far beneath her station would find anything going on in the household strange.

Before Elizabeth could ponder more about John, he returned and impatiently motioned her to follow him into a receiving room at the far end of the hall. She was not accustomed to being treated thus by servants, but held her tongue. Taking into consideration the fact that her costume belonged to one of her house maids, it was understandable that she would be taken for a woman of a lesser station. It just proved her disguise worked. If she was to get out of London undetected, no one except her new guardian, the good Doctor Jameson, should know her true identity.

The rustling of a young, fragile looking servant girl rousing from her slumber caught Elizabeth's attention. She peered into the small cupboard beneath the stairs as she walked by just in time to be captured by a pair of large brown sleep infused eyes that spoke of the hardship of a servant's life in eighteenth century England.

Taken aback by the stark reality of the girl's situation, Elizabeth thought of how different her own life might have been had she not been born into society. An orphan never fared well. Even in her position of privilege, her life lacked one of the most important necessities for happiness. Love.

Her uncle, an earl by birth, reluctantly took on the task of caring for Elizabeth and her brother after the death of his sister. He made it abundantly clear fairly early in their relationship that he preferred a different arrangement, but he refused to provide more gossip. His sister's rebellious ways managed to create plenty.

Lord Roberts made certain Elizabeth was well fed and impeccably dressed. He saw to it that she received the best education available for young women. He hired the best governesses and tutors that money could buy. He even provided her opportunities to do some light travel about England in order to broaden her view of their country.

Sadly, his heart stayed forever locked to her.

Elizabeth's mother, Lady Vanessa Roberts, shocked her family and society by rejecting the man of her parent's choice. She ran away and secretly married for love instead of openly marrying for wealth and status. To make matters worse, Vanessa married below her station to a man of middle class society.

Ironically, both of Vanessa's parents died of consumption not long after her shocking announcement of her marriage to a bright and promising young doctor. No ministering by the family physician or their new doctor son-in-law could reverse the course of the illness that ultimately claimed them. Rumor spread quickly that the Roberts were driven to their grave by their daughter's shocking display of rebellion. Surely the consumption would never have consumed them had they not lost their will to live from the shame of their daughter's actions. Years later, whispers could still be heard amongst the more rigid members of the ton.

Although Vanessa's new husband, Thomas Nottingham, worked hard to develop an earnest reputation of being the best physician in London and even earned the respect and eye of King George, Cyrus would not move past the fact that his sister publicly shamed the family by marrying him. Even the king's gifting Thomas with the title of knighthood, a grand estate in the country, and a generous fortune did not change her uncle's stubbornness. Cyrus harbored the bitter belief that the nuptial between Vanessa and the noble imposter was what drove his parents to their death.

The only son and heir to their parent's fortune, Cyrus denied Vanessa her rightful inheritance and any recognition as family, even though to look at them you could not deny the connection. His obstinacy continued until her husband's increased status with the king forced him to do otherwise. He may have eventually relented and given over Vanessa's inheritance, but he never truly befriended Thomas and there was a strain between brother and sister right up to the day she died.

Elizabeth's brother, Herald, as per the customs and laws of their country, inherited their parent's estate immediately upon their death. Three years her junior, the estate remained in trust with the law office of Simon and Jameson until Herald reached his sixteenth birthday. Elizabeth was left with a small fortune with the majority of it to act as a dowry. She was allowed to draw from it a small allowance for the day to day needs that were not met by her uncle while in his care.

She often wondered if her uncle would have been different toward her if she had been lucky like Herald and inherited her mother's fair hair, ruddy complexion and crystal blue eyes. Herald so resembled their uncle that those who were not aware of the circumstances often thought Cyrus was indeed the boy's true father. Cyrus favored the boy with so much affection that those unfamiliar with the situation would naturally mistake him for the boy's father.

She often pondered her uncle's disgusted reaction when he first laid eyes on her, 'Would that you would have taken after the Roberts, girl. Ye have your father's thick and unruly raven curls and perpetually rosy cheeks. Your skin may be that of your mothers, but those deep violet eyes are not of our bloodline. We have clear blue eyes. 'Tis your father's blood that dominates ye, child. All I see from your mother are the deep dimples in both cheeks and your petite and rather fragile looking physique. 'Tis a disappointment, to say the least.'

The fact that she would never feel the love that was showered upon her brother simply because she looked like her father was a painful realization to come to terms with. She often reminded herself how many girls in her situation found themselves in far less desirable circumstances and accepted the care he provided with humble gratitude. In fact, she was the model niece right up until the night he held a small, yet extravagant dinner party where he surprised her by announcing her engagement to the man she found herself seated next to all evening.

Elizabeth shuddered as she recalled the mixture of looks on the faces of the distinguished men and elegant ladies when her uncle stood at the end of the table that was laden with an abundant display of meats and fruits and raised his cup of newly imported coffee in a toast to the future nuptials of his niece and Lord Stephen Carlson. Some shone with admiration while others –primarily those of the ladies- displayed jealousy and envy.

Seated a little too snugly next to her, Lord Carlson immediately placed his hand over hers in a somewhat timid, yet possessive, manner while he smiled and nodded in response to the guest's applause and well wishes.

Could he detect her surprise? For surprised she was.

Stunned in fact.

Her uncle never even consulted with her on his decision. Was she not allowed even the slightest bit of say in respect to her future? Uncertain what to do, Elizabeth simply sat in her chair and stared at the oversized finely etched silver platter in the center of the table. It bore the weight of an enormous venison roast surrounded by baked apples, cherries and pears.

Having lived with her desires and wishes ignored since the fateful day her parents died, Elizabeth spent her years fantasizing about meeting a man who would love and adore her. She wanted a husband who would care about her needs, thoughts, and feelings. Most of all she wanted to marry for love. She clearly remembered the happiness and love her parents shared and longed to have the same for herself.

She knew very little about the man to whom she was just publicly promised other than he stood about a foot taller than she and sported a handsome mustache when first they'd met; which he since shaved off. He possessed steel gray eyes that reached deep into a person's soul when he looked at you. When he smiled, women -herself included- tended to become weak-kneed. But, was this enough to make her want to marry him and spend the rest of her life with him? Hardly!

Having just returned from the colonies, Lord Stephen Carlson was the talk of London society, as well as one of its most sought after bachelors in the ton. Thirteen years Elizabeth's senior, he sailed from England in search of adventure fifteen years prior and returned only recently at the request of his father, who suffered from an acute breathing affliction.

The heir to a dukedom with an estate that could rival that of a king's, Stephen set his affairs abroad aside and dutifully assumed the role of estate master. Within days over his father's badly neglected duties were in his competent hands.

Elizabeth considered her plight. Most women would have

swooned with delight at the prospect of becoming Lady Carlson. After all, Lord Carlson would one day be amongst the most influential men in England. His tall, muscular frame filled out his jacket and breeches in a way that was certainly pleasing to the eye. His ruddy complexion, chiseled jaw, and steel gray eyes -that were accentuated by sun-kissed auburn hair that looked as if it might become dark brown if left without exposure to the sun for any length of time- could certainly take one's breath away. On the rare occasions when he donned a wig, it seemed to accentuate his magnetism. Yes, any woman would consider herself fortunate indeed to become the wife of Lord Stephen Carlson.

But, she was not any woman.

After living for the past nine years as the ward of a man who could not, or would not, open his heart to her, she was determined not to spend the rest of her life in a loveless marriage. Remembering how happy her parents were together and knowing they defied convention and married for love, she promised herself she would do the same. She fully in-tended to honor that promise.

It did not matter to her that Stephen Carlson was to inherit a king's fortune. Nor did she care about the impressive fortune he reputedly acquired on his own while abroad. It did not matter to her that she would one day become a duchess with grand households at her disposal, both in England and abroad. It did not matter to her that this marriage gave her an opportunity to redeem the family name that had been sullied -in the eyes of her uncle and some stiff-lipped members of the ton at least- by her mother's actions. It did not matter to her that he was extremely handsome and vigorous. It did not matter to her that his adventures abroad left him with a charismatic air of mystique. What did matter was that he acted cold, reserved. He was clearly incapable of loving her the way she wanted to be loved.

The way she needed to be loved.

The way she dreamed of being loved her whole life.

Since Stephen returned to England less than a fortnight ago -after an absence of almost a decade-, Elizabeth found herself in his company on multiple occasions. They were first introduced at

Molly Regent's party and spent the briefest of time discussing the weather. Both were guests of the Countess Weston in her private box at the theater where they found themselves seated scandalously close during a performance of William Shakespeare's Comedy of Errors.

Although Elizabeth found Lord Carlson's good looks and the fact that he did not follow the trend of wearing makeup to enhance his features appealing, and their conversation proved entertainingly light and trivial, she was wary of the unfamiliar hot and fluttery sensation she felt in the pit of her stomach whenever he was near. Having grown up lacking the privilege of being allowed a circle of friends like youngest girls of her social status enjoyed, she had nary a confidant to explain these occurrences and was forced to resort to her own reasoning. Since the feeling left her confused and uncomfortable, she determined it must be bad. Since Lord Carlson was the instigator of these bad emotions and sensations, he too must be bad.

Stephen called upon her uncle on numerous occasions after her initial introduction to him. Each time he spent most of his visit barricaded behind the thick walnut doors that secured her uncle's private study from prying eyes and ears. He was sometimes in the company of just her uncle and other times joined by a few of his business associates. After the meetings dispersed, Stephen religiously made his way into the parlor where he spent the briefest of moments with her in trivial conversations followed by awkward silence.

Elizabeth noted how their private interactions were in stark contrast to the animated, light hearted interaction she experienced during their public meetings. Since they both traveled in the same social circle, she took this menial, uncomfortable attention as the ever popular and socially conscious Lord Carlson merely fulfilling an obligation of being polite before taking his leave. Never, in her wildest dreams, would she have considered he was courting her.

When her uncle shocked her by publicly announcing he agreed to give her hand in marriage to this aloof man who left her uncomfortably unsettled whenever he was near without even discussing it with her prior, she wanted to scream and run from the dinner table.

Of course, social etiquette would not allow it.

Life was a tortured blur during the few short months that led up to her wedding day. During this time, the visits from her fiancé dwindled in length and frequency, which suited her just fine.

Her governess, Madeleine Hardy, already completed the term of her contract, but agreed to remain in residence as Elizabeth's companion and waiting maid. She was also to act on behalf of Elizabeth's deceased mother by assisting her with the selection of her gown and trousseau.

Madeleine was a mere ten years Elizabeth's senior. Having been raised the daughter of a gentleman before her father's death necessitated she take up a position as governess, she dove into the task with excited zeal. She was so excited by the events that she failed to recognize how Elizabeth did not share one ounce of her enthusiasm.

For Elizabeth, her days were spent in despair. Was there no one who understood or shared her sense of over-whelming loss and confinement?

She was pondering just this fact while shopping for ribbons to match the new silk brocade she commissioned to be made into a morning robe. She was walking down Market Street when she ran into a very old colleague of her father's, Dr. Jameson.

Although her uncle Cyrus cared little for the distinguished doctor, her father had been a close friend. In fact, her father thought so highly of the Jameson family as a whole, Dr. Jameson's brother -the Jameson in the law firm of Simon and Jameson- was entrusted to manage their inheritance until they came of age.

Dr. Jameson took it upon himself to visit the earl's home and inquire on Elizabeth and Herald's wellbeing on more than one occasion. The fondness the young woman and the old doctor developed for each other was a result of these visits.

"My dear, I understand you are to be wed to Lord Stephen Carlson," Dr. Jameson bowed enthusiastically before taking her hands in his. "He is to inherit a dukedom, is he not? Well done, I say. Well done."

So pleased was she to be in the company of this comforting older man, Elizabeth easily excused the fact that he ignored the latest fashion trend of a clean shaven face and sported an outdated waxed salt and pepper mustache and goatee and an overly powdered, ill fitted wig that sat mildly askew on his head. His attempt to follow the trend to enhance his features with a little makeup here and there proved entirely unflattering and could easily be labeled gaudy. The combination of such gave him a comical appearance. Despite his ill fitted appearance, Elizabeth's eyes shone with genuine friendship. She was completely oblivious to the stares of passersby.

Her old friend's brows knit together with concern while he listened to Elizabeth stammer her gratitude for his well wishes. This was not the excitement of a young woman about to be married. Upon closer study, he could see how her normally rosy cheeks were paled and her usually brilliant, deep violet eyes looked dull and hallow. Could she be unwell?

Feeling the need to confide in someone, Elizabeth accepted the doctor's offer to join him for coffee. Fortunately, they were not far from one of the few coffee houses in London inclined to entertain women.

The rich aroma of freshly ground coffee beans tantalized her senses as she allowed the doctor to escort her to a more secluded table toward the back of the dimly lit room. She motioned Madeleine to place herself in a distant yet suitable location away from them, allowing her some privacy before entering into the doctor's confidence.

During a lengthy conversation, over freshly brewed coffee lightened with lightly browned sweet cream and complemented with sweet almond biscuits, Elizabeth expressed her despair about her uncle's promise for her to wed without even so much as a whisper to her prior to announcing it publicly. She felt even though her uncle adequately attended to her basic needs, he had not considered her feelings since that fateful day her parents died and she became his ward. She was positive the match between herself and Lord Stephen Carlson was intended to serve the earl's ego and political station far more than it was to serve her happiness and wellbeing.

Having been denied the privilege of marrying the love of his early years due to her improper station in society, Lord Michael Jameson opted to remain a bachelor and all but walked away from mixing and mingling with the nobility. He dove into science and medicine as a means to help him heal is broken heart. Yes, he fully related to Elizabeth's desire to marry for love and, yes, he certainly understood how she might feel her uncle was simply trying to unload her at the first opportunity to the highest bidder. After all, a girl of seventeen with a hefty inheritance and respectful allowance could certainly not be considered someone destined to become an undesirable spinster and was hardly a burden to her ward. Surely Lord Roberts could have waited a bit longer and have allowed his young ward the opportunity to fall in love.

Elizabeth's dissatisfaction with her uncle and her situation was a boon for the quirky doctor. He saw before him a golden opportunity. For some time, he'd longed to travel and explore the recently emancipated colonies. Alas, being the middle son and not heir to the family's wealth, he could not fund such a journey. Since his brother was in charge of Elizabeth's inheritance until she married, he was privy to certain information and was well aware that she had the means fund a trip around the world several times.

Since the girl fully intended to run from her present situation and start life anew, why not really run? Why not venture somewhere the earl would never think to look?

With great enthusiasm, the doctor used his persuasive abilities and painted a picture of freedom and happiness like no other with his description of the newly formed country. A country founded on the preface of freedom.

Elizabeth had not really thought of traveling far away from the only home she ever knew, especially as far away as across the ocean. She had never been to sea. To travel across the expansive ocean to a land as raw as that of the colonies was a frightening concept to her. There was a copious amount of whispers in good society concerning the barbarians who fought against the king's army alongside half-naked natives. It was reported they even practiced slavery, something that was no longer done in civilized countries. The colonies the doctor described sounded nothing like the barbaric land the gossip so vividly portrayed. When he reminded her that the very refined and respected Lord Stephen Carlson, the very man her uncle chose for her to wed, spent the last decade of his life there, she agreed it must indeed be the kind of land he was describing to her. It truly must be the land of new beginnings and freedom.

The picture the good doctor painted for Elizabeth made the newly emancipated country sound like a dream come true. Noting that a trip of this magnitude would prove costly, she agreed to fund their travel as long as he took care of the arrangements and acted as her escort for not only the duration of the trip, but also once they reached land.

The doctor assured her it would be an honor and a privilege to become her guardian until she met and fell in love with the man of her dreams. He urged her to tell no one of their plans. Her uncle was an influential man and the Carlson's equally so, if not greater. Should their plans be discovered before they were executed, the consequences could be far too dire to even whisper about.

They parted company with the promise to meet again within the week. Both walked with a lighter foot. Both moved with an air of excitement. They had a plan. For Dr. Michael Jameson it represented the adventure of a lifetime. For Lady Elizabeth Nottingham it held freedom and the promise of a new life with love and happiness.

****

"Beyond the pale, girl, tell me you did not come alone!" Dr. Michael Jameson bellowed as he entered the room with his steward, John, close at heel.

The genuine petulant fretfulness expressed in the doctor's

voice as he strode across the thickly woven wool carpet and took his seat in an overstuffed, green tapestry chair startled Elizabeth. She had not witnessed this side of her old friend during his short visits over the years. He had always been jovial and warm while telling her stories of when he and her father were young doctors making their way in the world.

"Why, yes I did," she replied stoically.

"Now, why would you do something so bloody stupid? Why, 'tis unheard of! Do you not know how dangerous the streets are at night? And... devil take me... what nonsense did I hear? You came through the alley?"

They were about to embark on the adventure of a lifetime and he was nervous and decidedly anxious. The last thing he needed was undue stress upon his aging countenance because of the thoughtless actions of this young woman.

"'Twas faster sir," Elizabeth replied hesitantly.

Hearing her response to the doctor's fury, Elizabeth, regrettably, had to agree with him. What had she been thinking? His reaction to her thoughtless method of travel was surprisingly vivid. What would he say if he knew the rest? Dare she tell him she confided, just a little, to Madeleine about her plans and the fool woman turned her in? Dare she admit that her uncle insisted on marrying her immediately to Lord Carlson in order to avoid yet another family scandal? Dare she tell him she had been Lady Carlson for well over a week?

She dared not.

"I thought it best to keep as few people as possible in-formed of our plans, thus I did not hire a carriage and took a route that would prove speedy and require less walking. I am sorry if I upset you, sir," she replied as she looked at the floor.

She suddenly felt quite foolish.

"No matter, dear child," the doctor sighed. He seemed to re-alize his harshness and put his temper in check. Returning to the man she knew so well, he continued, "You are probably right on that account. The less informed the better. Even a cabbie knowing your whereabouts could prove a risk. 'Tis a might scandalous an act we are up to, I dare say." He shook his head, allowed a broad smile to consume his face, and chuckled, "'Tis indeed an adventure."

"Indeed," snorted John, seemingly not enthused. "One that could cost you dearly, you, old fool. You are very likely sailing to the heathen colonies to be scalped or worse."

Elizabeth raised a brow in surprise at the unusual familiarity Dr. Jameson's man servant used while in his company. Noticing her reaction, her new guardian threw his head back in hearty laughter.

"Lady Elizabeth Nottingham, might I introduce my brother, Sir John Jameson? I realize you have met, but I am certain you were not properly introduced."

John bowed low, concealing his amusement as best he could.

"Your brother," Elizabeth gasped, "but, I thought..."

"Yes, and you are correct. He does indeed serve as the household steward," Dr. Jameson chuckled. "Not because he needs to, mind you. In fact, he is my eldest brother. The family fortune," the doctor swept his arm around the room, "this house, and all that is in it belongs to him. No, he does it not out of necessity, but out of desire. For some unfathomable reason, he enjoys playing the role of my man servant."

"Quite right," John nodded enthusiastically as he did his best to conceal his amusement.

"How very strange," Elizabeth mused.

"Indeed," the doctor agreed.

Somehow Elizabeth did not feel she was privy to the entire story, but she accepted their explanation. For the moment, there were more important issues to tend to. John's strange behavior could be addressed at a later time, if it was to be addressed at all.

"Am I correct in understanding that you stepped in a rather strange substance while journeying here?" her host asked.

"Yes, I am so very sorry. It was extremely difficult to see my way tonight." Upon noticing the dark look returning to the doctor's face, Elizabeth checked her words, "Your house maid did her best to get most of it off to avoid my tracking it through the house.

I am sorry to say my slippers did not fare well, but I believe nothing was tracked in."

"I am not as worried about you mucking up my house as much I am about you infecting yourself. These alleys are full of disease. I shall have a bath set up for you. Sally will help. We shall burn those clothes. The wardrobe I ordered for you arrived yesterday. Select a sensible travel costume after you have cleaned up and meet me in the dining room. We shall have a light fare before heading down to the docks." He stood up to leave, "I beg you do not dawdle, my dear child. I have no doubt that they will be looking for you at first light. We must make haste if we are to accomplish this."

Fortunately for all concerned, Elizabeth had not discussed the whole of her plans to Madeleine and Dr. Jameson's identity was spared. Knowing the good doctor as she felt she did, she was certain he would not have followed through with their plans had he realized that she was already wed to the very man she sought his help to escape. She decided that it was best to keep that fact a secret until after they set sail for the emancipated colonies.

TWO

Stephen leaned against the ship's weathered rail and made a mental note of its need for maintenance while he watched the English shore transform into a tiny, thin line that looked about to fall off the edge of the ocean's waters. It was good to be back on the open sea, even if it was under such unhappy circumstances. Sailing always made him feel free and alive. It was a feeling he especially craved after the heartache and trauma the last few months provided.

The stuffiness of London society was in stark contrast to the freedom of his life in the raw and newly formed United States. Even if he had not learned of his bride's voyage to the new world, he would have returned to it eventually. His bride's outrageous antics provided him with the excuse to do so earlier, and with his father's blessings.

Upon summons of his ailing father Stephen returned to England immediately, although reluctantly. The affairs of his family's estate were in turmoil and he was required at home to assist. The duke was unwell and his physicians were unable to diagnose the cause of his ever worsening breathing ailment. To add to the upheaval, the overseer, Mr. Eversmith, suffered a tragic fall from his mount while chasing poachers off their land and died from a broken neck. With his father bedridden and the overseer deceased, the lands and management of the estate were in dire need of attention. His mother's letter begged him to make haste in returning to assume his father's duties as the duke of their grand lands, even if he had yet to inherit the title.

Concerned that his son was still unwed and the possibility that he may not see the birth of the future of his bloodline, the duke made inquiries about eligible young ladies for his son. He finally settled on the daughter of Sir Thomas Nottingham.

Although born a merchant's son, Nottingham had been a distinguished physician who caught the king's eye and was awarded a title and a fortune. He also managed to marry into an old and established family, which took away a considerable amount of the sting of his less than noble birth. Whatever the girl lacked in pedigree, she made up for with her delicate, aristocratic beauty and sizable dowry. The Duke was taken by the way wisps of dark, unruly hair framing her delicate oval face. It accentuated her deep violet eyes, prominent cheekbones and thick, lush lips. She proved well-schooled in etiquette, displaying ever the demure and well-bred lady whenever seen in public. Although slight in frame, she seemed hearty enough. Inquiries provided nary a report of illness to her credit. Yes, Elizabeth Nottingham would do nicely to add to the duke's legacy, very nicely indeed.

Along with the identity of his choice of brides, Stephen's father provided him with a brief history of her family. As the only surviving heir to the family's mercantile business, Thomas Nottingham inherited at an early age after his mother, father, sister and brother were stricken by a gripping illness that took hold of their bodies and possession of their lives so quickly there was no time to diagnose, let alone treat the horrendous affliction. When Thomas returned from a buying trip, he discovered he was not only an orphan, but the new owner of a business he cared little about. Grief stricken, he decided to sell the business and study medicine. He was determined to become the best in the medical field so he could help prevent what happened to his family from happening to others. His choice in vocations proved to be a very wise decision. Skilled as a physician and eager to progress in life and make himself worthy to stand beside the woman who stepped down in her station the day she agreed to be his wife, Thomas managed to catch the King's eye and affection enough to be awarded a knighthood and a rather extensive estate. To this he added his own considerable inheritance. Out of this estate, Elizabeth stood to receive a respectable fortune upon her wedding day. The duke felt these factors far outweighed the scandal of her parent's defiant elopement.

The earl's description of Lady Elizabeth to the duke was that of a dutiful, young woman who was well schooled in the social graces and worldly events. Although he would sometimes witness an occasional high spirit not suitable of a lady –no doubt inherited from her father's common side- he was certain was well influenced by proper society and educated enough to be a model wife, mother, and head of household to compensate for any undesirable residue that may have remained within her common breeding.

Stephen wrestled with telling his father he developed an acquaintance with a socialite in the colonies. She was a striking southern belle from the plantation nearest his in Georgia. He found her witty as well as lovely to look at. He was considering courting her prior to being summoned to return home. It even crossed his mind to court her in spite of the summons.

After much thought, he decided against it. He knew that once his father made a decision of such magnitude, he would not be prone to change it. There was also the fact that, even though she was not of the purest pedigree, the Lady Elizabeth Nottingham was still of a higher and much more acceptable station for the taste of British society than Miss Paulette Moore. This was something a future Duke needed to keep in mind.

Stephen sighed and braced himself for the inevitable. He would have to shift his attentions from the fiery warmth of his beautiful and charming southern belle who he had grown quite fond of to the cold aloofness of a prim and proper English gentlewoman whom he knew nothing about, but had somehow passed the scrutiny of his father enough to be selected as his bride. Such an undertaking might take a bit of getting used to.

Keenly aware that neither the earl nor his father's description of Elizabeth included beauty, Stephen appealed to be allowed to view her on a few occasions without her knowledge of their intended nuptials. He explained that he wished to see her in her own element when she was not necessarily at her best behavior as a woman might be should a man be courting her. To himself he admitted that if she was not comely -which he assumed she was not- he would like to be prepared for that fact and have time to adjust to the sacrifice he would be making for his family's sake. It would also afford him the opportunity to discover what it was about the young chit that gave his father cause to overlook her less than perfect pedigree and acceptance into the family. It was a puzzlement that weighed heavy on him.

Had he not been absent from London society for such a long time, Stephen would have been aware of Lady Elizabeth's rich, exotic beauty and witnessed her impeccable manners and perfect etiquette during the many events she attended since her coming out ball. Taking into consideration the ten years that Stephen was away from London society while residing in a primitive land, Earl Roberts humored him and granted his odd request. Besides, there was the matter of the marital contract to be worked out before they could even think of going public with such an announcement. A marriage was a serious business venture and need not be rushed. He would allow Lord Carlson the time he requested to observe his niece, although an odd request it was.

Stephen was invited to several events where he was able to interact with Elizabeth. Although his young bride-to-be was far more reserved thank his fiery southern belle, Miss Paulette Moore, she still displayed a warmth and innocent zest for life that Stephen had not anticipated and was extremely pleased to discover. As a bonus, and much to his relief, he found her beauty to exceed any of the women he ever laid eyes on, including Miss Paulette.

I all his travels he had never seen such a combination of porcelain skin, rosy cheeks, rich violet eyes, and thick, carefree raven hair on a petite, perfectly proportioned female body. The fact that she appeared fragile, but healthy, only served to make her even more appealing.

He found her irresistible.

It took every ounce of his strength and reserve to hold back and not declare his love for her the moment he was introduced at the Regent's party. Knowing she was his betrothed, he struggled vehemently with the jealousy that swelled within him each time he watched her dance with the most eligible gents in the room. Never before had he found his emotions so difficult to keep in check.

The tortuous delight of being seated so near Elizabeth during the opera Countess Westbury invited him to almost proved to be Stephen's undoing. Upon a few stolen glances in the countess's direction, he could have sworn he caught a fleeting look of amusement on the Countess's gracefully aged face before she pulled it into check. Was her amusement at his expense? Did she realize his torture? He would put nothing past the bored aristocracy that was always in search of some small amusement to help them get through their days.

The terms of marriage negotiations with the earl were decidedly more complex than Stephen would have expected. He heard whispers here and there that Earl Roberts found caring for his niece troublesome and tedious. Wagging tongues insisted that the earl would have much preferred taking on the care of his nephew and being spared that of his niece. When his negotiations with Stephen proved in favor of his niece's future wellbeing, it came as a great surprise.

Although the earl's demands were fair and just, they took time to arrange. This caused a delay in the announcement of their intended nuptials, which was something Stephen found regretfully tortuous. He would have much preferred to have London know the beautiful Lady Elizabeth would soon belong to him. He particularly wanted to flaunt this fact to the wolf-like gents who flocked around her at every public event she attended.

Stephen found his meetings with Lord Roberts difficult to endure when he knew Elizabeth was somewhere under the same roof. He struggled with a burning longing to be sitting in her company and would have agreed to anything to shorten the meetings to be free to seek her out. Much to the earl's delight, he practically did.

It was common for women to seek the company of Lord Stephen Carlson and he found them easy to entertain. It was because of this fact that he was so frustrated when he finally had the opportunity to be alone with the beautiful Lady Elizabeth and could not summons his manly charms. He thought her lovely and delicate;

like an exotic bird. For some unknown reason, he could not shake the gnawing fear that his exotic bird might fly away. Her overall effect on him was overwhelming and he inevitably became embarrassingly and uncharacteristically over-heated and tongue-tied. Within minutes of seating himself in the room with her all wittiness and gifts of conversation left him. Frustrated by his boyish behavior, he found himself making excuses to shorten his stay and escape to the welcoming embrace of the fresh air outside.

Immediately upon his first encounter with Elizabeth, he realized how ridiculous his request to have their arrangement kept secret was. He loved her from the minute he set eyes on her. When the earl finally surprised him and announced their engagement during the intimate dinner party, Stephen's heart almost leapt from his body with excitement and anticipation. Without thinking, he placed his hand over hers in open display of affection.

The cold clamminess of Elizabeth's velvety skin as he enveloped her hand with his own was the first indication that perhaps the beautiful and delicate Elizabeth was not as happy about their intended union as he. It was like a bucket of ice thrown in his face. He never expected her to be non-desirous of a union with him. It was every woman's goal to make a fine match. He was so accustomed to women practically throwing themselves at him in pursuit of marriage that the possibility of a woman not wanting to marry him never even crossed his mind.

He cursed himself for catering to his own selfishness and not courting Elizabeth properly right from the start. If he learned nothing else, he was certain that a woman expected and desired to be wooed and cooed into loving her future husband. Even those who were in loveless marriages gone awry at one time enjoyed the pleasures of a courtship. His selfish fears had denied this lovely woman one of the most important experiences of a woman's life. He was woefully sorry. Fully intending to make it up to her, Stephen made a silent vow to court her for the time remaining in their short engagement.

Since Stephen's father was seriously ill, the doctor whispered concerns on more than one occasion that if he did not improve soon, death would more than likely ensue. Because of this, the wedding was set for less than forty-five days from the announcement, providing only enough time for the banns to be read, Elizabeth's wedding gown to be made by the best dressmaker in London, and a menu to be planned by the best cooks and pastry makers in the city. Lord Cyrus Roberts may not have concerned himself with Elizabeth's happiness, but he certainly monitored his own reputation with great care. Therefore, only the best of the best would be allowed to create a wedding that would be the talk of London society for months to come.

Sadly, before Stephen was even able to begin his courting ritual, his intentions came to a crashing halt. His opportunities were severely impaired when his father's health took an acute turn for the worse. The demands for the wellbeing of his family's estate that were placed on the newly engaged Lord Carlson were of such that he found little time for anything other than keeping a close watch on business affairs. Sadly, his visits with Elizabeth were far and few between. What worsened the situation was how his continual and irritating shyness impaired his ability to express his thoughts and feelings whenever he did find the time to be in her company.

Even though the earl's sudden request for a quick and quiet wedding took Stephen and his family by surprise, it was generally well received. His father was most anxious to see his only son and heir to his fortune and title satisfactorily wed before he died, and Stephen as equally eager to take this beautiful and exotic goddess, Elizabeth, as his wife. The groom and his family were more than happy to oblige.

Even so, reasons for the rushed marriage danced through Stephen's head as he stood in the cozy, ancient chapel with only a few of their closest relatives in attendance and watched Elizabeth slowly make her way down the aisle toward him. Since their engagement was not a lengthy one from the start, he was certain something was amiss to cause this unexpected shortening of it.

Stephen frowned as he took in the vision of beauty that was now standing so near that he could revel in her sweet, delicious scents. She was robbed of the pleasures of a proper courtship and now her right to experience a dream wedding was crushed. He did his best to peer through the silver threads of the thick, white voile shrouding her beauty. He may have been a man who appreciated and respected customs, but at this particular moment he wished they had forgone the custom of the veil. There should be a law against covering such beauty for even the briefest of moments.

The fact that Elizabeth was wearing the latest in wedding gown colors did not go unnoticed. She looked a vision in her billowing layers of rich, white satin adorned with creamy pearls. She decided against the modern hip and buttock pads, opting for the older and more traditional pannier beneath her skirts; creating a somewhat regal swag when she slowly made her way down the aisle. They may have eliminated the big wedding, but they at least managed to procure the perfect gown. Surely this fact pleased his beautiful young bride.

His frown deepened as he thought about the social association with the color of her gown. Although white was the latest rage in fashion, a white wedding gown was also intended to portray virginity and innocence. For a while, the church was in an uproar over the open flaunting of what should be kept private, but with both the fashion world and social mind-set insisting on it, the church eventually calmed down and accepted the new trend.

Could Elizabeth's virginity be a factor in rushing this wedding? After all, their marriage was unexpectedly and most urgently pushed forward by several months and practically being held in secret. They had not even completed the reading of their banns. This lack of the completion of the reading of the banns was a concern Stephen expressed. He was assured by the earl that it was a small issue that they could work around as he urged the young lord to move forward with the wedding. The earl's determination to marry his niece off so quickly could only mean one thing. The lady was wearing virgin white falsely and was probably with child.

Although the thought that another man enjoyed what he coveted as his own and had planted his seed within her velvety depths was difficult to bear, Stephen did his best to look past it. He was, after all, a man of the world and therefore should understand such things. The closed doors of London society did not necessarily promote the chastity in their women like one might assume. Since he became her betrothed but a few short weeks ago, he would accept her indiscretions as the actions of a foolish girl who grew up without the proper guidance a mother would have normally provided. One could hardly expect a governess who was very nearly the age of her protégé to give the girl the same guidance as a mother might give. As for her uncle... it was clear from the start that he was neither up to, nor desirous, of the task.

Suspecting something was amiss, Stephen engaged in a brief discussion with the earl about the possibility of Elizabeth having experienced an interlude and the need to marry being so great that even a day's delay would not do. He expressed clearly that although he would oblige the earl with his request, if his niece was with child, he must insist on reserving the option of sending the child to the earl for care. Not only did Stephen feel he should not be expected to care for the result of the foolish girl running amiss due to improper supervision by her guardian, there was also the possibility of a male child being born. Surely the earl realized that it would be impossible for him to claim such a child as his own when the laws required the family fortune go to the first born son. After all, his primary purpose for marrying Elizabeth was to produce an heir to carry on his family bloodline. Of course, something of such a delicate nature would not be further addressed until the sex of the child was known.

Although it was obvious that the earl was put out by Stephen's assumptions, mode of conversation, and insult to his guardianship, he readily agreed. His desire to be free of his niece seemed overwhelmingly acute.

Now, -seeing his bride-to-be standing so lovely and so near-his body quivered with anticipation. Stephen regretted his words with her uncle. It did not matter if Elizabeth was with child. It did not matter that she had gone amiss. All that mattered was that she was going to be his. He was marrying the sweetest, most beautiful woman in the land. No... in the world. That was all that mattered. All he had to do was shed his foolish awkward nervousness whenever she was near and life would be perfect.

Although Elizabeth never voiced as such, her actions made it painfully clear during their brief engagement and equally brief wedding ceremony that she did not desire marriage to him. Assuming her heart was captured by the father of the child budding in her womb, Stephen overlooked her obvious sulking and resigned himself to the possibility that theirs was likely to be one of the typical marriages of arrangement. Such marriages were all too common in London society. Although he prayed she might one day love him, he hoped they would at least work things out enough to be friends. After all, the bonds of a genuine friendship could prove to be quite rewarding. He regretted his arrogance and thoughtless assumptions as he recalled their wedding night.

Thinking he was not dealing with a virgin, his only focus in mind was to possess her wholly and wipe away any trace of the man who tasted her pleasures before him. To add to the situation, he drank his fill of courage during the reception as a precaution against that cursed nervousness that always arose in her presence. It would not do to have his body fail him during the sealing of the nuptials.

She fought him, of course, but that was to be expected. They were, for the most part, strangers and she was forced to marry him when she loved another. Curiosity for her lover's identity entered his mind only fleetingly before his intoxicated lust for his new bride took over. It did not matter that she resisted. He was certain she would come around after a few evenings in his bed and forget all about the man she left behind. He was, after all, a very accomplished lover.

If only he had not been so foolish and drank so much during their small, but elaborate reception.

She'd remained by his side as a new wife should for the majority of the evening, excusing herself only to take care of necessities. As per usual, her nearness caused his emotions to run rampant. He wanted to hold her close and whisper that she was the most beautiful woman he had ever seen and declare how he loved her from the moment he met her, but his tongue would not cooperate. His loins ached with excruciating anticipation. He would have given anything for the opportunity to take her there and then, but social etiquette kept them apart.

While he remained distorted inside from the tortures of her nearness, yet calm on the outside for all eyes to see, those in attendance praised what a lovely couple they made. Stephen could hardly endure it. He saw only one recourse for a man who suffered so.

Drink.

So, drink he did.

By the time he finally found himself alone with his beautiful bride in their newly acquired townhouse and was free to adorn her with his professions of love without the risk of a room full of listening ears, his mind was duly dulled by champagne and cognac. He was unable to articulate a single word. His body, on the other hand, came alive with a mind of its own. Frustrated over his incapacitated speech and unable to keep his urges in check, he wasted no time in bedding his new bride and claiming her sweetness as his own.

That was an act he would regret for the rest of his life.

Had Stephen's mind not been so fogged with alcohol, he would have realized his new bride was not fighting him off with all her might because of her love for another man. She was battling out of fear and confusion over what was happening to her.

Had Stephen's senses been more alert, he would have recognized that his delicate flower was not educated as to what went on between a husband and wife. He would have realized that she needed coaxing and caressing to bring her to a state of acceptance of what was about to occur before he plunged his manhood deep into her velvety depths so unceremoniously.

Had Stephen been sober, he would have noticed the resistance that her virgin body gave him.

Alas, Stephen had not been sober.

Upon awakening the following morning with a head that felt

like someone bashed it with the dull side of an ax. He was immediately humbled by his drunken folly. His heart twisted and he was filled with remorse when he rose onto one elbow and looked down at his still sleeping bride laying pinned beneath his bulk. Elizabeth's eyes were swollen and red from a tear-filled night and the remnants of her finely sewn dressing gown were all askew. In his haste to possess her, Stephen had not even taken the time to remove it and spare the expertly sewn silk from his ravaging. Needless to say, the gown was ruined.

It was painfully clear that he passed out atop her small, beautifully shaped bosom upon completion of their consummation. If not for the softness of the thick feather mattress, his muscular body would have surely crushed her petite and delicate frame. As Stephen moved to the side of the bed the unmistakable signs that he'd bedded a virgin boldly coated Elizabeth's gown and the bed covering, as well as parts of his own body. He groaned, sickened by his own actions.

Never before had he been so brutish with a woman – not even with the whores he occasionally bedded. How could he have been so idiotic as to allow himself so much drink? How could he have been such an animal, such a monster? What was it about Elizabeth Nottingham that caused him to act outside himself?

Stephen found the experience of a willing seductress much more compatible to his tastes and had therefore never bedded a virgin. Even so, he knew they needed to be treated much differently than the way he treated his poor young bride. His recollection of their battle was a hazy fog. From the bruises on her tender flesh, her swollen eyes, the torn gown, the stained bed covering, and the scratches on his chest, he was positive he treated her more like a whore than a new bride. No, worse than a whore. He provided no cooing and coaxing her fears away. Even a whore would have received that courtesy. The unbridled lust Stephen worked so hard to control got the better of him. The fact that it was released by an excess of alcohol magnified the situation.

Ashamed and embarrassed by his barbaric actions, he debated what to do. Since it was clear she was not pouting over the loss of a lover, he could only assume that his new bride simply did not find him appealing enough to want to marry. Of course, after last night, he could hardly expect her to like him enough to be his friend, let alone love him.

Resigning himself to his self-inflicted fate, Stephen decided to bed her until she got with child. Then he would leave her alone and allow her to live as the rest of London society seemed to live. He had no desire to force himself on a woman who truly found him repulsive any more than he had to. If it were not for the fact that he was expected to produce an heir, he would have walked away and never touched her again.

He sighed. Such is the lot of the aristocracy. Surely Elizabeth understood this. She may not have had a mother to instruct her, but she was a lady born and bred and some things were simply common knowledge. She would have to endure bedding him until the family line was secure and then he would set her free. She could remain in London and he would travel between his estate in England, his plantation in Jamaica, and his plantation in Georgia. Surely she would be tolerant of the rare visits this type of schedule would allow him.

The only flaw in Stephen's plan -besides the tortuous fact that he loved her- would be if the first child Elizabeth bore was a girl. If that should happen, he would have to remain in England and bed her until an heir was presented.

He would worry about that later.

Stephen avoided Elizabeth all day. He was far too ashamed to look at her, let alone enter into a conversation. If their paths did happen to cross and they had a need to address each other, the bare minimum was spoken.

When evening came and he once again entered her chambers, he found her reluctantly huddled in the middle of her bed with the richly embroidered covers pulled tight around her neck. His petite young bride looked small, innocent, and frightened on a mattress that looked spacious enough for her entire wait staff to slumber on.

He moaned with remorse for his own stupidity. If he had not

been expected to impregnate Elizabeth immediately for his ailing father's sake, he would have left the room and allowed her the peace her rich violet eyes so clearly begged him for. If only his father was not so ill, he could delay things and give her time to recover from their wedding night fiasco. Actually, he too would have appreciated some time for the memory and guilt of his drunken abandonment to dissipate.

Stephen did his best to avoid Elizabeth's haunting stare as he crossed the room and poured himself a hefty amount of brandy in a straight stemmed, intricately etched, wide-mouthed crystal goblet.

Her wide eyes never left him.

Tossing back the amber liquid as quickly as he could, he had another, and then another. Relaxation spread through his body almost instantly as the brandy's warmth reached his stomach. Its artificial power surged through his veins, giving him the courage he needed to finally face her.

Glancing in Elizabeth's direction, he poured a small amount into another glass and walked to the bed.

Cringing as far away from her new husband she was able, while still retaining coverage over her slender body proved impossible. The weight of his bulk as he sat down on the edge of the bed tossed her closer and the covers no longer guarded her as they once did. Her chemise slipped, exposing her silken shoulders, as she struggled to regain composure.

He absent-mindedly traced her exposed flesh along her collar bone with a finger as he offered her the brandy. His thoughts fought his lustful anticipation of what was to come. She was so lovely, so delicate and beautiful. His body responded on its own. He told himself it would be different this time. He consumed only enough brandy to take the edge off his boyish nervousness, not enough to make him drunk. He was in complete control now and would move slowly, sensually. He would woo her and show her what it was like to be loved by a man. He would wipe the memory of last night with his kisses and tender touch.

"Drink this. Twill loosen you up," Stephen said gently.

"I do not wish to drink." Elizabeth spat with squeaking emotion.

She may not know her husband well, but she conversed with him enough over the months to know she detected a mild slur in the handsome man's voice and wondered how much he drank before he entered her bed chambers and downed half a decanter of brandy before her very eyes. It was all too obvious that Stephen disliked bedding her just as much as she disliked bedding him.

"Tonight you do," Stephen commanded with a little more force than he intended.

Upon seeing Elizabeth's eyes open wide with fright, he heaved a deep sigh. This was not going well. He had no experience wooing a reluctant woman. If only she could like him just a little. This would be so much easier... and pleasurable. He wanted to walk away and leave her at peace. He was at a loss at what to do or how to act.

Taking a deep breath, he continued in a manner less abrupt, "Please drink this. 'Twill relax you just a little."

Elizabeth raised her chin defiantly, "I do not wish to..."

"Drink it," He blurted in frustration with a controlled voice that was barely above a whisper.

Stephen found the entire situation incredibly frustrating. He was not prepared to deal with a woman who resisted him in this manner night after night. He had no idea how he should be acting. The fact that Elizabeth was so obviously repulsed by him when he wanted nothing more than to lay with her forever surprised, infuriated, and devastated him.

Elizabeth was stunned by her new husband's sudden display of aggression. What type of man had she married? Her uncle assured her he was a well-bred young man who came from the finest of the finest. He would be able to provide for her and her children better than most husbands could. He seemed so quiet and, well... dull during their brief times together. He certainly managed to fool people by hiding this horrific side of his nature quite efficiently. One would never guess this side of his persona when he is out and about. Never.

It was no secret that Lord Stephen Carlson was the most sought after bachelor in London society. Her good fortune was pointed out to her by more than one person on many an occasion. If they knew about his drinking problem would they think so highly of him?

Had it really been good fortune? Remembering Stephen's drunken assault on her tender and innocent flesh just the night before, and hearing his aggressive manner just now gave Elizabeth cause to wonder just how fortunate she really was to have married the most sought after bachelor in London society.

Having watched him drink far more in a short period of time than was recommended over the course of a full night she determined she had the misfortune to have married a drunk. She heard whispers about such things. Would he beat her now? She prayed for a reprieve until she and the doctor could execute her plan of escape.

Thinking it best not to provoke him, Elizabeth took the glass and unceremoniously tossed the amber liquid down her throat. She rarely found cause to drink brandy. On the few occasions she did she found it quite distasteful and rarely let more than a few drops touch her lips. Therefore, she was not prepared for its fiery assault as it caused her throat to contract. Spinning into a fit of coughs and gasps, she struggled to suck in air.

Stephen pulled her close and patted her back in an effort to ease her discomfort. The sweet scent of lavender that mingled with the coarse heavy curls of her shiny, thick raven hair filled his nostrils, accentuated his headiness, and tantalized his loins. He groaned with dismay as unbridled lust twisted and beat at him in an unmistakable demand to be set free. It was like a wild beast seeking freedom from its cage.

Stephen summoned all his might to subdue his urges, for subdue them he must. He had no intention of repeating his actions from the night before. Tonight he would move slowly, carefully. Even if his wife did not desire him, she could at least enjoy the experience. He pleasured enough women to know that the mind did not require love for the body to enjoy its pleasures.

Realizing his intentions, Elizabeth pushed Stephen away with all her might while she struggled to free herself. In doing so, the lace of her loosely draped chemise fell off her shoulders, exposing a small, perfectly formed breast. Was this seemingly innocent goddess torturing him on purpose?

"Please. Not tonight. I... I hurt," Elizabeth wailed in frustration.

Although she did not want to anger him, she wanted even less to repeat the nightmare of the night before.

"Sadly, my dear wife, I know of no way of avoiding the hurt. I assure you that you will not feel hurt tonight like you felt last night, if you feel hurt at all." Stephen looked away and sighed, "Had I realized, I would have done things differently."

"Realized?" Elizabeth had no idea what he was referring to.

"'Tis no matter," Stephen smiled. "Now, remove your gown please."

Elizabeth froze. Was he serious? Did he actually expect her to remove her clothes like a wanton woman? Surely he was jesting.

"Shall I remove it for you?" Stephen asked gently.

When Stephen moved to do just that, Elizabeth scrambled quickly to the other side of the bed. She had no intention of baring her body for this brute of a man. Not now, not ever. A sudden decision struck her and she was no longer concerned about angering him. Let him beat her until her body was covered with bruises. Surely the pain would be less to endure than a repeat of the night before.

Stephen caught the edge of her gown and tugged in an effort to subdue her. He wanted nothing more than to make this night a pleasurable experience for the young exotic beauty before him, but her repulsion of him was not making things easy. He never had to force a woman to bed him. He found the experience degrading. He was at an absolute loss at what to say or do.

"We must create an heir," Stephen growled in frustration. Perhaps if he explained the situation to her, she would calm down. "Then, my dear wife, I shall leave you alone."

Elizabeth stopped short. What was it that she detected in his tone of voice? Could it be that her new husband found this situation just as distasteful as she did? She had not taken into consideration the fact that perhaps Lord Stephen Carlson married her to appease his father and not out of a desire for her. It had not occurred to her that he may have been forced to marry her, like she was forced to marry him. Was that why he drank himself drunk on their wedding night? Was it to block out the fact that he must bed her? Did he find her so undesirable?

Having no mother to confide in and no married friends, Elizabeth was not clear on what really went on between a wife and a husband. She assumed what she experienced the night before was typical behavior. That being the case, she was not anxious to repeat it. Could it be that he too was reluctant? Had it hurt him like it hurt her? These were things she did not know and had no one to ask. She certainly was not going to ask him.

The thought that the two of them were coupled against their will never entered her mind. Until now.

Noticing his wife was deep in thought, Stephen took advantage of her unguarded state and reached for her shoulders. His large, weathered, yet well-manicured, hand barely gripped her gown before she spun away, leaving him with a fist full of fabric. As she pulled against his hold, the delicate trimming of her light weight garment tore from its meticulous stitching. He scowled. It was not his intention to ruin yet another gown. What would the servants think? If he kept this up, he would not have to worry about how to get the gown off this breath taking creature for she would have nothing left to don.

In her struggles to release herself from Stephen's ever increasing grip, Elizabeth unwittingly forced an arousal in him that he could no longer deny. With a goodly amount of brandy coursing through his veins, all sensibility and caution was lost as his body took charge on its own accord. It ignored anything his mind might think that would stop him from fulfilling his needs and desires.

His lips burned against her skin, while he wantonly explored her feminine treasures. Within seconds he regained control of his senses and his love making shifted from that of a heated animal to the soft and sensual caresses of a most adept lover.

Stephen spoke the truth. The experience was not painful for Elizabeth as it was the night before. In fact, his tender ministrations were so wildly enjoyable that she was sure she would lose herself in ecstasy at any moment. Her mind reeled in confusion. Was she supposed to enjoy it like this? Was she expected to respond or should she simply allow him his pleasures like a dutiful wife? She had no idea.

Although Madeleine proved more than efficient when it came to her education on etiquette within society, a wife's house management duties, and world affairs, not once had she carried on a woman to woman discussion with Elizabeth about husbands and wives and what happened between them behind closed doors. The subject seemed practically taboo. If it was referred to at all, it was with a whisper that crept out from behind her hand. Elizabeth attributed it to the fact that Madeleine never even possessed a beau to kiss, let alone a man to marry.

Accustomed to being on guard so as not to displease the man of the household, Elizabeth decided it was best to remain as still as she could while her husband took his pleasures. She held her breath and closed her eyes as tight as they would close and used every ounce of strength she could find while she struggled to keep her composure in check. It took all her strength to subdue the moans of pleasure that threatened to escape her throat. It would not do to upset him with her selfish wiggling and squealing from this absolutely incredible experience.

The thought of having to remain stoic and stiff while she endured such delightful pleasures for the rest of her life was crushingly sad. Was this her fate? How did wives around the world do this? Those who did received her humble admiration, for she did not think she could possibly bear it night after night. It was no small wonder why so many women encouraged their husbands to take a mistress. Being alone in bed would be far less punishment than the tortures of having to subdue one of the most pleasurable sensations a body could have.

Elizabeth did her best to remove her thoughts from the pleasures of the flesh in hopes it would help her retain her calm demeanor under Stephen's wildly arousing ministries. In doing so, she found herself recalling the laughter and pleasurable conversation that transpired between the two during the many social engagements they simultaneously attended. She recalled how handsome he looked as he stepped onto the dance floor at Lord Milo's ball. His deep throated laughter caused shivers of delight up her arms and down her back at the Andersen's picnic. She recalled how well his muscular thighs rippled when he maneuvered his stallion next to her carriage while outing in the park. He was a handsome and virile man any woman would be overjoyed to claim as hers. Yet he was hers. He was hers and he was here doing the most marvelous things to her body while whispering the most wondrous devotions in her ear. She loved him for it. She loved him for everything. Oh dear, she loved him.

The ecstasy of realizing the truth of her feelings for Lord Stephen Carlson clashed with the knowledge that he married her out of duty and nothing more. She was crushed to the core. She loved a man who did not love her. Yes, he spoke devotions while in the throes of passion, but surely they were simply words in a moment of passion. He made no mention of love outside their coupling. He'd made it perfectly clear that once she gave him a son they would have nothing more to do with each other. What joke of fate? How could God be so cruel? She was a dutiful ward of her uncle and a model young lady to society. She accepted her situation after the death of her parents with grace and dignity. All she desired in return was one thing and one thing only... to be loved. Now, her dreams of that happening were crushed. She was married to a man who did not return her love. She was no fool. She listened to enough conversations to understand that men enjoyed women without loving them. This was certainly what must be happening now. It was impossible for him not to be enjoying the sensations of their coupling, was it not? He certainly seemed to be enjoying himself.

The situation was just too saddening. Thank goodness her plans to escape with Dr. Jameson were still in the making. Would the doctor come through with a message that all was in order soon? She fervently prayed that it be so.

Feeling Elizabeth's stiff body beneath him frustrated Stephen even more. After his initial lustful attack on her person, his senses returned and he did his best to show as much tenderness and consideration as he could. It was a difficult task to be sure. The woman's beauty and appeal was of such to drive the best of men mad. One could not be too harsh on him for his occasional loss of control.

He pulled himself up and looked down on Elizabeth's slight frame while she lay looking anywhere but at him. She looked so small and vulnerable. Her eyes were dry of tears but filled with what looked be sorrow. He sensed her mind preoccupied. Did she wish herself away? Did she find being with him that distasteful? Did he sicken her to such an extent that she could not allow her body to relax and enjoy his expert ministries of pleasure? Never had he failed in bringing a woman to the heights of passion, yet it seemed he had failed now... and with his own wife.

Stephen prayed Elizabeth would conceive an heir soon so he would no longer be required to force himself upon her. As beautiful as she was, he found the situation sickening. There were plenty of women wherever he traveled who were willing to throw themselves at him for just one night in his bed. He had no need or desire to keep returning to a woman who recoiled and remained like a piece of wood beneath him, even if she had captured his heart and he thought her to be the most beautiful creature he ever encountered.

Having been summoned by his father to assist with matters of estate after only a few weeks with his passionless bride, Stephen expected to be gone the better part of a fortnight. Although he was remorseful about leaving his young wife so soon without having accomplished the removal of the cold barrier between them, it could not be helped. Their fortune, and the inheritance of their future heir, required his immediate attention.

He questioned the waiting maid selected from his staff by Elizabeth upon the dismissal of Madeleine Hardy after her treason

-at least that was how Elizabeth viewed it- about her mistress's female cycle and learned she was expecting her moon time soon. He would have liked to have continued to lay with her in the night for at least another week to fortify the possibility of producing an heir as well as break through that shell of resistance and get her to realize, understand, accept and respond to his love. Unfortunately, there was nothing to be done about it. If he was unsuccessful at begetting her with child already he would simply have to start again when he returned. At least it would provide him with a greater opportunity to win her over – not to mention additional time making love to her.

His duties at his father's estate took surprisingly much less time than Stephen anticipated and he found himself returning home after only a few days of absence. Those few days were all it took for his reluctant bride to slip off in the night and disappear. He would have never thought his socially proper Elizabeth capable of doing such a thing. Was the concept of being his bride that reprehensible?

He initially joined in the general panic of the household while they speculated on what could have become of their young mistress, but after questioning Lord Roberts about the possibility of him knowing something of his niece's whereabouts and discovering that thwarting her original plan to run away was the reason behind their rushed marriage, he quickly realized that the earl's insistence of an early marriage had not in the least deterred his headstrong niece's plans. His bride had not been kidnapped or taken against her will. It was clear his beautiful, reluctant wife ran away.

Furious with the earl's deceitful actions, Stephen commanded he remain silent about what occurred. He was certain that the man's pride would keep him so. After all, he was still suffering -in his mind, if nowhere else- from the shame of his sister's actions so many years ago. Stephen then put on a ruse to the rest of the world. He claimed his wife longed for time away from the city, so they took up residence in a small cottage his family owned in the upper country and would remain there until she was ready to continue their honeymoon abroad.

People smiled and nodded in agreement about how lucky Lady Elizabeth was to have secured such a loving husband. Few husbands would grant his wife's every wish like Lord Carlson was doing, even if they were just newlywed.

Fortunately for Stephen, his family was long standing in London society and had strong connections in influential places. It took but a few days to trace Elizabeth's actions to the doorstep of the Jameson household. After a lengthy, heated, and impending conversation with John Jameson, Stephen was able to learn of the doctor's scheme to act as Elizabeth's guardian in exchange for her funding their journey to the emancipated colonies.

John explained to Stephen how he was the eldest brother and the doctor lived on his good graces. Because of this, the doctor convinced Elizabeth to use her inheritance money to fund their trip. Knowing how naïve Elizabeth was to the ways of the world, Stephen imagined that would not have been too difficult a task. Somehow, the conniving scoundrel also managed to solicit his other brother -who was a lawyer and the trustee to Elizabeth's inheritance- to release a considerable amount of her inheritance money to them. It mattered not to Stephen that John was uncomfortable with the idea and acted practically against his will. He held the entire Jameson family accountable.

Stephen's first concern was to find his wayward minx of a bride and bring her home. Once that was completed, this family of scoundrels would be duly dealt with.

THREE

Elizabeth leaned against the rail on the deck of the intolerably crowded ship and tugged the oversized hood of her fur lined, thick red lamb's wool cloak closer around her face. Its softness provided a touch of comfort to her poor suffering head that felt like it had been struck by a massive blunt object. Her stomach fared no better. It was so incredibly twisted from the incessant tossing of the unkind sea it was impossible to hold anything in it. In fact, she emptied it to such an extent she feared the actual stomach lining was next to rise. At times, when she leaned against the rail and silently begged the waters for mercy, she was certain she heard the waters laughing wickedly at her misery.

Not wanting to raise eyebrows or suspicion, the doctor purchased tickets for their passage as uncle and niece. Realizing she would be required to walk out of her home without luggage, he commissioned a new wardrobe and toiletries to be made ready in time for their voyage. Although the cut of her clothing was slightly plain in comparison to the dresses hanging in her wardrobe back home, they were made of the finest satins, silks, wools, velvets, and brocades available and they fit her exceptionally well. Elizabeth felt she sacrificed little, for which she thanked the good doctor profusely.

Dr. Jameson maintained his identity of a nobleman turned physician, explaining to Elizabeth the importance of immediately laying the foundation of his relationship with the good people of the new world. Since the overly crowded ship was taking all of its passengers there, they were technically already in the company of their new neighbors. Hence sparked Elizabeth's first question about her wisdom in making such a trip, for her fellow passengers seemed an unsavory lot indeed.

Elizabeth kept her thoughts and feelings to herself and focused on the freedom that awaited her in her new life and her deep appreciation that her father's once good friend and colleague, who was now her guardian. She found it a great boon to be traveling with a doctor. It was handy to be able to easily seek his ministrations on behalf of her unruly stomach and equally miserable head.

Even with the vivid imagination Elizabeth possessed, she could never have fathomed how long and grueling the voyage would be. For reasons unexplained to her, the ship navigated south and stopped in several ports down the coastline before going out to the open sea. Because of this, their trip was extended from that of an anticipated six-week voyage to an overwhelming two-and-a-half-month test of endurance. She directed her concern to the good doctor on various occasions and was always met with the same pat on her hand and nod of his head, with nary an explanation to be heard. She deduced that he knew just as little as she on the matter.

It was rumored the ship took on a small group of African slaves, but Elizabeth saw no sign of them. Therefore, she considered it rumor only.

When the word finally came that land was sited, she jumped and applauded in an elated child-like manner. She endured just about all she could of her fellow passengers. The incessant odor of unwashed bodies and their unsuitable talk that was common amongst her fellow passengers, along with the constant torture of her overly taxed stomach from the rocking and rolling of their vessel had her nerves shattered and her body exhausted. If relief did not come soon, she was certain she would either go mad or, at the very least, vomit herself into nothingness.

Although faring far better than Elizabeth, Sally was equally happy to hear they would soon be on dry land. She'd never acted as a waiting maid. Having to tend to a perpetually vomiting aristocrat was a challenging way to start. What made it worse was that she also experienced a few days of sickness before she acquired her sea legs. Her duties were those of a house maid since she was of age to be employed. When Elizabeth presented herself at the Jameson residence unattended, lack of a lady's maid needed to be rectified before they could begin their journey.

It was John who suggested that Sally accompany them and tend to Elizabeth's needs. Since the two women were close in age, he felt Sally could also serve as companion for his brother's new ward. Elizabeth's uncle instilled within her the belief that familiarity breeds contempt and, therefore, she should never befriend a member of the wait staff. She decided that, since she was starting a new life, perhaps she should start it with new ways. Thus, she made no mention of the impropriety of a house maid turned waiting maid acting as her traveling companion.

Sally had never been on a ship and did not find the idea enthralling. She was equally uncertain about leaving her homeland for the notoriously primitive and barbarous colonies. After all, it was not that long ago that the colonies were warring against England for their freedom. Would they really be receptive to the arrival of more faithful subjects of the crown? It was the promise of being promoted to waiting maid and the wages that came with it - not to mention never having to scrub a single floor ever again- that outweighed her fears and prompted her to agree to their scheme.

A comely girl of common origin, Sally possessed intelligence far superior to those of her class and up-bringing. It was not long before she learned what was expected of her and accomplished her duties to the extent that everyone, including herself, was hard pressed to remember that she had been a lowly housemaid not long ago.

"Ar' ya doin' alright, Lady Elizabeth?" asked the seedy looking captain as he slid up next to Elizabeth and looked out onto the brilliant blue, sun-kissed waters. "I understand ya 'ave been feelin' a bit poorly for the majority o' the trip."

"Yes captain. I am sorry to say that I have," Elizabeth replied politely.

Elizabeth slid her hand over her tender stomach absent mindedly. She was acutely aware of the captain's improper nearness as well as how boldly his eyes follow her hand as it slid to her stomach. Had the deck been less crowded, she would have questioned such impropriety. Although uncertain of the customs of the sea, in English society his actions would be considered a blatant display of disrespect for a lady of her stature. But then, as far as the captain was concerned, she was not the wife of a future duke. She was the niece and ward of a nobleman turned physician. Even so, under normal circumstances, such close proximity between strangers would not be acceptable; no matter what level of society a person held. Then, these were anything but normal circumstances.

"I was looking for the land. They said 'twas near, Captain Kline," she said in an effort to each the uncomfortable feeling that welled within her. "I cannot see it. Did I hear incorrectly?"

Elizabeth held her breath while she awaited his response. Oh please have land be near.

"Ya heard right, miss. We shall be touchin' shores soon 'nough," the captain chuckled.

"That is just wonderful." Elizabeth' said with obvious relief. "I wonder why I do not see anything," she stated softly as she craned her head to look hard over the expanse of waters.

She saw only a dark mass off in the distance which looked rather formidable, like it would swallow them up when they finally did approach it.

"Do ya see that dark mass way off yonder?" the captain pointed in the same direction that Elizabeth was looking. "'Tis the land we ar' aimin' for. It don't look like much now. Bu', as we grow closer yu'll be able ta make out a thing or two."

"My goodness, your men have good eyes to have been able to spot such a faraway thing before it even grew large enough to see," she exclaimed.

Elizabeth was amazed. She had searched the waters from all angles for the better part of the morning for any sign of land. It only just appeared a few moments before the captain joined her. Yet, his crew announced it at first light.

"Ah, milady, we 'ave special equipment ta 'elp us with ar' navigation an' search. Come... allow me ta give ya a look," the captain said with a smile that was warm and friendly.

Had Elizabeth been a little wiser to the ways of the world, she would have realized the captain's smile was a little too warm and far too friendly.

Although taken aback by her first encounter with the captain's seedy looks and unrefined mannerisms, the doctor and Elizabeth were included amongst the honored guests at his dinner table for the duration of the trip. The doctor developed a liking to the captain despite his obvious lack of propriety and seedy appearance. If her guardian trusted the captain, then so did she.

Feeling comfortable and safe in his presence, Elizabeth placed her hand on the arm he offered and allowed him to escort her across the weathered deck. The forged their way through the packed sea of passengers and up to the captain's deck just above his cabin. The aromatic smell of leather and wood seasoned by the salty sea air was thick as they entered the small open room at the helm of the ship. She welcomed their rich, exotic scents after moving through a crowded mass of bodies devoid of perfume and in dire need a bath.

A rather grizzly looking first mate gripped an oversized wheel fastidiously while he steered the ship steadily toward their destination. Although polished and well cared for, the thick wheel showed signs of wear from years of service to the captain and his crew.

"Over 'ere, milady," the captain cooed, as he urged Elizabeth toward the large telescope that was positioned on a sturdy looking stand. He caressed the highly polished brass tube, lovingly, "Ar' ya familiar with the telescope, milady?"

"Why, no captain. I have heard of them, but I have not come upon the opportunity to inspect one," Elizabeth responded with rising curiosity.

"Well ya 'ave that opportunity now. Come closer an' take a look." The captain's voice was salacious as he motioned for Elizabeth to move forward. "Just take a look through 'ere an' tell me wha' ya see."

Elizabeth giggled with delight while she stepped up to the telescope. Forgetting all pomp and circumstance, she gasped in awe as she peered through the telescope at the jagged land mass that seemed so distant to the naked eye, yet so close through this looking glass. Not only could she see it clearly, but she was easily able to capture the people bustling about in busy activity on the harbor docks.

Elizabeth was so engrossed in her new found ability to view the people long before they were aware of her that she did not catch the captain's exchange of looks and nods with his first mate. Nor did she realize her circumstance when the first mate secured the wheel and left them alone.

Upon hearing the captain clear his throat in an exaggerated manner, Elizabeth pulled her head away from the telescope and turned. The man was standing shockingly close, making it difficult to turn without crushing her body against him. The faint, foul scent of his unwashed body blended with the stench of his cheap cologne assaulted her sensitivities. She could feel his hard muscles rub against her as she forced herself to face him.

Looking around quickly, she saw no sign of the first mate. Alarmed, she pushed the flat of her hands hard against his chest in an effort to move him far enough way to let her pass. All her strength was not sufficient to budge him even a fraction of an inch. He chuckled at his captive's feeble attempt for freedom before crushing his lips to hers.

The world spun out of control as Elizabeth did her best to fight off the captain's pugnacious attack. What was happening? She should have known better than to allow herself to be escorted to one of the most private and off limits location of the ship. The only place more private would have been the captain's cabin, just below. She had only herself to blame for what was happening now. She could kick herself!

Elizabeth was supposed to be napping. Dr. Jameson feared for her safety on a ship that was overrun with common people traveling to the new land in hopes of escaping heaven knows what. The constant watching between him and Sally proved stifling. In order to access a small reprieve, Elizabeth begged off for a nap. When sleep would not come, she decided to take some air.

Her companions would not be looking for her for at least another hour, if not longer. Even if they were looking for her, would they think to look here? She sincerely doubted it. How foolish she was to step away from her protectors and believe no harm could come to her on a ship such as this. She would have expected an assault of this nature more from one of the dodgy looking crew members or even some of the unsavory looking passengers, rather than the captain of the vessel. Where was his honor? Where was his integrity?

She cursed herself for wearing such a costume of undress. The lack of a pannier created a much easier access for his coarse, sea splintered hands that wandered at will. The hip and backside pads that swept the fashion world and become quite popular were now being replaced by simpler, high waist gowns that flowed and draped a woman's body, similar to that of a Grecian goddess. Sally released her stays in preparation for her fabled napping. Once her maid left the cabin it was impossible for her to do them up again. Grateful that her breasts were of a manageable size and structure without the stays, she'd selected a gray lamb's wool gown and a matching cape lined with green satin to conceal her improper, unconfined bosom. As long as no one touched her, the absence of a properly laced corset would not be noticed.

Sadly, someone was touching her - and in a manner that only a husband should do. She was powerless to do anything about it.

She felt weak from the shock of this unexpected turn of events, as well as exhausted from several months of daily vomiting. Even with the exertion of as much strength as she possessed to waylay the assault on her person, it was not long before Elizabeth was overtaken by it all. Unable to cope with the chain of events, she swooned.

Seizing the opportunity, the captain whisked her petite, feather-light form into his arms and made haste to a more private location by way of a secluded stairway that led to his cabin below. The burly man tossed her limp body onto his damp, dank bed. Even in her foggy state, Elizabeth's senses were alerted to the mold that made its home deep within the thick horsehair and cotton batting mattress. It was obvious he had not aired and sun dried his bedding to protect it from the constant dampness of the sea in quite some time, if ever.

The captain harbored no qualms about raping a woman who was not even fully conscious and quickly went about his business. Realizing what was happening through the fog that coated her reality, Elizabeth pulled on the puny bit of strength left within her and kicked wildly.

Rather than deter her assailant, this only proved to arouse the captain's vile intentions to greater heights. No matter how hard Elizabeth tried to prevent it, the inevitable was about to happen. She was going to be raped by the captain of the very same vessel that was intended to provide her with the opportunity of a new life of freedom and safety.

The sound of fabric tearing echoed as she felt her bodice being pulled away from her easily accessible breasts. Within seconds the captain's hot lips encircled her tender rose tipped flesh. She was not sure which hurt more, the harshness of his ill-kept, wiry, and abundant facial hair or the severity of his intense suckling. She pulled at his greasy, coarse curls with all her might, hoping to deter his enthusiasm and bring him back to reason.

"Captain, please!" was all she could get past her lips before his foul tasting mouth smothered hers, forcing the remnants of her sentence back into the recesses of her throat.

The cool, moist air assaulted her flesh as his calloused hands raised her skirt, allowing him access to her most private area. Her mind spun on what to do. This was a nightmare of the worst kind. It just could not be happening to her. Any moment now, she would be waking up from the nap she was supposed to be taking and realize this was all a nightmare inspired by her stomach's poor countenance.

When the captain's lips finally released her own bruised ones, all she could do was gasp for air. Before she was able to stabilize her breathing, his body came crushing down upon her slight frame. The painful impact of his manhood as it slammed unceremoniously into her velvety, unprepared depths validated she was not dreaming. This nightmare was real.

The smell of his sweaty, unwashed flesh was poorly masked by heavy cologne. Her tender stomach lurched into a torrent of protest. She could not imagine there could be anything left to release, but the urge persisted anyway. Her mouth burned from the foul tobacco residue he shared while he forced his thick tongue past her clenched teeth. Her stomach moaned and rocked with the motion of his body as he continued to assault her for his own pleasure.

Elizabeth realized her battle was lost and resigned herself to laying limp beneath him while she prayed he would find release quickly. Since she found absolutely no pleasure in what was occurring, staying stiff as a board was incredibly easy. She focused her mind on other things to help take her away from the reality of her nightmare. Bile rose in her throat from the after taste of his repulsive kisses. She remembered how fresh and clean Stephen smelled when he came to her at night. His kisses tasted sweet, like the brandy he partook of prior to coming to her. His strong hands looked weathered, but were actually smooth and well-manicured. They were certainly not hands that would cut flesh with their multitude of harsh calluses. His face -his oh so handsome face- although tanned and thickened from the sun, was clean shaven and smooth against her flesh. Her senses were actually heightened when she was with Stephen. His flesh was so different than what assaulted her now. She felt certain her skin was being sanded away, bit by bit.

Although she had lain with only one man, the captain's sudden groan as his body's full weight fell upon her did not sound like the groan of a man reaching his peak of passion. This fact was made certain when she felt the warmth of his blood as it trickled across her bare breast. The sticky fluid was even more sickening than his foul scent and horrendous actions. Her screams were muffled by his almost unfathomable weight.

Gathering up every ounce of strength she possessed, Elizabeth positioned her hands against his chest and heaved his limp weight with all of her might. The captain's shocked eyes stared directly at her. She somehow managed to lift his body a few inches above her in order to get a better idea of what was happening. Seeing the pool of blood that was transferring from his back to her bosom made her almost delirious with fright. It also gave her the strength she needed to muster up one more powerful push and heave his body to relieve herself of his oppressive weight. The continual blood curdling screams she knew in the recesses of her mind were coming from her own lips, only magnified the situation. Sitting up and gasping for air, she struggled to quiet her screaming and control her breathing.

Looking around, she stared in disbelief. There, still as a statue, stood Sally. Elizabeth was horrified as she looked from Sally' blank face to the bloody knife she still gripped.

"What have you done?" Elizabeth gasped, as she jumped as far away from the captain's still body as she could. "Sally, what have you done?"

"He was... He...," Sally stuttered.

The young lady's maid was frozen from the shock of her own actions.

Hearing the thunder of boots clambering in their direction, Elizabeth struggled to wipe the captain's blood off her bosom with a piece of his rank bedding and adjust her clothing, as best she could to its original state.

"Help me... hurry!" she demanded.

Elizabeth's tone of voice spurred Sally out of her frozen state and into action. She dropped the knife on the nearly thread bare carpet and rushed to Elizabeth's aid. They barely finished making her presentable before the ship's first mate flew into the room; followed by a few members of the crew.

"Bloody 'ell, what 'ave ya done?" The first mate roared as he ran to inspect his captain's condition. "Did ya kill 'im?"

The first mate ordered his men to hold the women while he carefully positioned the captain on the bed and inspected the wound from Sally's knife. The fact that the captain was engaged in the act of taking his pleasures was obvious. The first mate looked long and hard at both women while their wrists were being bound in preparation of removing them from the room. Judging by the disarray of the lady and the look of defiance on her maid's face, he had a pretty good idea what occurred.

"It looks like 'e'll live, but 'e'll be one angry 'ound ta be 'round for some time, of tha' I am certain." The first mate directed his words to Elizabeth and Sally. "Ya do know tha' the cap'n is king of 'is ship, don't ya? Ya do realize the consequences of your actions. I 'ope."

Elizabeth could not guess what those consequences might be, but she was positive the first mate would inform her of them soon enough.

"'Twas me that did the stabbing'," Sally blurted.

"Hush!" Elizabeth snapped.

The first mate looked from Sally to Elizabeth and then back again.

"Don't matter who done it," he said directly to Sally. "Ya ar' the servant of milady." His focus switched to Elizabeth, "So, milady be responsible for wha' ya done just as if ya done it yourself!"

The crowd at the door was growing in size, making Elizabeth painfully aware of the implications her appearance presented.

"May I go to my room and freshen up?" she asked in a slightly haughty manner. When the first mate simply smirked at her, she grudgingly added, "Please?"

"You'll 'ave a new room from now on, milady," the first mate said with a snarl before turning to his men and adding, "Take 'em both below to the 'old and keep 'em there 'til I tell ya different."

If Elizabeth thought that no greater degradation could have been bestowed upon her than the recent rape by one of the filthiest bodies she ever encountered, she was wrong. The sneers and comment of the crew and a few fellow passengers as she was pushed and shoved through them, with her hair in total disarray and her torn clothing askew, felt like humbling spears being tossed at her from all directions. Her humiliation from the gasps made by the few notable passengers as they stared at her unkempt appearance and listened to the explanation of what happened and where she was being taken was unbearable. She would never be accepted in society after this. She was certain of it. Her only saving grace was that she was not using her true identity on this voyage.

As a few members of the crew roughly shoved the two women into the small cell that would be their prison, mindless of the lewd grabbing and shoving in intimate places the crowd witnessed, she gave thanks for Dr. Jameson's foresight in her using an assumed identity. While she was at it she gave thanks for Sally stabbing the captain before he was able to reach his peak. The thought of a possible pregnancy resulting from the touch of such a vile beast was too horrid to even fathom.

The doctor! When he discovered what happened, surely he would make arrangements to free them. The good doctor would also see to it that the captain received his dues for the injustice he bestowed upon her person. She held on to the that that it would not be long before she would be rescued from this horrid place, which lacked fresh air and assaulted her senses with the stench of urine and rot.

"I am so sorry, miss. I was not thinking. I only meant to help," Sally whispered.

Traumatized and too exhausted for words, Elizabeth cuddled up to Sally and leaned her head in the young woman's lap.

Sally placed her hand sympathetically on Elizabeth's bare head and pushed a stray raven curl from her face while she looked around them. It was incredibly dark. Little by little Sally grew accustomed to the pitch black enough to make out a few shapes and develop a sense of depth perception. When she did, she found herself staring back at a group of eyes belonging to the darky slaves picked up at the last port and unmercifully crammed in and chained to the opposite side of the hold.

FOUR

Rain pelted against Stephen's hunched back as he paced the deck, oblivious to its bitter cold. The ship's captain, Jackson Sims, had just forged his way through the wet fury to advise him it was unwise to remain topside. The waves raged like giant mountains of bluish white foam around them, roaring thunderously while they tossed the sparsely manned frigate to and fro.

Stephen grudgingly thought it his right to do as he chose on his own ship while he nodded to the captain as a means of appeasement. His mood was as angry as the waters. They suited each other.

Stephen's choice to stay topside was soon changed when he was almost seized by a wave determined to make him a prisoner of the water's depths. Saved by his good footing and quick reflexes, he decided to heed his captain's advice and go below.

His cabin was a fraction of the size one might expect the ship's owner to occupy. He spared the more spacious quarters for Jackson Sims' use, since it was he who spent his days in command of the ship and its crew. Even so, what the room lacked in size, it made up for in comfort. Great pains were taken to find the best furnishings money could buy whenever the ship made port along the coastlines of the Atlantic Ocean, and occasionally along the Mediterranean Sea.

Stephen long ago claimed this particular frigate for his own personal use. He purchased it shortly after leaving England to explore and make his fortune in the newly emancipated United States. It was his intention to use it as a means of transportation for not only himself but for goods he was either selling or buying. Over time his fleet grew, but the fond attachment to his first frigate remained strong.

He'd booked passage for the initial voyage he'd made fifteen years ago. He'd hired the services of cargo carriers when he first started doing business on his tobacco plantation in Jamaica and his cotton plantation in Georgia. He soon discovered owning such undertakings in two different locations with such a considerable distance between them required speedy and frequent travel. It was not long before he determined that the wiser, more convenient, and less costly thing to do was to own the ship. In his case, he owned several.

It was an added boon when he was introduced to the very capable Captain Jackson Sims while traveling the South Carolina coastline. The captain he originally commissioned to head the operations of his frigate at the time of purchase found himself in a scuffle up the coastline just prior to beginning his duties on board Stephen's ship. He was fulfilling a prior commitment for a brief commission that was to last less than a fortnight when his ship fell under siege by pirates. While defending the ship, the captain was severely wounded and was forced into early retirement. Stephen, having urgent business in Jamaica, made a few inquiries around the Charles Town docks for a replacement and was directed to a tavern where Captain Jackson Sims was dining on fare fit for a king.

Right up until the three weeks prior, Sims was in charge of a small fleet of vessels for a highly established family in Charles Town. While traveling to the orient on holiday, the entire family was overtaken by a mysterious ailment that the ship's doctor was at a loss to treat. Fortunately for the captain and his crew, the doctor was able to contain the plight to the family members only. As a result, all but a young daughter perished while at sea. The doctor, captain and his crew were not afflicted.

At a loss at what to do, Captain Sims returned the vessel to its home port. It was confiscated by the estate lawyers and placed into a trust for the surviving daughter when she came of age. The captain was left with no ship to command and his crew forced to search for a new post. It was as big a boon for Sims to be found by Stephen as it was for Stephen to find Sims, for a captain without a ship was a sad state indeed.

Captain Sims proved invaluable with his knowledge of the waters and vessels. It was not long before Stephen added more ships to his fleet and placed Sims as chief commander. Not only did the arrangement work well for all concerned, but the old sea dog of a captain and the handsome future duke developed a bond that went beyond that of employer and employee. It was a special kind of bond. One destined to last a lifetime.

Although one could not consider them to be original, Stephen's name for each ship was quite explanatory of the vessel's function. The Jamaican tobacco plantation's merchant ship was named Jamaica and the Georgian cotton plantation's merchant ship was named Georgia. Both ships were large and cumbersome when filled with merchandise. They were often accompanied by one or both of his two frigates, the Duke, and the Duchess. Each was suitably manned and armed to fend off possible attacks from pirates or privateers.

The ship that transported him in response to his father's summons from the colonies to England was the Duke, his favorite and fastest vessel. Although sparsely manned, its crew was efficient enough that one would never notice an absence of manpower. Stephen and Captain Sims selected the best seamen they could find and he paid them handsomely for their services. They were also an extremely loyal crew, not just because of the money, but because of the captain himself. For never a fairer captain could they find in all the seas and harbors.

Stephen's valet, Morris, helped him out of his soaking wet coat and breeches. slipped off his coat and breeches. He rubbed his wet hair vigorously with the thickly woven linen towel that rested on the back of an ornate wooden chair. The miniature coal burner in his room contained just enough hot coals in it to remove some of the damp air and provide the small quarters with much needed warmth.

Not that he really noticed. Stephen was so engrossed in his desire to catch the brigantine that swept his wife away that he was hardly aware of his surroundings or any occurrences such as inclement weather.

How could Elizabeth have been so foolish as to board a ship such as the Lady Fair? Did she not know it was a vessel of questionable repute? He heaved a heavy sigh. Of course, she would have no idea. The life she led under the guardian-ship of the earl shielded her from such gossip and scandal as was floating around the seaport about the seedy Captain Kline and his even more scandalous crew. Furthermore, she more than likely put all her faith and trust in that scoundrel Jameson.

Surely the doctor learned of the rumors when he made his inquiries for their passage. Nary would a man's lips part when speaking of the Lady Fair without including her rumored participation in a very vulgar side of the slave trade. He was also rumored as a possible privateer against the British on behalf of social outcasts in the colonies.

Stephen was actually surprised to discover the ship had even been allowed access to British ports. Somehow the captain of the Lady Fair managed to slink into London's busy harbor and slink back out with a cargo consisting primarily of disreputable passengers willing to pay higher than the normal passage for the opportunity to leave England quickly and quietly. There were only a few passengers of status aboard, his wife being one of them.

Learning this was no easy feat. He was reduced to practically pummeling whatever information he was able to squeeze out of more than one sailor and fish vendor before he managed to determine the doctor of considerable dress, traveling with a petite niece whose unusual beauty included thick, unruly raven hair, notably rosy and dimpled cheeks and the most unforgettable violet eyes, were his wayward bride and that scoundrel Jameson.

Stephen was relieved to learn that the Lady Fair was destined for Charles Town, South Carolina. This was one of the few ports that welcomed her sort since Charles Town ports were far busier than those of Savannah. Since hos plantation outside of Savannah was only a few days ride from Charles Town, Stephen made many a trip there. Thus, he was quite familiar with the city and its docks. He was thankful for that, at least.

He threw the dampened towel onto the impeccably clean floor

and slammed his fist into the palm of his hand while he went over in his mind what he intended to do to that rogue, Jameson, when he finally caught up with him. To risk the wellbeing and reputation of a naive young daughter of a deceased family friend was bad enough, but to take off with a man's new bride – well that was unconscionable.

The fact that the banns were read on only two of the necessary three Sundays during the church service before they took their nuptial vows weighed heavy on Stephen's mind. If Jameson was aware of this fact, then claiming Elizabeth as his legal wife would be difficult, if not impossible. The earl assured him it would be taken care of and hoped he was successful in doing so. Things were a complete mess.

A man who liked his affairs to be orderly, Stephen cursed himself for being so swept away by Elizabeth's beauty that he did not have sense enough to delve deeper into the earl's motive for marrying them before the agreed upon date and time. Not that knowing she preferred to run away rather than marry him would have swayed him from going through with the wedding. It was quite common for young brides to be concerned about their future with a man they hardly knew. Many a future bride rebelled with the threat of running off. If he had known Elizabeth was so set against becoming his wife, he would have taken greater pains to allow more time to court her. He would have wooed her instead of forcing her to do something she was so obviously repulsed by.

He was certain that, had he been given more time, he could have changed her mind about him. As it was, he managed to make her desire to be free of him even stronger. This was obvious since even with all of her uncle's precautions, she fled in spite of their marriage. Could it be that she knew the marriage law of seventeen-fifty and planned on using it to free herself from him? Was it her intention to nullify their nuptials because of an absence of the completion of the third reading of the banns? She and Jameson were privy to the council of his brother who was the very same lawyer who was privy to all of Elizabeth's most personal affairs. He was also the very same man who helped them slip away.

Stephen clutched the back of a chair until his knuckles turned white. How could he love a woman who disliked him to the extent Elizabeth clearly did? With so many women literally flaunting themselves at him daily, why would he fall for the one woman who wanted nothing to do with him? What was wrong with him?

At least his father managed to see him wed to the woman he chose for him. If all went well, his father's desire to see a grandson born into the world would also be fulfilled. Had Stephen realized the duke's health was going to become so suddenly compromised and deteriorate so rapidly, he would not have procrastinated on marriage and his father would have been enjoying several grandchildren by now. The duke always seemed so healthy and strong. When his lungs weakened to such a precarious state a few years ago -struggling daily to pull enough air into them to allow him to maintain a normal lifestyle- everyone was taken by surprise. Since Stephen was off proving himself and building a fortune of his own that surpassed the inheritance awaiting him in his homeland, those concerned thought it best not to burden him with news of his father's weakened state. With the overseer dead and his father's health in such a seriously impaired state, they felt they had no choice. He would have to abandon his adventures and return to England post haste. The future of his family's legacy depended on it.

Taking the duke's health into consideration, Stephen decided to keep Elizabeth's flight from him. News of this nature would only be torture to a sick man who was powerless to be of any assistance. He sent a message by courier claiming a small business matter that could not be ignored called him back to his plantation in Georgia. He and his new bride would be making haste, but they would stay no longer than necessary. He felt terrible about lying to a distinguished old man who lay so sick in his bed, but it seemed the better thing to do under the circumstances.

Morris silently went about his business tidying up the room and made ready for the long evening ahead of them while watching Stephen out of the corner of his eye. He decided to extinguish the fire in the miniature coal burner in lieu of the raging waters becoming even more troublesome than they already were. The cabin was constructed as such that its heat would hold for several hours before Stephen would feel the effects of the cold and often intolerable damp and salty air. Hopefully, by then the storm would have passed and Morris could bring the small box back to life.

After assisting Stephen with his dressing and aiding him into bed, he extinguished the lighting and fumbled his way to his own cot. He was grateful for its softness and warmth. His master may be young and still hot headed at times, but he was also considerate and appreciative of those who served him. Although smaller in proportion, Morris' bedding was almost as plush and grand as Stephen's own.

"Good night sir. Sleep tight," Morris uttered softly.

"'Till the morning, my good man," Stephen replied before he rolled onto his side and pulled the thick woolen blanket high around his neck. He was eager to let slumber take him away from his worries and the storm.

The incessant pounding of a fist against wood not two hours later startled both master and servant awake. Morris leapt toward the door and opened it just enough to allow the blinding light of the globe protected candle the ship mate held high to assault his eyes.

"What is it, man?" Morris whispered with mild agitation. He looked over his shoulder in hopes the intrusion did not disturb Stephen.

"I am awake, Morris. What is it?" Stephen bellowed through the darkness.

"'Tis the captain, sir, 'e sent me for you," the mate said firmly, but hesitantly.

He'd begged not to have to be the one to awaken Lord Carlson at such an hour. Although the storm passed and the waters were calm, the sun was still not risen. Disturbing the slumber of someone as grand as Lord Carlson seemed very wrong. He wanted to have no part of it, but the captain was stern with his orders. So here he was, doing exactly what he wished so vehemently not to have to do.

"What time is it?" Stephen growled as he struggled to shake the sleep from his head.

"'Tis not yet daylight, sir," the mate replied with a groan. Why did he always get the dirty jobs? Why could that scum Williams not be set to a task such as this?

"'Tis important then?" Stephen's voice sounded a little more reasonable.

"Aye, I believe so, sir," the mate replied, mildly encouraged by the change in Stephen's tone of voice.

"Tell the captain I shall be there shortly," Stephen stated flatly as he heaved his body out of bed.

Stephen felt stiff from the chill of the storm he so foolishly stood engulfed in for a questionable period of time. Rubbing his hands together, he watched as Morris lit a lantern and did his best to pry a little heat out of the few barely glowing coals in the coal box.

"I shall have this place heated up in no time, sir," Morris stated enthusiastically.

"All well and good," Stephen said, "but for now, just help me dress to go atop."

"Very good sir," Morris responded. He set the well-used iron poker back in its cradle and began assisting Stephen with his ritual of dress.

Morris served Stephen since he was a young boy and was overly fond of him. A lover of travel and adventure, he was more than delighted to accept Stephen's offer to join him on his adventures and remain in service.

Watching young Stephen transform from an over-privileged young boy to a man who earned his own way in the world by accumulating such wealth on his own that he suffered no requirement for the inheritance of his father's vast fortune earned the valet's respect and everlasting devotion. Like the crew felt about their captain, Morris was certain that a finer man could not be found than the employer he was now assisting with dress.

Stephen made haste to the captain's cabin. Entering without knocking, he was greeted by a notably unkempt Captain Jackson

Sims seated at an ornate, sturdy looking mahogany table holding a small piece of paper. A dead carrier pigeon lay before him.

"'Twas a terrible storm he struggled through," Sims said as he nodded toward the dead bird. "'Tis a shame to lose him. Homing pigeons what can locate ships are difficult to train. This was one of our last," he mumbled. "'Tis a wonder the little guy made it through a storm the likes of what we just had. You're lucky the message even reached you."

"Aye, 'tis true," Stephen replied as he seated himself on a bench secured to the floor on the opposite side of the table from the captain. He gently nudged the bird with his index finger; as if by doing so he would bring it back to life. "What did it bring?"

"This," Sims stated flatly as he shoved the small message sheet he disbanded from the bird's leg at Stephen.

Stephen unrolled the slight bit of paper and read the words that were written in the tiniest of scripts, *The Duke has died. Our sincere sympathies.*

Although he knew the news would come one day, he felt overwhelmed with sadness.

FIVE

Elizabeth stood up and slowly paced around the room while stretching her aching back and legs in a cat-like manner. It was three weeks since she and Sally were dragged ashore and shoved into a dank, sparsely furnished and poorly lit room. The small window, that was far too high above the floor for either of them to see out of, afforded their only cool, fresh air. This came only in the wee hours of the morning before the blazing Charles Town sun arose high in the sky and turned their tiny room by the sea into a veritable steam room. The intense heat accentuated the pungent smells of the active streets beyond the confines of the tiny, box-like prison.

They were told little about where they were or what fate lay in store for them. Although no one touched Elizabeth in the same manner as the captain, Sally was not so lucky. At least once daily and sometimes more often, she was forcefully dragged out of the room, kicking and screaming, and returned several hours later, bruised and subdued. Unable to stop what was happening and not knowing what to say, Elizabeth remained silent while doing her best to make Sally as comfortable as she could during the time the once happy house maid was allowed a reprieve from the assaults and invasions of her person.

As the door was opened and the poor girl once again tossed into the room, Elizabeth managed to peer past the filthy, burly man, who delivered her maid so unceremoniously. She managed to see that they were on a very busy street near the sea port. The docks were visible and the smell of rotting fish was acute. She covered her nose with her hands and held her breath while she waited for the roughhewn door to slam shut and the thick iron lock to turn.

Elizabeth stared with pity and remorse as Sally sat crumpled just inside the door. The once comely companion's bonnet had long gone missing and her thick, waist length auburn hair, which had not seen a wash or a comb since their capture, clung to her head in a matted mess. Her originally crisp, white apron was coated with dirt and dried blood.

Was it Sally's blood? Elizabeth thought so. She pinched her eyes shut when Sally's bruised and bloody face looked up at her. The sparkling light in her green eyes that once danced with hope and dreams of a new life was replaced with a deathly dullness.

"'Tis not what I thought 'twould be like; coming here," Sally moaned as she held the corner of her apron to her nose in an effort to stop its bleeding. "I wish I never stepped foot on that bloody ship."

Elizabeth rushed to Sally's side and fell down beside her. She agreed with the poor girl completely. If she experienced any regrets at all, it was trading the safety of her husband's arms and boarding that ship of ill repute. Cradling the weeping woman, she allowed her own tears to flow and rocked Sally until both their tears dried in thick streaks down their cheeks.

Blood from Sally's nose soaked Elizabeth's sleeve, but she made no move to pull away. Some things were more important than attire. She only wished she was not so powerless in this situation. She wished even harder to know why Dr. Jameson had not managed to secure their rescue. He certainly would have had ample time by now.

"They beat me, miss," Sally cried softly. "They ripped at me clothes an' did things to me person that no man ought to do. Look," she wailed as she lifted the shredded edge of her light weight muslin skirt, "they tore me skirts while they laughed."

Elizabeth shuddered. Although she was unclear exactly what was meant when Sally referred to *things had been done to her person that no man should do'*, she suffered at the hands of that vile captain, and, on a much lesser scale, from her drunken husband on her wedding night. Thus, she possessed a vague idea of what Sally was referring to. The thought of men, one after the other, touching her companion in that way was unthinkable. For the first time in her life, Elizabeth longed to be a man. If she were a man, she would beat them all to a point near death.

"I am sorry I could not stop them, Sally. I truly am," she moaned.

"I know, miss. 'Tis not your fault. 'Tis me own fault for stabbing the captain like I did," Sally replied.

"You did the right thing. He... he was... well, you know," Elizabeth stammered.

Her cheeks flushed even more than their normal rosiness as she thought about the fact that Sally witnessed her shame.

Sally chuckled wryly as she said, "Oh hell, miss. he was only doing what men do. I should have let him finish and then we could have been on our way and no one would be the wiser to look at you. Instead, I condemned us to this life of misery."

Elizabeth gasped, "I cannot believe you would say such a thing!"

"Which? The fact that I should have let him have his way with you or that I've condemned us for life?" Sally spat.

"Why... both," Elizabeth replied.

Sally threw her head back and laughed a sad laugh, sending curdling shivers down Elizabeth's spine.

"Miss, you are a naive one, ain't you?" she said. "Do you even know what they are planning for us?"

Elizabeth stared at her waiting maid with shocked surprise. What had come over her? It must have been the trauma of the latest events. Even so, she should not speak to her mistress in a manner that was beginning to reek of contempt.

Sally pulled her body to its full height as best she could while remaining seated on the floor.

"Well miss, let me fill you in," Sally spat.

"I am sure I do not appreciate the tone you are using with me, Sally," Elizabeth clipped.

Elizabeth was fully aware that Sally was new to serving her mistress, but this type of familiarity, which bordered on contempt, was not acceptable under any circumstances. Elizabeth was of noble status, and as such expected to be treated so. It did not matter that she was traveling incognito. Sally knew her true identity. Well, not fully. Sally believed her to be Lady Elizabeth Nottingham. Elizabeth told no one of her marriage to the future Duke of Eastwick.

"I guess it don't much matter wha' you appreciate anymore, miss. Since you and me are equals now. I shall be serving you no more," Sally purged.

The hostility in Sally's voice was as shocking as her words. It stung like a slap in Elizabeth's face.

"I beg your pardon?" Elizabeth was at a loss for words.

"It seems the good doctor was no match for the captain," Sally practically hissed. "He ran off with your money and left us to the mercy of these ruffians. You are just as poor and helpless as any woman out on the street. In two more days, if the bastard who had his way with me was telling truth, you go to the slave auction an' I shall be working on a floating brothel... whatever that is. It sounds like a dream life; don't it miss?" She laughed sarcastically. "Forget about being a lady. Those days are gone. You ain't no lady here," Sally said with snarled sarcasm.

"This cannot be true!" Elizabeth screeched.

Why was Sally being so cruel?

Sally' tone softened as she continued, "Ah, but that ain't the worst of it."

"There is more?" Elizabeth said as she fell onto the room's only cot in disbelief.

"For you there is, miss. Not for me," Sally replied. Compassion floated briefly over her face as she looked at Elizabeth like one would look at someone for the first time. "The captain is telling people that you have darky blood in you. You are to be sold at auction with the other darkies that he had in the ship's hold with us. I saw their eyes, but I did not know who they were, did you?" She wrinkled her nose, "That must have been the stench that kept coming up so strong."

Elizabeth jumped to her feet.

"That's preposterous!" she screeched. "I am nothing of the kind. How can he even say such a thing? Just look at me. Do I look like a darky?"

"Well, miss," Sally hesitated, "'Tis hard to say. Your white for sure, but then the men say that lots of darkies get the black bred out of them by plantation owners. This new country has plenty of darkies that look white working in the main house. Most of them are the sons and daughters of the master. You only need a drop of darky blood to be labeled a darky... only a drop. Then there is...," Sally stopped, as if afraid to continue.

"There is what?" Elizabeth snapped.

The pitiful woman took a deep breath before answering.

"Your hair, miss. 'Tis black as night and as thick and unruly as a darky's hair. I don't rightly recall ever seeing a white noble woman with hair such as yours," Sally cooed with a sinister tone.

Elizabeth was taken even more aback when she realized how much pleasure Sally experienced delivering the horrendous news of her fate. The thought made her seethe with rage.

The maid's superior satisfaction faded and she gasped with regret for her words and attitude when she saw the look on Elizabeth's face. She quickly leaned back to avoid the blow the enraged woman looked capable of delivering at any moment.

To calm herself, Elizabeth focused on her breathing. She filled her lungs with the putrid air she had gradually grown accustomed to and let it out in a slow, concentrated manner. She could hardly contain her anger. Slapping Sally would have eased some of it, but she could not do such a thing to someone who already suffered an extensive amount of abuse no matter how badly the girl needed to be put in her place.

"You have never seen any noblewoman's real hair; silly twit," Elizabeth growled. "You have only seen the wigs or caps they wear. House maids do not have the privilege of seeing a woman with her hair in its natural state, like a waiting maid would."

Sally looked to Elizabeth in stunned silence at the realization of the truth of her former mistress' statement. Quiet echoed between the two women for the remainder of the afternoon. When a burly, foul smelling sailor came and yanked Sally away once again, Elizabeth was actually relieved. Sally's new found boldness and open resentfulness was stifling.

Elizabeth needed time to think about the news Sally present-ed, as well as Sally's new treatment of her. How was she to cope with all of this? She knew all too well the type of kindness she extended to the servants was a rarity. For her to be placed in a position where others could reap cruelty upon her at their leisure was unconscionable. What added to its severity was the fact that she knew full well she would not be able to hide her pampered background from the other servants. Resentment would be sure to arise, just as it had with Sally.

When the ruffian's finally returned her former servant to the room a few hours later, Sally was sporting even more bruises and blood. Although Elizabeth questioned how long the woman would be able to survive under such cruel conditions, she made no move to comfort her. A wall was formed between them from the con-tempt that Sally so clearly held for her mistress.

SIX

The night proved to be long and tortuous.

Sally took on a persona that Elizabeth hardly recognized. She grew more and more abrasive and bold with every return from the ravishing of their detestable captors.

When they were first placed in the tiny, smelly room, it went without saying that Elizabeth would be the occupant of the single lumpy cot in their tiny box-like environment. Other than a worn looking wooden table and two dangerously rickety chairs, it was all the furnishings provided. Sally made a bed on the pile of rags and hay tossed on the floor in the corner. Since Sally never experienced sleeping arrangements even remotely as comfortable while in the service of the Jameson estate, she was content with the arrangement.

That night Sally laid claim to the cot, suggesting Elizabeth start getting accustomed to living in the style of a slave and be thankful that there was at least some softness beneath her. Elizabeth recognized the truth in Sally' words. Her thoughts went to the young girl curled up in the cupboard beneath the stairs when she arrived at the Jameson estate on the morning that altered her fate forever.

Since Sally was much taller and stronger than Elizabeth, there was nothing for Elizabeth to do but submit herself to the degradation of being tossed from bed to floor.

It was actually the least of her worries. The news of Captain Kline's vile lie and plans for the sale of her person at a slave auction weighed heavy on her mind.

She could not fathom how Dr. Jameson could abandon her like this. It made no sense to her. Was it not she who funded his trip to the emancipated colonies? Was it not she who signed a significant portion of her trust over to him for their care while traveling and settling down? How could he repay her for her kindness and generosity in such a manner? Where was he now? Was he off enjoying her money as a free man while she was being sold into slavery? She simply could not believe the friend of her father to be a coward and a thief, but it appeared he was.

Elizabeth wiped a tear that was trickling slowly down her cheek. How foolish she was to have run away from Stephen. How silly of her to fantasize about marrying for love. More than once Stephen proclaimed his love for her while in her bed, but she refused to listen. She chose to believe his words a product of the alcohol he enjoyed imbibing his mind with instead of the truth of his heart. So convinced was she that her love was one sided, she never gave him a chance to prove his love outside of the bedroom. She left far too soon to give their marriage a chance. Maybe he did really love her as she loved him. If so, she would never know. He was lost to her by her own foolish actions.

She shuddered as she remembered bits and pieces of the horrors of Captain Kline's sweaty, smelly body crushing hers while he violated her. The clean scent of Stephen and his tender, overwhelmingly arousing ministries were stark in comparison.

Although her husband was zealous in his desire to possess her fully, he was never vile or cruel, not even on their wedding night. Her initial viewpoint of their nights together was the viewpoint of a naïve virgin who lacked the female guidance afforded most ladies of her station. Had she known then what she knew now, she would have realized that her new husband was stating truth about doing his best not to hurt her while he struggled to keep bridled his lust for the beautiful young wife who made him wild with desire. After all, the nights following were certainly pleasurable. or would have been had she not been tortured by her duty to be silent and still.

Elizabeth was furious with herself. A husband desiring his wife was a rarity among the socially elite. How foolish she was to have treated it so lightly. If she could do things over, she would have stayed and gotten to know her virile and handsome husband. From her conversations with Sally, she discovered the feelings she felt for him were truly those of love. She was not mistaken in this. She never discussed her feelings with another woman before. She had no validation that what she felt was real until now. If she had it to do all over again she would have stayed and nurtured her relationship with Stephen in hopes that he would grow to love her as she loved him. She would have never run away.

She slid her hand over her stomach. Their voyage kept them at sea for two and a half months, the majority of which her head was hanging over the side of the ship's rails or over a chamber pot wrenching up the contents of her stomach. She and Sally were imprisoned in this locked, box-like room for several weeks now and yet she continued to wretch and vomit, particularly upon rising. Sally was worldlier in the ways of the female body. She examined Elizabeth's breasts and still flat stomach closely before proclaiming that her mistress was with child.

Since the captain's violation of her person was only a few weeks ago and Sally stabbed him before he satisfied his lust, there was no guessing who the father was. She was carrying the heir that her father-in-law, the Duke of Eastwick, so badly desired. She was carrying Stephen's child.

Her trunks never found their way to her. Needless to say, she assumed her belongings were sold or given to some of the sordid women whose hawking their wares permeated the night as a trinket of appreciation for some sexual favor or the like. She was without clean clothes or toiletries and there was no mirror to be found. It was probably for the best. She was certain she made a frightful sight. Even so, she would have liked to inspect herself. Was she showing signs of wear and fatigue from all she endured? Was she looking worn and haggard? Did her eyes still have that brilliant glow that consistently won over the hearts of so many or were they hollow and lackluster like her companions? They say that a woman with child radiated a special glow. Was she radiating? She just did not know.

Elizabeth longed for the opportunity to clean up. Her teeth were coated with a foul tasting film and her body odor offended her at times to the point of nausea. The itching that tormented her was a strong indication she was bit sleeping in the lumpy cot. Soon she would be covered with sores and some type of disease would more than likely consume her. She heaved an enormous sigh. It was probably the lesser of the evils that was about to occur.

The women spent their days wearing only their shifts and light linen skirts in an attempt to avoid being overcome by the heat. Elizabeth stood in the light that poured through the small window by complements of the full moon. She looked down and sighed at the filth and stains that coated her once pristine attire. Its lace trim fell away in several places and would soon be off completely.

The coolness of the night was slowly replacing the incessant stifling heat from the impact of the afternoon sun, making it a little easier for Elizabeth to relax and fall asleep. She stole a glance at the silhouette of her cell mate's body as she sprawled comfortably on the cot Elizabeth once claimed and emitted an indignant humph. After pounding at the hay in an attempt to make it just a little fluffier, Elizabeth arranged the rags as best she could and sunk down onto them. Sally was right. She was grateful to at least have some type of padding beneath her. The truth be known, the hay was actually more comfortable than the cot and probably housed fewer critters.

She closed her eyes and allowed herself to remember her younger days at their country estate. Her mother and father had taken them on a picnic. Her scamp of a younger brother, Herald, was trying to coax her into the icy cold lake, knowing full well she would freeze, but he was too young to realize the possible repercussions of such freezing. It was all in good fun and there was plenty of laughter.

Elizabeth's bond with her brother was so strong she never even thought to be jealous over how he commanded and received the love from her uncle that she so desperately longed for. She missed Herald. She missed his rich sense of humor and zest for life. She never considered the fact that her escape from her imagined bondage with Stephen would also separate her from Herald. That fact never even entered her mind. The fact that she did not have a chance to tell him she was leaving and say good-bye filled her with sorrowful remorse.

It seemed like Elizabeth only just fell asleep when the thud of the door being thrown open and slamming into the thick, salt-weathered wooden wall roused her.

"Wake up, me beauties," chortled an old sailor as he pulled a dented tin wash tub that saw better days into the room. "'Tis time ta wash up!"

Elizabeth had grown so accustomed to the appearance of her motley looking captors that she barely noticed the old sailor's decayed and partially toothless grin and matted bristly whiskers. Even the accentuated stench of his unwashed body, as a sudden breeze found its way through the door, did not assault her like it used to. Her focus was on something that represented a reprieve from the horrendous existence she was forced to endure these past weeks. This grizzly old sailor brought in a bath! It did not matter what he looked or smelled like right now. To her he was the most wonderful person in the world.

The old sailor finished placing the severely dented and slightly misshapen tub in the center of the room and shot a look toward the cot where Sally sat, indignantly watching him. His eyes found Elizabeth kneeling in the corner of the room on the pile of hay.

"Ya are ta 'elp the lady wash up. D'ya 'ere?" he growled at Sally. "You'll do it right, girl, if ya know what be good fer ya."

Two skinny, scraggly men, who Elizabeth noted could surely benefit from a bath themselves, followed the gruff sailor into the room. Their hands were laden with buckets of steaming water. Shortly afterward a third sailor arrived with a small trunk containing Elizabeth's toiletries. This was just too good to be true.

Sally waited for the men to close the door behind them before leaping off the cot.

"Wow. A bath! I never..." she squealed as she stripped her night shift off and eased her naked body down into the steaming tub.

Elizabeth, who was not accustomed to seeing another person totally naked -least of all a servant- reddened and turned her head. Unfortunately, it was not before she witnessed the clear water cloud from the caked blood and soil that quickly washed off Sally' scarred and battered body.

"That bath was intended for me. He told you that," Elizabeth grumbled.

"I did not hear him tell me that'," Sally replied saucily. "I heard him tell me that I needed to help you clean up. And I shall just as soon as I have finished with me own wash up," she chuckled from deep within her throat.

Elizabeth was livid. The water was a light brown from the filth of her former maid's body. Even though she was well aware of the circumstances that caused their current filthy conditions, she was certain the woman had not experienced a true bath in at least a year; if ever.

A gasp of horror escaped the forlorn aristocrat's pursed lips at the sight of tiny dead bugs floating in the surface scum. There was absolutely no way she would allow one drop of that water to touch her body. If her captors wanted her clean, then they would just have to provide a fresh bath.

Had Sally not become such a belligerent shrew, Elizabeth might have felt compassion for the woman's present state and condition. As it was, she felt only revulsion and contempt.

Although the faint knock at the door alerted Elizabeth to back into the corner, it went unnoticed by her bath engrossed companion. Sally's surprise at being caught in the act of stealing her former mistress's fresh, steaming bath water was apparent when she found herself looking into Captain Kline's angry, beady eyes.

"Wha' the bloody 'ell is going on 'ere?" the captain roared. "Who the 'ell told you to filthy up the tub with your bugs an' scum, wench?"

The captain's face was almost purple with rage as he glowered at Sally while she struggled to shrink as best she could from his sight. He stood in an openly indignant stance with his hands placed firmly on his hips while he waited for the frightened young woman's response. When she did nothing more than whimper, he emitted a roar that resembled that of a wild animal and kicked his heavy boot against the tub with such a force he caused the tub to topple onto its side. Thus adding another dent to its well cratered walls.

The loud thud of Sally' body as she hit the roughhewn planked flooring mixed with the gushing of the filthy water that quickly spread across the room. Sally' cry of indignation blended with Elizabeth's screech of dismay while she watched the filthy, bug infested water flood her makeshift bedding. Her dream of a new life in the United States became a living nightmare.

"I 'ave a right to clean me own body more than that of a darky" Sally wailed.

"Ya 'ave only the right ta spread your legs until we ar' through with ya, wench. Nothin' more!" the captain spat with disgust. His eyes slowly searched the room until they settled on Elizabeth's small frame. She shriveled under his lustful drool, wishing herself invisible. "An'," he chuckled, "we both know she ain't no darky."

"She ain't?" Sally bolted upward in surprise, negligent of the fact that she was standing naked in the presence of a man.

The captain twisted his head back in Sally' direction as if he forgot she was in the room. Seemingly unmoved by the sight of her nakedness, he roared, "I'll be orderin' fresh water fer the lady an' I 'ad better not 'ear tha' ya did not take care of your mistress proper. Do ya 'ear me, wench?"

"Yes, sir," Sally moaned from the safety of the corner of the room where she retreated to almost immediately after feeling the wrath of the captain's foot.

It did not go unnoticed by the two women that the captain realigned their stations in life.

As the captain started out the door, Elizabeth found the courage and strength to step forward and speak, even if it was only above a whisper.

"Captain Kline, please wait," she said.

Startled by her request, the grizzly sea dog stopped in his tracks and waited for her to find her voice again. Struggling with her emotions, it took Elizabeth a little longer than she would have liked to manipulate the question past her lips. The captain seemed only too happy to wait, since it provided him time to devour her slowly with his eyes.

"If you know that I am not a darky, then pray tell why are you telling people that I am?" Elizabeth was finally able to ask.

"'Tis business, milady, just business," the captain replied in a light hearted manner as he flashed a wicked grin and continued out the door.

"Then 'tis true," Elizabeth mumbled, more to herself than anyone else, "I am to be sold at auction as a darky"

"Aye milady," the captain's muffled voice floated through the closed door, "'Tis indeed true."

The shock of the reality of what was about to occur was so intense, Elizabeth's body shook until her legs were no longer sturdy enough to hold her and she crumbled to the floor.

SEVEN

The sun was exceedingly hot for such an early morning hour as Paulette Moore grudgingly left the pleasures of a lazy hammock nestled in the shade of the hemlock grove to join her brother, Arthur, inside their Georgian mansion. He promised to take her to market in Charles Town and purchase a slave for her birthday. She could hardly wait.

Her damned fool personal attendant, Jane, a comely mulatto who was a gift from her parents on her tenth birthday, smuggled herself into the bed of a field hand, got pregnant, and died giving birth. Now she was left to struggle with the clumsy ministrations of the unschooled hands of one of the second floor maids. Of course, the child Jane bore still lived and now belonged to Paulette, but he was of no use to her until he was at least three or four years of age.

It certainly would not hurt if her brother gifted her with another slave or two as part of her dowry. Slaves were a commodity, after all. It was no secret the greater the dowry the more desirable the lady. Not that she needed to worry about a man desiring her. Paulette was considered one of the state of Georgia's most sought after southern belles. Her beauty was enough to capture a man even without her dowry. Many a man had already offered his hand in marriage. Most were rich men with large cotton and sugar plantations. She was holding out for that proposal from the one man who managed to capture her heart as well and the friendship of her brother. As soon as her darling Stephen Carlson returned from tending to his sick father's estate, she had no doubt in her mind he would be on bended knee proposing to her. She was certain, had the summons for his return not arrived when it did, she would have been engaged to him by now. In the meantime, she saw no harm in padding her dowry just a little more.

Arthur Moore extended his arm as his sister glided up beside him and casually guided her to the breakfast table

"Are you ready for an exciting trip to auction, my lovely half-sister?" he asked enthusiastically.

"I do not know, my handsome half-brother," Paulette whined as she feigned boredom. 'Tis such a long ride and the days are so hot. Isn't there an auction in Savannah soon?"

Accustomed to her theatrical antics, and knowing full well how much she enjoyed traveling to Charles Town, Arthur played along.

"There probably is, dearest, but I understand the stock at the Charles Town auction house is quite spectacular. There is even a darky who looks white. What a novelty that would be, dearest," he drawled. "I hear she was raised to act and be amongst the ladies. I should think her likely to know all of the latest styles for you and possibly some gossip as well. But, if you would rather wait for the auction here..."

"Oh hush. You are well aware that a white mulatto at auction is a commodity I should not wish to pass on. You can be such a devil at times," Paulette cooed as he helped her into her chair next to his at the end of the sixteen-foot Louis XVI style, mahogany dining table.

"Well then, let us eat up and get going," Arthur said with a chuckle. "We have a full day's ride ahead."

Arthur also noted the weather. The sun had barely risen and it was already necessary to seek shade from the effects of its blistering rays. The barouche would likely be intolerable and require a block of ice for some semblance of comfort. They would also have to take their horses into consideration and go slower than usual.

"Do not worry, my dearest," Arthur said when he noticed Paulette looking out of the window with concern. "There will be plenty of stops and water on the trip."

"Will we be stopping at Aunt Mildred's at Beaumont?" she asked.

Arthur's eyes lit up. What a splendid idea. He should have thought of it himself. Beaumont plantation was just about halfway between Savannah and Charles Town. It required just a short detour from the road they would be traveling. It would make a perfect place to stop for the night. They had not seen their father's widowed sister in months. Mildred suffered with her health for some time now and found travel tedious and taxing. A brief visit with her would be welcome on all accounts.

"I say," he said with genuine enthusiasm. "A visit with Aunt Mildred would certainly serve us in many ways, would it not, my dearest? How clever you are."

Arthur smiled as he reached across the table to stroke Paulette's smooth ivory cheek that sported just enough blush color to be within the boundaries of fashion.

Paulette was smug with satisfaction. If her brother found her clever with the suggestion of their breaking up the tedious drive with a visit to their aunt's plantation, perhaps she could earn even more praise by suggesting they spend more time there.

"Since the auction is not for a few days and 'tis so unbearably hot, perhaps we could spend an extra night to really break up the dreariness of the trip," she drawled lazily, "I would much rather house the spare night with Aunt Mildred than in some stuffy hotel in Charles Town." She giggled mischievously, "I remember that pond in the north pasture. I am certain it would feel just lovely after a long day's ride in this heat. Why not stay a day to enjoy it and continue on after?"

Arthur popped the last of his hardboiled egg into his mouth and chewed slowly, emphasizing the fact that he was considering her suggestion. He dramatically swallowed his fare and washed it down with a mouthful of freshly brewed coffee from a newly arrived shipment he recently procured from Jamaica. He savored its flavor before he swallowed with a loud unmannerly gulp. With a crisp linen napkin that matched the tablecloth perfectly, he dabbed at the corners of his mouth with meticulous care before standing up slowly. His lean, well-muscled physique provided a fine form for his fashionable light weight costume. He wore only a pale gray linen vest over his natural cotton shirt and rich burgundy breeches. They were made from cotton grown on their very own plantation and milled in their very own mill house.

Next to Stephen, Paulette thought Arthur the most handsome and virile man in all of Georgia. Stephen was the only man who could even come close to her brother's impossible good looks, wealth, and social status. If things went her way, she would soon have both of Georgia's most desirable men at her beck and call.

Catching a glimpse of Arthur's richly tanned chest beneath his open necked shirt and loose hanging cravat, she smiled.

"You have been baking in the sun again," she said in a tone that was a mix of whimper and cooing. "Have you been to the pond without me or are you simply weathered from doing our overseers job?"

"Sister," Arthur chuckled as he walked behind her and wrapped his arms around her slim shoulders, allowing his fingers to lightly slide up the nape of her neck. "Do you really think I would go to the pond without you?" He sighed heavily, "My, oh my, you are so beautiful, my lovely, sweet sister." Leaning close to her ear, he whispered, "If you were not my sister I would take you as my bride."

Reveling in the sensation of his hot breath against her ear lobe, Paulette giggled and boldly placed her hand over his, forcing his fingers deeper into her flesh. She so loved the effect she had on men, even if this one was her half-brother.

"I know, dearest," she sighed, "but, alas it cannot be. We share our father's blood, after all." She turned her face to look at him and continued, "You know that no matter who you marry... or I... you shall always have my heart." She leaned her head back against his arm and felt the heat of his body radiating through his cotton shirt against her bare neck. "Well," she said with renewed energy, "I could do this all day, but we should be going."

"Indeed," Arthur mused as he reluctantly pulled his hand away from her silken skin. Unable to resist, he caressed the exposed flesh that peeked from the lace that covered her upper shoulders and lowered his lips to her neck. Placing a feather light kiss just below her ear, he whispered. "Your idea of spending a few nights in Beaumont is perfect... as are you."

Paulette closed her eyes while she struggled to maintain her composure. Arthur was such a scoundrel. It was no wonder women swooned over him so. She was tempted to call his bluff and demand satisfaction and release right then and there, but, of course, brothers and sisters did not engage in such actions in polite society.

Many a time Arthur bemoaned his fate for being born long after the time of the acceptance of siblings marrying. Even though they were half-brother and half-sister, the laws still held since they shared blood from the same father. He was six years old when his mother died giving birth to a brother who also died within a few days. It was not long afterward that his father remarried. Less than a year later Paulette was born.

They first realized their love for each other was more than normal siblings possessed when Paulette was fourteen and Arthur was twenty. It was on one of the hottest summer days the state had seen since it was founded as one of the thirteen colonies and per-haps even prior to that. Paulette begged her parents to let her go to the swimming hole on the far end of their plantation. Since the threat of an encounter with a renegade Cherokee was prevalent, her parents adamantly denied her. After thirty minutes of non-stop lamenting from Paulette, the frustrated couple ordered her to her room for the remainder of the day. Her waiting maid, Jane, was given the task of washing her down with the coolest water avail-able. It would have to suffice.

Spoiled beyond any sense of reason by both her mother and her father, Paulette disobeyed their orders to remain in her room and stole out of the house and off to the swimming hole. She threatened poor Jane with the beating of her life if she uttered one word of her whereabouts to anyone. Knowing full well that a beating from Paulette's parents would be far easier to endure than a beating from her mean and spoiled mistress, Jane obediently fol-lowed Paulette's orders.

Although Paulette did not meet up with any Indians, she did encounter Arthur; who was also there against their parent's wish-es. Paulette removed her skirt and stomacher, leaving only her light corset and shift to swim in. She managed to loosen enough of the corset's stays to make it comfortable and was gaily splashing around the cool body of water by the time Arthur arrived and joined her. The two laughed, giggled and played in the water well into the afternoon. The sun was fading behind the trees when they finally pulled their soaked and tired bodies out of the cool liquid and flopped onto the lush grass beneath an ancient black walnut tree.

Arthur's shocked surprise was barely masked while he watched Paulette boldly walk from the pond, seemingly unaware that the light-weight and water soaked fabric clinging to her already voluptuous body left nothing to the imagination. She moved without a care in the world. Admittedly unschooled in what happened between a man and a woman, Paulette was still very aware that she was misbehaving in the worst of fashion. She was thrilled by the naughtiness of it. Life on the plantation could be so dull.

Arthur spread a thick blanket that was kept in the boot of the imported hunting fourgon he was so fond of driving onto a shaded section of ground and coaxed his beautiful, young half-sister to join him. He spread the fabric of her full skirt across some low hanging branches and created a covering for her to lie under for protection from the few rays from the blistering sun that managed to weave their way through the thick foliage that intertwined between the close growing trees. The set up was deliciously ingenious, since it still allowed the warm breeze to pass over her body while protecting her delicate creamy skin from being ravished by the fierce Georgia sun.

The two spent the better part of the hour basking in the warmth of the balmy afternoon while they waited for their clothing to dry sufficiently for them to return home. Unbeknownst to his innocent sister, Arthur struggled vehemently with his manly urges the entire time.

With the sun almost set and their clothes fairly dry, he leaned on his elbow to suggest they start back for home. His heart almost stopped from the beauty of Paulette's profile as the shadows, created by the sun's hint of relinquishment of the sky to the full moon, blended with her creamy skin. With the fabric of her shift still damp and molded to her pert breasts, her thick golden curls splayed down her back, and her sultry blue eyes half closed, she resembled a statue of a Greek goddess displayed in the home of a friend in Savannah. It was more than he could bare. Before he could stop himself, he leaned over to steal a kiss.

For the briefest of moments Paulette kissed back, but then rapidly came to her senses. They were brother and sister! What were they thinking? Her innocence and naivety took over. She considered herself ruined for marriage and her future prospects for a husband destroyed. Leaping to her feet with lightning speed, she grabbed her skirt and stomacher and disappeared into the nearby grove before Arthur was able to come down from the clouds, regain his senses, and realize what he had done. For weeks following the incident she would not spare a word or even a look in his direction.

Arthur's humiliation and regret for his thoughtless unbridled actions toward dear, innocent Paulette ran deep. He did not blame her for hating him. He hated himself. Even so, they were closer than most siblings could ever imagine being and he found her refusal to acknowledge him so crushing he did not think he could go on living.

When Arthur's father complained of Cherokees raiding their livestock at some of the plantation's outposts and asked his son to join him on a small outing for the purpose of securing their boundaries, he was more than eager to go. They anticipated being gone for a month. Perhaps that would allow enough time for Paulette to cease being angry with him and for him to think of a way to make it up to her.

It was during that outing that James Moore died.

The rains were excessive, making visibility more than a few feet away almost impossible. They were approaching a ravine flooded with raging waters that resembled a miniature version of the ocean waves on a recent voyage Arthur took to Virginia, when his father's gelding was spooked by a bobcat and broke its gait. Thinking his father in control of his mount, Arthur gave chase to the bobcat for about a quarter mile. To his horrified surprise, when he returned he found his father was face down in the ravine and the gelding struggling a few yards away with a broken leg. In denial of the situation, it took minutes of agonizing tear-filled begging for a response from his father while he inspected his limp body for him to accept the fact that the man was dead.

What followed was a complete blur to Arthur. After the ordeal of putting his father's gelding out of its misery, he tackled the heartbreaking and arduous task of loading James Moore's broken body onto his own mount and taking him back to the plantation.

To Arthur's surprise and dismay, not only did he have to suffer witnessing his father's death, he was forced to endure the brutal accusations of his step-mother, Margaret Moore. The woman never managed to find room in her heart for the Arthur from the day she met him. When she realized how bonded he was with her daughter, she made certain to emphasize regularly the fact that he was not her son and not a full blood relation to Paulette; hence, such a bond was unsuitable.

Riddled with grief and concern for what the future might hold for a widow who never encouraged a warm relationship with her step son, Margaret convinced herself and a few influential friends that her husband's death was the deliberation of Arthur's actions. In short, she insisted Arthur murdered his own father in his eagerness for his inheritance.

Margaret Moore's accusations spurred a rather lengthy investigation that cultivated tremendous hurt along with a serious amount of added animosity on Arthur's part toward her.

If Paulette knew nothing else about her dear half-brother, she knew he loved their father whole heartedly. Feeling her mother's accusations unfounded and unfair, she sided with Arthur. She took great pains in comforting him as best she could, but more importantly she forgave him for his foolish blunder that afternoon at the swimming hole.

Arthur was eventually cleared of Margaret's accusations of the murder and his inheritance -which included the plantation and all that was in it- was presented to him as per the law and the contents of his father's will. Paulette and her mother were left a tidy sum, but certainly not enough to allow them to maintain the lifestyle they knew, loved, and expected to continue without Arthur's good graces.

Unable to stand the sight of his step-mother a moment longer, but not the type of man to simply turn his back on the woman who captured his father's heart and helped raise him, he bade Margaret leave his home and made provisions for her elaborate keeping in nearby Savannah. Margaret was more than willing to oblige. Being an active socialite, she found this arrangement most agreeable.

Paulette was given a choice of remaining in residence with Arthur or leaving with her mother. By now, Paulette comforted and ministered Arthur to the point where she was convinced that she was in love and could not bring herself to leave him.

Arthur was at a loss as what to do when Paulette's fantasy love gradually grew into an obsession. As time unfolded, she sought to act upon it in little ways that were far from appropriate for a young lady toward a gentleman, let alone for a sister toward a brother. To her mounting frustration Arthur matured enough to keep his wits about him and she was not successful. He blamed his own sinful love for her, excessive doting, and providing her with her every want for the pickle he now found himself in.

A visit by Aunt Mildred occurred just in perfect timing for his dilemma. With their father's sister in house, Paulette was forced to tame her behavior. She kept her clumsy advances restricted to whenever her aunt was absent, which Arthur made certain was a rarity.

This enforced time of abstinence from her antics, as well as insightful feminine conversations with her favorite aunt, gave Paulette room to think and ideas to ponder on. She began to realize the folly of her ways. No matter how much she and Arthur loved each other, it was impossible for them to be together the way she longed for them to be. They would never be able to exist in society if they were to act on their attraction. A tortured Arthur new this and had been trying to get her to see it for quite some time.

Arthur's genuine affection for her was so strong, he could deny her nothing. If Aunt Mildred had not arrived when she had, he could not be sure whether he would have given in to Paulette's pleas and brought shame to them all.

Having been influenced strongly by her mother, social status meant a great deal to Paulette. She placed it above most everything else. As much as she wanted it to be different and shout out her love for her darling Arthur, common sense prevailed. She would eventually have to marry a man who was not him, just as he would eventually have to marry a woman who was not her.

As time went by and Paulette developed into a stunning young woman. She reveled in the attention the young beaus introduced at her coming out ball were continually bestowing upon her. Even so, this did not stop her from being excessively possessive where her half-brother was concerned.

As the years rolled by and they both matured and grew more accustomed to the feelings that could never be acted upon, they decided it was time they consider the prospects that existed for Paulette to secure a husband and Arthur a wife. Promising neither would move a distance away from the other, they each launched their search in earnest for a spouse to complement their social status.

When Arthur befriended Lord Stephen Carlson and introduced him to Paulette, brother and sister were certain their search for a suitable husband for her was over. Not only did Arthur and Stephen become the best of mates, but his profitable plantation neighbored theirs. Since he was the best of mates and Paulette found him exceedingly handsome, who better for Arthur to share her with?

A wife for Arthur was yet to be found, but they were certain once Paulette was married and settled, he would find the right woman and settle down quick enough.

The long journey loomed over them and Paulette knew that every minute delayed would allow the sun more time to increase its assault on the Georgian countryside.

She pushed her chair back as hard as she could, jabbing its

ornate, gilded backing into Arthur's stomach, and smiled as she heard a 'humph' escape him. Enough of his silliness, it was time to be on their way.

EIGHT

The weight of the coarse iron cuffs on Elizabeth's tiny wrists was excruciating. Rough edges cut into her skin, staining the pale pink linen frock the surly captain rescued from her trunk in anticipation of the auction with tiny crimson droplets. The remainders of her belongings were distributed amongst the men to use as gifts for their lady friends.

She struggled to keep up with the long legged slaves who shared the shackled line of human stock. The only white skin amidst a sea of darkness, her presence caused quite a stir.

After Elizabeth threatened to inform the crowd of her vile injustice just as soon as she was able, the captain took precautions and ordered her drugged with a dose of laudanum. She was given just enough to fog her mind and subdue her manner without the crowd recognizing her drug induced state. Barely able to utter her name, Elizabeth was helpless to announce her truth to the seemingly endless crowd she was tugged and pulled through so unceremoniously.

Eager to display her rich raven waves, her captors denied her a bonnet. Her scalp burned under the searing sun as she stood in line and awaited her turn to be pushed onto the block and bargained over like an animal.

Since slavery was abolished in England, Elizabeth had never witnessed such a sale. Even if slavery was still legal, she would never have been allowed to attend such an event. It was unseemly for a lady to be exposed to such. Even in her state of murky twilight, she was acutely aware of how horridly humiliating it was for the captives who preceded her.

More of the laudanum the ship's doctor provided for the captain to force down her throat was brought along for good measure. Its effects kept her emotionless while she watched men and women being stripped of their clothing and their naked bodies poked, pawed, and at times caressed in their most intimate places.

The bidders discussed each slave's usefulness for labor, breeding, and his own personal pleasure as the auction dragged on. No one escaped this degradation. Men, women and children alike were marched onto the auction block and subjected to variations of this humiliation before being sold to the highest bidder. Tears and wailing pierced the air as babies were forcibly wrested from their mothers, wives from their husbands, and siblings from each other.

Elizabeth watched as the last of her shackled companions was led up onto the auction block. He was a tall, broad shouldered man with skin the color of rich ebony. Moist from the sun's burning rays, his rich black skin glistened and reflected the sunlight like the fine gem she commissioned her jeweler to place in a setting for a necklace she greatly favored. She had worn it so often its gold was worn precariously thin so she tucked it away in a box she kept her precious things in for safe keeping until she was able to take it to the jeweler for repair. That box was now long gone, as was the necklace.

The chained man's face was expressionless as his eyes met hers. The auctioneers unceremoniously removed his threadbare breaches to display his generous anatomy to the potential buyers. What his facial expression hid, his eyes did not. Elizabeth cringed at this poor man's shame.

Her expression stirred him in some way and his back straightened and chin raised a notch. They were not exaggerated gestures and probably went unnoticed by the bidders who were absorbed in their scrutinizing of his various body parts. The fact that she noticed seemed to please him.

Elizabeth realized her mind was hazy, but she doubted it was so hazy as to misconstrue that look. He though she was a darky slave. The thought was almost overwhelming.

She looked quickly away, doing her best to pull herself together. She was to be the last one sold and her time was coming soon. She needed to clear the fog from her head, regain the composure a lady of noble birth and breeding was expected to have at all times, and tell this crowd the wrong done to her. Surely, once the truth about her situation was discovered, the crowd would hang that captain for his vile ways. Although she was anxious to return to England, apologize to her husband for her foolishness, and become the faithful and doting wife she knew she could be, she would not mind sticking around long enough to watch that disgusting ship's captain hang. In fact, she was certain she would enjoy it.

The moment Elizabeth both longed for and dreaded arrived. She straightened her back as best she could under the weight of the chains and cuffs and stumbled up the wooden steps to the platform. She shook her head and cleared her throat in preparation for the plea she was prepared to shout out just as soon as her feet touched the platform. To her horror and dismay, the ship's doctor greeted her in the center of the stairs and forced one more dose of laudanum down her throat for good measure. He explained to the auctioneers that she was a high spirited mulatto from special circumstances and it would be much easier to get top dollar if they kept her sedated until the auction was over. Although not a common practice, the auctioneers experienced situations of the like before and, since it was their duty to get the highest bid they could, they simply nodded their heads in agreement and proceeded with the auction.

Elizabeth's heart sank as her head swirled from the effects of the newly ingested laudanum. She would never find her voice now. She could barely focus three feet before her. The world was a blur.

The thick, wooden stairs were worn smooth in the center by excessive use, but the sides still threatened an uncovered foot with filthy slivers of various thicknesses and lengths. Although they gave her one of her gowns to wear, she was not provided with a pair of shoes. When her tender bare foot stumbled off the smooth center, her soft flesh was immediately assaulted by a three-inch sliver of decaying wood.

A loud scream escaped her lips as she jumped from shock

mixed with pain. Her captors stumbled to and fro while the crowd rolled with laughter.

Angered and embarrassed, one of the burly men pulled his fist back and sent it flying right into the middle of her back. Although its force pushed most of the air out of her lungs, she used what little remained to wail with painful indignation before falling to her knees and doing her best to replenish her air supply.

Pulling her to her feet, the disgruntled man half dragged, half carried her petite frame to the top of the steps and dropped her, unceremoniously, onto the platform. Without thinking about the fact that she was on public display, Elizabeth pulled up her skirt; exposing a bit of ankle while she inspected her wounded appendage through blurring eyes. Murmurs spread through the crowd while they watched her intently work at getting the sliver out of her foot, seemingly ignoring their presence.

Paulette leaned into her brother and whispered, "The chit acts like she has not one care in the world. Buy her for me, will you dearest?"

Arthur bowed to his regal looking half-sister and made his way to the front of the crowd where the bidders waited for the sale to begin. When he reached the edge of the platform, his eyes locked with the deepest violet pools of enchantment he had ever encountered. He was so taken by surprise that he almost forgot his reason for being there.

The snap of the auctioneer's whip across Elizabeth's back sent him into a tail spin. He roared his indignation so loud his fellow bidders joined in. It was clear this woman was a gem amid a pile of rocks and they did not appreciate one flaw being place on her body by a bully such as he.

The crowd's outrage only added to the auctioneer's angst and embarrassment. He stepped away, but not before his boot found the softness of poor Elizabeth's backside in a swift, hard kick and his hand grabbed the back of her bodice. With a vice-like grip, he held firm to the fine fabric while the weight of her tiny body plummeting forward created the resistance needed for the material to tear all the way down the back to her waist. The auctioneer pulled aggressively until he was satisfied that her corset-less body was exposed for all eyes to see before he released it and stepped back, glowering with disdain.

The crowd got a good solid view of her wares before Elizabeth, who was still dulled by the laudanum, realized what happened. It was even longer before she gathered enough wits about her to scoop up her bodice and hold it firmly to her breasts.

The forlorn aristocrat looked at the pool of blood forming around her foot on the platform and sighed. She was not sure which needed her hands more, her bodice or her foot.

Painfully aware of the auctioneer's prompting for her to stand, she saw no way out. For now, there was nothing to do but obey.

Since she was unable to remove the entire sliver from her tender flesh, Elizabeth's foot was not only swelling, but the pain was intensifying. Her wound throbbed to the beat of her heart. She received an injury similar to this a few years ago and Madeleine had placed a healing salve on it. She wished she possessed such a salve now, along with a needle and thread.

Her mind felt weak and her body was tired. She wanted nothing more than to lie down and sleep until this nightmare was over.

Noticing her condition, Arthur guessed she was drugged. He scowled his disapproval, but said nothing.

As the bidding began, Elizabeth tried to speak out to tell the crowd who she was and how she had come to be placed in such a position. She strained against the effects of the drug to summon up the right words. She barely uttered a syllable before one of her captors approached her quickly and, jabbing a miniature dagger into the small of her back, whispered a threat to her life. If she did one thing to upset the sale he would kill her on the spot and no one would care because, when all was said and done, she was nothing more than a darky. It was a threat she was certain he would follow through with should she disobeyed him.

The bidding went higher and higher as, little by little, the number of bidders dwindled. When it was left to just Arthur and an older man on Arthur's right, Arthur's opponent insisted on seeing more of the merchandise he was bidding on.

The thought of the young beauty baring more of her goddess-like body before ogling eyes, not to mention her tender private parts being pawed by strangers, made Arthur's skin crawl. He just could not allow it to occur. In an ordinary slave auction, this would have been considered completely normal, but this was not an ordinary slave auction and the chit before him was not an ordinary slave woman. Besides, she already inadvertently displayed her small, well-formed breasts to the crowd.

Arthur was a rich man. In fact, he was one of the richest men in the newly emancipated United States. Now, like no other, was a time when he was extremely grateful for this fact.

"I intend to buy this mulatto, sir, and I do not wish to have any more of her wares displayed for all to see. So, kindly step back and admit your defeat," he said boldly.

"Do you not know my identity, good sir?" the man replied indignantly.

"By name, no," Arthur stated flatly, "but I do know you are not the man who will be walking away from this block with that mulatto."

"We shall just have to see about that." the man huffed. His face flushed with anger as he poked his walking stick toward the auctioneer. "You there! Kindly tell this young man my name," he demanded.

The auctioneer displayed rotting teeth as he sneered, looked down at Arthur as he bellowed, "This be Sir Martin Simone of Charles Town."

Although he had never been introduced to Sir Simone, Arthur was more than familiar with his social and financial status. He was a man of wealth that was surpassed by only a few. Fortunately, Arthur was amongst those few. Arthur also knew that Sir Simone met with his father on more than one occasion for business purposes and was obliged to his family as a result of some favors his father called in from his colleagues on the man's behalf.

Turning to the indignant old gentleman, he bowed low, "I am honored to make your acquaintance, Sir Simone of Charles Town.

Please, allow me to introduce myself," he drawled smugly, "I am Arthur Moore of Savannah. I believe you knew my father, James Moore. God rest his soul."

It may have sounded like a simple introduction to those near-by, but the exchange between the two men went far deeper than that. Sir Simone immediately understood he would not be the vic-tor in the competition to buy the breath taking mulatto. Even if he could muster up the means to outbid this young man, he was beholding to the family and therefore had no choice than to grace-fully back away.

"I am honored to make your acquaintance, sir," the old man stated grudgingly as he bowed low. "I had no idea I was bidding opposite such a distinguished gentleman. I will rescind my bid and allow you the spoils of the day."

Although livid about being referred to as a mulatto and the spoils of the day, Elizabeth was more than a little relieved to hear that she would not have to remove her clothing like the other un-fortunates who went before her. At least she was spared that in-dignation.

She was almost able to focus clearly enough on the man who purchased her to realize his striking good looks, when he startled her out of focus again by barking orders to his man.

"Take her to the wagon," he said flatly as he strolled past her to pay the cashier.

Arthur moved past Elizabeth without a second glance. The auc-tion was over and his interest with her apparently finished with it.

A tall black man, dressed in white cotton that could rival the best London had to offer, pulled her to her feet and gently escorted her by her elbow to a large side-less wagon. As he urged her into the rolling wooden structure with the other unfortunates of the day, she opened her mouth to protest but then thought better of it. Perhaps once they reached their destination and the laudanum was out of her system she would be able to speak with the strikingly handsome gentleman who just paid a ridiculous amount of money for her. Surely he would see the deception played. She was not a mulatto. She just needed a chance to prove it.

NINE

Elizabeth stood flat against the wall as she watched the seamstress draping, pulling, tucking, and pinning the exquisite white silk across Paulette's voluptuous body. Her amazing hands magically worked it into an evening gown for the Simpson ball the following week. Elizabeth posed many times while having dresses and gowns fitted to her slight body, but never had her seamstress been as adept as the middle aged woman serving Paulette proved to be. Yet, Paulette seemed not to notice the woman's exquisite talent as she moaned, groaned, and occasionally slapped at the poor seamstress over something Elizabeth thought incredibly trivial.

Witnessing such a scene outraged Elizabeth, but she knew better than to show it. She still stung from the beating she received the night before as a result of moving too slow for Paulette's liking. In fact, she questioned how badly one of her ribs was injured. Each breath she took caused a pain deep beneath the gash from the buckle on the thick strap Paulette unmercifully wielded. The buxom black woman -who ran the kitchen and everyone called Ole Sookie- put a poultice on her ribs during the night to help draw out some of the pain, stop infection, and help to keep any scarring to a minimum. Elizabeth was so grateful for the old woman's kindness she vowed that, if she ever got out of this mess, she would buy all the slaves owned by this horrid woman and set them free. In fact, she might just buy the plantation and personally usher this vile she-creature down the road on foot!

She was so deeply engrossed in her musing of Paulette's demise, Arthur's entry went unnoticed until he stood next to the beautiful southern belle and smiled at her reflection in the mirror.

"You look lovely, dearest, simply lovely," Arthur said softly.

"I do believe I must to agree with you," Paulette chuckled. "Mrs. Jones certainly does have a way with a needle and thread, does she not?"

A slight squeak of shock escaped Elizabeth's lips at the sound of an actual compliment coming from Paulette's lips toward the poor woman who she spent almost three hours verbally torturing. Immediately after exhuming it, Elizabeth wanted to kick herself for not having greater control.

The silence in the room was deafening as both brother and sister stopped their conversation and turned in her direction.

"Well, well, who might we have here?" Arthur murmured as he stepped closer toward Elizabeth. "Paulette, could this be the little minx I purchased for you last week in Charles Town?" He walked closer toward Elizabeth to get a better look. "Why, I believe it is." Elizabeth did her best to shrink away and become invisible when Arthur stood before her and lifted her chin. "Yes, I remember those eyes. They are like something I have never seen. They pull at you. I forgot about her. Why have you kept her hidden?"

Paulette snarled possessively as she watched her brother stare deep into Elizabeth's exotic violet eyes while he continued to caress her silken, porcelain chin. She kept the wench hidden from her brother after the chit was presented to her cleaned up and she realized how lovely a woman she actually was.

"I knew what would happen if I presented her to you," she stated jealously.

"What might that be?" Arthur chuckled.

"You know exactly what that might be," Paulette said with exasperation. "Really, you can be such a philanderer,"

She despised being taunted in this way.

"She is far prettier than I remember," Arthur mused; more to himself than to his sister.

"You bought her for me, remember?" Paulette snapped.

"Yes, dearest, I remember," Arthur replied as he dropped Elizabeth's chin and stepped back. "She looks to be a bit of a frail thing. She appears very tired and extremely white for a mulatto. Clearly she is in poor health. Had I realized this at auction, I might not have paid so dearly for her. I swear... the sun can indeed play tricks on the eyes, can it not?" he murmured. Arthur focused on Elizabeth's pale face as he walked, slowly, back and forth in front of her frozen body while he studied her more closely. "Are you certain she is up to task?"

"That is my business!" Paulette's words were so forceful they resembled a bark.

"Now, now, we shall have none of that. Do you hear me? Let us not forget that I have not yet gotten around to signing the papers that turn her over to you. Therefore, technically she is still mine. Thus, it is my business," Arthur stated in a tone that was soft, but firm. He moved back to Paulette's side and kissed her softly on the nape of her neck. "Send her to me in an hour." At Paulette's jealous snort, he reiterated in his still gentle, but firm voice, "In an hour, I say."

"What do you want to see her for?" Paulette's whine bordered on shrill.

"Just send her to me," he responded as he walked stealthily out of the room.

Elizabeth shuddered as Arthur passed dangerously close by her without as much as a look. He was a ruggedly handsome man, but he was an unreadable man who, through a twist of fate, now owned her. Her mind reeled with the possible reasons he could have for wanting her sent to him. None of them were good. She closed her eyes and moaned inwardly with despair.

Arthur barely left the room before Paulette escaped the ministering of Mrs. Jones and positioned herself threateningly in front of Elizabeth.

Being of small height herself, Paulette was but an inch or two taller than Elizabeth. Even so, her bone structure was as such that the gorgeous southern bell felt large, clumsy, and frumpy next to the petite and delicate English beauty. For this, Elizabeth suffered daily.

"I am sorry he ever bought you for me. You are a mulatto she-wolf!" Paulette hissed so vehemently that her saliva spattered into Elizabeth's eye.

Taken aback, Elizabeth quickly wiped it away with the back

of her hand.

"What are you doing? Did I say you could do that?" Paulette screeched.

Having been on the receiving end of her hand, belt, or a stick more than once since her arrival, and being fully aware of what would happen if she fought back, Elizabeth cowered. By now she was all too familiar with the woman's outbursts and was able to discern which ones would simply entail shouting and which ones foretold of a beating to follow. This one reeked of beating and, since she had not yet divulged the fact she was with child, she wanted to avoid any physical abuse that might well cause a miscarriage. Whenever she thought about divulging her delicate condition to Paulette, Elizabeth feared the knowledge might bring even more wrath upon her than what she already endured.

Before Elizabeth could protect herself, Paulette slapped her face with full force, causing the English aristocrat to spin on her heels before falling to the floor.

Paulette grabbed the thick braid that rested the length of Elizabeth's back. It was the only hairstyle she was allowed to wear. She pulled on the ebony braid with all her might. Elizabeth could not contain her scream from the sheer agony of it while she did her best to ease the excruciating pull against her scalp by standing up and closing the space between them.

Arthur was not far enough away from Paulette's quarters to have Elizabeth's screaming go unnoticed by him. He hurried back to the room and arrived in time to witness the cruelty his sister was delivering to his fragile, exquisite looking, and rather expensive slave.

"Here, here, now," he roared, "stop this at once!"

Stunned by the fact that she was caught displaying a side of her nature she reserved for the servants only, Paulette was mortified and speechless.

The brief reprieve was all Elizabeth needed to regain her composure and stand as proud and erect as she could. Arthur gently, but firmly, moved his sister aside and, with equal gentleness, extended his hand for Elizabeth to take. She looked from Paulette to Arthur and then back again while she debated what to do. The look in Arthur's eyes told her he was the better choice for the moment. She accepted his offering, allowing him to pull her from the room. It really did not matter what he planned on doing with her at this point. Anything was better than having to endure one more beating from that vile, spoiled, jealousy crazed woman.

Arthur handed Elizabeth a crisp linen handkerchief to wipe the blood from the corner of her mouth. He stood for a moment and watched her with silent interest before he guided her into his private suite. Knowing she was at his mercy, the London aristocrat steeled herself for the inevitable. To her surprise, he reached for a decanter of port and filled two crystal glasses before handing her one. Elizabeth accepted it gratefully.

Arthur watched the porcelain beauty for which he paid a pretty price with curiosity. Although beaten, bruised, and dressed in coarse rags, she carried herself with a regal air. The way she daintily dabbled at the blood with his handkerchief as well as the way she held her glass of wine denoted refinement and education. Her actions were smooth and automatic. It was clear she was exposed to the finer things all of her life. To his surprise and mild delight, her body language and actions even hinted of her expectation to be treated as the genteel ladies she so competently emulated. His dear Paulette would do well to take schooling from this wench.

He could not help being curious about what type of owners promoted such education and behavior in a slave girl. Her papers stated they were world travelers who met their demise at sea. That was a real shame. He was certain he would have enjoyed meeting people of such unusual character, providing they even existed. It was no secret that mystery owners would sometimes be concocted to camouflage the fact that the slave was stolen or purchased from the Indians.

Arthur pursed his lips. At closer look, Elizabeth's skin resembled rich white porcelain. It was far whiter than the creamy color a normal mulatto might have. The auctioneer stated she was purchased in Europe and brought to Charles Town along with other slaves acquired along the Mediterranean coastal cities. Looking at her more closely, he questioned if she was in fact mulatto. He heard of cases where women found themselves in prison for one reason or another. They either chose slavery over prison life or they were sold by their wardens for a pretty price into slavery. It was a way to keep the prison population down that no one bothered to challenge, since these women were commonly ladies of ill repute to begin with.

His curiosity was aroused.

"Please sit," he said in a manner reserved for the gentile.

The corners of Arthur's mouth hinted a smile as he watched Elizabeth take her seat with the grace and air of a woman of the finest of society. This was surely an unusual slave woman. Not only was she refined, but she was quite possibly the most beautiful woman, next to Paulette, he had ever laid eyes on. He did well with this purchase, very well indeed.

"Are you comfortable?" he asked quietly.

Not sure what the handsome master of the house was up to, Elizabeth nodded timidly. It had been several months since she had been treated like a lady, tasted good port, or felt the softness of an upholstered seat beneath her. It was all she could do to hold back the tears that threatened to flood the room at any moment.

"My sister named you Lizzy. Am I correct?" Arthur asked gently.

"Yes," Elizabeth replied softly.

"Sir," Arthur added.

"I beg your pardon?" Elizabeth asked with confusion.

"When you address me, you shall call me sir," Arthur stated as he settled back in his chair.

"I beg your pardon, sir. So much has happened over the last few months. I fear I have forgotten my manners. Please forgive me," she said as she pulled herself up as straight as she could.

She wanted to add 'And you can address me as Lady Elizabeth... sir!', but thought better of it.

"I shall excuse you this time but, should it happen again, I promise you shall feel my whip. Do you understand?" Arthur said.

His voice never rose above a gentle coo, but his words stung with their strength of meaning. He owned a large plantation that required an enormous number of slaves to keep it running smoothly and efficiently, not to mention profitably. In order to maintain obedience, he held a firm hand on them and required they act accordingly. He would allow no exceptions.

Elizabeth hung her head while she spoke her apologies. With the exception of viewing him from a distance, this was her first encounter with Arthur Moore since he purchased her from that nightmarish auction block in Charles Town. She had no idea if he was as crazy as his sister and she had no desire to find out.

"Turn around for me. I should like to view you better," Arthur said as he twirled his finger in the air to emphasize his meaning.

Elizabeth obliged without taking her eyes off her new master.

"Hmm," Arthur murmured. "I should like to see more."

Elizabeth sucked in her breath, remembering Paulette's accusation of her brother being a philanderer.

That was a term used to describe men who went with many women, was it not?

"Lift your skirts. I should like to see your ankles," he demanded.

Arthur adjusted himself in his seat while he watched Elizabeth slowly pull at the hem of her coarsely woven muslin skirt. At the sight of her soiled bare and swollen feet his face went scarlet. "What is this? You have no shoes?"

"Nay sir," she replied.

Elizabeth lowered her eyes to the floor and tried to huddle her body as tightly as she could in preparation for his blow. If his sister could pack such a powerful punch, she could only image what he might produce.

"Come closer!" he barked.

Aware that her feet were not a comely sight and thinking him angry with her for it, Elizabeth dropped her skirts and moved slowly toward him. She was not eager to be within his reach.

"Keep your skirts up," Arthur urged, in a gentler tone.

When Elizabeth was just a few feet away from him he raised

his hands for her to stop and looked closer at her bare feet. Although the sliver was removed and the infection thwarted, her foot was clearly not healing. He reached forward and pressed on her swollen flesh, causing her to wince.

She was certain she had earned herself a beating. Thick, salty tears slid freely down her cheeks while she cried openly. She was tired of being hit, tired of being mistreated and tired of being on her raw and swollen feet. Most of all, she was tired of being pregnant. Maybe it would be for the best if she did miscarry. At least that would be one less burden for her to suffer. Plus, from the way things were happening, she doubted if she would ever see her handsome husband again. The opportunity to beg his forgiveness and present him with the heir his family so desired was lost to her. Her child would be born a slave instead of the aristocrat he or she rightly deserved because of her folly. If she miscarried now, would it really matter?

A sudden wave of motherly protectiveness swept over Elizabeth and a new found strength emerged. Yes, it would matter if she miscarried. It would matter very much. She may have lost her chance to be happy with Stephen, but she still had a part of him inside of her. Even though her married life with him was ever so brief, she felt a bond with him through the child she carried and the love in her heart. Her baby was her tie to what she so foolishly tossed away. It was a tie she was not willing to relinquish. She wanted this baby. She would give the love that she had denied showing Stephen to his child. Who knows, perhaps one day she would find a way to give it back its freedom as well.

Feeling it was time to push the issue she prepared herself for the blow she was sure would come and blurted out, "Sir, I am with child."

To her relief and surprise, Arthur sat back in his chair and chuckled.

"What good fortune. I purchased one slave and received two," he said. "Well, well, 'tis mighty fine; 'tis mighty fine indeed. I paid a very dear price for you. This makes up for it."

TEN

Stephen folded the letter he just finished reading and placed it in the pocket he asked his tailor to sew on the inside of his satin lined waist coat. His brows knit together as he pondered its contents.

Life was becoming far more taxing and complicated than he could have ever imagined.

He was forced to abandon his search for his new bride upon hearing of the death of his father and return to England. There were unexpected affairs of the estate he inherited that required his immediate attention. These took time to deal with. Time he could have used searching for Elizabeth.

Now, a few months after his return, he received the most unusual letter from his neighbor and sister of his good friend, Miss Paulette Moore. Her letter informed him of the distressing happenings on their plantation since he took his leave. Arthur purchased a mulatto woman at the slave auction in Charles Town as an intended addition to her dowry. Instead, the woman bewitched him into behaving most foolishly. He took her to his bed more than was considered seemly for a master and a slave. What made it worse was that she was with child. Paulette had no idea if the child was Arthur's or some other man's, but it galled her that Arthur was so smitten with the mulatto witch that he refused to allow Paulette freedom to properly train her as her lady's maid. To add to the situation, because the woman was with child, her demented brother was commanding special treatment for her. It was all so wrong and Paulette was completely vexed. The mulatto woman was a genuine nuisance in her household. To top things off, she feared Arthur was falling in love with the little vixen. It might possibly be enough for him to consider marriage! As her brother's dearest friend, Paulette begged Stephen to return as soon as possible to help poor, spellbound Arthur see the folly of his ways and help her to convince him to sell the she-devil quickly, before more disruption occurred.

If the information about Arthur's bewitchment was not enough, the letter also contained within it, of all things, a marriage proposal from Paulette. How scandalous it would be if it were known by Savannah society that the beautiful southern minx took it upon herself to propose to Stephen instead of waiting for Stephen to propose to her. Stephen did not know if he should be amused or annoyed.

Paulette dared to be so bold as to put to pen her feelings for him and her willingness to wed as soon as he returned. She hoped he would put some thought into making haste to return and come to their aid, as well as join her at the altar.

He read her shocking words again. *Just imagine the possibilities of blending your money and social status with my own. Once we are properly joined in marriage, we can begin to find a suitable woman for our poor, bewitched Arthur.*

Stephen shook his head slowly as he thought of how incredulous he found Paulette's boldness. A proposal of marriage initiated from a woman. Stephen heard of such things, but never received one until now. British ladies of social standing would never have dreamed of extending such a shameless offer for fear of their reputation. Perhaps this was a practice in the colonies, or perhaps Paulette was a different kind of woman. He suspected it was the latter. He always thought her breeding to be of the highest standards. Apparently he was incorrect in this assumption.

He found Paulette extremely pleasing to look at, although she was blatantly spoiled. He grew up surrounded by women who were spoiled as such. Society women of wealth and good standing tended to be given the world on a golden platter more often than not. Therefore, he felt that Paulette's spoiled nature would not pose a problem.

It was true that at one time he was actually considering marrying Paulette. That was before all the family drama and his marriage to Elizabeth. It was a fleeting thought that he would have probably decided against after putting deep thought into it merely for the fact that her social standing did not meet British society's criteria. This was something a future duke needed to keep in mind.

None of it mattered now. He was already married and he happened to have fallen in love his beautiful young wife from the moment he set eyes on the petite English beauty. True, Elizabeth may have been lost to him for the present, but he was not ready to admit defeat. He planned to continue to look for her; for a while longer anyway.

Stephen fervently searched for an excuse to leave his clinging mother, who was more concerned with her needs than curious as to the whereabouts of her daughter-in-law. He was eager to set out once again in search of his bride. This letter provided him with just such an excuse.

He looked at the date that the letter. She posted it several weeks past.

Arthur was one of Stephen's best friends among the plantation owners of Georgia. He was well aware of the man's weakness for women. If he fell victim to a spell of a Mulatto slave who used trickery to bend his mind, Stephen wanted to save him for sure. From Paulette's letter, Stephen deduced Arthur was under some type of love spell. He witnessed people under the effects of spells a few times while in Jamaica, but never in Georgia. If this mulatto was practicing the same magic as what he witnessed being practiced by the natives at his plantation in Jamaica, Arthur would need a clear headed male to help him see reason and dull the effects of the spell.

Although Stephen's primary reason for setting sail was to search for his wayward new bride, he saw no harm in taking the time to help set his friend aright. He also felt it best to explain his inability to marry Paulette to her in person, rather than through the coldness of a pen.

He scribbled a note to Captain Sims requesting he prepare to set sail within two days' time and sent it off by courier before summoning his man servant, Morris, to inform him of their newest travel plans.

With that done, he set to pen a reply to Paulette; explaining that he should be arriving approximately one week after the letter reached her. He assured her he would immediately set to helping save Arthur from the evil vixen. Uncertain about how to pose the topic of her proposal, but still insistent that it was not the act of a gentleman to decline such an offer through pen, he added that he would discuss the subject of marriage upon his arrival. There was a frigate leaving on a direct route for Charles Town that very evening. If his man hurried, he could catch it before it set sail and the letter would be in Paulette's hands in plenty of time.

Stephen felt fairly confident the affairs of his estate were in good enough order for him to be absent for quite some time. He hired a new overseer and added a new accountant to look after the old accountant. Each accountant was to watch the other to insure an honest and accurate set of books. He sent a summons for them to meet with him within the hour and gave them one last set of orders along with an address for their reports to be sent on a weekly basis. Even though it would take several weeks for these reports to reach him, it was far better than having him be in the dark and find that he was bankrupt or worse when he returned.

Stephen's mother took to her bed after his father's passing. Although in good enough health, she was just not willing to toil through the day to day dealings of life. He attributed that to being part of her mourning over the loss of her life partner. He would be back to deal with his mother's sorrow and needs soon enough. For now, he would go to Georgia and attend to the salvation of his good friend before commissioning some aid from Arthur in the search for Elizabeth. With any luck, he and his bride would be back in England within a matter of months to take their rightful place as the Duke and Duchess of Eastwick.

He had just closed the estate ledgers and bid his accountants good-eve when Morris appeared at the door holding a note from Captain Sims. Stephen was uncertain why the captain would reply to his orders since he explained his need quite clearly. He quickly broke the waxed seal and moved to the nearest light to read the captain's clean handwriting.

Sir,

It grieves me to inform you of what has come to my attention. I have been informed Lady Elizabeth was mistaken for a mulatto and was sold at auction about six weeks past. Might I suggest you collect proof of her lineage to present when we arrive?

Your Servant,

Jackson Sims

Stephen stared at the note in disbelief. What type of nonsense was this? How could anyone think Elizabeth a mulatto? One look at her would tell differently. He was aware that certain plantations owned very white mulattoes. They were generally a product of the plantation owner's amorous lifestyle. Even so, Elizabeth's skin was too white to ever consider even a drop of black in it. It was not just her clean porcelain complexion and rosy cheeks, but her bone structure was all wrong for that of a woman with African or Island lineage.

This was preposterous.

Even so, Stephen took the captain's suggestion to heart. He considered the old sea dog to be a man far wiser than he in affairs such as this. Over the years, Sims exposure in the workings of the slave trade was great. Stephen inherited most of his slaves when he purchased his plantations. He was also aware that at one time Sims dabbled in the merchandising of slaves. If he felt proof of Elizabeth's family lineage would help free her more so than him claiming her as his wife, then so be it.

After all, since the legality of his marriage was questionable under England's damnable marriage act, her lineage would more than likely be the stronger argument.

In order to obtain Elizabeth's records, he needed to visit the office of Simon and Jameson. Being fully aware of the role they played in Elizabeth's disappearance, he was disgruntled at the thought of having to ask them any favors when all he wanted to do was pummel their faces with his fists.

What a foolish young woman his wife proved to be. Her silly notions about marrying for love placed her in the most compromising position. The sad fact was that he did love her, but perhaps that was not enough. Perhaps she wanted to feel that love flowing within her as well. He could not blame her. Again he cursed himself for his own part in this folly. If he had only taken the time to court her, perhaps she would have found the love in her heart for him like he instantly felt for her.

Stephen knew all too well the perilous possibilities that awaited a female slave. He owned several plantations, after all. In fact, he bedded a few of his own female slaves -not because he was their owner and it was his right, but because they were fine examples of female flesh. Their allure was irresistible. So much so that, had they not been slaves, he would have still managed to find a way into their beds.

Stephen held a slightly different position on slave ownership than his neighboring plantation owners. His views of slavery were mixed. Although well aware of their necessity if one was to develop a strong and powerful plantation, he also cringed at the concept of one man owning another.

In the beginning, he tried to walk the fence and hired a few free darkies to assist him with the development of his investments. He quickly learned that the majority had the mindset of a slave and not one of an enterprising laborer. Taking into account this fact, along with the snubbing the other plantation owners were doing as a result of their outrage to his not supporting slavery after they worked so hard to have it reinstated, he attended a few local slave auctions and even purchased a new slave for working both inside the main house and out in the fields. Once he appeased his peers, enjoyed their cooperation, and created a stronger slave base, it did not take long for his plantations to flourish and for him to applaud his own decision to go with the knowing flow of society.

He was deep in these thoughts as he made his way toward the office of Simmons and Jameson, causing him to practically run head on into his brother-in-law, Herald Nottingham.

"Good gad, man. Your mind must be on one of your ships a thousand miles away," Herald teased as he stepped aside to avoid colliding with the man sixteen years his senior.

"Master Herald, yes... please forgive me. My mind was indeed engaged elsewhere," Stephen responded. "How are you, my new brother-by-law?"

"I am well, Lord Carlson, quite well, thank you much," Harold replied.

Although Herald's words were jovial, they sounded stiff with reserve, similar to the greetings his uncle might have given. Since Lord Roberts took such an interest in the boy, it stood to reason that much of his mannerisms rubbed off on the young man.

"I am about to the law office of Simon and Jameson," Stephen volunteered.

"Well now, I happen to be on my way to the very same place," Herald stated with surprised delight. "Might I join you?"

Stephen perked his attention. It was too soon for Herald to take possession of his estate, so what business might he have with the trustees? Could it be concerning Elizabeth and not him?

"Indeed. I was just about to suggest the very same. Although, not because I knew you had business with them, but for the very fact that it would provide us an opportunity for conversation between brothers-by-law," Stephen said with a smile as he gestured for his new in-law to step alongside him.

Although a mere fourteen years of age, with his fifteenth birthday soon to come, Herald Nottingham appeared and acted a young man far beyond his years. One could easily believe him at least approaching twenty. His tall, well developed physique only served to add to the illusion his mannerisms instigated.

Having been no more than five years old when placed in the care of his uncle, Herald recalled only bits of his life in the country with his mother and father. What he did remember was plenty of laughter. This was something that he saw little of in the years that followed while in the household of his uncle.

Herald did his best during his visits from school to bring a smile to his poor sister's lips. Her happiness was his utmost concern. He loved his uncle, to be sure, but it was clear the man possessed little, if any, use for his niece. Since Harold had a reprieve from the strictness of his uncle's household, the fact that Elizabeth was required to remain in such a loveless environment troubled him deeply. He pledged at an early age to take his sister away from the overbearing life she lived and give her free roam of his household just as soon as his inheritance came into his possession.

When Elizabeth's engagement to Sir Stephen Carlson was first announced, Herald was concerned. Since Sir Carlson was considered the greatest catch in London, he found the fact that his sister never spoke of her intentions puzzling. It was only later that he discovered she only learned of the engagement at the same time as he. This was typical of Uncle Cyrus' treatment of poor Elizabeth.

Herald spent quite a bit of time checking into the character of Lord Carlson. He also found excuses to be in his company for the purpose of getting to know him. His conclusion was that there was no finer man around to which he —or in this case his uncle- could present his sister's hand to in marriage. What made it even more satisfying was the fact that Lord Carlson seemed to genuinely care for his dear sister. He may not have spoken to Herald of his feelings, but he did not need to. The slight upward curve that formed at the corners of the man's mouth and the sparkle that arose in his steel gray eyes at the mere mention of her name was all Herald needed to witness to know the man was helplessly in love with his bride-to-be.

He regretted not mentioning this observation to his sister. He knew she harbored reservations about the marriage, but was not in a position to deny her uncle. He started to broach the subject while battling her over a game of chess when their earl burst into the drawing room engulfed in a wild and furious rage after Elizabeth's waiting maid confided in him of Elizabeth's intentions to run away before the wedding could take place. The wedding date was moved forward, with only a few guests in attendance. Elizabeth was locked in her room with no visitors -not even Herald- or contact with the outside world until the day of her vows. Herald was granted only the briefest moment to wish her well at the small reception before she was swept off to her new home. He had not seen nor heard from her since. Of course, he needed to take into consideration the fact that the day after the wedding he returned to school, with this being his first visit home since.

"So, how goes it with my sister? She is well, I hope? It was my intention to call on your house this very afternoon. In fact, my card should have arrived by now," Herald said as he matched strides with Stephen.

Stephen's heart fell. It was not uncommon for secrets to slip out by way of servant's tongues and he hoped this might have happened where Elizabeth's absence was concerned. He sighed, it just proved the loyalty of his staff and he should be grateful. So, Herald knew nothing of his sister's running away because Stephen told no one. Instead he gave belief that they were in blissful honeymoon mode and traveling. He returned without her, he explained, because they discovered she did not travel the sea well and might possibly be with child. He had no idea how close to the truth his tale really was.

Stephen stopped and looked long and hard at Herald. He was, after all, not yet a man. But, it appeared his thoughts and actions were as such. Perhaps it would benefit to have another on his team when he searched for Elizabeth. It would certainly be of benefit when it came to obtaining, as well as proving, the family lineage. He drew a deep breath and suggested they find a private location to confer about a matter of the utmost importance.

The fact that this request was in response to his inquiry about his sister did not go unnoticed by Herald. His mind reeled with the possibilities of what Lord Carlson would like to confer with him about while he readily agreed to step into the back room of a nearby ale house. They selected a small table in the semi-dark corner of the room where they could talk privately, with only an occasional interruption from the serving woman.

Herald sat still and silent while he listened intently to Stephen's story of the chain of events that brought the handsome, virile lord to seek information from the office of Simon and Jameson that day. Although horrified to discover that the very men his father befriended and trusted with his children's fortune, future, and wellbeing, played a vital role in the horrific fate of his sister, he displayed no inkling of such emotion while he allowed the distressed and obviously heartbroken man sitting opposite him to speak.

When Stephen concluded his story, Herald took a long draft of ale and wiped his mouth with the back of his hand before looking his brother-in-law hard in the eye.

"Before we get into debate over my age and need for schooling or my Uncle Cyrus and his opinion of what I should and should not be doing," Herald stated boldly," I want to make it perfectly clear that I intend to join up with you in the quest to find my sister. So, kindly speak not a word on these accounts."

Stephen admired the fortitude and calmness the young man opposite him displayed. He had not considered the fact that Herald might insist on accompanying him, but it was not such a bad idea that he did so. Displaying the slightest of smiles, he closed his eyes and bobbed his head in acknowledgment of his brother-by-law's request.

"Good," Herald stated with satisfaction. "Now, with that being out of the way, I believe we are due a visit to the office of the soon-to-be-former trustee of my estate. Before we do such, I should like to make a quick detour."

Herald stood up without waiting for Stephen to agree and dropped some coins on the table.

Stephen couldn't help think with admiration how, although he was a mere fourteen years of age, his brother by marriage was wise in mind and action.

He decided not to question Herald about their destination and simply kept pace with him as they silently made their way several blocks east. Each remained deep in his own thoughts until they reached the law office of Sir John Halper, Esq. Herald entered the office without ceremony. He moved as if he were in a place of acute familiarity and forgot Stephen was still with him. Mildly taken aback, Stephen hesitated only briefly before following the young man through the door.

"Good afternoon, Master Herald," greeted a young clerk as he stepped from behind a small oak desk, "Is the judge expecting you? I apologize, for I was not aware."

"Good day, Thomas. I am not expected, but 'tis a matter of the utmost importance. I pray the chancellor will find a few moments audience for myself and my brother-by-law," Herald replied.

The young clerk nodded, looked in Stephen's direction, and nodded again before leaving the room through a narrow doorway in the back. Within moments he returned to beckon Herald and Stephen to follow him by way of a different, grander route.

Stephen was once again impressed as he watched the manner in which Herald was received by one of London's most powerful and distinguished judges. It was clear his young brother-by-law was very much schooled in social manners and understood their quirky ways. It was also quite clear he had already developed a head start in forging his place in preparation for the day when he would take over his inheritance and enter society as a man.

Stephen took the seat offered him and listened while Herald relayed the story that had only just recently been told to him. Like Herald had done when he was being told, the judge listened intently and did not interrupt. Once Herald finished, Sir Halper sat back and rubbed his chin in contemplation.

"If I understand this correctly, my dear young man, there has been a gross misuse of funds by the trustees that is not in accordance to your father's will," Sir Halper said as leaned forward and directed his attention to Stephen. "Tell me good sir, were you presented with your wife's dowry upon the day of your wedding, as per the will's provisions?"

Grateful that the judge was considerate enough not to comment on Elizabeth's rash and unseemly behavior, Stephen shook his head in response to his question about her dowry. He admitted to the room that with all he was required to attend to so soon after his wedding the presentation of the dowry never crossed his mind. He had no need for it and thus forgot about it.

"Your honor, I ask that these scoundrels be removed from the position of trustee of mine and my sister's inheritance and I further ask that I be judged fit to assume control immediately," Herald said.

He sat tall and confident as he made his request.

"Hmm," the judge mumbled as he looked long and hard at the young man.

Stephen's pride in his young brother-by-law was apparent as he watched him remain firm with his demands.

"You do realize this is most unusual," the judge stated as he lit a pipe and sat back. Drumming his fingers on the arm of his chair, he burrowed his brows together, indicating his deep concentration.

"Yes sir, I do," Herald replied with a calm, steady voice.

The young man radiated his confidence in his own ability to manage his affairs. The room was so silent that the clicking of the pendulum clock in the reception area could be heard while the judge and Herald looked at each other, neither one moving so much as an eyelid.

"Well, I must say it is an unusual request," the judge broke the silence as he repositioned his body in his chair, "but I believe it is a well-founded request. Here is what I shall do. First, I shall see to it that your sister's dowry is presented to her husband post haste."

"Thank you, sir," Stephen stated with a slight bow of his head.

He was really not concerned about the dowry. In fact, he had no idea what it even amounted to. He assumed it was a trivial amount since her uncle was so negligent of caring about her. Had Elizabeth been due to receive a small fortune, Cyrus Roberts would have surely provided her with the respect and consideration due a noble woman of wealth. No matter the amount, he felt he should acknowledge the judge's action with gratitude.

The judge nodded his approval and gave gracious reception of Stephen's thank you before he turned to Herald.

"As for you, young man, "the judge continued, "I shall see to the immediate freeze of the estate and all trustee rights that may be exercised by Simon and Jameson and order a complete investigation of their records and actions from the date of your father's death until this day." He leaned forward and looked closer into the young man's face. "This may prove to be a lengthy process,

I fear, but I must be thorough in order to be able to present your inheritance to you prior to your sixteenth birthday and have that decision be an incontestable and irrevocable decision."

Herald smiled, "Yes sir, thank you."

Sir Halper nodded, took a long draw on his pipe, and then stood up and called out, "Thomas! Come here and bring your quill."

With lightning speed Thomas appeared through the doorway. He stood patiently against the wall while he waited for the judge to give him further orders.

"Good sirs," Sir Halper stated in a friendly, but formal manner, "if you will excuse me I have a letter to dictate and send post haste to a certain law office."

"Sir," Herald stood up, "If I might suggest... We are on our way there this very moment. If you approve, we shall step outside and wait for your letter to be prepared and see to it ourselves that it reaches its destination and is read."

The judge looked at Herald as a broad smile spread over his face before replying, "Splendid idea, young man, splendid."

Stephen followed Herald out to the reception room and took a seat next to him on one of the wooden chairs that lined the walls. He noticed his surroundings for the first time. The walls were painted a pale rose with the mantle, trim and crown molding done in a rich, dark varnish. There were several comfortable looking wooden chairs with thickly padded tapestry seating lined along the walls and a small table in the corner. Stephen questioned the comely, yet unpretentious décor in an office of a man with such power and stature. It certainly was an oddity.

Unable to hold back his curiosity, he queried Herald on his relationship with Sir Halper. He discovered the judge was the father of Herald's oldest and closest friend at school. Herald was a guest in his house many times over the years. In fact, Sir Halper recently approached both Herald and his uncle about a possible union with his daughter when she and Herald came of age. In essence, the judge was Herald's future father-by-law. Thus, he had no desire to see his daughter's future fortune tampered with so unscrupulously by these dishonest trustees. Action would be taken for certain. Herald estimated it would be completed by the time they returned with Elizabeth.

Although Stephen was surprised to discover that a man as young as Herald was already planning his future nuptials, it fell into character with the young man he was discovering lived within this mature, fourteen-year-old body.

The unfortunate freezing of Herald's estate funds would place a hardship on the young man financially until things were cleared up, especially since he had no desire to inform his uncle of his whereabouts or activities. He was certain that the earl would protest to such a degree that Stephen would be forced to oblige and forbid him to make the trip. Sensing Herald's concerns, Stephen bid him not to worry. Believing it was to his benefit to have the young man join him in his search for Elizabeth, he assured Herald he would leave all communication about Herald's activities and whereabouts to his discretion. As for funds, he was happy to provide for Herald's needs, whatever they may be and would have no more discussion on the subject.

The streets were slowing down as people searched for respite and food to give them fuel to complete their day. They reached the office of Simon and Jameson just as the sun rose to mid-day. The men were surprised to find no one in the reception room to greet them when they entered.

Uncertain what to do, they listened for sounds from behind one of the three doors that led off the large, lavishly furnished room. Stephen smirked as he made note of the stark contrast between this office and that of the esteemed Sir Halper's. The walls were covered with deep ivory wallpaper flocked with burgundy colored velvet. Several small chairs upholstered in velvet that matched the wallpaper were placed around the room in pairs. Each pair of chairs had a small decorative table between them. The rich ambiance of this very inviting room was topped off with a gilded fireplace and crown molding. Aware of the impropriety of the Jameson part of Simon and Jameson, he could not help questioning whose money funded such lavishness.

Stephen's body froze as the voice of Dr. Michael Jameson filtered out from behind the door to the left of the oversized fireplace.

"Whose office is that?" he questioned.

"If memory serves me correctly, that would belong to the Sir Jameson, esquire," Herald replied.

Herald barely finished his sentence before Stephen stormed forward and practically kicked the door open. With lightning speed, he raced across the room and wrapped his hand around the doctor's Adam's apple as he slammed the old man against the wall.

"Where is she?" Stephen roared.

The doctor's brother did his best to free him from Stephen's vice grip, as did the stunned Herald.   He had never imagined his brother-in-law capable of such passionate rage. This was more than a simple thwarted husband's pride This behavior belonged to a man very much in love.

Finally calming down enough to realize he might very well kill the doctor before he successfully pulled from him the information he needed. Stephen released the old man and stepped back.

Michael Jameson slid to the floor while he struggled to pull air through his crushed windpipe.

"I suggest you answer him, Dr. Jameson, or I shan't be responsible for what happens here of," Herald flatly stated.

"I... I do not know where she is," the doctor managed to choke out. "Somewhere in the colonies... err... the United States, I would guess." Michael looked at Stephen with tear filled eyes. "She said naught of your nuptials. I did not know, I swear, I did not know!"

Having lost his battle against Captain Kline on Elizabeth's behalf and being too old to be of any value on the market, the doctor was given a choice of returning to England on a ship that happened to be leaving within the hour or to be set ashore to continue on his journey. The captain made it perfectly clear that if the good doctor chose to continue making a life for himself in the new world, he would forever be in need of watching over his shoulder. They would be continually curious to discover if the old man made mention of what occurred on his ship to anyone who should not be told in or near Cape Town.

The old doctor did not even need to think about it. Although he hid it well to those around him, he found the voyage not to his liking. The thrill of an adventure actually faded before the ship was half-way across the ocean. He desired nothing more than to return home.

What happened to Elizabeth was appalling and something needed to be done. Judging from the attitudes of his fellow passengers, he was certain he would have more success getting the help he needed for her from his side of the waters. He was grossly incorrect about the newly formed United States. From his exposure to the fellow passengers who were making the new land their home, it was clear the rumors that the country was filled with barbarians were not far from truth. Its population was filled with social cast offs from his country and the countries of others. He had no desire to step one foot on their soil.

It was not long after he returned to England that he learned of Elizabeth's marriage to Lord Carlson. Furious with the young lady for not telling him the truth about her nuptials and fearful of addressing the duke directly, he sent word to the captain of Stephen's ship about Elizabeth's possible fate. He fervently hoped the captain would send word to Stephen and that they would sail off to rescue poor Lady Elizabeth. In turn, he fully intended to use their absence from London as an opportunity to make provisions for his own departure to more friendly grounds before Stephen and his bride returned. He surely could not remain in London after being a party to such a horrendous act as what just occurred to an English duchess and the daughter of his deceased friend. He was so ashamed of his part in the tragedy he would be lucky if he could ever find it in himself to look in a mirror again.

As fate would have it, his plan went awry. There, before him, stood a monstrously angry, thwarted husband. If that was not difficult enough, the angry, thwarted husband was a rich and powerful duke. The doctor shuddered to think what was to become of him.

"Whether you were aiding a foolish newlywed bride to flee from her husband or a bride-to-be to flee from her promise of bonds, 'tis equally appalling," Stephen roared as he pushed his angry face as close to the doctor's as humanly possible while still allowing him the ability to look in his eyes. "You best start talking. I want to hear every detail from the beginning. Spare no feelings or shame. Do you understand?"

Stephen's normally sun kissed face was scarlet from the rage within him that threatened to burst into a wild fury at any moment.

ELEVEN

Herald sailed several times in his short life, but never on such a long journey as this. Although he was concerned about Elizabeth's wellbeing, he could not help feeling excited about the opportunity for a new adventure. Not many young men of his age and station could boast such an experience. It certainly would help rank him higher within his circle of friends once he returned to relay the details of the journey to them. He spent his first day at sea quizzing Captain Sims as much as the old sea dog would allow. He was filled with curiosity about the ship and its navigational instruments. The grizzly old captain had never encountered a young man of such intelligence and, although he was not by nature the most hospitable of men, for the most part he enjoyed Herald's youthful enthusiasm and eagerness to learn.

They were deep in the high seas when Herald overheard a conversation between Stephen and the captain that set him on his heels. In order to reduce their travel time, they made some changes with the ship as well as their route. The ship carried minimal armament and an even lighter crew than normal. This meant that the utmost precautions must be made to avoid the pirates that hovered along the Virginia and Carolina shores.

They debated about dropping lower in their route. This would bring them up the Florida waters near Jacksonville. It was a small deviation from their direct route, but the Spanish kept the waters fairly well guarded and the threat of pirates was lessened. Unfortunately, the threat of storms was not. They reached a point in their travel where a decision needed to be made. Having the final decision placed in his hands, the captain decided to head for Jacksonville waters and take their chances with the weather. Once they reached Brunswick waters the wind's current should pick up and there was a good chance it would help them make up for lost time the deviation in the route could potentially cost them. This was something he experienced many times while traveling those waters and he was banking on experiencing it again.

Herald's heart pounded in his ears at the thought of their vulnerability. He struggled to push back fear that was threatening to paralyze him. This was a factor he had not counted on when he insisted on accompanying Stephen. He watched the two men part company and steeled himself to confront the captain about what he heard. It was his hope that he would be able to keep his fear undetected.

"Excuse me, Captain," Herald called as he stepped out of the shadows and alongside Sims. "I did not mean to listen in. I just happened along and could not help hearing. Is it true we are powerless against pirates?"

"Well son," the captain said with a scowl. "I do not like the term powerless. We are just a wee bit light on our defenses."

"Is that wise?" Herald queried.

"I never question the orders of the master, young sir," he said firmly. "I suggest you refrain as well. I will say that there is no accounting for the thinking of a man crazed by love. Wise or not, 'tis the way it is and we all have to make the best of it."

Feeling suddenly chagrined by the captain's referral to Stephen's desire to reach his wife at all costs and his apparent failure to realize it, Herald excused himself and went to his small room.

The captain was right, of course. Stephen probably was not thinking clearly. Who could blame the poor man? His wife was encouraged into running off by an old fool and now suffered the tortuous life of a plantation slave. He could only imagine what horrors might be being forced on her this very moment. That had to be first and foremost in his brother-by-law's thinking. As her brother, it should also be his. Getting to her as quickly as possible, no matter what the risks, must have been Stephen's reasoning. Given the same circumstances, Herald would have probably done the same thing.

Herald entered his small cabin and smiled when he discovered Stephen's man servant, Morris, took the liberty of serving him as well. He left London in such haste he had not time to procure his own man-servant. He did not have one at school and he certainly was not about to return to his uncle's residence and request William be allowed the trip with him. As far as his uncle was concerned, Herald was safely at school diving deep into his studies.

The room was barely large enough for the hammock that extended from one wall to the other. There was no miniature coal burning stove such as those in Stephen and the Captain's cabins, but a small square box that was filled with hot coals that radiated delicious heat was placed not far from his hammock. It produced just the right amount of warmth to take the chill out of the air, but not enough to make the room suffocating. There was a clean nightshirt draped across the back of a wooden, straight backed chair that was placed close enough to the box to warm the shirt, but far enough away to prohibit a fire.

Herald donned the inviting cotton nightshirt quickly and snuffed out the flame of his candle with a long handle snuffer that hung on a hook near the table by his hammock. The embers that glowed through the holes in the box provided enough light for him to make out the furnishings in his room. He recalled how he marveled over the fact that the small wooden table and chair were solidly secured to the floor to prevent unwanted movement on the rocky ocean waters. He had never taken this into consideration before. It made perfect sense.

Herald was uncertain about how much comfort or sleep he would find in the hammock. Much to his surprise, its swaying kept rhythm with the movement of the ship and had a therapeutic effect. It practically rocked him to sleep like a babe in a cradle. The finely woven cotton sheeting on the bottom and soft, fine woolen coverlet on the top certainly helped. Because of the dampness in the air, the captain did not allow many items that were stuffed or upholstered on the ship. The few that did find their way aboard were aired regularly and kept dry in order to discourage mold from forming.

Morning came all too soon for Herald. He pulled his tired body out from the warmth of his hammock and into the assaulting bitterness of the morning air. The coal box had long since ceased to produce heat and he could see his breath crystallize in front of him. The ship rocked more than usual and his stomach was not dealing well with the sensation. If it did not stop soon, he was certain that, even though his stomach was empty, it would undoubtedly attempt to shed whatever contents it possessed.

Pulling on his vest, breeches, thick woolen stockings and shoes as quickly as he could, he grabbed his waistcoat and hat and hurried topside. The crisp, moist morning air plunged into his lungs. He coughed uncontrollably.

The firm slap of Stephen's hand on his back helped to calm his coughing fit enough for him to say good morning. The steaming cup of coffee his brother-by-law presented to him finished the process. The rich dark liquid warmed his insides and soothed the rawness of the salty sea air. Whoever discovered coffee was a saint to be sure.

"How are you this morn?" Stephen bellowed over the roar of the wind and the crashing of waves that was growing steadily stronger.

"I know not, sir. I am drinking this coffee and enjoying it as it goes down, but I question if it will be back up shortly. If so, I cannot imagine enjoying it one bit," Herald said as he did his best to be heard above the distressing chaos.

Stephen threw his head back in a robust laugh. He recalled his first days at sea were spent in a similar manner. It took several trips before he grew accustomed to the incessant rocking and feeling of unsteadiness, especially when the seas were restless. It was enough to send the best equilibrium into a tail spin.

"You shall get used to it soon enough," Stephen said assuringly.

The ringing of cook's bell alerted them that their breakfast awaited them. Stephen stepped aside and motioned Herald to take the lead to the captain's cabin where the table was set for the three of them to dine. At first Herald was inclined to pass on putting anything more into his troubled stomach, but thought better of it. Perhaps a solid meal of coddled fish and warm biscuits would be just the ticket to steady him up.

The cook presented a meal made with the last of the large Halibut caught just a few days earlier. He amazed the Harold with his versatility of recipes since he boarded. Alternating between the pork, lamb and chicken that were brought along, the fresh fish made a light and enjoyable interlude.

"I 'ave rightly enjoyed avin' fish on the trip," Captain Sims noted as he dove into his meal. "'Tis a shame the way we travel the waters like we do, yet we see so little of the ocean's stock on our table."

"I have to agree. I do not know why it took so long for us to set up those fishing rods," Stephen stated enthusiastically as he spooned some halibut onto his biscuit, "although, I prefer Sea Bass. 'Twould be great if we can catch a few before the voyage ends."

"I shall put your order in, sir," Sims chuckled.

Herald looked at the captain in surprise before joining the other men in their laughter over a fine joke. The more he observed his brother-by-law the more he admired him. The man knew how to rule with a tight fist while being gentle enough to earn respect and loyalty from everyone who served him. This was an art he vowed to acquire.

"Do you know when we might reach our destination?" Herald asked as the ship jolted, causing his stomach to lurch as he reached to save his biscuit from doing the same.

"We have reached the southern waters so it should only be a day or so now," the captain replied.

"So soon," Herald gasped, "we only just switched direction."

The captain and Stephen laughed simultaneously.

"Where did you get that notion?" Stephen asked.

"From... I heard," Herald stammered as he looked at the captain who simply looked back at him with a raised brow. "I heard you discussing it with the captain last night."

"You did, did you?" Stephen said with amusement. "The trouble with eavesdropping is that you run the risk of not hearing all of the facts. We altered course about a week ago."

Herald looked embarrassed at the thought of being called an

eavesdropper.

"I did not mean to be eavesdropping. I was just walking on deck and I heard talking and... I did not want to interrupt. I am truly embarrassed," he said humbly.

"No need," Stephen stated gently. The look of chagrin on his young companion's face made him regret his joking comment about eavesdropping. He simply had to remember that, although Herald looked a man, he was still a boy. "I was simply teasing. A poor joke at best. Please forgive me."

Herald perked up instantly and was off onto another subject as if nothing had happened.

The sound of thunder cracking brought everyone to attention as the ship's mate rushed into the room and beckoned the captain to follow. Sims suggested Herald and Stephen retire to their rooms to weather out the storm that brewed. It appeared to be far more serious than the signs led them to believe.

Noting Herald's nervousness, Stephen suggested they retire to his cabin for a game of cards to help pass the time. Herald accepted the invitation readily. The last thing he wanted was to be sitting in his cabin alone while he wondered if the howling winds, pelting rain, and angry waves would see fit to show them mercy.

TWELVE

Arthur paced the floor of his study while he waited for Paulette to enter. He opened the letter in his hand and folded it again with nervous agitation. When his sister finally did arrive, he tossed it into the fireplace, only to rescue it before the flames could do more than singe its edges.

"Good heavens Arthur, whatever is amiss?" Paulette asked as she glided across the floor to stand next to him.

"Two letters were delivered to this house this morning." Arthur sighed.

"And?" Paulette asked impatiently.

Arthur reached in his pocket and handed a letter addressed to Paulette. It was the letter Stephen posted just before he set sail. Its seal was unbroken.

"'Tis from Stephen!" Paulette squealed as she snatched the letter from her brother's outstretched hand and held it to her chest.

Closing his eyes, as if by doing so he could change the scene that was about to occur, he held out the letter that he recently retrieved from the fireplace. "And this..."

Paulette stopped short and stared at the letter in Arthur's outstretched hand. From the dark and sullen look that covered his handsome face, it was clear the letter was not the bearer of good news.

"What is this?" Paulette asked.

Her voice was barely above a whisper as she took the letter hesitantly.

"Would you like me to read it to you or would you prefer to read it on your own?" Arthur asked gently.

Silence cut through the room as Paulette's eyes locked with Arthur's. With hands that trembled as they closed around Stephen's letter, she dropped her eyes to the one in Arthur's outstretched hand.

"Perhaps 'twould be best if you read it," she practically whispered.

Arthur opened the letter slowly, cleared his throat, and began to read aloud, "Dear Arthur, 'Tis with a grievous heart that I inform you the frigate, Duke, was taken by a storm off shore. Its occupants were forced to abandon ship. Although the ship's captain and much of the crew found their way ashore near St. Augustine, your good friend and mine, Lord Stephen Carlson, has not yet been found. It is our greatest fear he did not survive the ordeal. My deepest sympathies accompany this note. Your humble servant, Matthew Walters."

The blood curdling scream that pierced the air brought the main floor servants running from all directions. They arrived just in time to witness Paulette's shocked body crumple to the floor.

The old cook rushed forward and pulled out the small vile of smelling salts she kept in her skirt pocket for the many times a lady in a tight corset might need assistance. She waved it vigorously under Paulette's nose. Once Paulette was sufficiently revived, the house butler assisted her into a chair.

Arthur knelt on the floor near his sister and held her hand.

"What can I do, dearest?" he asked with heartfelt earnest. "Tell me what to do and I shall do it."

"Find him!" Paulette wailed. "I just know he is alive. Find him... please."

"Aye," Arthur said with obvious resolve as he stood up and started pacing across the thick woven imported carpet that dominated the study floor. "I shall make preparations to leave immediately."

It was a good idea to go looking for Stephen. It gave him a sense of purpose, rather than wandering the house waiting while he struggled to find a way to comfort his sister's intense distress. His own was difficult enough. Stephen was, after all, his closest friend.

It was all too terrible.

He ordered a few things packed for his leave and called a small meeting with some of his staff to make sure things ran smoothly in his absence. Once satisfied, he bid Paulette good-bye and raced down the long drive toward the main road.

Traveling from Savannah to St. Augustine on horseback was no pleasure trip, but it was a welcome trip in this case. Hopefully, by the time he arrived his head would have cleared and his twisted heart realigned. Not since the death of his father had he felt so ripped up and forlorn.

Paulette stood on the veranda while she watched her brother race away on his fastest mount. He just had to find Stephen. She refused to believe that the love of her life was dead. It just could not be.

Remembering his letter still clenched in her hand, she called for Elizabeth to prepare her a bath and made way to her rooms for some privacy while she read her precious correspondence from her love. Elizabeth heard Paulette's screaming, but opted to keep her distance. The other slaves may have felt a sense of duty to the woman, but all she felt was hatred.

Life at the plantation became a little easier after Arthur took notice of her. The news of her being with child created both a positive and negative situation for her. On the positive side, Paulette was forbidden to hit her for fear of causing a miscarriage. Her child, at least, was safe. On the negative side, since she was already with child, Arthur had no worries of impregnating her and made free to bed her at every opportunity.

Although Elizabeth's duties shifted from being Paulette's waiting maid to Arthur's sex slave, Paulette's venomous jealousy caused her to take every opportunity she could to make Elizabeth as miserable as possible.

Even though Elizabeth had no soft feelings for Paulette, she did for the situation. It was obvious the woman was very much in love with the man lost at sea. Such a loss would be crushing. She could not help the feelings of compassion that ebbed from her for this poor wretched woman.

She wondered on occasion what it might have been like if she met Paulette on even ground. What if she was introduced to this high and mighty socialite as the person she truly was, Lady Elizabeth Carlson, the future Duchess of Eastwick? Would they become friends? She could not be certain. What she could be certain of is that the woman would have striven to show her best side at all times.

Elizabeth sighed. On a few occasions she was witness to that side of Paulette. She truly could be pleasant, as well as charming, when she chose to be. Elizabeth recalled the many beaus who battled for Paulette's favor almost daily and felt a tinge of envy. Her life in her uncle's care was confining with only the basics of social interaction. If a beau desired to call on her, he suffered such incredible scrutiny from her uncle that he would give up and seek out a new female to dote on. The only man who actually made it through to the finish line was her darling Stephen.

She wondered what her life might have been like had she been allowed to receive as many beaus as Paulette received. Perhaps all that attention would have driven her to act spoiled like Paulette. Even Arthur doted on Paulette. Never having experienced such a lifestyle, Elizabeth could not help wonder how it would be.

****

"Are you day dreaming again, Lizzy? Get over here and add more heat to my bath!" Paulette barked as she folded a wet cloth and placed it over her eyes.

Arthur was gone several days with no word about his progress; leaving Paulette frayed with anticipation. She buried herself deep beneath the sudsy water, hoping it would work its magic on her frazzled nerves.

Elizabeth obediently emptied the bucket of heated water that was left on the floor by the tub. As she did, she studied Paulette's tortured face carefully. When she was unaware and her guard was down, she resembled a beautiful young woman who was innocent to the ways of the world. Even so, the pain she suffered over the loss of her fiancé permeated the room.

Something came over Elizabeth and she forgot her own sorrow and anger. Her only thought was to try to do something to ease the pain that radiated from this poor woman who lay vulnerable in the soaking tub. Without a second thought, she reached into the water and pulled out the thick sponge. Wringing the warm liquid from the heavily laden sponge over Paulette's shoulders, she gently washed the woman's body. Slowly, as Paulette relaxed, Elizabeth relaxed.

The room radiated a sense of peace for the first time since Elizabeth arrived. It was at this moment that she experienced the first movement of her unborn child. She placed her hand on her stomach and smiled. She spent the last few weeks concerned about her baby's wellbeing. Bertha was tortuously adamant that she was far enough along now that she should have a round belly that kicked on occasion. Being of slight frame and severely over tasked, Bertha assured Elizabeth it was natural for her to have a rather small belly verses the rotund one Sally Jean, who was about as close to giving birth as Elizabeth was. Small stomach aside, her baby should be moving around and showing some liveliness. The fact that Elizabeth felt nothing during her entire term was something that concerned Bertha greatly.

Arthur commented on the fact that Elizabeth's figure remained intact for a considerable length of time considering the progression of her condition, but he saw that in the past with some of his other slave women. She appeared healthy enough, so he was not concerned. Unlike Bertha, he harbored no concerns and felt confident his unborn slave would be born healthy.

The agony of the reality of the turn of events in her life was almost unbearable. What made it even worse was that she had submitted an innocent child to this fate. It was no longer just herself who would suffer from her folly. She spent her evenings lying in bed while her tormented mind struggled to think of a way out of the nightmare her foolishness created.

Paulette's moan from the sheer pleasure of her ministries jerked Elizabeth away from her thoughts. She once again focused on her surroundings and her task at hand. Elizabeth was a quick learner. She allowed her mind to stray once while in Paulette's presence and was forced to endure its consequences. She was not about to allow that to happen again.

"Get out," Paulette snapped. "I wish to be alone."

Startled by her mistress's sudden command, Elizabeth stepped back and stumbled over a dressing stool she had not noticed prior. She quickly caught her balance. She was grateful Paulette's eyes were still covered with the damp cloth and she did not witness her clumsiness. Even though Arthur gave his sister strict orders to behave in his absence, Paulette's abuse simply shifted to behind closed doors. Now, with Arthur out of the house and no one to curb her, it was truly unbearable. More than once Elizabeth was forced to remind herself that she suffered Paulette's abuse for the sake of her unborn child. Had she not been expecting she would have surely fought back and shown this haughty Southern Belle what an English aristocrat thought of her terrorism, no matter what the consequences.

The letters that caused such a traumatic reaction in Paulette lay on the floor where they landed after her recent display of fits. Elizabeth stared at them for a moment, longing to know the contents of the one that was reported to have been written by her lover. She had never received such correspondence and her curiosity was all consuming.

Making certain she was clear from prying eyes, Elizabeth quickly scooped up the lover's letter and tucked it into the folds of her skirt before heading back to her room. It would be a while before Paulette's bath grew tepid. This gave her plenty of time to sneak a look at the letter and then return it.

With the letter tucked securely in her pocket, Elizabeth's attention was drawn to the sounds of Arthur's horse as its hooves clashed against the cobblestone drive.

THIRTEEN

Every muscle in his body hurt. What happened? Herald rolled over onto his side and looked around. He did not recognize his surroundings, nor could he identify its strangeness.

His attempt to sit up was thwarted by a piercing pain in his skull. Raising his hand slowly, he felt the bandage covering the gash over his right eye. As he gradually grew more alert, he felt for more bandages. He found one on his right thigh. As he eyes slowly focused, he was able to look at his leg to see that it had not fared well.

Herald struggled to recall the chain of events that led to his being trussed up like a mummy in what looked like a hospital bed, although he could not fathom what hospital it might be. As hard as he tried, he could recall nothing beyond the card game he was winning in Stephen's cabin on board the Duke.

The gentle rustling of skirts nearby caught his attention. His attempt to speak produced something that resembled a cross between a laugh and a moan, but it was enough to get the nun's attention.

"Padre, creo que uno de ellos ha despertado," she said in a low tone just above a whisper.

Although the woman's voice barely audible, he was able to make out the words enough to identify them as a language not his own. Yet, it was a language he understood. The woman had said, "Father, I believe one of them has aroused". What language was she speaking? Think Herald, think!

"Son... son, can you hear me?" asked the padre.

The heavily accented voice of Padre Rodriguez was low and gentle as he seated himself in the humble chair next to Herald's cot. Although he spoke with an accent, his English was clear and distinct.

Herald's eyes rolled in his head as he tried to focus on the padre's face.

"¿Quizás él no es el inglés? ¿Francés, quizás? ¿Dice usted el francés, padre?" the woman whispered.

Realizing the nun suggested he did not understand Spanish and perhaps they should try French, Herald struggled to force his tongue to cooperate. I speak English, his frustrated mind roared, and Spanish. You do not need to speak French to me.

"I... I speak..." was all he managed to get out amongst groans and gasps, but it was enough.

"Ah, very good my son. I am Padre Rodriguez and you are in my mission. Do you remember how you got here?" the padre asked gently.

Herald tried to shake his head, but quickly abandoned the idea. His lips were parched and his mouth felt as if he had swallowed a considerable amount of sand. He was not sure where he was or how he came to be in the hands of these gentle people, but he was sure he required water. Although his voice would not cooperate, his lips managed to mouth his needs enough for them to understand. A ladle of cool water was carefully placed against his lips. He rolled the liquid around in his mouth, savoring its sweetness for as long as he could. When he finally relinquished the inviting liquid to his throat, his body did not accept the water as willingly as he would have expected. He coughed uncontrollably.

With his vision still trying to focus, Harold managed to make out the color and design of the woman's costume. He realized that she was a nun just before she held a small beaker to his lips and poured its contents into his mouth. He swallowed the laudanum willingly and within a matter of seconds was once again drifting off into a dark, pain free abyss.

Padre Rodriguez patted Herald gently on his shoulder before standing up and questioning the nun about the condition of the young man's companion. She guided him to a room nearby where Stephen lay on a cot at the end of a row of similar cots, each containing a wounded man.

"He fared much worse, padre. The doctor questions whether

he will awaken," said the nun, who was also one of the mission's nurses.

"Well, then, sister, we shall pray for him," he replied.

Padre Rodriguez and the nun lowered their heads as he uttered a small prayer while standing at Stephen's side. When he finished, he made his way down the row of wounded men; stopping at each cot and asking about the man's condition and repeating the prayer in accordance to the information given to him by the nun who remained ever present at his side.

The arrival of a tall black man who was accompanied by a few Seminole Indians interrupted the padre's ministries. He excused himself to go speak with them.

The holy man led the small group of men out of the hospital to a small garden. It was one of his favorite places in the mission. He found it soothed him and gave him a stronger sense of closeness with the heavens. Because of this, he visited it often for quiet contemplation. He seated himself on the sturdy wooden bench that a mission member only recently gifted him and beckoned the men to make themselves comfortable. While most of them sat in a semi-circle on the ground at the padre's feet, the tall black man and two of the Indians remained standing.

"Tell me, my good men, have you any news?" asked the padre.

"They belong to the ship that went down in the storm," offered the black man.

"Thank you, Sam. I assumed as such," replied the padre. "Have we any clues to his identity?"

Sam scratched his closely cropped head.

"I ain't sure, padre," he said, "but I think the older one was the boss of the ship."

Padre Rodriguez raised an eyebrow and studied Sam closer. He joined the mission a year ago after escaping a life of slavery at a plantation in Savannah. The mission was a haven for many runaway slaves as well as dispossessed stragglers from various Indian tribes from Georgia and the Carolinas.

"What makes you say so?" the padre asked.

"I saw him once when he visited my masta's place. I talked

with his livery man whilst he was visitin'. His people liked him. They said he was not like the others. I remember," Sam replied.

"Interesting," Padre Rodriguez replied, "I will look into this immediately. Gracias, Sam."

The smile on Sam's face as he took his leave warmed the padre's heart. It was not so long ago the padre was barely able to get Sam to look at him, let alone smile. Such was the extent of Sam's suffering.

Born the son of a free black couple in Pennsylvania, Sam lived a life like many other boys of his color and station in the northern colonies. His father was the town's blacksmith. As he grew older, Sam helped his father in the shop and grew to know the trade. It was not long before he developed his own following to enhance their customer list. Life was good and Sam was happy.

When he came of age to marry, he fell in love with Jasmine, a cream skinned mulatto in the next town over. Sadly, she was not free.

Sam and Jasmine planned her escape and might have succeeded if they had not been taken in by the guise of a man who was secretly connected to the slave trade. The minute his beady eyes took in the beauty of Jasmine's creamy olive skin, their fate was sealed.

They were taken south and auctioned during one of Savannah's festive events. Sam was purchased by a local plantation owner and Jasmine to another. Sam lost connection with his love and could only wonder about her whereabouts and welfare.

Upon hearing his story, the padre did his best to ease the pain of the young black runaway. He sent word to Sam's parents that he was well and safe and offered to aid him in returning to Pennsylvania, but Sam declined. He felt safe and secure within the confines of the mission and did not trust that the same thing might happen to him again while in transport to Pennsylvania. Father Rodriguez completely understood the black man's fears and concerns as they were well founded. Therefore, he did not press him. Instead, he welcomed him as part of their family and no more was said on the subject.

As he grew more comfortable in his new surroundings and trusting of those who came and went, Sam fell in love with a local Seminole woman. He was welcomed by her people most heartily. Sam finally found happiness.

"Excuse me, Sam," the padre called, causing the former slave to turn his attention back to him. Stopping patiently, Sam waited for him to continue. "Do you recall the name of this man's plantation?"

Sam creased his brow in thought. "No sir, but I can ask."

"Mucho gracias, my good man," the padre replied.

He watched Sam lead his band of relatives out of the mission's parameter and into its wild surroundings.

****

Herald sipped the broth that Sister Lilly offered him gratefully. He was famished!

"How long have I been here?" he asked.

"My goodness, I believe señor has been here at least two weeks now, possibly a little longer," she replied.

The sweet melody of her voice was like music to his young ears.

"Is there anyone else from the ship here?" he asked timidly.

Herald was not entirely certain he wanted to know the answer.

"Si, there is one. He is in the ward down the hall," Sister Lilly replied hesitantly.

The nun was uncertain if she should continue with the direction his queries were going. Herald recently revived enough to tell them his name along with bits and pieces of their journey's purpose. She thought it might not be in his best interest to discover that his friend had not yet gained consciousness. She would have preferred to see him stronger before such a conversation transpired.

"I would like to know his name," Herald stated firmly.

"I am sorry, señor, but we do not have that for you. He has not yet awoken," she said softly.

"Then I must look upon his face so that I may know who he is," Herald stated calmly.

Surprised by his controlled demeanor and commanding mannerism, Sister Lilly found herself assisting him out of his cot and aiding him through the door. She obediently guided him down the narrow, roofless corridor to the ward at the end. Other than the few times Herald needed to stop and regain his footing on the cool slated floor, he made it to Stephen's side with ease. Sister Lilly took note of this accomplishment with great delight.

Herald stared down at the newly bearded face of his brother-by-law and scowled. There was no bandage indicating he suffered a wound to the head, so why had he still not risen? He identified Stephen as his companion and brother-by-law and then asked to confer with the physician about his condition. Something seemed amiss.

"He has not moved?" Herald asked, never taking his eyes off Stephen's still body.

"No señor, nothing to tell of. He moved a little when he first arrived and made a few sounds, but that is all," Sister Lilly's voice stated. Her voice was filled with compassion.

"When might the physician be available to speak with me?" Herald asked.

Sister Lilly responded to the young man whose questions sounded more like a command with an appraising look. His companion was identified as the owner of a cotton plantation in Georgia as well as the owner of the sunken ship. Clearly this young man who claimed to be the brother-by-law also led a life of privilege, for a man of common upbringing would not command in such a manner. Even so, she was not upset by his obvious air of superiority. She found it somehow gratifying. Before her stood a young man who would grow to be a man of power and strength. Judging by his mannerism, she also guessed he would become a man of compassion and honor.

"I will summon the doctor for señor," she replied softly. "Please, señor must first return to his cot. The doctor will not like to see that señor is up and wandering around before he has had an opportunity to inspect your condition."

Herald was happy to oblige. The prolonged standing and movement caused his head to resume the pounding that he was certain existed even while he was sleeping. He longed for a dose of laudanum to ease the pain, but knew that it must wait until after he spoke with the physician. He required a clear head for their conversation.

He did not have to wait long before the mission's physician was scurrying to his side. They discussed Stephen's condition at great lengths. All of his organs seemed to be working just fine and he suffered no broken bones or lacerations. The doctor prescribed laudanum when he first examined Stephen to help him rest and recover, but that order had since been removed and yet the man still slept. It was a mystery to the medicine man.

Herald could not shake the feeling that something was amiss. He knew this was why Stephen had not regained consciousness, but he could not say what that something might be. Feeling the need to watch him more closely, he asked to be moved next to Stephen. When the doctor expressed the fact that the ward was already overcrowded, Herald recommended, in a manner that re-sembled an order more than a request, that his brother-by-law's cot be placed in his room next to his own. Since there were only two other men rooming with Herald at this time, there seemed to be plenty of space available and no reason for the doctor to refuse him his request.

Herald accepted his dose of laudanum readily and settled in for a nap. The doctor agreed to his request and Herald was confi-dent that by the time he awoke he would find Stephen resting in a cot next to his.

That is exactly what occurred.

Herald refused to believe Stephen would not awaken, nor would he accept that Stephen could not hear what was going on in the room. He spent hours upon hours conversing with the silent man as he scrutinized every inch of his body. There must be a clue somewhere as to why he remained sleeping.

The nurses came in twice a day to administer laudanum to Herald and to care for his sleeping companion. Since they tended to him first, Herald's eyes were closed and he was well on his way to drifting off to his favorite abyss before they turned their ministering to Stephen.

He and his silent companion were roommates for the better part of a week when Herald stopped the nurses before they could get the laudanum down him and asked to know the manner of care they were administering to Stephen. To his shocked horror, they were still giving him laudanum. Worse, the dosage exceeded his own. He called for the doctor with an angry growl. The mystery of why Lord Stephen Carlson remained in slumber was solved and someone had some explaining to do.

The chagrined doctor admonished his nurses severely for their incompetence and inability to pay attention to his orders while skimming over the topic that he was the physician and should have questioned his nurses about the care they were providing long ago. Herald pursed his lips as he listened. Adding his own opinion into the mix would do no good and probably not be the wisest of actions, especially since he was a guest and under their care.

After a few days of reprieve from the excessive administering of laudanum, Stephen stirred. His fight for survival ended. Unfortunately, both he and his younger brother-by-law faced a new battle. Their bodies now craved the drug.

The days that followed were tortuous with both men begging for a dose of the hallucinogenic liquid at all too frequent intervals. Little by little they were weaned from their dependency. Surprisingly, Herald took the longest to overcome his addiction. After an excruciating cleansing period, they were eventually free from the interminable vice.

FOURTEEN

Arthur returned saddened, defeated, and without his good friend. Finding his search produced no results, Paulette's devastation caused her to be even more vicious than normal to those subservient to her.

Fearing for the safety of her child, Elizabeth begged an audience with the plantation's forlorn master. She could respect his sadness and need for mourning time, but this was a situation that could not wait. Paulette had already struck her and knocked her down several times in his absence. The last time caused her to fall against the railing of the second floor. She narrowly escaped tumbling down the steep flight of stairs. The old cook practically kept her hidden in the pantry the days following to protect her until the master returned.

Being summoned strictly for his personal pleasures, speaking freely was a luxury Elizabeth did not enjoy while in Arthur's bed. Although he agreed to allow her an audience and the opportunity to tell her story, his look of apathetic detachment led her to believe that he either did not believe her or was not listening. She returned to her room feeling disappointed and dejected.

The air in her tiny and sparsely furnished quarters felt abnormally stifling. Positioned on the attic floor of the elaborate mansion, it provided minimal ventilation under the best of circumstances. The fact that they were in the midst of the hottest months of the year only served to worsen the situation. Elizabeth stripped down to her shift and poured a small amount of water into the wash bowl. She was almost at the end of her daily water ration and needed to conserve what little was left. She was far too tired to walk down to the kitchen and explain to cook why she required more. What was in the pitcher would have to suffice for drinking, as well as cooling and washing, until morning.

The odor emitted from her person from the toils of the day was offensive, but there was little she could do to remedy the situation. She was so very tired. At the moment, she valued a restful sleep far more than a clean body. She would rectify the situation the first thing in the morning. Besides, a night in the oven she occupied would surely create even more necessity for a thorough washing up before she started her day.

Elizabeth stretched out on her cotton stuffed mat. It felt flat and lumpy. It most definitely was in need of a shaking, but, not tonight. Tonight it would have to suffice.

Grateful her stomach proved such a small burden, Elizabeth positioned herself as comfortably as she could. She closed her eyes and fell immediately into a deep sleep while she dreamt of a lavish, lavender scented bath in the copper tub that rested in Paulette's suite on the second floor. Elizabeth's exhaustion was such that she did not hear the scratch on her door in the wee hours of the night. Nor did she hear the latch lift as Arthur's prize field hand, Big Jim, slowly open it and crept inside. He was followed by his wife and Arthur's head of housekeeping, Bertha.

"Miss Lizzy... wake up," Bertha whispered as she gently shook Elizabeth awake.

Sitting up with a start, Elizabeth stared into the acute darkness that made it impossible for her to discern who was in her room. Even if the night was not devoid of the light that was normally provided by the moon and stars, it would still be black as pitch in her room since the window was boarded over at the onset of the summer by orders of Paulette. The woman was forever searching for ways to torture her.

"Who is it?" Elizabeth hissed.

"'Tis I, miss Lizzy, 'tis Berth an' Big Jim," Bertha replied.

"What? Bertha? Big Jim?" Elizabeth was completely at a loss as to why the only true friends she had on the plantation would be standing in her hot box in the middle of the night.

"Phew, is hot in here, miss Lizzy. How do ya breathe, poor child?" Bertha wailed in a deep throated whisper.

"We come ta take ya away, miss," Big Jim said in a voice that could barely be heard. The slaves at the plantation had long ago mastered the art of speaking clearly in a tone that was just above a whisper yet barely audible to the untrained ear.

"Pardon?" Elizabeth replied.

She was completely at a loss. Was there something she was supposed to do before the masters of the house awoke? Had she been so tired that it slipped her mind?

"Hush now, miss. Ya have ta trust us now. We come ta take ya way from here," Big Jim continued.

"Trust us, honey. We have it all worked out. Just wrap your arms around Big Jim and we are gonna get outa here," Bertha stated in a commanding whisper. When Elizabeth hesitated she added, "Do it now, girl."

Still overcome with exhaustion, Elizabeth obediently reached up and felt for Big Jim's arms. Once connected, she allowed him to scoop her into them. As she laid her head against his broad chest, she could hear the strong, steady beat of his heart. Its steady rhythm offered soothing assurance. She was in good hands. She had no idea what they were about or where they were taking her, but it somehow felt alright. They were her friends and she trusted them.

As they made their way down the servant's steps and out the back kitchen, Elizabeth was relieved to see that precautions were taken with the guard dogs that were set free to roam the house at night. Old Sukie saw fit to feed them stew laced with enough laudanum to keep them dreaming whatever dogs dreamed well into the morning.

Big Jim and Bertha stopped just long enough to retrieve a few things they hid behind the smoke house in preparation for their escape and then set out as fast as their feet would carry them across the field and into the woods. Elizabeth held tight to her transport, praying she was not too cumbersome a load to slow them down, but knowing that she was not capable of running alongside them.

The trio made it to the river where a dozen other slaves were waiting. Once they were sure all were present, they uncovered a raft tucked deep in the brush and positioned everyone on it.

The amount of bodies almost exceeded the space on the raft. This was something they had not counted on. After a few miles of clambering over one another to prevent capsizing, Big Jim and a few other men entered the water and held onto the edge of the raft. They all prayed fervently they would not encounter a hungry alligator on their journey.

Once everyone was settled, Elizabeth questioned Bertha about their destination.

The woman stroked her hair gently and drawled, "We be on our way ta freedom, miss. That be all that matters."

Realizing that was all the information she was going to get out of Bertha for the time being, Elizabeth leaned into the black woman's generous body and rested her head on her shoulder.

"Oh child," Bertha whispered in her ear, "the first matter o' business when we git safe is ta wash ya up!"

Elizabeth's embarrassment was overwhelming. Never in her life would she have ever thought that she, a woman of noble birth and privilege, would be told that she stunk by a servant; slave or free. What had become of her?

The lapping of the water as they slowly moved with the river's current had a hypnotic effect on the overworked slaves. Many fell into a light sleep. Feeling insecure on such a flimsy platform and anxious to reach their destination so she could feel dry land again, Elizabeth remained awake and alert.

A boy of no more than five watched her carefully from behind the folds of the skirt of the buxom woman who cuddled him close to her. Under normal circumstances Elizabeth would have instantly thought the woman to be his mother, but in the crazy world she found herself trapped in where people were bought and sold like mere animals and mothers and fathers rarely remained with their sons and daughters for long, she was not about to jump to conclusions. The woman could have been the boy's mother, but the odds were high that she was a fellow slave who adopted him when he was purchased by his master. Just like Bertha adopted her.

Elizabeth gave the boy a timid smile. He quickly buried his face in the woman's bosom. As she looked around she realized the boy was not the only one looking at her. The few passengers who were not slumbering had unfriendly eyes focused in her direction. She had no doubt as to their thoughts. More than once she heard the whispers amongst the other slaves of the unlikelihood of her being a true mulatto. Even if the Masta' could justify her porcelain skin, her bones just did not match.

It was just such whisperings that prompted Bertha to confront Elizabeth shortly after her arrival. She found Elizabeth with her head hanging over the chamber pot after her stomach's morning expulsion. Recognizing instantly the signs of motherhood, Bertha pulled Elizabeth to the side and quietly asked her who she was and why she was masquerading as a slave woman. Bertha listened intently to Elizabeth's story and shook her head. Never in her life had she heard of such a thing. A lady of society being sold into slavery; it was unheard of.

The story of Elizabeth's demise spread rapidly amongst Arthur's house slaves. Much to Elizabeth's surprise, the majority of them took pity on her and did their best to keep her load light, as well as protect her from the wrath of Paulette as best they could. Unfortunately, the one thing they were helpless in preventing was their master's regular summoning of her for his nightly pleasures. This was a burden she had no choice but to endure as best she could. Since the master was young and handsome, it certainly was not the worst thing that could happen to her. There were tales of woe that curled Elizabeth's toes from so many others around her. If the worst that had happened was that she had been forced to bed the handsome masta' she should consider herself lucky.

The fact that the slaves from various plantations might not welcome her on the raft hit her straight in the chest. She burrowed closer into Bertha, seeking the protection she inherently felt she required.

She was right.

As the trip progressed and the raft grew exceedingly cramped and uncomfortable, her fellow passengers started mumbling amongst themselves about the need for more room and the possibility of a few more passengers climbing into the water to make the raft more comfortable for the others. Normally the choice would be from amongst the men aboard the raft, but the fact that Elizabeth had not one drop of darky blood did not go unmentioned. Hearing their rumblings, Bertha's body appeared to almost double in size as she puffed herself out and dared anyone to lay a hand on her girl. A formidable woman in the best of circumstances, she was not to be reckoned with in this matter and the rumblings ceased almost instantly.

Grateful beyond words, Elizabeth laid her head in Bertha's lap and closed her eyes. Perhaps it was best to just allow sleep to take her away from it all until they reached their destination. She feared the tension directed toward her would be her end if she did not find a means of escaping it.

She felt the reassuring touch of Big Jim's wet hand on her ankle just before she slipped off her welcomed world of dreams.

****

The morning sun escaped the confines of the horizon before it beat mercilessly down on them. They made excellent time and actually arrived at the meeting place for the second half of their trip a little early. The men covered the raft with brush and urged everyone to be as quiet as they could while they waited for the wagon to arrive.

Bertha finally divulged their intentions to Elizabeth. To Elizabeth's surprise, but much to the awareness of all slaves in captivity, there existed a secret society made up of whites and darkies alike. This society did not support the reinstatement of slavery in Georgia. It sympathized with the plight of slaves to the extent that its members were willing to break the law in order to help them escape. The wagon for which the tense group of runaways waited belonged to just one of these sympathizers. It would take them to a plantation run by a couple who hired free darkies. They would spend the night there and then move on. Their goal was to reach Spanish territory where they could live freely.

The feel of the grass beneath her bare feet was wonderfully

refreshing. Bertha stole a chemise and skirt from a section of Paulette's wardrobe that she barely touched for Elizabeth to change into, but Elizabeth wanted to wait until they reached their destination before donning it. She had no idea what this place was like, but she intended to look as decent as she could when they arrived. To her surprise, Big Jim produced her own worn and soiled muslin.

He managed to grab it from its dropping spot after she haphazardly stripped it off in her state of exhaustion. How the man was able to see one thing in that pitch of darkness was beyond Elizabeth's comprehension, but she was certainly grateful. With a smile of delight, she scooped it up and started to put it on. The loud sound of Bertha clearing her throat grabbed her attention. Was something wrong? This was her skirt, after all. Looking at the soil and stains in the folds of muslin, she realized Bertha's message. Her skirt was not the only thing that needed washing. How horrid it was that she had grown so accustomed to her own odor that she was no longer offended.

"We best go upstream a bit, miss. There will be more privacy for ya," Bertha coaxed as she led Elizabeth passed the ogling eyes of the male passengers to a more secluded spot.

Bertha worried about straying too far from the group. It would not do to be caught by a whitey, or even worse, an alligator. She considered expressing her concerns to Lizzy, but thought better of it. The young miss had enough worries without her adding more to the pile.

Elizabeth looked at Bertha briefly before stripping off her shift and walking into the cool water. It felt like heaven. Not since that fateful bath in preparation for her sale had she experienced more than a small basin of tepid water to wash from. She wanted to wade out as far as she could and float beneath the sun's rays, but knew that would not be the wisest move. As it was, she needed to hurry before some scamp decided to sneak up and view what wares her body, thick with child, had to offer.

Bertha looked long and hard at Elizabeth's belly. Although still not large, it showed signs of dropping. The baby was preparing to be born. This was not a good sign while they were traveling.

She cursed herself for not doing a physical inspection of Lizzy's womb to get a better idea of the baby's birthing time before they carted her off with them. Then, one of the motivating factors for their timing was to protect Lizzy's unborn child from being registered as the slave property of the Moore's plantation. The masta was kind enough as masta's go, but that sister of his was a she-devil. It was bad enough for a darky to be born into such evilness, but for a child who was, in essence, above that wicked woman's station... well, that was downright wrong.

Remembering Lizzy's soiled skirt, Berth prepared to give it a light wash. The rustling of paper in its folds caught her attention. She could not read, but she did not need such a skill to recognize the letter she removed from the skirt pocket. She saw it plenty of times during the fits of heartache and temper Paulette threw. It was the letter Miss Paulette's lost love wrote to her. What would possess Miss Lizzy to take it?

Realizing what Bertha was holding, Elizabeth caught her breath. She was so tired that she forgot to read and return the letter. Now, instead of thinking her naughty and nosy, Bertha would think her a thief. This was awful... simply awful.

"Miss Lizzy?" Bertha's look openly scolded her as she held up the letter.

"'Tis not what you may think, Bertha, I was only going to read it once and then give it back. I was so exhausted, I forgot it as quickly as I borrowed it."

Elizabeth listened to her own words and groaned. What was she thinking?

"Ya know that be just not right," Bertha scolded.

"I know," Elizabeth replied as she held her head in shame.

"Invading Miss Paulette's privacy like that," Bertha continued, shaking her head.

"I cannot explain what came over me. My life has changed so and I longed for... well... I longed for..." Elizabeth apologized.

"Poor child, what have they done to ya?" Bertha scowled.

Elizabeth looked at her feet, unable to respond.

"Well," giggled Bertha, "as long as we have it here, can ya

read it?"

Elizabeth looked into Bertha's mischievous eyes and laughed. She was relieved at the change of mood.

"I certainly can," she said with a giggle in return.

"Well then, come on out of that water and so we can see what it says," Bertha urged.

She helped Elizabeth out of the water and quickly pulled her shift over her nakedness. The two found a comfortable bit of shade and positioned themselves for the invasion of Paulette's privacy. Elizabeth opened the letter carefully while Bertha looked on eagerly.

"Read it all, now. Leave nothin' out," Bertha insisted.

Elizabeth smiled and began reading, "My dear Miss Paulette, What joy upon receiving a letter from someone whose grace, charm, and whit is only surpassed by her beauty. It is a pleasure that I will treasure always. I beg your forgiveness, for I write in haste. Therefore, I write little. My haste is to be certain that this note finds post this evening in order to arrive in time to alert you of my return shortly after you receive this message. When I arrive I beg an audience with you and your brother. Our topics shall be my change in circumstances due to the death of my father, your brother and my dear friend Arthur's wellbeing, and the possibility of a marriage between us. I dare not dawdle with details as the courier has arrived. I eagerly look forward to once again being in your memorable company, at which time we may speak in more detail. Your servant, Stephen Carlson, Duke of Eastwick."

Elizabeth's voice trailed off as she realized that Paulette's lost love and her husband were one in the same. At first Bertha was so wrapped up in the romance the letter implicated that Elizabeth's pale face went unnoticed. It was not long before she questioned the young woman about her reaction to the beautiful words on the paper. She sighed with genuine sadness when she discovered the poor girl's reason.

Poor Lizzy! How impossible it would seem to have the very same vixen that held her captive and punished her daily be the woman who managed to capture the love of the man she herself loved, was married to, and whose child she carried. In a world as big as this, how could such a thing happen?

"I met your man, Miss Lizzy. He be a fine one, that man," Bertha blurted, without realizing the insensitivity of her words.

"He loves her," Elizabeth said with shocked disbelief. "He loves the evilest woman in the world."

Her shoulders slumped low, accentuating her engorged stomach.

"It sounded ta me like he was proposin' ta Miss Paulette. How can he do that if he is married to ya?" Bertha asked.

She was still oblivious to the harsh blows her words were striking.

"'Tis complicated," Elizabeth replied, not knowing what else to say since she was thinking the very same thing. Since slaves were very accustomed to not being allowed a true relationship or loved one, Elizabeth did not take Bertha's attitude to heart.

"Well," Bertha stood up and brushed off her skirts, "we better go on back afore we miss the wagon."

Elizabeth did her best to disguise her emotions as she rose to allowed Bertha to help her don her already dry, lightly rinsed, and freshened skirt before following her robotically back to the group. Stephen Carlson, the man she regretted leaving, the man whose arms she dreamt about each night, the man she dreamt of returning to and regaining his love and trust, the man whose child she carried, loved Paulette Moore. Her heart felt so heavy she was sure it would fall from of her chest and settle near her feet at any moment.

They almost reached the group when the realization of her discovery struck her. Not only did her husband and the father of her child love another woman and intend to marry said woman, but this very same man had been lost at sea! Elizabeth may have appeared docile on the outside, but she was screaming on the inside. How could this be happening? She was a runaway slave who was about to give birth to a baby in a foreign land that was filled with barbarians and to top it all off she was a widow.

The sound of a man's anguished cry brought her quickly back to reality. Bertha burst forward with the speed and strength of a raging bull, leaving Elizabeth to make the rest of the journey back as quickly as her cumbersome body allowed.

The horror of what she witnessed when she finally caught up with Bertha would cause nightmares for years to come. Before her, lay the upper part of a man. The bottom half of his torso was removed by an alligator during a tug of war between the alligator and a few male slaves trying to free its victim. When his hips tore free, the alligator took his prize and left. Blood poured out from what was left of the poor man's belly as he screamed in blind trauma. Elizabeth wondered if he even realized what really happened to him. Bile filled her throat when the man's thrashing caused his intestines to slide out of his torn torso and onto the grass. Someone had to do something. But what?

Unprepared for anything of such proportion, the slaves stood frozen while they watched the poor, half-eaten man flail and thrash around the embankment. It was Lizzy who finally took action. Realizing the man would die a slow and painful death, she searched for a stick heavy enough to mercifully beat the poor man to his death. When she returned with one she felt suitable for the horrific task it was too late. The alligator, or possibly its mate, rose up from the waters with lightning force and plunged its body close enough to retrieve the rest of its meal. With the power and speed that belied its awkward build, the beast claimed the rest of the poor wretched man and was back in the water before any of the onlookers had time to blink their bewildered eyes. Fearful they might be next, the group scattered as quickly as they could.

Elizabeth dropped her stick and pushed her body into a speed like she had never known as she ran in the direction she saw Bertha and Big Jim flee. Suddenly remembering her, Big Jim returned and scooped her up in his arms. His legs never slowed down or lost their rhythm. They reached the road just as their wagon approached.

Hiding in the bushes until they were certain of the driver's identity, they rushed up to the wagon and scrambled onto its bed. No one spoke as they covered themselves with the heavy tarp the driver provided.

The intense heat of the day was immediately accentuated as their bodies huddled together under the heavy covering that provided no ventilation. No one complained. It did not matter that the sun's rays threatened to suffocate them under the thick canvas. They had endured worse. They were safe from whips, safe from beatings, safe from alligators, and most important...they would soon be free.

The relief Big Jim provided by carrying Elizabeth came too late. Her overtaxed body could stand no more trauma or shock. It rebelled in the worst of ways. The searing pain that ripped at her stomach was all consuming. Since it was not a steady pain and would come and go at will, she did her best to endure it and not burden her companions.

After what seemed like eternity, their driver stopped the wagon and lifted the tarp to speak with them. They were dangerously close to both the road and the river that slave traders traveled toward Louisville. Louisville was so noted for its auctions that slaves only whispered its name. The dangers of their being caught were high.

He looked into the faces of the overly heated runaways with sorrow. It pained him to have to transport them in such a fashion, but it could not be helped. They had less than five miles left for this part of the journey. Surely they could last until then.

Apologizing profusely for their discomfort, his gaze rested on Elizabeth, who looked even more uncomfortable than the rest. After a quick assessment of the situation, it became clear that she was in labor. The driver longed to place her in the front of the wagon with him where she could at least breathe fresh air, but the risk of being stopped out of concern for her condition was too great. They decided to continue on with their journey for as long as they were able. It was just as easy for Elizabeth to endure the labor pains in the back of the wagon as it was for them to stop and watch her suffer.

Beyond herself with misery, Elizabeth gratefully sucked hot, dusty air into her lungs through the rip the driver created in the dusty tarp on her behalf.

Remarkably, they made it to their destination without any interruption. They were at the residence of Sir Matthew Caldwell, a wealthy sympathizer who tipped his nose at society and stood his ground in his beliefs by working only free darkies on his land. He took pride in the fact that he paid his free darkies a fair and honest wage.

Without a moment's hesitation, the driver explained Elizabeth's condition to their new protectors. They directed Big Jim to carry her into the cabin that the plantation used for delivering the babies born to the hired help. A mid-wife was sent for post-haste and a new plan of action was devised.

Bertha provided their hosts with a brief explanation of the reason the white woman was with them. Duly shocked by the story, they transferred Elizabeth from the cabin to a guest room in the main house and did their best to make her as comfortable as possible. Although the midwife was still allowed to tend to her, the Caldwell's also sent a summons for their family doctor. He would probably not make it in time for the delivery of the child, but he could at least make sure that all was in good order with the unfortunate woman after the event.

The runaways could stay no longer than a few hours. They were to be given food, shelter, and the opportunity for a little rest and sleep, but then they must continue. Rumor was spreading throughout the countryside of Sir Caldwell's possible participation in aiding runaway slaves and a safe haven was no longer something he felt he could provide. Transport that would see them on the rest of their journey had already been arranged.

Elizabeth, of course, must remain behind. This would not create such a problem since she was not a darky and they could claim her as a distant relative. She would be cared for until the child and she were well enough to travel and then the Caldwell's would assist her in returning to her homeland. The disgrace the people of their land bestowed upon a lady of her stature was shocking!

Elizabeth relaxed for the first time since sailing away from the docks of London. She had finally met people of grace and dignity. Perhaps now her nightmare was ended.

The baby arrived just a few hours before Bertha was to take her leave. She held Elizabeth's surprisingly healthy newborn son while grinning from ear to ear with so much pride one would think the child her own. What a strapping young boy he was. So big to have come out of such a tiny woman with no belly. Where did she hide him? It had all been worth it. Miss Lizzy and her baby were safe and free and she and Big Jim would soon be the same. It was a great day indeed.

When asked his name, Elizabeth smiled and replied, "James, of course." This brought joyous tears to Bertha. Hearing the new baby was named after him, Big Jim swelled with pride.

Bertha kissed the exhausted mother and her swaddled infant good-bye and swore never to forget her as she reluctantly made her leave. The waiting maid assigned to Elizabeth pulled the draperies wide open to allow the new mother a view of the wagon that carried her dear friends away. She kept her eyes glued to it for as long as it was visible. Although she doubted she would ever see those dear, compassionate slaves again, she vowed to hold them in her heart forever.

FIFTEEN

Arthur did not call for Elizabeth's pleasures after hearing her tale of how she came to be in his household. Instead, he spent the night pondering its validity. Her story was so preposterous that it just might be truth. The fact that she knew so much about Stephen Carlson and his family was remarkable. His mind wrestled with the amount of information she had been able to provide without a moment's hesitation or slip of the tongue. Could she have discovered this from Paulette? He thought not. It poured forth like truth. Yet, he did not want it to be true. He did not want to believe it. He did not want her to be the wife of his best friend.

His night of contemplation brought to light the fact that he had fallen in love with her. He held himself back from his true emotions by the fact that she was a slave, but now...

Although crushed to discover that the one woman whose beauty confounded him almost instantly was not available, he was happy and delighted to have been the one to have rescued the wife of his best friend from a fate worse than death. With the exception of a few beatings from Paulette, Elizabeth suffered little under their ownership. Her situation could have been far worse had she gone to another plantation. He pushed the fact that he bedded her almost nightly for the last few months into the recesses of his mind. He could not be held accountable for such actions while under the impression he was bedding a slave he paid a tidy sum for. Stephen would simply have to understand, if he was even alive to discover it.

As he sat at the breakfast table toying with his scrambled eggs and grits. Reality struck as he realized the wife of his best friend was in fact most likely a widow. Even more so, she was a widow who was about to give birth to the child of his best friend. This matter required immediate attention. He could not change what happened in the past, but he could most certainly correct what would happen in the future. Lady Elizabeth would be treated as just that... a lady... a duchess at that. Arthur was so overwhelmed by the situation; he did not know whether to laugh or cry.

It was unusual to keep a seamstress in residence, but then Paulette's demands were often most unusual. If it pleased her, then so be it. Today was the first day Arthur was grateful for such an arrangement. He summoned the resident seamstress and ordered her to immediately begin to put together a wardrobe suitable for a lady of society. Cost was not to be considered. He could not have a member of British nobility dressing in rags while she was under his protection. He expected at least one new gown within the next three days. She bowed and scooted out to begin her task as quickly as possible.

Although not a slave, she was always eager to do their bidding, for the pay more than compensated the occasional inconveniences and fits of the household members.

His next act was to summon for the doctor to examine Elizabeth's condition and then a midwife to take up residence in preparation for the birth of her child. He noticed of late that her stomach, although still quite small, seemed heavy and dropping. He was not an expert, but he sensed she was approaching her time.

Breaking this news to Paulette would be difficult for Arthur. She was already vehemently jealous of Elizabeth. Discovering that the little minx was married to the man she set her sights on would not go over well. The fact that she carried Stephen's child could potentially send Paulette into a rage like no one had ever seen before.

In some small way Arthur understood Paulette's position. She was denied his love because they shared their father's blood and was forced to stand by powerlessly while he took Elizabeth to his bed night after night. Now, the only man she felt could buffer the agony of being denied the love of a man she could never have was lost to her. He was not just lost to the sea, but to the very woman who had captured his attention as well as his heart! Yes, although he dreaded her rage, he would understand it.

Arthur scratched his head. Had not his sister reiterated the contents of Stephen's letter stated his intent to propose? Had she misread his words? It had to be, for otherwise it would not make sense.

When he thought about Elizabeth's looks, mannerisms and her acute knowledge of Stephen, he felt he could not deny she was telling the truth. Then again, if it was the truth, why then would Stephen be proposing to Paulette? Something was amiss. To be safe, he decided to send to England for verification.

Had Stephen not perished at sea, he would have only had to seek verification from him, he thought sadly.

Arthur's joy at discovering Elizabeth's true identity wrestled with his sorrow at the fact that she was the widow of his closest friend. Things would have to be handled delicately from this moment on. He ordered another place set at the table and summoned for Elizabeth to be brought to the dining room. There was no better time than the present to start making things aright.

When Sukie slipped timidly through the thick double doors a few minutes later to announce that Elizabeth and some of the other slaves were nowhere to be found, his roar was so powerful she was certain it could be heard clear to Savannah.

****

Paulette watched from her bedroom window as Arthur rounded up a hunting party to go after his runaway slaves. He lost six in all; with Elizabeth included.

She smiled smugly at the thought of her finally being freed from that petite spell-caster. She was actually sorry she had not thought of it herself. Losing a few slaves was a small price to pay for being rid of that horrid witchy woman.

Arthur told her the story Elizabeth relayed to him the night before, as well as the fact that he believed it to be true. Paulette would hear nothing of it. The mulatto pest was a liar and a she-devil who bewitched her brother. It was as simple as that.

She sighed as she listened to the faint sounds of Arthur barking orders in preparation to leave. He was abnormally obsessed with the little slave witch. It was not healthy. She fervently wished the little whore was miles away by now, never to be returned.

Although there were few slaves in residence who cared if she lived or died, Paulette did have one or two who were loyal to her and that was all it took for her to discover the fact that Elizabeth was on her way to freedom in Florida courtesy of Big Jim and Bertha. She wished with all her might that the runaways made it to Florida before her brother caught up with them. It would grieve her greatly to see that troublesome witch returned to her household.

Paulette's disappointment at her brother's return without Stephen was acute. She just knew he was not dead. She could feel his life's breath all around her. He was alive... he was alive... he was alive!

Her handsome Stephen was not married. How could he be when he had clearly proposed to her in the letter he posted in such haste? She decided to seek comfort and reassurance in the words he wrote in the only thing she possessed of him right now, his letter. Calling her waiting maid to fetch it for her, she watched the last of Arthur's posse trot down the lane and disappear. In preparation for reading Stephen's letter one more time, she settled herself onto her Marie Antoinette influenced, gilded settee. When her maid returned empty handed, her rage could not be contained.

Who could have taken her letter? Certainly not Arthur and none of the slaves could read; none except one.... Lizzy!

With her fury far beyond a sense of reason, she barked orders for preparations to be made for her to follow her brother. She would hunt down that devil-witch herself if she had to. How dare she steal her letter!

Throwing caution to the wind, Paulette thought of only one thing; finding Lizzy and retrieving her letter. Then she would sell the little mulatto witch to the nearest plantation before anyone was the wiser. Her brother's illusions of the little wench being of nobility be damned!

Although Arthur and his posse had a goodly head start, Paulette was not worried. She traveled light on horseback with only her bodyguard, Manley. She found Manley's strong muscular body pleasing to the eye and rarely over-dressed him. As bodyguards go, he was one of the best. He was schooled in a variety of fighting methods while traveling the orient as a young boy with his former owner, now deceased. She had no worries about her safety while Manley was at her side.

From the information provided her, the slaves were headed for St. Augustine. She had rummaged through Arthur's office for the map that would aid her in following prior to leaving. She had never been further south than Savannah and never without escort. The need to follow a map was never at hand. Hopefully she could catch up with her brother before she was required to call upon the map's guidance. The thought of venturing into unknown territory with only a map that she barely knew how to use was intimidating. Even so, it did not deter her from moving forward with her intent.

With Elizabeth's slave papers tucked inside her skirts, Paulette smugly mounted her mare. She would look back on this with fondness for years to come.

The southern belle started her journey much later than she would have liked. She would consider herself lucky to catch up with Arthur before dark. She regretted not sending a man ahead to either notify him of her coming or to arrange for housing before they arrived. Although she would never admit this to others, she had to admit to herself that this was not a well thought out venture.

The sun was blistering as Paulette and Manley urged their horses to cover as much ground as possible without overheating them to a froth. The map Paulette guided them with showed several roads that looked to be shortcuts leading to the main road Arthur would be more than likely be using by now. As they neared one of them she noticed it appeared to give a considerable and much needed respite from the blistering sun. Elated with her find, she ordered Manley to follow her down it.

Wary of taking a road with so much foliage to hide behind,

Manley did his best to dissuade Paulette, but to no avail.

Sukie had hastily packed some meats and biscuits and they found a tree to rest and partake of the fare. Feeling more vulnerable than she anticipated prior to starting out, Paulette surprised her guard by asking him to sit close to her. This was something she never did before.

Manley's exotic scents as he sat so near were surprisingly arousing. With the exception of her waiting maid, she had never allowed her slaves close enough for her to touch or feel their nearness, especially the males. His scent was raw and alluring. He smelled of chicory smoke, leather, horse and some type of herb she assumed was used in the soap recipe they brought from their country. The sensation that trickled through her body was almost alarming.

Sensing her arousal from her obvious body language, Manley casually stood up and made busy with the horses. Feeling thwarted by her slave, Paulette commanded that he return. Reluctantly, he secured the horse's tether and re-seated himself next to his mistress while he lamented to himself about how no good would come of these actions. They didn't encounter another traveler all day. Even so, they picnicked on the edge of the road. Should someone happen by to witness a white woman sitting so close to a darky, it would not be viewed well at all.

"I should like to take a little walk before I get back on that horse," Paulette blurted as she stood up, licking the grease from the cold, roasted spiced meat from her fingers. Marching into the trees that lined the road without a moment's hesitation, Paulette looked back at Manley and scowled. "Come on, Manley. You heard me."

"But, miss, what 'bout the horses?" Manley stammered, hoping she would come to her senses when she realized she was about to abandon them.

"Oh fiddle-dee-dee," she scoffed, as she placed her hands on her hips. She forgot about the horses. "Bring them along then."

"No good can come of this," Manley mumbled, "no good at all."

"What did you say?" Paulette barked.

"Nothin', Miss Paulette," Manley said quickly. "I be just takin' the shackle off this here mare. I be right along."

"Good," Paulette mumbled as she scoped the thick foliage for a direction that looked inviting as well as easy to navigate. "Follow me, then."

Manley pulled the horses behind him as he trekked behind Paulette into the thick greenery. He experienced terrains like this before and thought her foolish for dragging her horses into such. These horses were used on clean roads and manicured pastures. They certainly were not accustomed to pioneering through thick brush and possible swamp. There was no telling what they would encounter in this untouched territory. Also, the branches of the trees were so intertwined that it would be easy to get lost.

The air grew thick and humid, indicating that they were nearing a body of water. Paulette mopped the back of her neck with her linen handkerchief.

"I think there is water up ahead," she said eagerly. "Oh, I truly hope so. 'Tis terribly hot."

Encourage by the sound of running water, she picked up speed, making it difficult for Manley to keep up while pulling the reluctant horses.

Relief flooded Manley when he reached a clearing that edged a rather large pool of water near the base of a small waterfall. The water would be cool and refreshing for sure. He watched longingly as Paulette slipped off the majority of her costume -leaving minimal to the imagination- and raced into the water. He was not sure what he longed for more, her luscious, voluptuous body or the cool, inviting water.

Paulette paddled around the pool while her eyes followed Manley as he watered the horses and then tethered them to a sturdy walnut tree. His body gleamed with sweat from the exertion of the day, accentuating his finely chiseled muscles.

"Come in the water and cool off, Manley. Just stay over there when you do!" Paulette shouted as she pointed to the side of the body of water that was closest to the falls.

Manley was so happy he could hardly contain his joy. He felt as if the heat of the sun scorched him almost to the bone. He wasted no time hopping into the water and immersing himself from head to toe. The swirling of the cool liquid as it rushed from the falls past him was an added boon.

The sight of her body guard's scantily clad, muscular frame in the water sent a shiver through Paulette that she experienced only once before while swimming with Arthur those many years ago. Although it excited her, it also made her uncomfortable. Doing her best to subdue the unsettling sensations that flowed through her, she climbed out of the water and sat on the bank to let the sun dry her off.

"That is quite enough, Manley. Get out now," she called as she lay back on the silky grass and closed her eyes.

Aware that she could not stay in the sun long, Paulette recalled the make-shift tent her dear brother made for her so many years ago and told Manley to make some kind of mat out of foliage or whatever else he could find for her to rest on and instructed him to stretch her skirts between branches so that she could dry off in the shade for just a bit before they resumed their trip.

Manley reluctantly stepped out of the water. He was instructed to enter the water near the falls, were it was much colder than the rest of the pool. He found its icy waters hitting his scorched skin incredibly invigorating and was not yet ready to leave. For a brief moment he allowed himself to remember the days when he was the property of Masta' Orlando. A man of the world, Orlando took Manley with him on all of his travels. This allowed him the exposure and education of a world that even most debutantes were hard pressed to experience. His life as Paulette's bodyguard paled excessively in comparison.

He did not mind her spoiled ways. He witnessed far worse in his day. There was something about Paulette that made it alright. The only thing he wished was different was the way she treated Miss Lizzy. That was cruel and uncalled for. Some say it was because Miss Paulette wanted her brother in a way a sister should not and was jealous because Miss Lizzy had him that way. If that was true... well, he just did not know. It just seemed improper for a sister to want a brother like that. Then, looking at the way Miss Paulette was lying in front of him with barely a stitch to cover her creamy skin was not very proper either. Her corset was loosened just enough to allow him a tantalizing glimpse of the lushness of her rosebud tipped breasts as she shifted her body on the mat he created for her.

He sometimes wondered if the masta' should have sent her abroad for some education in the ways of a proper lady. Unless they recently arrived from abroad, he found that women of the colonies were not schooled in the ways of a lady. Manley had seen enough of the world to know the difference. Take Miss Lizzy for instance. She was clearly well schooled in the ways of a proper lady. Anyone with eyes could see that.

Paulette watched Manley from beneath the half closed lids of her large, almond shaped eyes and admired his powerful muscles as he moved past her. He was a fine specimen of manhood. So fine, in fact, that Arthur often bred him to several of his female darkies who he felt produced strong, healthy children. There were even a few occasions when Arthur rented Manley's stud service to neighboring plantations for that very same purpose. The scuttle about Manley's abilities as an accomplished lover amongst the women darkies reached Paulette's ears more than once. Having never been with a man, she could only speculate on what the stories meant.

He had almost moved past her reach when she extended her foot to trip him, giggling as she watched him crash to the ground. His muscular bulk landed within inches of her person. Catching himself with his powerful arms, he lay as stiff as a marble statue.

Surprised and uncertain of what to do, Manley remained still. Perhaps if he played possum she would stop with this game and let him get up. If the masta' knew what she was about he would lock her in her room and flog her for sure. He wanted no part of this... none at all.

"I want you to face me," Paulette said in a husky voice that seemed to come from deep within her throat. "Turn around and face me."

Manley closed his eyes and rolled his body to face hers. He could feel the heat of her breath on his face and his skin tingled from her nearness. She smelled of fresh flowers. He did not know the name of the flowers, but he knew it was sweet like the flowers they had on the plantation. She probably washed her hair in water scented from the flower's petals. His favorite woman worked in the house and told him about such things.

His manhood came alive from Paulette's sensual touch as she slowly traced the muscles on his broad chest through his water soaked cotton shirt. Her ministries were torturing him and if she did not stop soon he could not guarantee that he would remember that she was the mistress and he just a lowly slave. Did she not realize he was highly sexed; which was why his masta' used him as a stud? She was coming dangerously close to calling forth the beast within him. If he was not careful, he might lose control and take her where she lay. Is that what she wanted? He had to wonder.

Paulette paid little attention to Manley's response, nor did she realize his agony. Her mind was far away in another place and time as she absent-mindedly stroked her bodyguard's chest. She was thinking of her missed opportunities with Stephen. If only she decided to marry him earlier. Then maybe he would be lying here with her today. She tried to visualize herself lying half naked in the shade of the Georgian sun with Stephen Carlson, but as hard as she tried she could see only that she-devil Lizzy's petite body in his arms. It was tortuous. To make matters worse, her mind refused to be bridled as it moved on to replace Stephen with Arthur. Paulette almost exploded with despair at the vision before her. It just was not fair! She must not think about it!

Pulling herself back to the here and now, she forced herself to let her senses take in Manley's presence. Within seconds her body was responding and the man beside her became her fantasy.

SIXTEEN

Paulette lay outstretched on the grass wrapped in euphoria from of the visions that swirled in her head. She heard whispers from others in her social circle about mistresses bedding their stud darky, but she never really considered it a possibility for herself. Now, here she was contemplating that very thing!

She shook her head to clear it. What was she thinking? Obviously the combination of the shock and disappointment of Stephen's disappearance, the theft of his letter by that wicked devil woman, and traveling in this intense heat in unfamiliar territory took hold of her senses. She pushed at Manley's chest to create some space between them and rolled her back to him. He did not move. Why was he not moving? She could feel the heat of his breath on the back of her neck. It was sending soft shivers up and down her spine. This just was not fitting. She needed to stop before things went too far. Unfortunately, her body had other ideas and was responding to his nearness whether she thought it fitting or not.

Feeling a mild sense of panic and distrust in her ability for restraint, Paulette sat up quickly and looked down at him. He had changed positions and was now lying on his back with his arm resting over his eyes. It seemed a rather casual, not to mention sensual, pose for a slave in the presence of his mistress. This was a fortunate thing, for it was enough to prompt her mind to overtake her body's obvious rebellion and allow indignation to replace her lust.

"Get up!" she snapped, a little rougher than she intended. "'Tis time to leave."

Saddened that the beautiful dream he thought himself in was at an end, Manley stood up and adjusted his breeches to cover the fact that he had not yet returned to normal. He scurried over to the horses without being told. This gave his suddenly shy mistress the privacy she claimed to require to don her skirt and chemise and regain some semblance of her normal composure.

She had barely turned around to investigate the reason for Manley's loud grunt when a hand slapped over her mouth and she was pulled unceremoniously close to the body of the Indian who snuck up behind her without so much as the snapping of a twig. The scent of musk and grease mixed with an indefinable aroma that almost resembled sweat filled her nostrils.

Looking around wildly within the range of her terrified eyes, she could see Manley was overtaken by several equally half-naked Indians. She focused on their costume and hair style and tried to recall her lessons while growing up. The tribe they belonged to would determine the fate of herself and her slave. From what she could remember, they were either Creek or Cherokee. Neither of which favored the white man.

****

Adahy held tight to the white woman he had silently observed from behind the trees while she kicked and struggled to free herself. The only thing her efforts managed to accomplish was to tangle her legs in the fabric of her riding skirts. Her costume was made of so much material he was forced to squeeze tight to find the woman within it. His friend and hunting buddy, Degotoga walked by smirking at the fact that Adahy could barely be seen amongst all of the fabric and wild waist length blonde hair that came loose from its pins and billowed around his face.

When Paulette finally settled down enough for Adahy to remove his hand from her mouth, she made a loud sucking sound while she filled her lungs with much needed air. Realizing her struggles were futile, she forced herself to calm down enough to assess the situation. This pleased Adahy greatly. He feared he would have to strike her if she persisted and it was not something he relished doing. They were actually after the black man, but he sensed the woman might be of some value as well. White women were fragile creatures. He had no desire to damage her before he realized what value she held.

Paulette was almost paralyzed with fear as she took in the scene before her. Several half naked Indians with outlandish headdresses and colorful paint on their bodies were tying Manley's wrist and shackling his ankles. From the blood on his face as well as that on the face of two of his captors, she deduced he put up a fair amount of fight before they managed to subdue him.

Seeing the party was ready to move on, Adahy's hand put pressure against Paulette's back. He nodded his head in the direction of the others; indicating he wanted her to follow them. She was not given an opportunity to don her riding boots and winced as she felt sticks, stones, and rough foliage under her feet. She pointed to her bare appendages that peeked out just below the hem of her skirts and asked for covering, but her captor either did not understand or did not care. She was forced to continue on while her feet suffered the unfamiliar treatment.

She deduced by the porcupine hair roaches on their heads that they were Cherokee. Although she took little interest in the Indian population of Georgia, Arthur insisted she learned a bit for self-preservation. After all, they were not on the best of terms with these savages and it was not unheard of for small raiding parties to steal their slaves and then resell them elsewhere. They were even known to take them back to their village for their own use. They took few whites, for they disliked them too much. That did not mean a white person was exempt as one would go missing on rare occasions. Therefore, great measures were continually taken to avoid the Indians at all costs.

Paulette did not consider the Indians when she dragged Manley deep into the trees to allow privacy for her wickedness. This was her punishment. She was certain of it.

Her feet screamed with pain. It was beginning to creep up her legs and would soon consume her entire body. They had only walked a few miles, but it felt like one- hundred to Paulette, who hardly walked anywhere.

Manley did his best to keep an eye on Paulette. She wondered how he thought he could possibly help her if she was in need of his aid. They tied her wrists together, but left her legs free. Manley, on the other hand, was bound in every way possible. It was a wonder he could even walk.

She hoped to be allowed a bit of rest when they reached a small clearing that ran along a narrow road she did not recognize as being the one she and Manley traveled. When she tried to sit without permission, Adahy –who confiscated her mare and was now riding it– tossed a rope around her neck and she was dragged along behind him. The slightest hesitancy or slowing down of her gate would tighten the rope around her neck to the point she was fearful she would choke to death. She feared death in such a manner so she pushed her body onward.

The party walked their captives down the middle of the deserted road, giving Paulette the impression she was a distance from any plantation or town that would be occupied by her kind. She was at the mercy of these savages and had no idea where they were taking her. Were they still in Georgia?

Shadows danced across the landscape as the afternoon sun slowly prepared to retire for the night. Paulette was exhausted to the point she was sure her body would fail her and she would die from strangulation while being dragged behind her own prize mare. She strained her eyes to see as far as she could down the long, narrow path they turned onto a while back. It was actually worn down enough to qualify to be labeled a road if a person felt so inclined to give it such.

Darkness was rapidly sweeping the land, but even so there was still enough light for her to make out what looked like a group of thatched buildings. As they drew closer, she recognized them as being homes. Was she being taken to the village of these savages?

Stories of the fate of a white person at the hands of the Cherokee during the war raced through her mind. The fighting was over, but the anger and hatred between the races still ran strong. Even though things calmed down between the red man and the white people, there was still the occasional renegade or angry plantation owner who would lash out in vengeance, often in the most horrific and unmentionable manner.

With her exhaustion the overwhelming factor, Paulette hoped they were going to at least stop for the night at the village. It did not matter who it belonged to. She needed to rest. Her pampered body was about to break at any moment. At this point she hardly cared what they did with her once she arrived in the village. She just wanted to rest. Be it tethered with the horses or next to the dogs, it did not matter. Just please let her rest.

Since the king of England made the colonial's practice of forcing an Indian into slavery illegal, the focus of the slave traders and slave owners turned to the darkies from Africa and the islands. Capitalizing on this -as well as feeling the dark people inferior to the lighter, browned skinned people- many tribes linked up with the slave traders. They captured runaway slaves and turned them in for pay or sometimes stole them from one plantation and took them far enough away to sell at an auction without their theft being discovered.

When Adahy's party stumbled on the white woman bathing alongside the darky, it was too good an opportunity to pass up. He was a strong, powerful looking ebony man who would command a very good price. As for her, well Adahy still had not thought about what to do with her yet.

As they approached the village, strange guttural noises filled the air as women, children, and old men piled out of what looked to Paulette like thatched covered hovels. She later learned the Cherokee name for these shacks was asi.

The closer they got, the easier it was for her to make out her surroundings. She was indeed in a small village with about fifty asi strategically placed around a large center circle. It was in this circle that she and Manley were led.

The party stopped and Paulette felt the rope around her neck loosen. She was finally able to give her body a break. She slumped to the ground without care of how she might appear to the onlookers.

Several women approached Manley. They poked at him with a stick to force him to stand up. Paulette could not help feeling sorry for her poor body guard who stood tall and proud while at the mercy of such savages. They poked at his wounds with long sticks until the bleeding resumed, but he never moved a muscle.

Her concern for Manley soon shifted to herself as she felt the strong hands of the Indian women tugging at her clothing. Were they trying to strip her tortured body? She screamed for them to stop and did her best to push them away, but there were too many of them and she was weak from exhaustion. The tearing and shredding of the fine fabric of her costume pierced the air. It was not long before she found herself standing naked in front of the entire village. The shouts and sounds of the women who threw fistfuls of dirt at her seemed distant as the world spun out of control. Her mind spoke to her from the recesses of her head. Her body was pushed to the breaking point. She was going to die at the hands of savages. With that thought, everything went black.

Adahy's father was a member of Dragging Canoe's army during the revolutionary war. Up until a few years ago he continued to join in small raids here and there. From the time Adahy took his first breath, he was warned about the evil that dwelled within the hearts of the white colonials. He was never to trust them and always to fear and hate them. It was as much a natural part of the young Indian as his need for food, water, and sleep.

He left the circle to check on the condition of his father, whose illness was reported to him upon arriving. When he returned to find his property being treated as such, he went into a rage. True the woman was white and as such was their enemy, but she was his property and he did not appreciate them destroying her before he had a chance to determine what to do with her. He barked orders for the crowd to stand back and stood over her with a disgusted scowl. Her naked body was covered with dirt and bleeding in several places. Careful inspection of her feet showed they would need some attention from the medicine man. All in all, his prize did not look like much of a prize. He considered leaving her there and letting whatever happened, happen. After all, it was the dark man they really wanted. The white woman was just extra baggage. At the last minute he decided differently.

Adahy had just completed his twenty-fifth year of life. Having fallen in love with a beautiful girl from a nearby clan when just fifteen, he sought the approval of her grandmother and married her as soon as she came of age. His transition into her tribal village had not gone well and he never quite felt like he belonged. Having come from a warrior lineage, he married into a passive clan who did not share the same thoughts and sentiments about the white colonials or the practice of slavery. When the Mohawk, Shawnee, and Ottawa asked them to join up in battle during the onset of the revolutionary war, his wife's tribe declined. They chose to remain peaceful and as free from the white man's company as possible.

Adahy's wife tried to bring three sons into the world. Each one died within a few days. The birth of her last son was so difficult she died along with the child. When his wife died delivering his third stillborn son, he considered it a sign that he did not belong with this clan and returned to his clan of birth. Now, he spent his days hunting, fishing and helping with the crops.

On occasion, he would house with his good friend Degotoga and his wife, Yona. Although not a common practice, the village would look the other way on the rare occasions when two males would live in a household and share a single wife. Yona found Adahy handsome the moment she met him and was glad when he approached Degotoga about the arrangement. Degotoga was close with Adahy since they were young boys and found his company, as well as his assistance in putting meat on the table, a welcome pleasure. He questioned whether he would be able to share Yona in such a manner, but discovered almost immediately that it did not bother him in the least. So, whenever Adahy felt the need, Degotoga and Yona welcomed him with open arms.

Noticing Yona standing at the edge of the circle with a scowl on her face, he ordered her to prepare a mat for the white woman inside his hut. Reluctant to oblige him, but seeing no way of denying his request without having to explain her reason for doing so, she stomped off to do his bidding. Adahy watched her silently. He noticed a change in her mannerisms lately. She was beginning to give him attention outside of their night sac that a woman should not be giving to a man who was not her husband. This made him question the wisdom of the arrangement he kept with his good friend. Although it originally seemed workable for all concerned, perhaps they were wrong.

Adahy found Yona's body warm and pleasing, but his mind never touched on her once his needs were met. It was beginning to appear like that was not the case with Yona. Being fully aware of the feelings Degotoga had for his wife, Adahy did not wish to be a party to her approaching the clan leaders for the right to divorce because she wished to be with him. Arrangements such as he had with Degotoga and Yona were a rarity and he was starting to understand why.

Heaving a sigh, he plowed his way through the crowd and grabbed Paulette's ankle. Dragging her limp and seemingly lifeless, naked body as it bounced unceremoniously across the rough dirt, pebbles, and twigs that covered the ground, he made his way back to his hut. He called over his shoulder for Degotoga to follow with Manley. It was lucky for Degotoga that the enormous black man was alert and able to walk.

SEVENTEEN

Stephen stood in the missionary office and watched Padre Rodriguez through the window. The black man, who looked to be the leader of the small band of Indians that stood a short distance behind him, hung his head low as he listened to the padre's words and responded. The two were obviously deep in conversation.

Stephen was pretty confident he knew the topic of discussion. After learning that he was in a mission just north of St. Augustine, he quickly explained himself and his circumstances to Padre Rodriguez and requested aid in returning to his plantation. It was his original intention to purchase a new frigate to make his way up coast, but his poor brother-by-law was not yet ready to brave the water. In a way, he could not blame the young lad. Instead, he requested the assistance of the good padre to help him find a guide and transport over land. It would take longer, but it was a small concession after what his brave companion suffered.

At the sight of the padre and very familiar looking darky parting company, Stephen made his way out the door and walked toward him.

"Ah, my good man, I see you are moving around very well," Padre Rodriguez said with a smile of satisfaction. "I believe you are well enough to leave the mission whenever you wish it."

"Thank you, Padre. You and those of your mission have been most kind. I should like to repay you," Stephen replied. After a brief moment he continued. "I could not help notice that you have an abundance of runaway slaves and Indians within the walls of your mission."

Padre Rodriguez looked nervous as he nodded in agreement. He was fully aware that he was speaking with a plantation owner who owned a fair share of his own slaves. It could even be possible that he was providing harbor for a slave or two who had run away from this man. Although Georgia slave owners were powerless within his mission walls, he was still uncomfortable with the topic.

"Fear not, padre. I mean no malice," Stephen assured the holy man after noticing how uneasy he suddenly appeared. "I was just intending to suggest that perhaps a donation of goods to help feed and clothe these refuges might be in order. 'Twould be a privilege and an honor to arrange for such."

Padre Rodriguez expelled the air that had collected in his lungs during his long anticipation of Stephen's admonitions of his aiding and abetting the runaway slaves and renegade Indians. Escaping such a confrontation was joy enough, but to hear an offer such as the one being placed before him was a wondrous gift from above. The mission was sorely in need of food and supplies. They struggled daily to provide the basics for the sick and the refugees. Just yesterday the padre engaged in a most sorrowful discussion with the mission's doctor about the possibility of them having to select who they could assist and who they must turn away because their supplies were so depleted. Surely this man standing before him was a saint they scooped out of the waters.

"My good man, we would welcome your assistance with the utmost gratitude," the padre replied with genuine appreciation.

Seeing Padre Rodriguez's heartfelt response to his offer touched Stephen deeply. This man truly cared for the people he helped. Stephen watched the way he interacted with members of his staff, as well as the sick and those who simply lived amongst them, and thought it so. The genuine gratitude in his voice confirmed the depth of his charity.

"Well then, 'tis settled. Once I am returned to my plantation, I shall arrange for a supply of cotton to be delivered to the mission to be sold for the funding of supplies. I shall also arrange for an account of trust to be set up on the mission's behalf." Stephen looked at the padre's overwhelmed look and smiled. "I give these gifts unconditionally, padre, but I ask a favor that I pray you see fit to grant."

"What be the favor, my good man?" Padre Rodriguez prayed

with all his might that the favor would not be some outlandish request that he would not be able to fulfill.

"I ask that you accept these gifts as if they were from an anonymous donor," Stephen replied.

It was a narrow road he was walking. He was eager to repay the mission for saving his and Herald's lives, but he dreaded the wrath that might befall him should the other plantation owners discover his generosity. Since he needed no recognition for good deeds done for his ego to savor, it was best his identity be kept secret to avoid confrontations that were sure to arise.

Stephen did not like being forced into such a position and made a mental note to change things once his mission was completed and he was once again united with his wife. He needed workers to work his plantation, but perhaps he could free his slaves and then offer those who wanted to stay a payment by way of housing and a small wage. Although he tried it before, perhaps he had gone about it the wrong way. He heard of other plantation owners who adapted such a practice. He would investigate more closely how well it worked for them and then reconsider it for himself.

There was a small tobacco plantation one county over that he was considering purchasing before his father summoned him home. It bordered the wilderness and was rather remote from society. He could experiment with that one before he brought such a practice to his Savannah plantation.

Padre Rodriguez had never met a man who was selfless enough to request anonymity for such generosity.

"You truly are a saint," the holy man stated with heartfelt wonder in his voice.

"I think not," Herald interjected as he entered the room, "but he is one of the most extraordinary men I have ever encountered and I am proud to call him my relation."

Stephen looked at Herald and chuckled. The boy looked to have grown a few inches since they set sail. Or, perhaps it was an illusion as a result of the way he was carrying himself these days. Their time in recuperation provided them an opportunity to get to know each other better. They found they liked each other immensely. After confiding in Stephen his opinion of his sister's foolishness, Herald spent hours in discussion with him on how to locate her and prove that she was who they claimed she was.

Discussions with Padre Rodriguez on the matter proved extremely helpful. Being a man who abhorred slavery of any kind he studied the laws of slavery for the colonies over the years and could recite them verbatim. It was by his insistence that they replace the proof of Elizabeth's lineage that had gone down with the ship.

Hesitant at first and fully expecting to receive a scathing letter from the earl about the disappointing actions of his niece and nephew, Herald eventually relented and wrote to his uncle. He requested the papers be sent immediately to Stephen's plantation in Georgia. Now all they needed was to go to the Charles Town auction and check the records to find out who purchased Elizabeth and get her back. Stephen would buy her if he had to.

The bell rang for dinner and the three men eagerly made their way to the dining hall. Herald took an instant liking to the food prepared by the mission's Spanish cook. In fact, he enjoyed it so much that Stephen noticed the young man's body filled out a little in the mid-section. He jokingly made mention of the possibility of having to seek a tailor's attention to let out the waist of Herald's breeches before they began their journey and was met with a hearty laugh and an agreeing nod. If that was the consequences of his enjoying such tasty fare, then Herald was willing to pay the price. His only regret was that they would have to leave the cook behind.

Dinner consisted of some re-fried beans atop a crispy flat bread made of corn the cook toasted to make a crispy wafer that burst with flavor when it hit one's mouth. It was accompanied by a spicy shrimp stew. Although Stephen enjoyed the cook's food, his admiration paled next to Herald's. He looked at the women, children, and a few old men who left no seat empty in the great hall and smiled. The padre was right. His gift of charity would be very useful.

On the morning of Stephen and Herald's scheduled departure,

Sam and six Indians waited at the entrance of the mission. The padre saw to the acquisition of some fine horseflesh for Stephen and Herald, along with making certain that they had sufficient supplies to keep them fairly comfortable on their journey back to Savannah. Stephen promised to return the horses as soon as he arrived at his plantation. If they stayed steady on the course they could make it there in two days' time. The padre provided them with a letter of introduction to present to a family in New Inverness who were anti-slavery sympathizers and general sympathizers of those in need. He felt confident they would open their home to the weary travelers for the night.

Stephen and Herald were informed that Sam would accompany them as far as the St. Johns River. After that it was not safe for him or his men, since the possibility of them being captured by either slave traders or renegade Indians was too great. They would travel on their own from then on, but the padre packed a good map in their bags and prayed diligently that they should not run into any trouble along the way.

Stephen traveled to St. Johns Island on more than one occasion and felt fairly confident that he would be able to manage without a scout. He and Herald bade the padre, doctor, head nun, and cook good-bye and climbed onto their mounts.

Herald followed Stephen out of the mission wearing a broad grin as his senses bathed in the rich aroma of the small bundle of food the cook tucked inside his jacket while bidding him a good journey.

EIGHTEEN

Arthur's search took him near the town of New Inverness with no sign of his runaways. As nightfall closed in around them and they found themselves still miles from town, he gave the order for his weary men to make camp in a clearing just off the main road. The fast flowing stream that was only a few yards away from the spot they selected for their camp provided fresh water for cooking and drinking, as well as a cool bath for those so inclined.

Although he kept a steady hand with his slaves, Arthur was not as strict about segregation with his darkies as most of his fellow slave owners. He walked a fine line between their distinct opinion that a darky was born to work hard and would not be able to survive as a free man and his friend Stephen's viewpoint of them being on the unfortunate side of a difficult lifestyle structure.

He attributed his thinking to the many conversations with his father, who owned slaves out of necessity, but did not necessarily support slavery. The two had partaken in many evening discussions, with a glass of brandy and a good cigar, about slavery, man, and God.

Having wrestled with the concept of slavery after many of his close friends became sympathizers, James Moore poured over their matters of estate to see how he might possibly follow the examples of his friends and work the plantation with paid labor instead of slaves. Unfortunately, at the time his father was considering this, their matters were not in order sufficiently to support such a shift. Twisted inside, James turned to the church for answers. After several days of praying on the topic, the chapel priest presented him with the passage of scriptures – *Leviticus 25.44* – which stated ...*You may buy male and female slaves from the nations that are about you... you may bequeath them to your sons after you; to inherit as a possession forever...* This provided him the justification for his need to maintain slaves. Arthur's father relaxed about the subject of slavery, making certain that he kept order without cruelty, as per the scriptures.

As Arthur stripped off his clothes and plowed into the cool, refreshing water along with the rest of his posse, he chuckled at the outrage his fellow plantation owners -with the exception of Stephen- would feel at the thought of him bathing with his darkies. He looked around at his men's overly tired faces. They laughed and played with each other while delighting in this brief reprieve from their day to day drudgery. Was he doing the right thing by keeping them in bondage? Was the plantation now at a point where it would be able to support freeing them and hiring those who wanted to stay as paid labor? Arthur shook his head to clear the thoughts from his mind. This was a topic he would have to address at a later date. Now he had other, more pressing, matters to deal with, such as finding Elizabeth and bringing her home before she fell into harm's way.

Disheartened with his inability to catch up with his runaway slaves who were obviously being aided by anti-slavery sympathizers, Arthur finished bathing and dove into the task of considering the best and shortest route to St. Augustine as best he could with the light his candle provided. Had he not been seeking to retrieve Elizabeth, he might have been tempted to abandon the slaves as lost. If he did such now, he would also be abandoning the woman who captured his heart. Not since he realized he loved Paulette had he felt so drawn to a woman. How often did a man feel an all-consuming emotion such as this? Not often, he reckoned.

****

The sun was barely risen when Ollie, one of the slaves who attended Paulette, raced into Arthur's camp. He rode at breakneck speed in search of the posse to make certain that Paulette managed to catch up with Arthur and was safe. He had no desire to suffer the wrath of an angry masta' because he did not do what was expected of him.

Having just finished breakfast himself, Arthur ordered his cook to feed Ollie and had one of members of the posse rub down the horse that Ollie pressed to its limits in his effort to reach them as quickly as possible. Positioning himself on a tree trunk with a tin cup filled with steaming coffee in his hand, Arthur listened to Ollie tell of how Paulette ordered Manley to get her prize mare and the fastest horse he could ride and the two of them had set out riding. Paulette had not confided her intentions with any of the slaves, therefore they could not spread the word for Ollie's ears to hear about what was amiss.

Ollie never noticed Paulette and Manley riding down the lane. When he did discover they rode off on horseback, he assumed the mistress was just going out for her daily ride. When she did not return by late afternoon, he began to make inquiries and that was when he found out about the fit the mistress threw over the missing letter from her dead beau and her insistence that Miss Lizzy stole it. Although no one was certain, since Sukie was asked to pack a goodly amount of food for them, Ollie determined Miss Paulette must have gone on a hunt of her own to find the slave woman herself and retrieve the letter. It did not take long for him to pick up their tracks and figure out that Miss Paulette was following Arthur's posse.

Although Manley was a loyal and competent guard, Ollie took it upon himself to find them and tag along because of the dangers of Indians along the way. He saddled one of the masta's fastest geldings with minimal tack to encourage speed and hoped to catch up with his mistress and fellow slave within a few hours. To his dismay, he lost their tracks on a side road somewhere near Richmond Hill. The side road was not far from the infamous road slave traders used to travel to auction. He was worried about getting caught -him being alone and all- and was unsure what to do. He decided to abandon his search and continue on to find the masta' and let him know Miss Paulette was missing.

Arthur's ears roared as if trying to drown out what he was hearing. His heart twisted while it struggled to continue pumping life giving blood through his body. His chest contracted to the point he was hard pressed to take in air. Ollie was a well-rounded darky who deceived the world with his slight, wiry body. His fearlessness and ability with his fists went unsurpassed. He could ride any horse he was placed on like he was raised on its back and was also one of the best trackers he owned, second only to his man Bishoff, who was leading the posse. If Ollie lost signs of his sister, it was extremely serious. He dared not even think about how serious a situation it was, let alone voice it out loud.

The possibilities of what could have happened to Paulette raced through Arthur's mind. He prayed they simply lost their way and were in some town right now with Paulette ordering Manley around in her sassy manner. The fact that Ollie lost all signs of them near the river that many slave traders used to travel to Louisville was ominous. Manley was a fine specimen of a darky and Paulette was no match for a trader wanting to steal him away. In fact, Arthur shook his head at his sister's foolishness for taking Manley instead of Ollie. If she was going to go ahead and do such a fool hearty thing, she should have taken her best man for protection, not her prettiest. In fairness to Manley, had Ollie not been available he too would have selected him. Although not as well rounded as Ollie or nearly as quick in the mind, Manley was fearless, strong, steadfast, and skilled in many methods of combat. These were excellent qualities for a body guard.

There was nothing to do except abandon their mission. As much as he loved Elizabeth and wanted to bring her home, he loved Paulette more. She was his blood, after all. Not to mention the fact that she had occupied a significant place in his heart for the greater part of his life. Arthur closed his eyes and forced back the panic. If anything happened to his dear Paulette, he would not be able to bear it.

After first admonishing Ollie for traveling alone and risking his own safety, he went on to praise him for his quick thinking and devotion. He ordered his men to break camp and make ready for a change of course. They would be returning north. With both Ollie and Bishoff with him, he felt confident that he would be able to pick up their tracks. The less time wasted the better.

NINETEEN

The blistering sun was positioned in the sky high enough to cook an egg on a flat stone if someone so desired, but not high enough to indicate midday. Paulette was grateful for the cool water she stood ankle deep in and would occasionally dampen the cloth around her neck in as well. She hurt from her head to her toes. The pampered existence she led over the nineteen years of her life never once hinted of the trials she was enduring now. She questioned if even her strongest slave would possess the strength and stamina that these barbarians expected of her.

Upon the thought of her slaves, she craned her head over the tall grass to see if she could locate Manley. Both edges of the river were filled with bobbing heads as the workers bent down, cut the reed at its root base with a sharp piece of bone, and then stood up to place it in piles to be bundled. They were gathering reeds for basket weaving. Some would be used by the village and others taken to trade for other supplies that their simple set up did not provide.

Her eyes slowly surveyed the bobbing heads for the one that looked familiar. Since there were only a few darkies mixed in with the Indian workers, it should not be that difficult to find Manley. He was nowhere to be seen.

It was days since their capture and she saw him only once from across the center circle. He was standing proud and tall like an ebony statue in a small circle of tribal women who were giggling while diligently washing his finely chiseled body. Unable to communicate with them, but fully aware that much of the Indian nation dealt in the slave trade as well as kept some of their own, she assumed they were preparing her body guard for market. After that one time, she saw him no more. Had they sold him already?

An incredibly sun weathered white woman approached Paulette with caution.

"I speak English," she stated in a voice just above a whisper. "You look for your black warrior?"

"Pardon?" Paulette asked.

"Your slave. The women call him black warrior because he is a strong fighter. They praise his beauty." The woman continued as she moved closer and placed her hand on Paulette's elbow. "I am Elsa. I been here ten years now."

Although Elsa's speech lost a great deal of its lilt from lack of use, she still had a command on the English language, for which Paulette was grateful. The two women worked side by side while Elsa filled Paulette in on the village, her slave, and their captors.

Elsa was a mere girl of eight, while traveling with her family and a small band of farmers heading for the western edge of Georgia when they came across a party of displaced Creeks. The men in her party grew aggressive and fearful. They forced an altercation between them that Elsa later learned was not the intent of the Creeks. As a result, most of her party was killed and the few who survived were taken prisoner.

There was a gathering of several tribes, hosted by her captors, five years back. It was at this gathering that Elsa caught the eye of Atul, her new owner. Atul paid a good price for her and brought her back to tend to his needs in the day as well as the night. Atul recently fell in love with a woman from a nearby village and planned to marry. Once married, it was tradition for the male to move to the village of the female's grandmother. He would not be taking Elsa with him. Now new arrangements would have to be made for her. Elsa heard Adahy intended purchasing her, but was not certain if it was correct.

The sun bronzed woman picked up enough of the village's language to communicate slightly and listen well. She kept the full extent of her knowledge of their speech and traditions hidden. She found those around her more comfortable and free with their topics of conversation that way. This allowed her to keep up with things that she might normally have not been privy to knowing.

Manley had not been sold. Adahy was still debating what to

do with him. Although it was clear Manley would bring a fine price at market, he was discussing with others in the tribe his potential as a stud for breeding more fine slaves for trade and market. Adahy could either sell him at auction for one good price or sell his offspring for many good prices.

Paulette thought of how Arthur had seen the same value in Manley's genes, even to the point of renting his services to other plantation owners. She was surprised at how astute these Indians were when it came to matters of business and profit. She would not have expected such.

"There is something else you should know," Elsa murmured hesitantly.

Detecting a change in Elsa's mannerism and voice pattern, Paulette stopped laboring and looked directly into her face. She had no idea what this woman was about to tell her, but from the way her faded brown eyes looked at her from beneath lids that aged prematurely and the sound of her voice Paulette knew it could not be good. Were they planning on selling her into slavery? What could it be that was causing this woman to hesitate in telling her?

"Go ahead," Paulette urged.

"They plan on breeding him to you and me," Elsa stated flatly.

"What?" Paulette almost screamed the words. "You are jesting, of course."

"Nay, 'tis no jest. Adahy spoke to the others in the village and they think that it would be better to sell his babies to the plantation owners. They say babies with white blood command a high price."

Paulette could not argue that point. Had she and Arthur not made the trip to Charles Town because they heard about a mulatto for sale? Arthur paid far more than he should have in order to outbid the others in the bidding war that ensued when Lizzy was placed on the auction block. A wave of nausea consumed her as the reality of her situation burrowed into her mind. She was in denial since her capture. She was aware of her surroundings and what was going on, yet somehow stayed detached from it as it if was happening to someone else. She could do that no longer. This was no bad dream. It was something very, very real and it was happening to her.

Everything she had been desensitized to in her daily existence -owning people, beating people, breeding people like they were livestock, overworking them to the point that they dropped and then beating them back into motion- she witnessed and sometimes participated in it all. It was now being done to her... right down to the planned breeding of her to her former stud slave as if she was an animal.

Unlike plantation overseers, the Indians who monitored the captive workers were not as cruel and allowed them to partake in conversation as long as it did not interfere with their work flow. However, should they stop working even for the briefest of moments, it could bring forth great consequences. Paulette knew this, but it completely slipped her mind as she stood in stunned silence at the prospect of being bedded by her own slave. Elsa, having learned early how to escape the switch that was now headed their way, immediately moved away and resumed working as if she had never been in Paulette's company.

Even Elsa's abandonment was not enough to snap Paulette back into action. It took three lashes with a razor sharp willow switch across her hip before she realized where she was and what was happening. She immediately cowered and resumed her work while tears flowed down her cheeks. She was not sure what pained her more, her torn flesh or her torn heart.

The morning dragged as Paulette toiled near the river. Ignoring the fact that Elsa blatantly left her to the mercy of the switch, Paulette made her way close to the young woman and struck up another conversation. Elsa was the only female in the village who she was able to converse with and who would help her understand what was happening. It did not matter that under normal circumstances she would have barely spared a glance for the rough looking woman who was born of humble farmers. Her life was not normal and probably never would be again.

The two women took their lunch huddled together against the

trunk of a black walnut tree. Their conversation continued while they scooped the remains of their potato soup out of the bowl with their soil embedded fingers. Paulette's soup blended with the taste of the bloody wounds on her fingers that refused to heal as a result of the scabs being continually torn away from the work she was forced to do.

"There will be one good thing if they breed us," Elsa mumbled from behind her bowl.

"Do tell," Paulette stated flatly, as she dropped her bowl in her lap and watched the last of its contents drizzle onto her deerskin shift.

She was simply too exhausted to pick it up again. As for the soiling from food on the disgusting shift they provided for her, it simply could not worsen its already foul condition. At this point, it just did not matter.

"If they breed us, they will not work us. I bred for them a few times already. The slaves they breed get a good house, good food, and clean clothes. 'Tis a much easier life," Elsa offered.

"I can hardly wait," Paulette snapped as she struggled to stand once again.

She spotted Adahy coming their way and did not want to be in a compromised position when he reached her. More than once she felt the wrath of his foot in her ribs because she remained seated when he wanted her to stand. If he did not want her standing, it would be far less painful to have him push her down than to suffer his kicking her to stand up.

"I regret so much in life," Paulette sighed.

Adahy approached her rapidly and slapped her hard across the face, sending her body slamming into the tree trunk behind her. He yelled words she could not under-stand and then moved on across the circle without looking back at his captive who was slowly sliding down the trunk.

"You should not speak when he approaches. 'Tis considered disrespectful," Elsa whispered as she helped Paulette to her feet.

"You understood what he said?" Paulette gasped in shocked realization.

"Every word. I told you I learned," Elsa responded.

She found it irritating that either Paulette was not paying attention to her or had not believed her.

"Tell me more... please. If I can understand more then perhaps I can avoid the beatings and floggings they are giving me daily," Paulette pleaded in a tone that resembled begging.

"I will tell you more if you will finish what you started to say. What regrets do you have?" Elsa quizzed mischievously.

If Paulette missed Elsa's gossipy nature before this, she was fully alerted to it now.

"I regret the treatment I gave my slaves, for one. I never put myself in their places to know the pain and humiliation they felt. 'Tis quite humbling to be here, I dare say," Paulette stated earnestly.

"Aye, 'tis that," Elsa agreed.

Elsa's voice trailed off and a faraway look covered her face. She had been a captive for ten long years. Sometimes it was difficult to remember the life she led when she was free, but when she did it was bittersweet indeed.

Paulette squared her shoulders before asking, "Is there no way to escape?"

"Escape," Elsa said as she rolled with laughter. "Pray where would you escape to? Do you think your people would welcome you back with open arms after they discovered you bedded an Indian? Worse yet, your own slave?" Liza's eyes squinted with seriousness as she leaned nearer to Paulette so that her whispered words could be heard. "I hear tell you will be bedded with your warrior this night."

Paulette covered her ears. She could hear no more.

"'Tis not such a bad thing," Elsa continued. "If I must confess, I have already bedded the man several times and it was not at all unpleasant. In fact, it was a far greater pleasure than I have experienced up 'til then. 'Twill be alright. You will see..."

Elsa's words trailed off as she watched Paulette break into a run across the clearing toward the river. She shook her head when her new friend fell to the ground under the impact of a brave's body as it slammed against hers. She could almost feel the thud of his weight on the poor woman's body as it rumbled through the loose soil when they hit the ground. Her heart winced while she watched Paulette's wildly flailing body being dragged unceremoniously by her hair across the rough ground as they delivered her to Adahy's asi.

Elsa was raised in humble surroundings and taken captive at such a young age that she adapted to the ways of the Indians far easier than a woman of Paulette's age and stature proved capable of doing. She witnessed the capture of women like Paulette captured several times before. Paulette lived much longer than the others had lived, or even been allowed to live. She would have to speak with her about the perils she created for herself with such actions as today. It was no secret Cherokee spit on the life of a white settler. They put no value in it. It was unwise for her to toss away her only measure of survival. To breed with the black warrior and produce healthy children for Adahy to sell into slavery would keep her alive for years to come.

The thudding sounds of Paulette's flailing mixed with her piercing screams as Elsa walked slowly back to her hut. The Cherokee allowed their workers a short resting time for napping before resuming their chores and she did not want to miss one minute of her allotted time. She was sorry for Paulette, but the woman created her own hell as far as Elsa was concerned. If she would just stop fighting them and do as she was told, her life would be a lot easier and certainly less painful.

The deep open gashes on Paulette's body had not gone unnoticed by Elsa. They looked to be bordering infection. She was certain the poor thing suffered a cracked rib or two after her latest antics. Lizzy had a few remedies up her sleeve. When she was permitted enough free time she would gather what she needed to make a paste for the poor woman's wounds to help ward off infection and bind her ribs to prevent the bones from breaking completely apart.

TWENTY

Elizabeth sat on the edge of her bed and watched the wet nurse bathe her newborn son with a damp cloth. Since her arrival at the Caldwell's' plantation, she experienced the treatment due a woman of her stature. It felt wonderful. Although she had always held a kind regard towards the servants of her uncle's estate, her treatment of them was even kinder now.

The workers of the Caldwell's' plantation were free and could walk away whenever they desired to do so. This was not the case for the majority of the darkies who resided in colonial America. Some were brought over the waters to become slaves and others were born as slaves, but slaves they were and slaves they would remain.

Elizabeth thought about the freedom granted the Indians by King George when he passed a law making it illegal to hold Indians in slavery and wondered if such a law would ever come about for the darkies as well. She remembered the slaves she left behind with that horrible woman, Paulette, and wished with all her heart that she could, in some way, spare them her wrath.

Paulette was an incredibly spoiled young woman. Elizabeth witnessed such attitudes plenty of times back in London. The difference being that she was simply an observer and not the recipient. Had she truly understood what it was like to be on the receiving end of such unjust treatment, she was certain she would have done her best to stand up for the servants who were unfortunate enough to feel the wrath of one of her over privileged acquaintances. For even though they were free to leave, their position in life did not afford them the luxury of being without employment.

Most of the women Elizabeth associated with outgrew their tendencies to abuse the help as they matured and ventured out amongst society. Realizing Paulette's exposure was limited to the small circle that made up Savannah's elite, Elizabeth felt Paulette would benefit from a little more broadening of her social interacting with the world. A trip abroad might help her understand the power of kindness. Until then, Elizabeth would pray for the safety and wellbeing of those poor unfortunates who suffered her wrath.

Mrs. Sara Caldwell was a full figured woman who stood about three inches taller than Elizabeth. Her genuine warmth when she addressed a person overshadowed her overly large beak-like nose and deep set eyes that always sported dark circles. Even her crooked teeth did not deter from the sense of warmth and wellbeing that an individual felt while in her company.

Having been born and raised in London herself, Sara was delighted to sit for hours while she questioned Elizabeth about the happenings of the London society she left fifteen years hence. Elizabeth found her hostess' chatter uplifting. Her relationship with Sara quickly proved to be the type of relationship with another female she had longed for all of her life.

Sara led a life of affluence and was raised as such, but she never succumbed to the spoiled and selfish ways so many privileged girls with doting parents tended to do. Since Elizabeth's uncle was neither doting nor extravagant with her care, she always felt like an outsider when amongst the other women of society while attending teas, balls, and such. Now, for the first time in her life, she felt like she belonged. It was a glorious feeling that she never wanted to end.

Much to the dismay of the Caldwell's, the couple found themselves childless. Elizabeth thought this an enormous tragedy. A child lucky enough to have been raised in the Caldwell's household would have surely experienced all the love, joy, happiness and privileges that any human being could conceive. When the Caldwell's transferred all of their untapped parental love onto her and her newborn son, she welcomed it in earnest. It was an arrangement suitable for all.

Having met Lord Roberts on several occasions when he was a young man, Sir Caldwell felt it was his duty to send word that his niece was safe and in his care. Elizabeth tensed at the mention of her host's deed, but thanked him none-the-less. It would not do to trouble them with the truth about her estranged relationship with the earl. They simply would not be able to understand such ways or probably even believe it possible. Such was the type of people they were.

As certain as she was that her uncle would not wish her return for his sake, she was equally as certain about Stephen. She read his letter to Paulette, after all. It was clear Paulette was the woman her husband wished to have as his bride. Elizabeth did him a favor by running away. It gave him the way out that he must have been longing for from the minute their nuptials were announced.

Prior to her departure, while in idle conversation with the lawyer Jameson, Elizabeth learned that wedding banns must be read for three consecutive Sundays before a wedding could legally take place. Little did he realize that he was telling Elizabeth that her marriage was not legal.

Was Stephen aware of this fact? She thought not. If he was, he would have surely declined rushing the wedding and being bound to her when his heart was elsewhere. Surely he would have exposed her uncle for his trickery and justified his return to the Colonies to take Paulette as his bride as soon as he discovered the truth. True, Elizabeth loved Stephen, but Stephen loved Paulette.

The fact that her uncle was willing to shove her into the arms of a man under the ruse of a marriage that was not legal empowered her leaving even more. She had no doubt that scoundrel of an uncle planned on pulling strings to make up for the lack of the third reading of the banns. She wondered if he had yet succeeded. Was she truly a widow to the Duke of Eastwick?

To Elizabeth's relief, the Caldwell's questioned her little about her deceased husband since her arrival and were therefore unaware that he was the Duke of Eastwick as well as a plantation owner in Georgia. They simply knew her to be a widow whose husband was lost at sea. The details that connected the dots were omitted.

Would it make a difference in their eagerness for her to make their home her home if they knew she shirked her responsibilities as a new bride and ran away from the duke only two weeks after their nuptials? Would it matter to them that the banns had not been fully read and if her uncle was unsuccessful in pulling strings to compensate this fact she was actually not a widow and her son was not legitimate? She pondered on the subject for several days and decided to wait to see how her uncle responded to the news of her whereabouts before sharing any more information with them. Since all attention was on the newborn in their midst, that had not proven difficult.

"Ya be healing nice, miss," the wet nurse commented as she watched Elizabeth slip out of bed and make her way to the commode chair placed behind a screen in the corner of the room for her convenience.

"Thank you, Anna. I agree," Elizabeth replied as she stepped off the thick tapestry rug and glided across the highly polished flooring until Anna could no longer see her.

Anna had recently given birth to their fourth son. Elizabeth had held the infant and could attest to his robust health, making her quite confident in allowing Anna to suckle her own newborn son.

A former slave to a plantation in North Carolina, Anna was purchased at auction ten years prior by Sir Caldwell to work in their kitchens. She fell in love with one of his field hands, who was equally satisfied with his treatment on the plantation. When Sir Caldwell freed his slaves eight years hence, Anna and her love agreed to stay on. They felt there was no better place to raise their children than on the plantation of such generous and warm hearted people. She knew that if they left to make their way in the world as free darkies they would always be in peril of being captured and sold to evil slave owners. There was also the probability of having to live in hovels while they scratched out a living as so many free darkies were doing. Since the Caldwell's were seeing to it that all of the children on their plantation received a basic education, they saw no reason to take themselves or their children away from such a friendly and advantageous environment.

"I think ya might be fine going down to the garden for a bit today if you be so inclined, miss," Anna stated as she turned her head in the direction opposite Elizabeth.

The screen was between them, but even so, it was an intimate time for the miss and she felt she should provide her with as much consideration as possible. This consideration did not go unnoticed by Elizabeth, who had almost forgotten what it was like to be treated as such after the months she spent in forced slavery. She wanted to do something to show her gratitude for such consideration but had not yet decided what that might be. She was certain it would come to her soon enough. She thought to mention it to Sara. Having been Anna's mistress for over a decade, Sara would know better what type of gift would be suitable to give in a situation like this.

The fact that she felt free in discussing the concept of giving a gift of thanks to a servant was so elating for Elizabeth that her feet barely touched the ground as she made her way back to her bed.

"Perhaps you are right, Anna. It would do me good to get some sun, I am sure," she said jovially.

"Very good, miss," Anna said with a satisfied smile. "I shall inform Lady Caldwell of your plans and see what arrangements she desires for your outing. Would you like to take your afternoon tea there?" Anna asked as she swaddled baby James and placed him in a nearby cradle.

"That would be lovely, Anna. Quite lovely," Elizabeth replied as she smiled contentedly.

Sara was kind enough to go through her wardrobe and have the local seamstress alter a few day dresses to fit Elizabeth. Once Elizabeth was recovered enough to stand for a fitting, the Caldwell's promised to send for the local milliner who also provided a good stock of dress fabric to select from. She was anxious to don the pale peach linen chemise and matching skirt. They looked to be light weight and airy. It was the perfect costume for such a hot summer's day. Pulling the bell cord for her waiting maid, Elizabeth started the process of dressing without waiting for her to arrive.

By the time Janet, her recently acquired waiting maid, arrived on the scene, Elizabeth managed to tangle herself in her corset quite effectively. It took considerable patience, as well as time, for Janet to rework the laces correctly. Uncertain about the reason her mistress would do something so silly, Janet remained quiet.

Born into slavery, Janet's mother was Creek and her father was African. Her mother instilled much of her native mannerisms and beliefs into her before she was purchased by the Caldwell's at auction and then immediately freed with the option of remaining and working on the plantation.

Feeling like an outcast amongst the other darkies because of her mixed bloodline, she was quiet by nature and made it a point to blend as best she could with her environment so that she would not be noticed or stand out in a crowd. This type of anonymity was something Janet relished and enjoyed.

Embarrassed by her fumbling mess, Elizabeth remained silent and allowed Janet to dress her correctly. Once satisfied that her mistress was properly attired for her little outing, Janet positioned Elizabeth in front of the dressing table and began to work her hair.

Impatient, Elizabeth suggested a modest, unpretentious up sweep. A wig had been provided by her thoughtful hostess, but after such a long time going without one, Elizabeth now preferred her own hair. She would reserve the more fashionable wig for more social occasions.

The brilliant sun radiated warmth on her body as she sat in the shade of an old, black walnut tree and sipped on freshly squeezed lemonade sweetened with honey which was harvested from the plantation's bee farm. Elizabeth was certain life could not be grander than it was here at the home of the Caldwell's. She gave thanks for her good fortune in finding them.

She smiled as she watched the soft silhouette the sun behind Sara Caldwell created as she gracefully made her way across the greens of their oversized garden toward her. The figure of a man walked a short distance behind her. Elizabeth thought the man's walk looked familiar, but she could not place it. She did not think it was Sir Caldwell. Curious, she said up and shielded her eyes from the sun's glare, hoping this would give her a better view.

"Elizabeth, my dear, we have a visitor," Sara bubbled jovially.

As the figures grew closer Elizabeth's body froze. Her worst nightmare had happened. There, before her, stood the very same man who purchased her at the slave auction several months prior and used her body for his own pleasures night after night. The very same man she went through so much to escape!

Elizabeth's first thought was of her son. She remembered all too well Arthur's delight in discovering she was with child and the fact that he would get two slaves for the price of one.

Without a moment's hesitation, Elizabeth set off toward the house in a dead run. Stunned by her ward's unseemly actions, Sara turned to Arthur just in time to catch a candid look of hurt, sadness, and... could it be love?... fleetingly cross his face before he regained his composure and calmly suggested they go after her.

Sara was most gracious when Arthur and his men arrived at her doorstep a few minutes earlier seeking permission to rest on their greens for the evening. Of course, this was a matter for her husband, who was due to return from the overseer's office shortly. She really should have asked Arthur to wait in the parlor until then but, instead, she acted impulsively and escorted him to the garden where Elizabeth was waiting for her to join her for tea. It was her intention to have Elizabeth help entertain him until her husband's return.

Arthur Moore was a very comely young man. He was the owner of a rather large plantation to the north of them and he was single. She had to admit that a bit of match making may have been in the back of her mind. Certainly she would have worked fervently to match him to her own daughter, had she been blessed enough to have borne one. Now, seeing poor Elizabeth's fear at the sight of him, she truly regretted her impulsiveness. The curiosity that most puzzled her was the look on Mr. Moore's face when he saw Elizabeth depart in such a manner. It was clear the man knew her and probably loved her. How did he know her? More so, why was she so frightened of him. Was his plantation the one from which her dear Elizabeth only recently escaped? Dare she guess? This was most puzzling.

Sara declined Arthur's suggestion to catch up with Elizabeth and escorted him to the parlor instead. This was most definitely a matter for Sir Caldwell.

They did not have to wait long for her husband to return. Even so, it felt like an eternity to Arthur. When he knocked on the door of the plantation's main house that day it was to inquire about permission to rest his men on their greens for the night. He heard the Caldwells were an amiable family, even if they were anti- slavery sympathizers.

This fact did not concern Arthur, since he too was weighing the pros and cons of freeing his slaves. He could not say he was anti-slavery, but he was not a diehard supporter either. For the present, he required slaves to keep his plantation operating smoothly. Until the time came when that was not the case, he would own them with a free conscience. He was grateful when his father pointed out the fact that the scriptures supported slavery. Otherwise, he might have spent many torturous nights questioning the morality of his ways, as well as not be able to hold his own in conversations with anti-slavery sympathizers such as the man whose home he was a guest in.

His conversation with Sir Caldwell went well and he was given permission to settle his men on the north side of their garden. Discovering that Arthur was the son of one of his old school chums from back in the days of growing up in the motherland, Sir Caldwell also invited him to dine with them that evening.

As for the matter of Arthur claiming Elizabeth as a runaway slave, it was absolutely absurd. Sir Caldwell was certain he had the poor girl confused with someone else. Elizabeth was a grand lady from London society who would not take kindly to such gossip being spread about her.

Arthur read between the lines and understood. He had never met Sir Caldwell until today, but he was well aware of the man's power and political connections. It would not do to have the man as his enemy. Elizabeth did well when she secured him as her protector. Very well indeed.

He recalled his conversation with Elizabeth the night she fled his plantation as he watched Sir Arthur escort her impeccably dressed, petite form that was no longer encumbered with an unborn child across the thick imported carpet to the highly polished mahogany dinner table. If he doubted she spoke truth about her identity before, he doubted it no more. There were certain ways in which a lady of privilege acted and a special way she carried herself that even the best educated darky or commoner could never master.

The breath taking lady before him moved with the grace and confidence of a woman accustomed to being escorted to dinner in this manner all of her life. His heart swelled with pride as he drank in her beauty. Even in her simple turquoise trimmed lightweight linen day gown she was a vision of a princess.

Arthur thought Paulette the fairest woman in the colonies, but, looking seeing Elizabeth in this environment, he was want to differ. Elizabeth, with her dark exotic features may not be lovelier than his fair haired, blue-eyed sister, but she certainly proved to be a competitive rival. How lucky he was to have had two such beautiful women under his roof and how ashamed he was to think that Elizabeth was treated in such a manner while there. Even if he had been deceived into thinking her a mulatto slave, could she ever forgive him?

Sir Caldwell monopolized the conversation for the majority of the dinner, allowing Arthur the opportunity to interject at the appropriate moments. It would have taken the strictest of trained eyes to recognize that Arthur watched Elizabeth's every move out of the corner of his eye during the entire meal while he held an ongoing and lively conversation with his host. He noticed how carefully she laid her knife on the upper right side of her plate, with the blade resting toward its center as it balanced on the gold trimmed rim. He noticed the genteel way she dabbled at her full lips after sipping on her wine and the refined way she fed herself with her left hand.

The corners of his mouth curled as he remembered his governess and her lessons in table etiquette, 'Feed thyself with thy two fingers and the thumb of thy left hand.'

He even noticed the way she nibbled at her chocolate puffs, taking small bites in a display of restraint and manners. Surely something so appetizing and delectable would tempt one less schooled in social graces to pop it into one's mouth.

Arthur noticed all of this and more as the conversation rambled on about the future of Georgia State and where the country was heading as the turn of the century approached.

When dinner was over and the men retired for a smoke, Elizabeth seized the opportunity to step outside for some fresh air. Anna slipped into the dining room with little James and Lady Sara's attention was completely captured. After and long and tortuous dinner, Elizabeth was alone at last.

It was her first day out after her confinement and she was tired, so very tired. The shock of seeing Arthur walking across the green took its toll on her still recovering body. It suffered not just from the delivery of James, but from her ordeal at the hands of Captain Kline and months of slavery both in Arthur's bed and beneath Paulette's whip.

Arthur sought an audience with her earlier in the afternoon. A little resistant, she saw no way out, since Sir Caldwell felt it best to face the situation head on to clear up matters. After joining them briefly for a glass of port, Sir Caldwell made his excuses and left them alone to discuss the matter at hand. Elizabeth was grateful, at least, for the fact that Arthur did not press the issue concerning his ownership of her. He came to terms with and believed her story, even though it took time to settle in with him. He even apologized for the gross injustice done her by Captain Kline and all that followed. Even so, his remorse and apologies did not and could not erase what happened.

What occurred after his array of apologies was something that Elizabeth, in her wildest of dreams, would never have imagined. The man who held her in bondage and used her body for his pleasures night after night kneeled before her and attested to his undying love. If that was not shocking enough, what followed surely was. Upon discovering Elizabeth was the widow of his truest friend, Arthur felt it was his duty to see to her welfare. When she ran away from the plantation, her absence brought forth the realization that he loved her. It came to him that the best for all concerned was to marry her. Since she was not of darky blood and a widow, it would be quite possible. He spent the better part of an hour explaining and describing the benefits of her becoming his wife, not just for her benefit, but for the son of his best friend as well.

To Elizabeth's surprise, his words made sense. She asked for a few days to contemplate his offer, of which he was glad to oblige.

The matter of Arthur locating his minx of a sister still needed to be dealt with. After discussing the facts, as he knew them, with Sir Caldwell, they mutually concluded that, since neither Paulette nor Manley were adept at reading a map, they simply took a wrong a road and were probably honored guests of one of his many amiable neighbors.

He sent Ollie and Bishoff off to pick up their trail where Ollie lost it, with orders to bring them back. Once he had Paulette safe and sound he would decide how to deal with her. In the meantime, Arthur would be a guest of the Caldwells.

Arthur expressed his sincerest hoped that Elizabeth would see her way clear to give him the answer he longed for and agree to marry him before his men returned with his wayward, and often disagreeable sister. He assured her that if she needed more time he was willing to wait, but also was clear about how agonizing he found waiting to be. To his surprise and delight he did not have to wait long at all.

After a brief stroll around the gardens under the moonlight, with her mind reflecting over what she had done to destroy her life and what she could do to correct it, Elizabeth made her decision. She had lived at Arthur's plantation long enough to see that he was a wealthy and generous gentleman almost to a fault. He kept a firm hand with the slaves, but not a cruel one. Even when he bedded her, he was considerate and gentle. Other than the fact that she was miserable over her misfortune of being placed in the lowly position of a slave in his household and she longed to replace his arms for those of her husband, she had to admit she could not complain about his treatment toward her. He may not make her feel the wild pleasure that she felt when Stephen took her to his bed, but he had not proven unbearable either.

His sister, on the other hand, was a different matter altogether. She was a matter Elizabeth would most definitively have to converse with him about. If he wished to take her as his wife, his sister must move out of the house. Elizabeth cared not whether Paulette moved into her mother's residence or her own. Surely Arthur was financially able to support Paulette's private household, should she choose to live alone until she secured a husband. Although this sort of thing was not done in England, the land she found herself in now had a way of thinking that could be quite different from her home land. Elizabeth doubted if Paulette's taking up residence alone would create much of a stir. If Arthur would agree to this, she saw no reason to deny her son the kind of life he could have under the care of such a wealthy and powerful man and she would marry him.

Although saddened at the thought of having Paulette move out of his home and not being able to see her on a daily basis, Arthur knew the day for them to part would eventually come. He and Paulette needed to move on with their lives and if this was the only thing preventing Elizabeth's agreeing to marry him, then he would have to comply. Once that was decided, he insisted they speak with Sir Caldwell right away.

Delighted with the prospect of acting on Elizabeth's uncle's behalf in such matters, Sir Caldwell determined the wedding would be held in his estate chapel. He would send word, post haste, to Lord Roberts about the blessed event.

Elizabeth requested that her brother be notified as well. Although certain he would be shocked at the events that occurred while he was tucked safely away at school, she wanted him to be aware and prayed her uncle would allow him to travel and attend the wedding. It would give her great pleasure to have Sir Caldwell give her away during the ceremony, but even more if it could be done by her dear brother who she missed grievously.

Arthur was so overwhelmed with joy that he could not contain himself. That night when the house was asleep, he found his way into Elizabeth's room to taste the sweetness he had grown accustomed to from his soon-to-be bride. After admonishing him about his lack of understanding of the healing process a woman endures after giving birth, Elizabeth hustled him back to his room. She was no longer a slave and deserved the consideration and respect due a lady of her station. Duly chagrined, Arthur apologized profusely and slipped through the dark and quiet house back to his quarters.

TWENTY-ONE

Stephen's back screeched in agony with every step his geld-ing took. Their trip proved difficult as he and Herald came to the realization their bodies were not quite healed enough to withstand the grueling trip through the Georgia wilderness.

Stephen's primary land travel was over the countryside near-ing Savannah which was rapidly developing and Herald had only read of the wilderness in his school books. Theirs was not a jour-ney for the weak of constitution. Although they were well cared for at the mission, they suffered greatly at the hands of the ocean's raging waters and their constitution was not yet returned to nor-malcy. Therefore, a trip that should have taken no more than two to three days was well into its fourth day with at least one more day's ride ahead of them, possibly more.

Their escort turned back two nights before, leaving them to forge their way as best they could. True to his word, the padre provided a detailed map that they put to use to help them in their journey.

Nothing could have prepared Herald for the humidity, insects, and abundant wild and gnarled foliage they found themselves for-aging through on a consistent basis. Having been warned of the perils of alligators, and recognizing their threat was a reality, only served to heighten the tension in his tired and achy body. As a result, he resisted the motion of his mount instead of combining with it, making him eager to stop long before they should have.

Herald shook his head as he looked at the back of his brother-by-law while he led him, once again, along a barely detectable path that was lined with brush so gnarly and thick it threatened to swallow them up if they rode too near. The adventure he was so excited to embark on was now an ordeal he dreaded and longed to end. He thought of his poor sister having to make her way in this untamed wilderness and straightened his back while mustering up his determination. He needed to remember the reason he came. He had always been focused on finding Elizabeth and bringing her back to England, but now, more than ever. He could not stand the thought of her being left in a place like this. It was far too crude for such a delicate lady as she. In fact, as Herald saw it, it was far too crude for any civilized human.

The sound of something moving in the distance caught their attention and they stopped their mounts to listen more closely. It sounded like someone was running toward them. Before they could confer on the matter, Big Jim and Bertha bounded out of the brush and fell breathlessly to their knees only feet in front of them. They were breathing so hard from the exertion that they had no breath left to explain the reason for their running.

Stephen and Herald waited patiently.

At first the black couple hedged slowly toward the bush. They were prepared to flee just as soon as they regained their wind. When it became apparent the two men on horseback meant them no harm, they visibly relaxed and begged for food instead.

Stephen tossed them a hunk of bread from their food sack and questioned them on their whereabouts. They ate the bread gratefully and took the water offered hesitantly. Having never been allowed to drink from the same flask as a white man before, Big Jim held the flask clumsily while he stared at Stephen. Stephen closed his eyes, smiled and nodded. With a look of satisfaction and self-importance, Big Jim drank his belly full before tossing the flask back to Stephen who, with a gesture that stated more than any words could say, took a long drink before capping it back up and securing it over his shoulder.

Recognizing Stephen as Paulette's lost beau and Miss Lizzy's dead husband, Bertha crouched behind Big Jim. Whether he was a ghost or a man, she wanted as much space between herself and the man who caused so much pain to these women as she could get.

Big Jim, on the other hand, had no idea of Stephen's identity and Bertha had no way of warning him. Feeling comfortable and safe with their new found friends, he opened up and told just enough of their story and answered just enough of Stephen's questions for him to realize that they were runaway slaves from the plantation of his best friend, Arthur Moore. This information placed him in a very difficult position. As much as he disliked slavery, he himself owned slaves and Arthur was his dearest friend. It did not seem right for him to converse with slaves who ran from his best friend's plantation as if they were a free couple he met in passing. What seemed even more wrong was the concept of returning two human beings who suffered so much to gain their freedom and were obviously willing to risk dying to be free.

Determining his plate was already overflowing with problems that needed attention, Stephen decided to let Arthur take care of his own troubles and allow the darkies to go on their way. So, he simply wished them well.

Relieved by the fact that the masta's neighbor and friend did not recognize them and remembering Miss Lizzy's despair at the thought of her husband's death, Bertha eagerly made mention of a plantation about four miles north that would be likely to offer them food and shelter.

Big Jim broke a sturdy branch off a nearby bush and scratched a make-shift map in the ground while he explained the landmarks for the men to look for as best he could. He also told them of a road not one-hundred yards to the east of where they stood that was far more established than the path they were following. In fact, they were traveling that very road when they saw a man on horseback riding toward them. Frightened of who he might be and what he might do to them, they ran off the road into the thicket, which was how they came to stumble into Stephen and Herald.

Chuckling at the looks of disgust on Stephen and Herald's face when they heard they suffered such a grueling trip when a much easier one lay so close, Bertha begged them to give their love to Miss Lizzy and kiss her sweet baby James on their behalf when they reached the plantation. Then she and Big Jim disappeared into the thick foliage in the direction from which Stephen and Herald just came.

Stephen looked at the sun's position in the sky while Herald pulled out the pocket watch he purchased from one of the residents of the mission. The sun was high and hot, but Herald's watch registered not yet noon. If they road steady and rested little, they should make it to the plantation the runaway slaves told them about before dusk.

Getting off the cumbersome path and onto an actual roadway helped matters considerably. Before they realized it, they were nearing the landmarks Big Jim mentioned that would help lead them to the plantation.

Stephen stood at the end of the long, tree lined lane that led up to the great white mansion and took in its elegant beauty. His life had exposed him to some of the grandest and finest homes in existence. Even so, he found this place impressive. They stopped a darky who was herding a small flock of sheep from one part of the garden to another and verified the identity of the plantation's owner before making their way up the long lane to the mansion's front door.

An ebony black footman in a brilliant white muslin shirt and blue breeches raced down the impressive stone steps to greet them. He beckoned yet another footman of similar look and dress to tend to their horses before beckoning them to follow him into the front foyer. Once inside, the butler politely led them to a small parlor immediately to the left of the front door where they waited patiently for Mr. Caldwell to join them.

Herald was amazed and almost overwhelmed by the finery that surrounded them. Since he was washed ashore he encountered nothing but crude and roughhewn buildings and furniture. His experiences during his recent journey caused him to formulate his opinion of the American colonies. Now he would have to rethink that opinion. This was not the home of a barbarian. This was a home that could rival the best of any England offered, save the king's. He looked out of the tall, multi-paned windows that afforded a panoramic view of the expansive gardens and smiled.

Stephen found Sir Caldwell to be witty and hospitable. The men had barely made his acquaintance before he was calling for rooms to be prepared and baths to be set up. After listening to the stories of their perils at sea and of their stay at the Spanish mission that rescued them, he insisted Stephen and his young brother-by-law remain his guests until they were truly in the state of good health. He would hear nothing of the contrary.

Calling his wife for a brief introduction of their new house guests, he joined her in an amusing chuckle about the business of their guest rooms of late. It seemed their previous company departed just the day before.

Promising to spend more time with them once they were rest-ed, Sir Caldwell sent them off to their respective rooms to bathe, eat a cold supper, and get a good night's sleep. He urged them to remain abed as long as they desired, promising to send hot fare to their rooms for their convenience and pleasure in the morning.

Herald listened to the caring instructions his host was spout-ing both to him and Stephen, as well as his staff, and thought how efficient he would have been at the mission. He dared say he felt that although they received kindness and care at the hands of the missionary nurses, they might have fared far better had they been washed up to this man's shoreline.

As they made their way up the wide, winding staircase and down the corridor of the second floor toward their rooms, Ste-phen stopped to listen to the cries of a baby. Realizing that the Caldwells were beyond childbearing years, he raised his eyebrow in question at the young man who was guiding them.

"'Tis Lady Lizzy's youngin'. She keeps this guest suite," whispered their guide.

Remembering Bertha's request and feeling that Miss Lizzy and Lady Lizzy were one in the same, Stephen decided to wait until morning to send their regards. If Lady Lizzy was a resident of the household and not a runaway slave as he originally thought, there would be time to keep his promise to the old slave woman.

Herald reveled in the comfort of his room and followed his host's suggestion of remaining in his room and having breakfast in bed. Stephen, on the other hand, felt abnormally restless. His room was next to that of Lady Lizzy and her newborn babe, who saw fit to cry through most of the night. If there was one thing

Stephen was certain of, it was the fact that the baby had a power-ful set of lungs.

Early the next morning, Stephen poked his head out into the hallway just in time see Anna as she stepped out of Lizzy's set of rooms with a swaddled infant and quietly closed the door behind her.

Startled at first, she quickly regained her composure and put her fingers to her lips in a request for silence. After hearing first-hand, the child's wails through the night and noticing his eyes were closed, Stephen assumed this was the first good sleep the baby had fallen into. He nodded knowingly. He certainly did not want to be the one responsible for waking such a tired infant.

Accustomed to the members of the household insisting on ogling over little James, Anna padded over to Stephen and posi-tioned the infant so that he could look at his sleeping, cherub-like face. Stephen chuckled to himself as he noted certain features of the child that looked remarkably like his father. This boy could have easily passed as his lineage. He would be interested in dis-covering the boy's parentage. They could very possibly be distant relatives.

Stephen waited for Anna to disappear down the far end of the hallway into what he believed to be the area that was turned into a nursery before he made his way downstairs. He allowed his mind to drift only briefly on the fact that Miss Lizzy allowed the crying baby to remain in her room with her throughout the night rather than shuffle him off with his wet nurse to the other end of the house so that she could have a good night's sleep. This was the ac-tion of a doting mother and something rare amongst the aristocrats back home. He had not yet met the young woman, but he already held her in high regard.

The sun was still rising. It created beautiful panoramic view through the row of plant adorned windows that made up the out-side wall of the casual dining porch. Stephen stood, awe struck, as he watched the massive grounds of the plantation illuminate and come to life under the powerful rays of the Georgia sun. He did not know which was more impressive, the grounds outside or the garden-like décor of the dining porch.

"Today will be another scorcher, I fear," Sir Caldwell said as he entered the room and walked directly to the French provincial buffet server. "I swear my cook is a miracle worker in the kitchen. In all my years I have not tasted a sausage that could compare with hers. Help yourself, my good man."

Stephen followed Sir Caldwell's lead and worked his way down the line of warming dishes, filling his plate with a little of everything that was offered. Realizing it was impolite to comment on his guest's ravenous appetite, Sir Caldwell simply patted him on the back with the most jovial of mannerisms as he made his way to the larger of the square tables that was strategically centered amongst the potted plants. On evenings when the Caldwells held casual gatherings the room often doubled for a game room.

"I hope my appetite does not offend you, good sir. 'Tis just that I have not tasted such fine fare in months and I am afraid I forgot myself," Stephen said after placing his overly laden plate opposite his host's sparse one.

"Nonsense my good man, nonsense. 'Tis a complement to the cook, to be sure. I shall be certain to extend the message to her. She will delight in such a robust appreciation of her cooking," Sir Caldwell replied.

Stephen found the Caldwells to be a remarkable couple. Shortly after he seated himself opposite Sir Caldwell, Lady Caldwell joined them. Her bubbly personality was infectious and it was not long before they were talking gaily about mutual acquaintances back in London. It seemed Lady Caldwell had, as a young girl, set her cap on Stephen's father, but it was a one sided affair since she had not even had her coming out when his engagement to Stephen's mother was announced.

Wounded, the young debutant was certain her life was over. She somehow managed to continue living and during her coming out ball she had the good fortune to meet Sir Caldwell, who recently returned from pioneering the colonies. It was love at first sight and he swept her off her feet and then off to her new life in Georgia. Although she missed London, she had to admit that her life on the plantation was pampered and easy going. If she had it to do all over again she would not change a thing.

They were so engrossed in conversation that no one noticed when Elizabeth entered the room. Nor did they hear her shocked gasp at the sight of her deceased husband sitting at the breakfast table in casual conversation with her benefactors. It was Lady Caldwell who realized her presence her first.

"Ah, my dear, come in. Come in and meet one of the most interesting men I have ever had the pleasure of crossing my path. He is the image of his father," Sara chuckled. "You know, I had aspirations of marrying his father when I was a young girl." She heaved a sigh while refueling her lungs to continue, "but, of course, I met my wonderful Sir Caldwell."

Turning to Stephen she smiled, "Lord Carlson, might I introduce the latest addition to our household? This dear young lady is Miss Elizabeth Nottingham. Soon to be Mrs. Moore, I might add. We are planning her wedding this very moment. 'Twill be a grand affair... the grandest in Georgia, if I know my Matthew." She gestured for Elizabeth to join them, "Come Elizabeth, come in and meet our guest."

Elizabeth was dumbstruck, frozen in place. This could not be. How could this be? He was dead. They told her he was dead. Emotions whirled around and through her until she could feel only the air swoosh past her face as she slumped to the floor.

Completely taken aback, Sir Caldwell had already leapt to his feet and was at Elizabeth's side before Stephen had an opportunity to allow the blood that seemingly drained from his body upon the news that Elizabeth intended to marry another to return, come to his senses, and assist him.

Did he hear Lady Caldwells correctly? Was Elizabeth planning on marrying someone else? Was she claiming their marriage a farce? Was he too late? Had he lost the only woman he ever loved, he could ever love?

Although Sir Caldwell offered to call for one of his men to carry Elizabeth back to her room, Stephen insisted on doing so himself. Thinking his actions terribly romantic, Lady Caldwell waited until she was alone with her husband before blurting her suspicions that perhaps there might be rivals for Lady Elizabeth's hand up and coming. It was only a fleeting second, but she was certain Elizabeth's fainting spell was a direct result from the shock of seeing Lord Carlson. If she was correct with this, then Lady Elizabeth knew Lord Carlson, even if he had not volunteered such information.

After much ado, Elizabeth was left in her room with Janet at her side, Stephen and his hosts returned to the breakfast room for a soothing cup of tea. Such excitement had not been witnessed in their household for many a year.

Sir Caldwell expressed his concern for Elizabeth's condition and lamented over the fact that her fiancé, Mr. Arthur Moore, was off searching for his lost sister and thus could not be there to assist them with her care. For truly such a fainting spell in the morning could only mean one thing. With such a young babe in arms and them not yet wed, why this was a matter that needed conversation indeed.

Although more than a little taken aback about the fact that his wife was now engaged to his best friend, had obviously delivered his baby, and might possibly be carrying another, Stephen's disconcertion grew even more upon the news that Paulette was missing. He pressed the Caldwells for as much information as they could provide and then made his way to Herald's room.

After updating Herald on the fact that they stumbled upon the very place where Elizabeth was residing and waiting for his elation to calm down enough to continue, Stephen relayed the news about Elizabeth's engagement to his best friend, the child she bore Arthur, and Sir Caldwell's assumption that she might yet be carrying another.

Stunned, Herald was at a loss for words. Before he could summon his vocal cords into action, Stephen went on to explain that his best friend's sister, who he also held dear, was missing and he felt duty bound to join him with his search. He was leaving immediately and once Paulette was found and returned to safety he would address the matter of Arthur Moore wanting to marry his wife.

Herald completely understood and bade him a safe journey. He waited until Stephen rode out of sight before he crept to find Elizabeth's room. He was not sure why his brother-by-law asked him to keep his questionable marriage to Elizabeth a secret, but he promised he would. This meant he needed to also hide the fact that he was her brother.

Life was becoming overwhelmingly complicated.

TWENTY-TWO

Paulette lay on the corn husk mat that was covered with an enormous bear skin as she watched Manley move about the hut. They were locked in together for three days with an occasional visit from Adahy or one of the other male leaders of the village. From Elsa's whisperings through the cracks in the walls, they would remain together until it was certain that she was with child.

Their first coupling proved to be a horrendous ordeal. Although accustomed to being used for stud service, never had Manley been asked to plant his seed in a mistress of society. His fear of the repercussions he would encounter from the plantation owners, should he ever break free from the Indian's captivity, far outweighed his fear of what Adahy and his friends might do to him. He blatantly refused to perform.

When the village's old women examined Paulette the following morning and discovered her virginity was still intact, Adahy went wild with rage. One did not need to understand his language to understand his meaning. Realizing that his refusal to bed Paulette could actually cost him his life, Manley apologized profusely and, with Adahy standing in the corner observing while two women held Paulette steadfast, he took her swiftly.

The degradation was almost more than the pampered young lady of society could fathom. To be mounted like a brood mare by one of her slaves was bad enough, but to have an audience was beyond anything she thought she could endure.

Adahy remained planted firmly in place and ordered Manley to mount her again, and again, and again. By the time their captor was satisfied enough to leave the hut, Manley was spent and Paulette was devoid of all senses.

"I be so sorry, miss. Ya know'd I would not be doin' this if they did not make me," Manley said as he moved to Paulette and wiped a stray tear away from her cheek. "Can I get ya anything, Miss Paulette? Is there somethin' I can do?"

Paulette's stony stare sent creepy shivers down Manley's spine. He did not want to be there. He did not want to be left in the same hut with this woman. She had obviously gone crazy. Her look frightened him. Pounding on the door, he demanded that they let him out.

Several women responded to Manley's commotion. Pushing past his shackled body, they stood staring at Paulette, deep in discussion on what to do. Finally, one of them untied her bindings. They held steadfast while they dragged her naked body out of the hut to the river. Fully prepared for a fight, they were taken aback by her complaisant mannerisms. The leader of the women adamantly insisted it was a trick and cautioned them to hold tight at all times.

Manley stood at the doorway of the hut and watched them drag Paulette away. He was unable to go further as a result of being bound to the wall with one of the thickest hemp ropes he had ever encountered. The rope was sealed in a permanent knot around his ankle and then coated with melted bees wax. He would need a sharp tool, plenty of time, and sufficient energy if he were to free himself from such bindings. The rough hemp rubbed the top layer of skin off his ankle, making it painful to move around more than necessary.

The sight of Paulette's limp body being tossed unceremoniously into the cold river was not nearly as disturbing as watching her flail about while she struggled for her footing. Taking advantage of the fact that they were near water, the woman grouped together and washed Paulette's resistant body vigorously. They rinsed away all signs and scents of her recent coupling as they prepared her for more to come.

Manley watched the women's hands as they slowly maneuvered over Paulette's voluptuous curves and found himself oddly aroused. His tongue moved slowly over his lips while he watched one of the women run her hand over Paulette's soft mound, washing it thoroughly with cool clean water. He found himself gripping his engorged manhood for want of release. Certain he would be expected to perform shortly, he refrained from releasing his pent up lust on his own and backed away from the door. Perhaps a few deep breaths would help keep his manhood under control. Having been used as a stud most of his life, Manly was accustomed to arousing easily, but there was something different about his reactions of late. He questioned if his food was being laced with something to accentuate his manhood. He knew it was done with slaves to assist them in performing, but it was never needed with him. Perhaps his refusal to perform at the onset instigated the lacing of his food. If so, his arousal at simply observing the women washing Paulette's nakedness would certainly make sense.

By the time Paulette was returned to the hut, Manley had once again regained control of his urges. He watched as the women secured the bindings on his reluctant lover's ankles, making sure they could not be removed. One of the women approached Manley with a sack of scented grease and rubbed it vigorously over his body while he stood obediently still. By now he was familiar with their ritual of rubbing bear grease containing herbs to promote fertility over him before he set about his duties. From the looks of Paulette's body, they did the same to her. The women looked from Manley to Paulette and giggled before leaving the hut to resume their daily duties.

The color returned to Paulette's cheeks and she appeared more aware of her surroundings.

"Okay now?" Manley asked hesitantly.

"Get me with child," Paulette blurted unexpectedly. "Get me with child so this can stop."

Manley looked at Paulette's freshly scrubbed and rosy skin and felt his urges returning. She was ripe, lovely, and finally willing.

Since there was no longer an audience, he decided to use a different approach with her. It was the least he could do for the poor woman. Surely such treatment was horrid enough for a woman born to slavery, but for a woman born of privilege it had to be... well, he could not even say. He could at least make it a pleasing experience for her. She did not need to be made to feel like an animal.

Manly moved to her slowly and knelt beside her. Pushing her gently onto the mat, he allowed his large hands to roam over her body, barely touching her oily skin while his soft moist lips found her most sensitive areas. It was not long before she was a relaxed and willing partner.

The experience was like nothing Paulette could have imagined. His touch, his scent, and his feel created such a heady sensation that she quickly lost control. Manley's rich ebony skin gleamed with sweat and other scents from his exertion. He smelled of musky sweat and the scented grease that the women rubbed all over him. Feeling heady from the newly discovered ecstasy that love making could provide, Paulette tasted his neck, his shoulders and finally his lips. He was salty, yet sweet and woody. It was a very odd combination.

The more she tasted Manley, the more wanton she felt. It was as if his taste acted as a type of aphrodisiac. She moved against his kisses with such exuberance that Manley almost lost control. Not wanting to proceed before he was certain she was ready, he focused more on showering her body with kisses. As his lips encompassed her erect nipples he could taste the unusual sweetness of the grease. Along with its delicious taste came an equally delicious sensation. He suckled greedily. The more he tasted, the more he wanted to consume every inch of her.

Wild with an animal-like abandonment that neither one could control, his tongue traced down her body until he found her most private area. Surprisingly receptive to his ministries, Paulette wrapped her legs around him, entrapping her willing partner while her pleasure mounted to a point of explosion. Twining her hands deep into his thick nappy hair that had started to grow out, she pulled his head level with hers and kissed him with a passion she did not know existed. His thick tongue consumed the cavity of her mouth, driving deep into her throat while sending chills of sensual delight all the way to her groin. She forgot all about the pain in her body. She ignored the fact that her movements against the coarse bedding were tearing open some of deep welts on her back from the abundance of lashes she received since her capture. In its own way the pain magnified the sensuality of the moment. She wanted more. She needed more.

As Paulette slowed with satiety, Manley he was back in action with the power of a stallion. He caressed her gently in her most private areas while he coaxed her back into receptivity for his engorged manhood. Her body arched as she matched her movements to the rhythm of his deep thrusts. She felt sure she was about to explode from the inside out. Her aggression grew stronger as her passion rose. Her fingers dug into his flesh as she urged him to continue. When it seemed like they would both burst from sheer ecstasy, Manley let out a roar that would rival that of a bear as he emptied his seed deep into Paulette's womb.

Although she had nothing to compare it to, Paulette was certain the experience with Manley would be difficult for another man to replicate. She closed her eyes, wanting to burn the memories of this delicious experience into her mind for all eternity.

As they lay beside each other, still desiring the sensation of being touched, pinched, and rubbed, but were too spent to move, a few of the women who had coated their bodies with the mysterious grease smiled with satisfaction as they moved away from the crack in the wall that allowed them to observe their coupling. There was no doubt they would be hearing that bear roar more than once before the moon gave way to the sun.

*****

Elsa stood up and arched her back. She had not lain with Manley since he and Paulette were locked into the asi Adahy had vacated and turned into a breeding hut for his captives. Having given birth to more than one half-breed, Elsa was no stranger to bedding a man. Never had it ever been so enjoyable as it was with that black warrior. Her experience with Paulette's darky was beyond compare, which is why she felt so resentful about being forced to work while Paulette lay sprawled under his solid mass of muscle as he took her to heights of ecstasy that Elsa was positive the inexperienced society woman would not appreciate to their fullest.

Sharing a man never mattered to Elsa before. It was a new emotion that she was not certain she liked. Paulette was the first white woman to live long enough for her to get to know. It was nice to speak the English tongue again, even if she spoke it poorly. It was also nice to speak with a woman whose skin was whiter than her own. She did not want to ruin this budding friendship with jealous emotions.

Noticing her guard moving toward her with a long switch extended and ready, she quickly resumed her work. When Manley's exuberant roar reached her ears, her face grew hot. He had not done that with her. He had been as silent as a mouse with her, ending with a low grunt. What did Paulette have to offer him that she did not? Was she prettier or more willing? Jealous, frustrated, and angry, Liza dug at the soil with renewed vigor.

Manley's roar also caught the attention of the guards, who were now laughing, jeering, and slapping each other on the back – which was why no one noticed Ollie and Bishoff creeping silently along the edge of the clearing.

TWENTY-THREE

The tracker Stephen hired in the nearby village proved his worth. Within hours Stephen was caught up with Arthur and his posse. Shocked, surprised, and happy that Stephen was not dead, Arthur greeted him with the enthusiasm of a true friend who was relieved to discover he had not lost their friendship.

Although it was in the back of his mind, Stephen refrained from mentioning the fact that he knew Arthur intended to marry his wife. He also did not broach the subject of the newborn baby. He had not had time to do the math where the infant was concerned, but since Elizabeth's waiting maid was relatively certain he had not impregnated her before she ran away, he could only assume that Arthur did the deed immediately upon purchasing her. The dis-appearance of Paulette proved devastating for his friend and he felt the timing for such a discussion not correct. There would be time to sort out these matters once Paulette was found; hopefully unharmed.

Arthur sent a message back to his plantation to make certain Paulette had not returned home after Ollie left. He was seated under the shade of an enormous oak tree reading the response when Stephen approached him.

"'Tis good news, I hope?" Stephen inquired as he dropped to the ground next to his friend.

"I hoped as such, but I fear not. Paulette is not at home," Arthur replied. "There are times when I think that when I find her I shall ring her neck for her foolishness and then times when I think I shall hold her and never let her go," Arthur choked on his emotion.

"You love her truly," Stephen stated.

He had always been aware of his friend's intense bond with his half-sister. It had to be ripping at Arthur to not know where

Paulette was. Arthur's affection for Paulette surpassed any Stephen witnessed between siblings prior, even those of full blood. Perhaps his agony equaled Stephen's when Elizabeth disappeared. He thought possibly.

"Aye, I do that, but you love her too," Arthur said as he looked directly at Stephen. "She told me of the letter you posted just before you set sail. It came the same day we received word that the Duke capsized and you were lost at sea. You were planning to propose to her."

"What?" Stephen practically gasped as he pushed his body to a position that allowed him to view Arthur better. "You have it wrong, my friend. She proposed to me by post. I could not accept even if I wished to. I married while in England to a woman of my father's choice, but also, to a woman I fell in love with the minute her smile lit up the room. I did not wish to cause dear Paulette embarrassment and pain by refusing her through pen. I felt it best to break this news in person and so I made mention of our need to talk." Stephen groaned. "I apologize. I wrote in such haste so that I might catch the ship leaving that eve so that my note might arrive on time. I did not think to question if my words would be taken otherwise."

Silence permeated the air. It seemed even the birds muted their song as the two men looked at each other. Neither was willing to broach the subject that hovered so heavily between them.

It was Arthur who finally broke the silence.

"We thought you were dead," he said softly.

"Aye, I almost was," Stephen replied, "but as you can see I am very much alive thanks to the generosity of the good padre and his staff at a mission near St. Augustine." After filling his lungs with the sweet scented air of the Georgia shoreline to their maximum capacity and releasing it ever so slowly, he continued, "I believe we have a lot to discuss."

Arthur closed his eyes and slowly nodded his head. The moment he came down from his height of elated joy at the discovery that his good friend was not lost to him and realized that Stephen's being alive meant Elizabeth was not a widow, he knew that he would eventually have to have this conversation. He had been dancing around the subject while he waited for the right moment. Now he wished to be anywhere but here. For surely nothing good could come of this conversation. They were both in love with the same woman. Such a curse should not befall two men who loved each other so.

"I love her," Arthur sighed.

"As do I," Stephen replied in a calm manner that belied the torrent of emotions within him.

The distant figures of Bishoff and Ollie as they slowly made their way on foot down the trodden path toward the two friends grew larger and more distinguishable as Arthur filled Stephen in on how he came to purchase Elizabeth at the Charles Town slave auction. Stephen listened intently, interrupting only on the rare occasion where he required a little more explanation to be clear on the occurrences.

Arthur watched his friend's facial expression carefully while he spoke. He knew Stephen almost as well as he knew himself. His friend was genuinely tormented by what his wife endured. The moistness in his eyes hinted of the tears of agony that he was crying inside. He questioned if his own love for Elizabeth was as strong as that of the man before him. Perhaps his friend had love for his wife that equaled his love for his sister. He thought yes.

Arthur's trackers drew close, forcing them to cease their conversation and tend to the matters at hand. They had still found no accurate tracks for Paulette, but they did discover an Indian village about fifteen miles southwest. While keeping their distance for fear of being captured themselves, they managed to spot a few darkies and a white woman. Unfortunately, they were not close enough to confirm the identity of the woman or any of the darkies. What they were able to tell was that these people were being forced to cut the reed along the river bank. They were obviously captives.

Stephen and Arthur put their heads together for the better part of the afternoon while they determined what to do. With the exception the Indians from the mission who escorted him and

Herald for a brief time, there was never a reason for Stephen to deal with them. His knowledge was strictly hearsay. Arthur did a small amount of business with a Cherokee tribe when he first inherited the plantation and was seeking more slaves for his fields. The two men hoped his limited exposure would prove enough to help them communicate when they arrived at the village.

Their plan was risky. If these Indians dealt in slavery, the possibility of them being captured and forced into slavery themselves was very real. Since Stephen and Arthur were wealthy plantation owners and white, they would not be desired for the auction and could probably escape their captivity by purchasing their freedom. There was also the possibility of them being put to death in order to cover the fact that their darkies were confiscated. It would all depend upon the value the Indians placed on the flesh that was preparing to march into their village.

It was a very great risk for the entire posse when they had no true confirmation Paulette was being held in the Indian's village. Since the scouts reported a white woman with sun blonde hair cutting reeds on the river bank, Arthur and Stephen could not walk away without investigating her identity. If Paulette was indeed a captive in the Indian village, she had been so for several weeks now.

Arthur could only imagine what horrors his poor sister might be forced to endure from the savages that held her captive. It was common knowledge the Cherokee had little use for white people. The fact that they didn't kill the woman and were working her in the field gave cause for thought. Paulette was certainly not built for hard labor, nor was she raised to do it. Surely she was not proving to be a good slave. Arthur began to question the identity of the woman. He mentioned his concerns to Stephen who expressed the same thoughts.

"I agree that it is a long shot at best, but we have no other clue. 'Tis as if she vanished into thin air. I question if I shall sleep properly if I walk away without confirming the woman's identity," Stephen said in earnest.

"You are correct. 'Tis a difficult decision. If the woman is not

Paulette we would have jeopardized the safety of a dozen men," Arthur murmured.

"Have you known any white women who have been taken by the Indians?" Stephen's voice quivered.

"Nay. There was a young girl captured just before you purchased your plantation, but when they brought her home she took her own life. Such were the horrors bestowed upon her. She could not bear to continue with life," Arthur choked.

"How long was she held captive?" asked Stephen.

"At least a month, maybe more," Arthur whispered as he wiped at a tear that was threatening to escape the corner of his eye with the end of his index finger.

"How long has Paulette been missing?" Stephen pushed.

"Close to a fortnight," he replied. Arthur's face was stone-like as he responded to Stephen's questioning. "No... longer."

"Let us pray she is not with them," Stephen said with empathy.

He patted his friend on the back and walked away. It was obvious to him that Arthur was having a difficult time holding himself together and needed time alone. As he made his way along the narrow path Stephen could smell the ocean off in the distance. Even though it was miles away, its scent teased the air. Memories of his last voyage flashed through his mind. Having a plantation in Jamaica, a plantation in Georgia and roots in England gave him cause to go to sea well over fifty times in his life. The waters were not always kind but they had never been so abusive as to destroy his vessel. In some ways he probably thought such a thing would not happen to him and his. It was something one heard of happening to other unfortunate sailors, not something he would actually experience. He never considered it something that would ever happen to him. Yet it did. It almost killed not only him, but a young man who he admired greatly. Until the fateful night that Captain Sims was forced to hull the Duke and place them at the mercy of the sea, Stephen had never considered his mortality.

Stephen thought of Herald's bravery and show of maturity both on the ship as well as at the mission. He was genuinely fond of the young man. The thought that they may not remain family caused him deep regret. Seeing Elizabeth fainting at the sight of him proved crushing. At first he flattered himself into thinking that she was overtaken with joy at the discovery that he was alive but, after speaking with the Caldwells, he realized that they had no idea that he was her husband -deceased or alive- and spoke only of the handsome Mr. Moore and the obvious love the two had for each other.

Hearing such news caused Stephen's chest to constrict as if someone had punched him deep into his rib cage and forced his lungs to freeze in defense. He'd struggled to get them working again without bringing attention to his torment. It proved a difficult task and he questioned if he too might find himself in a heap on the floor with salts under his nose. By the time he was able to control the trembling in his body enough to walk with a display of nonchalant confidence across the room, he had received an earful about Mr. Moore, Lady Elizabeth, and baby James.

It seemed they were not married yet, but had been living as man and wife for some time since Elizabeth had been cruelly sold at auction by some unscrupulous ship's captain under the guise of a mulatto and was purchased by the unknowing Mr. Moore. Although it was not ideal for a man to bed his female slaves, it was a common practice. At least he was not breaking any marriage vows.

It took a little time for Elizabeth to find the opportunity to bend Mr. Moore's ear enough to tell him of her misfortune. Miraculously, unbeknownst to dear Elizabeth, she happened to tell him on the eve of a planned escape by some of his slaves. The runaways carried the dear girl off on their quest for freedom before Mr. Moore had been allowed time to digest the shocking information she laid before him. It was by the hand of God that Mr. Moore arrived at their doorstep, not searching for Elizabeth, but for his sister... only to discover Elizabeth under their protection. Of course, as soon as Mr. Moore's shock subsided he insisted on making things right by asking for her hand in marriage. Since she was a widow and quite free to marry, she readily agreed.

Stephen clenched his teeth as he recalled how Sara Caldwell

took great pains to emphasize the romance of the situation. Elizabeth finally had her romance and he was nowhere in it. It seemed a bittersweet realization.

TWENTY-FOUR

Elizabeth's hands ached from her nervously ringing them while she paced the sitting area of her suite while watching out the window for Sara to return from her trip to town. Things were a mess and she needed a woman to confide in. Since her relationship with Sara grew stronger with every day she remained in their care and she felt no woman alive could match the good woman's clear head and sense of right and wrong, she felt privileged to have Lady Sara Caldwell available at such a time.

Herald sat in the corner of the room and watched his sister through lowered lids. To the onlooker who did not know him well, one would have assumed the young man had closed himself off to his sister's obvious despair and decided to take a nap. Elizabeth knew better. Her brother was an astute young man who developed the uncanny skill of not missing a thing that went on around him. This was true even if his eyelids were all but closed. It proved handy on more than one occasion when he wished to divert his uncle's attention from him yet still be privy to the situation.

After watching Stephen make his way down the lane to find his friend until he could see him no more, Herald followed Stephen's instructions and snuck quietly into Elizabeth's room. Her shock at seeing her brother was quickly replaced by joy. The siblings embraced so tightly their bodies emitted popping sounds.

She called for some tea for herself and her brother, who wished his presence in her room unknown. Still not certain why Stephen desired he not divulge that they knew Elizabeth but wanting to honor his wishes, Herald searched for a hiding place when the maid knocked on the door to announce the arrival of the tea. Entering the room, the young girl looked around while carrying her tray to the small tea cart positioned next to Elizabeth's chair. She silently questioned the possibility that the lady's fainting spell may have compromised her stability as she poured two cups of tea to serve Elizabeth's single person. Bidding the young maid a gracious but dismissing thank you, Elizabeth stirred some sugar into the tea and extended a delicate porcelain cup to her brother who was awkwardly emerging from the ornate, oversized walnut wardrobe with a smirk on my face.

"I certainly hope you did not crush my gowns," Elizabeth teased, "I am hard pressed for them these days."

"That shall change soon enough, sister dear. Your loving brother and equally loving husband are here now. You shall suffer never more," Herald assured her as he accepted his tea and seated himself in a plush tapestry upholstered winged-back chair that afforded a cool breeze from the opened window. His finger traced the intricate art on the fabric that clearly stated its fine origin. "Things are changing for you. Look," he swept his arm in a broad arch, "already you have secured surroundings that suit you."

Elizabeth lowered her gaze. How could she explain to her brother -a young man who appeared grown up but was, in essence, still on the cusp of being a boy- the details of her relationship with Stephen Carlson? How could she tell him that she ran from Stephen to find love because he did not want her and that his heart was occupied by the woman who tormented her so cruelly for months? To live a life in a loveless marriage was bad enough without the knowledge that your spouse's heart belonged to another. The fact that Stephen Carlson came to find her appeared admirable, but surely it was to claim his freedom from the bond of marriage -although a shaky one- so that he could be free to marry Paulette.

Such a thing was difficult to think about, let alone discuss with a young mind. The fact that she agreed to marry Arthur, the man who purchased her and held her in bondage for months, was even more impossible to explain. She needed help with this matter. She needed Sara.

The sound of Sara's white gilded buggy approaching the front of the house caught both Elizabeth and Herald's attention. Requesting that her brother remain where he was for the moment,

Elizabeth scooted off to meet her friend and hopefully gain some wisdom on what to do.

Sara listened intently to Elizabeth's story. She was secretly pleased with herself for detecting that both men were in love with her ward. This was a dilemma indeed and would take some serious consideration. Under normal circumstances, Sara would have seen a cut and dry solution and advised Elizabeth accordingly. Elizabeth had married Stephen and thought he was dead so she agreed to marry Arthur. Yet, Stephen was very much alive. Therefore, she needed to tell Arthur she was not a widow and could not marry him. After that she should go off to live life happily ever after with Stephen who was quite handsome, wealthy and seemed a fine man indeed. Yes, that was the advice she would have given if circumstances had been normal.

Alas, they were not normal. In fact, they were anything but normal.

Elizabeth was forced to marry Stephen prior to the completion of the reading of the banns. If Sara recalled correctly, according to English law, she was not legally wed to Stephen. Although it was understandable that Elizabeth may not know of such things, her uncle and the good Lord Carlson should have both been aware. The lack of completion of the reading of the banns made the sweet babe in arms born upon arriving illegitimate. Lord Carlson wrote a love letter to the very lovely Miss Paulette Moore whose reputation for grace and beauty easily reached the ears of Sara Caldwell once she put them up to the gossip line. This letter indicated his desire to marry Paulette. His words having been read by Elizabeth herself. Elizabeth had so desired to be free of Stephen that she risked her life crossing the ocean on a vessel headed by a seedy captain and found herself sold into slavery where, although she spoke not of it, Sara heard enough from the runaways to realize that the odds of Elizabeth's having to share Arthur's bed were quite high. Fortunately, Arthur fell head over heels in love with Elizabeth and was willing to overlook the colorful and unseemly events that transpired, as well as accept her bastard child as his own. These were most definitely not normal factors and therefore the situation could not be treated as such.

Sara suggested they take some time to think things through. It would not do to act rashly. She asked permission to share this dilemma with Sir Caldwell, feeling his input would prove invaluable. Elizabeth hesitated briefly before agreeing to Sara's request.

The two women pushed the topic off into the recesses of their minds and they summoned for Herald to join them in the back garden to enjoy the warm soft coastal Georgia breeze and the sweet scents of the day. Sara found Herald a delightful breath of fresh air and welcome addition to their home. In her typical zealous way, she mentioned it to the point that the young man grew self-conscious. Elizabeth chuckled at her brother's modesty and whispered that he would grow accustomed to the Caldwells' frank honesty in due time.

By the time Sir Caldwell returned from his weekly rounds of the plantation, he found the trio deep in conversation. He need not ask their topic of discussion, for he knew his wife far too well. With two young Londoners seated in her midst, what other topic than London society was there to discuss?

Herald found Sir Caldwell to be a level headed and amiable man. His impression from the night before was enhanced by the generous conversation toward the slaves and their situation that he engaged everyone in almost immediately upon his arrival. Sir Caldwell was most definitely a man of wealth, wisdom, and compassion.

Having had his uncle insist on exposing him to society at a very young age, Herald met many wealthy and powerful men in his short lifetime. Rarely had he encountered all three attributes in a single man. He found it impressive and refreshing.

Elizabeth was surprised when the evening meal was announced. The day simply slipped by. She could not recall a time when she was so pleasurably engaged in conversation like she was that day. Since the others seemed equally stunned by the time, she could only assume that they too were enraptured by conversation.

The diners were halfway through dessert before Lady Caldwell dramatically cleared her throat and asked for her husband's ear on a serious matter that involved everyone in the room. Wine was poured and candles replenished while Sara relayed Elizabeth's story, detail by detail, to her husband. Hearing it coming from someone else seemed odd to Elizabeth, not to mention dramatic. To think this all happened because of her foolishness, which is exactly what Sir Caldwell startled everyone in the room by stating.

"My dear Elizabeth, I am sure you know that you mean the world to my wife and me. You entered our hearts the moment you entered our home. You are the daughter we were never blessed to have. I feel you and that wee babe were sent to this house to fill it with life from corner to corner. I am certain I speak for Lady Caldwell, as well as myself, when I say we wish you would never leave. I must say things this day that may hurt you and that saddens me. Alas, 'tis my duty as such in the absence of your uncle," Sir Caldwell stated as he leaned back and held his glass out to indicate to the quick responding servant standing statue-like several feet behind him that he wanted it refilled. "I have met Lord Carlson and spent time in his company. I must say that I find him a jolly fine fellow indeed. He is well mannered, well educated, holds a nice title back in England and, although he has not openly stated as such, I still have enough of a connection with our mother land to know who is who and I know that his family is extremely wealthy. If you combine his inheritance to his own accomplishments 'tis clear he is as rich as a king, possibly richer. I have also met Mr. Arthur Moore and spent some very enjoyable time with him. I find him to be an equally jolly fellow who is equally educated and certainly not a poor man by anyone's standards. Both men would make a fine husband for you and father for the wee one." Lord Caldwell took a moment to fill his lungs before continuing, "The fact remains that your uncle chose Lord Carlson for this position and even rushed the wedding to insure it would take place before you had an opportunity to run away. Had you been less foolish, he would have kept the date as arranged and the question of the banns would not exist. In turn the legitimacy of the child you bore would not be a factor."

Elizabeth shifted in her seat. The new lace tucked into the neckline of her dress suddenly felt stiff and coarse against her tender porcelain skin and she was miserably hot and uncomfortable. Although she hesitated when Sara asked to bring Sir Caldwell into their confidence, she had not expected it would be because he would be so harsh on her once he learned the seriousness of the situation. She dipped the corner of her linen napkin in her water glass and wiped at the back of her neck, caring not a fig how her actions might have appeared or been taken by the others in the room.

"My goodness, Sir Caldwell," his wife exclaimed with genuine surprise, "you utter such harsh words to the dear girl."

Sir Caldwell closed his eyes and took a deep breath. The room seemed to join its inhabitants in anticipated silence while they waited for his next assault on Elizabeth.

"I beg your pardon, my dear. 'Tis true my words are harsh, but they are also true. As much as it pains me to say these things, they must be said and then we can be done with it." Sir Caldwell looked directly at Elizabeth. "I shall admit that I do not understand your Uncle's rash behavior in doing something so foolish as to wed you before the banns were completed," he sighed as he slowly shook his head. "I cannot pretend to know the mind of Lord Carlson for going along with it. But, I will tell you, dear child, that your uncle's insistence on an early and private wedding opened the door for many questions as to its reason, thus giving a man who does not wish to marry the woman just cause to probe said motives and most probably find cause not to marry. Stephen did not do such. This leads me to believe that he entered this marriage fully aware of the risk he was taking with the absence of the reading of the third banns because he wanted to marry you, not because he was forced to do so."

"But... the letter..." Elizabeth squeaked.

"Aye, the letter. Do you still have it?" Sir Caldwell asked.

"I do," Elizabeth replied.

"Might I ask why?" Sir Caldwell pressed.

Startled by his question, Elizabeth was tongue tied. Why had she kept the letter? Surely there was no reason. No reason except that it was written by Stephen's own hand. Many an evening passed with her cradling her son in her arms – Stephen's son- while holding the letter close to her heart. It was as if the letter would bring father closer to son and wherever he was he would know her love for him. She knew it seemed silly, but Stephen's letter was all she had of him to pass on to James. His penmanship was a direct reflection of his strength and character. When she held the letter she could almost smell his scent and recall those nights of wild ecstasy she experienced under his touch. It was something she had not known since and she was certain she never would.

"Might I see it?" Sir Caldwell continued.

With her face the color very near that of the scarlet velvet upholstered seat upon which she sat, Elizabeth reached into the folds of her skirt and produced the letter. Herald extended his hand for the letter and walked it to the end of the table where Sir Caldwell was waiting to review it.

After a careful review of Stephen's words while the others looked on with baited breath, Sir Caldwell slowly folded it and extended it out for Herald to retrieve and return to his sister. The young man did so quickly and graciously.

"I saw nothing in this letter that resembled an actual proposal from Stephen. I did, however see how you might interpret his words as such," Sir Caldwell stated with gentle firmness.

"My... oh... really?" Lady Caldwell stared at the letter longingly.

How she would have loved to have been privy to reading it, but it would have been quite inappropriate to make such a request. Of course if someone offered her a read...

"Elizabeth, my dear," Sir Caldwell said as he ignored his wife's obvious hint and leaned toward Elizabeth, "Do you love Mr. Moore? Are you in love with the man?"

Elizabeth sucked in her breath as Sir Caldwell's words roared in her ears. Did she love Arthur? Did she? No. No, she did not. She was marrying him for security and because her childish fantasy of marrying for love died long ago. She was a woman with a newborn baby who depended on her for his care. It was her duty to provide the best she could for him. She did not love Arthur, but she was not repulsed by him either. She knew life with him would be privileged, tolerable, and comfortable. Even though she did not love him, he at least was in love with her. That was more than she could say for Stephen.

Elizabeth's hesitancy was all the occupants of the room needed to realize that she was not in love with the man she intended to marry. Sara Caldwell closed her eyes as tight as she could to push back her tears. How sad to see this beautiful young girl who she had grown to love selling herself in marriage in such a way for the sake of security. How very sad. But, such was the way for many a woman. Elizabeth was not alone in this matter. She reached over and touched the back of her husband's hand while she silently gave thanks that she was not one of those women. She was lucky enough to marry for love, very lucky indeed.

"Might I make a suggestion?" Sir Caldwell's question was more of an order and they all knew it. "'Tis painfully obvious that you love neither the man you wed in England nor the man you intend to wed here in our chapel. We are all quite certain of the love Mr. Moore has for you, dear Elizabeth. He stated it quite plainly when he asked for your hand in marriage. Lord Carlson, on the other hand, has not had the opportunity to declare his feelings. Instead, they have been assumed. In my years of life, I have learned that assuming something can cause many undue complications. I feel quite strongly that Lord Carlson should be given the same opportunity as Mr. Moore to declare his love, should it exist, before he is cast aside as a loveless husband."

"He loves her," Herald spoke up, "He almost died while searching for her. I have been with the man enough to know he loves her truly."

"Herald," Elizabeth's tearful voice was barely above a whisper, "he sought me to secure his freedom so that he could marry Paulette." She turned to Sir Caldwell and continued, "Perhaps the letter was not direct in its proposal to Paulette, but she was quite clear that their intention was... and had been for some time... to wed. Of that I am certain."

"You are certain of nothing of the kind. What you are certain of is that your former mistress, who may very well come to be your sister-by-law, possessed high hopes and dreams of a wedding with Lord Carlson. Dreams that it is quite clear were not shared by him. For, if he harbored such desires, he would have wed her and presented her to his family. After all, she is quite renowned in Georgia for her beauty and her breeding. Her lineage can be traced back to some of the greatest families in England. I have no doubt her brother would have seen to it that she would offer a very attractive dowry. Surely there would have been no resistance accepting her into the family had Lord Carlson chosen to do this." Sir Caldwell's tone softened, "Instead he chose to marry the lovely Lady Elizabeth. Knowing this, I deduce from the words he wrote in the letter that the man was preparing Paulette -a woman for whom I am certain he has a very high regard- for a conversation relaying such. You must learn to read more than the mere words on the page, my dear girl."

Elizabeth was stunned. Never in her wildest imagination could she have acquired such an interpretation of the situation as had the kind, middle-aged, and rather plump gentleman at the head of the table. It was a tremendous amount to absorb. Her mind, which was now at the mercy of one too many glasses of wine, was not letting this information enter and settle. Instead it rejected it vehemently. She shook her head vigorously and tried once again to focus.

Sir Caldwell chuckled at the obvious drunkenness of his ward and gently suggested she be escorted to her room for the night. Perhaps in the morning, after they all had time to digest the situation, things would appear brighter and a solution would be presented.

Elizabeth's head swirled as she clung to Herald's arm while they ascended the grand, winding staircase. Her slippers fell off her delicate feet and she was now carrying them in her hand while she reveled in the coolness of the highly polished white marble against her flesh. The iron scones that were strategically placed along the wall illuminated the stairway with rich golden light. It was as if she was ascending the stairway to heaven.

Once in her room she accepted the chair Herald offered and rested her chin in the palm of her hand. Her brother stood before her at a loss of what to do. He had never seen a woman drunk; especially not his sister. Had she been a man, he would have dowsed some water on her face to shock her sober, but was that appropriate in this case? He simply did not know. He decided to call her waiting maid instead and have her assisted into bed. The hour was late and soberness would serve no purpose since they should all retire for the evening anyway.

Elizabeth waited for Herald to leave the room before she retrieved Stephen's letter from the folds of her skirt. Holding it firmly, she allowed Janet to assist her with her preparations for bed while never losing grip on the crumpled paper.

Alone in her room, with only the moon's rays to accompany her, Elizabeth slowly rubbed Stephen's letter across her stomach while she closed her eyes and imagined it was his hands instead of his words caressing her so.

TWENTY-FIVE

Elsa shifted her position as she sat on the natural stoop the low lying branches and tree stumps created for the asi that imprisoned Paulette and Manley. She had been there since the night before and her body was going numb. She would have to get up and walk around soon or she feared she might lose the use of her legs completely. Her mind was racing. Atul would be wed soon and she would be left to the mercy of the village, or even worse —Adahy. It was no secret Adahy despised the white man and the only reason he had not killed Paulette was because of the potential wealth to be had from breeding her to the virile dark warrior. She also knew that if Paulette proved baron she would die immediately. Since Elsa was the property of Atul as well as produced several strapping children, she was protected from Adahy and his evil thoughts about white people as long as Atul was around. That protection would be gone soon.

Elsa's moon time had come and gone, which meant her coupling with Manley was ineffective. She needed to mate with him and produce a healthy child to secure her place within the village, as well as her safety. If she did not produce a child soon she would be cast out or even killed -if the decision was left up to Adahy. This would especially be true if Elizabeth conceived.

She thought about what she might do if they cast her out. She lived with the Creek and then the Cherokee for over half of her life. She remembered very little of her life prior to being taken and what she did remember seemed a vague dream. She still spoke the white man's tongue, but very poorly and she possessed no family that she could recall. Where would she go? Who would accept her after she lived as a savage for so long? She envisioned herself lying on the roadside half-starved, while white people walked past her as if she were an animal that repulsed them.

She was accustomed to the ways of the Cherokee. She learned their language and spoke it nearly as well as those born into the tribe. She knew her place within the ranks of the people and was careful not to overstep herself around the ancient women who directed the daily activities of the village from the comfort of their asi. She worked hard and, truth be known, really did not mind it. Her children were taken from her at birth and given to women who proved unable to have a child. Therefore, she was quite accustomed to bearing children without calling them her own. She had also proven that she could bear strong, healthy children. It was she, not Paulette, who should be on the opposite side of that door enjoying the ministries of the strong, handsome black warrior.

Elsa moved closer to the hut and listened for signs of life within. She could hear nothing. Could they still be sleeping at such an hour? The sun was high enough to prompt the rest of the village to awaken. Surely they were roused by now. At the sight of one of the village girls making her way toward the asi with a basket containing warm corn pones, freshly picked strawberries, and a gourd of spice wood tea, she darted off the stoop and hid in the thickets a few yards away.

The young girl opened the door and entered without a moment's hesitation. Had Manley and Paulette been in the middle of coupling it would not have mattered to her. She was raised to think of white people as little more than animals and she witnessed many animals mating throughout her tender years.

The young girl glanced around the room until her eyes settled on Paulette's small, naked frame huddled in the fetal position as close to the wall as she could get. Her torn and inflamed, scabbed back was turned to the room, but her breathing was at a rhythm that spoke of sleep. Manley lay stretched out on the floor on the opposite side of the room. He too appeared deep in sleep.

Scowling, she left the hut quickly. Elsa managed to crawl to the back of the hut and find a crack large enough to allow her to see the majority of the hut's interior. She shook her head at the sight of Paulette sleeping alone. This would not go well for her. She could not understand Paulette's thinking. Did she not realize that she would die if she did not get with child?

Elsa longed to be able to speak with her to make her understand. Paulette tried to explain to Elsa the extent of abomination the act that Adahy was forcing her to perform with Manley was, but her co-captive could not grasp it. She had lain with the ebony stallion and it proved to be one of the greatest pleasures of her life. How could such an experience be such an unthinkable act for a lowly white woman? She should be offering gifts to the Great One for such good fortune. No, Elsa simply could not understand Paulette's way of thinking.

The young girl returned to the asi with several of the village's ancient women. The leader stood in the doorway of the small building with her hands on her hips and a deep frown on her weathered face. With a voice that could command an army, she ordered Paulette's private area be inspected for signs of mating. Not realizing that such an event would occur, Paulette spent a good amount of time prior to sleep washing away the very thing these women were now searching for.

Furious at hearing that they found no trace of Manley on Paulette's body, the old woman ordered her held down while she beat Manley with a willow switch until he crawled on top of Paulette and plunged into her. He was grateful he was able to perform under the most difficult of situations.

With the aphrodisiac oil having been washed from her body by her own hands, Paulette resisted Manley's thrusts as best she could while the women held her ankles and wrists. He whispered words of tenderness in her ear to try to calm her, but eventually ceased when he saw it was not effective. He decided instead to focus on planting his seed as quickly as possible to shorten the ordeal as best he could.

Satisfied, the women positioned both Paulette and Manley side by side against the wall and pushed their breakfast in front of them. Motioning her hand to her mouth to indicate they were to eat, the leader of the group barked another order at the other women and they filed out of the asi.

Paulette sat motionless with her eyes staring in front of her at nothing in particular. She wanted to die. The last few days were so incredibly humiliating that she was sure she would never be able to look at her own reflection, let alone anyone else. Besides that, her body screamed its pain and felt like it was on fire. She was sure that, if they did not kill her soon, she would die from the infection that raged in the agitated welts on her back. Manley suggested they shift positions for their coupling to spare any more reopening of her angry wounds, but Paulette had no desire to co-operate.

She thought of the female slaves who were selected to couple with Manley for the sake of breeding young slaves and shook her head. Although she had never attended, she had heard stories that the slave owners often remained in the room to observe and validate that the deed was done. After all, they were paying good money for stud service and wanted to be certain that the woman was given every opportunity to get with child before Manley's time with her had expired. Manley was required to plant his seed inside their woman a minimum of three times. There would be a midwife or physician on hand to validate such after each time he mounted the female. It was all very cold and calculated, much like it was for her now. She wondered if the Indians learned to breed their slaves from the white man or if it was the other way around.

The corn pone in Manley's outstretched hand caught her attention and she slapped it away.

"Get away from me!" she hissed. "I do not know what they put on me to make me react like I did, but it shall never happen again, you dog. You stay away from me!"

Manley lowered his hand and stared at Paulette with a dejected look. He knew that something was up when she responded so heatedly to his ministries. He had been a fool to think that someone as lovely as this sun goddess would actually enjoy being in his solid, ebony arms. She was so different, so warm and passionate. It was like a taste of honey that broke up his bitter day. Now, before him sat the Paulette he was all too familiar with – a spoiled, rich, vixen who looked down upon those who were not of her social class. He laughed at the absurdity of it all. Could she not realize that she was no better than he was? Had it not sunk in that she was actually considered less than he? In this village she held no more value or respect than a snake, maybe less.

"I been nice ta ya Miss Paulette. There be no need ta be mean ta me," Manley snapped as he stood up to cross the room.

Paulette jumped to her feet and pushed at Manley's bare chest.

"Do not dare talk to me with that tone, Manley," she hissed. "Remember your place or I shall whip that black skin off your back!"

Manley looked at Paulette, thoroughly puzzled.

"Have ya gone mad, Miss? Do ya not realize that ya no longer own me?" he said vehemently. "We is equals. In fact, I might be just a bit better than ya in the eyes of these Indians, since I be the stud and ya are the bitch."

Letting out a blood curdling screech, Paulette pummeled her fists wildly against Manley's bare chest. He stood steadfast while he gripped her shoulders and pushed her away so that her blows barely grazed his bulging muscles. Watching her bare, pert breasts heave and wobble as she twisted in anger sent a shiver of arousal through him. He was locked up with her nakedness for days, yet he still had not tired of feasting on her soft, white beauty.

Manley had lain with an abundance of women in his lifetime, but there was something about Paulette's smooth, milky suppleness that left him mercilessly wanting more. He almost dreaded the time when she would be with child and he would be mated with someone else. The memory of her sweet taste caused him to lick his lips in anticipation.

Elsa stood perfectly quiet while she continued to peek through the crack at the nude couple. What was Paulette doing? Had she lost her mind? Surely her loud screech would attract attention. Elsa had no doubt one of the old crones would be bursting back into the asi at any moment. If she witnessed this fit, it would probably cost Paulette a few lashes from her whip. From the look of her back, Elsa doubted Paulette could tolerate much more.

Looking closely at Manley, she could see that the dog was

actually getting aroused. Men were such strange creatures. Elsa shook her head. Only a man would find a beating sensual.

When Paulette finally fell to the floor from exhaustion, Manley walked to the other side of the room and leaned his face against the wall while he held his manhood. He was at a loss at what to do. During the times he mounted her against her will, there had been women to hold her down. Now, he was alone. Could he handle this wild cat without their help? He was not sure. His frustration with the situation took over.

"What be wrong with ya, woman?" Manley half-growled, half-wailed while still facing the wall, "Can ya not understand what's happnin'? Have ya lost your mind or are ya just so spoiled that ya do not give in?" He heaved a heavy sigh and turned to look at her. "You're in my world now. My world! Do ya understand? Ya ain't my boss and ya ain't no lady no more. You be no better than a bug ta these people. Do ya understand, woman?"

Paulette stared at Manley as if not seeing him.

"Answer me!" he roared.

The door burst open and Manley groaned before receding to the shadows. His manhood was ready to burst and his body ached from exhaustion. The last thing he desired was another lashing from that confounded switch that the old women seemed all too eager to wield.

Relief flooded him when he saw Elsa quickly close the door behind her and hold her finger to her lips.

"Hush. I came to see if I can help Paulette understand things. If she ain't gonna change she is gonna die for sure," Elsa whispered.

"Maybe she should die," Manley stated flatly.

"What?" Elsa gasped.

"She ain't cut out fer this and they ain't gonna set us free. Maybe she should die. I know sometimes I want ta die and I am a lot stronger than her," Manley said as he moved closer to Paulette. "Why should she go through this when we both know she ain't gonna last much longer? Look at her, she has plum gone crazy already."

Elsa moved between Paulette and Manley and planted her feet firmly. She was taller than Paulette but still a foot shorter than the enormous black man whose way she was blocking.

"You best not be gettin' any ideas of killin' her yourself," she hissed. "Do you know what Adahy would do to you if you did such a thing?"

"Adahy?" Manley had no idea who she was talking about.

"That is who owns you both," Liza explained as she shook her head. "He is the meanest in the whole village. If you kill this woman to spare her any more you will be causin' your own death and I can promise it shant be quick. I have seen what they do to slaves who anger them." Elsa shuddered. "Let me try to talk some sense into her. All she needs ta do is get with child." She smiled seductively, displaying several gaps where teeth once were. "I cannot imagine why she is resisting. I know if I was in here with you I would think myself the queen of the village."

Manley puffed his chest and smiled. His stud services had entailed force with a female so often that on the rarity that he encountered a willing partner, he drank it in greedily. He looked Elsa up and down slowly. She was slender, but still curvy. He had already tasted her and recalled her passionate response. It was similar to Paulette's reaction the day prior except there was no oil prompting her moans and her moves. Elsa responded the way she had out of sheer pleasure, not drugs. She may not be as beautiful and arouse him like Miss Paulette, but she sure did not repel him either.

Recognizing what was happening Elsa seized the opportunity. She needed to get with child right away. Her future depended on it. She quickly slipped off her newly made deer skin dress and moved closer to Manley. With gentle, expert hands, she caressed his solid body, feeling his muscles tense and then release under her gentle touch.

Paulette looked on, mesmerized, while Elsa seduced Manley. She found the fact that Elsa was not the least bit concerned that she was looking on amazing. Manley responded to Elsa's ministries with a passion Paulette found embarrassing. She wanted to turn away from the scene before her, but her eyes would not move. Instead they drank in every detail and burned it into her memory bank.

An expert in foreplay, Elsa taunted and teased Manley as she readied him for their coupling. He, in turn, used his own wiles to drive her passion so high that she was certain she would not survive the moment.

Paulette placed her hands on her heated face and patted her cheeks. If she felt out of touch with the world, this was certainly bringing her back around. She stood up and moved away from the couple. They seemed not to notice. Her foot touched the edge of Liza's dress and she bent down and scooped it up. It was an interesting piece of attire. The leather was stretched so thin that it felt almost like cloth. Elsa had bragged that she did the bead work on it herself. Paulette inspected it closely and had to admit the workmanship was admirable.

As she listened to the moans of the lovemaking, Paulette was struck with an idea. She snuck over to the door and peered out. The circle was empty. Glancing down at her ankle she scowled. The skin was rubbed raw by the hemp rope that was around her leg, binding her to the wall.

The sight of the pottery bowl that was placed in the room for her personal needs made her spring into action. Dumping out the urine, she slammed the bowl against the clay wall as hard as she could. Fearful Manley or Elsa would stop her, she stood frozen until she was certain they were too absorbed in their pleasures to take note of what she was up to.

Moving quickly, she rubbed the broken clay against the rope until she frayed it enough to allow her to force her leg free. Resisting the temptation to take time to coddle her legs and feet, she leapt up and donned Elsa's dress, forcing herself to endure the searing pain the leather caused as it rubbed against her infected body. Checking one more time to make sure Elsa and Manley's passion was still full force, she slipped outside and darted off into the thicket.

There was no time to waste. She headed to the fields where

she first met Elsa and started inching her way toward the woods while pretending to work. With any luck she would be able to pass for Elsa from a distance and if she did nothing to warrant reprimanding they would not come close enough to realize otherwise.

Recognizing that Elsa and Manley would not be in the state of ecstasy much longer and would surely report her missing to save their own necks, she took advantage of the guard's attention being drawn to a worker at the opposite side of the field and made a wild dash for the woods. Her legs screamed at her and her feet threatened to fall off, but she kept on going. When she could go no further she stopped to catch her breath. Her heart was pounding so hard that she could hear or feel nothing else for quite some time.

She waited and watched to see if anyone was following her before continuing on. She had no idea where she was or where she was heading. Wherever it was it had to be better than where she just escaped from.

TWENTY-SIX

Stephen looked over his shoulder as he watched half of Arthur's posse disappear in the direction from which he came. They pressed hard since early that morning after stumbling upon a tradesman who rode Paulette's mare. When questioned, the man told them that although he purchased the mare at auction up the river he had it from the best authority that the mare was brought to the auction by Cherokees from a nearby village.

Giving the man a fair price for the return of the steed, they rode with him to a nearby town where he could replace his mount and provide them with a map of the area to assist them in locating the Cherokee village more swiftly. When the man learned that they intended to enter the village to save Paulette, he did his best to dissuade them. The Indians of that village were hostile toward white people and only interacted when necessary. He was positive that, by now, they either killed or sold Paulette and impressed upon them the fact that walking into that camp would surely be tempting their fate.

Upon hearing of the potential horrors that his dear Paulette could be experiencing at that very moment, there was no reasoning with Arthur. He snatched the map from the tradesman's hands and raced his mount out of town before Stephen and the rest of the men could even grasp what was happening.

Stephen shouted for the others to mount up and raced off after his wildly distraught friend. How foolish the man was to heedlessly run toward danger like that. Stephen could only hope he could catch up with him before he found the trouble he was seeking.

The sound of branches cracking and a horse squealing permeated the air. Stephen spurred his horse onward. Within moments he was upon the most horrific scene. Arthur's horse lay with its leg broken on top of his rider. The horse was writhing and squealing while crushing his friend with each move. Arthur lay still. He was clearly unconscious.

Ollie pulled his horse up next to Stephen and sucked in air as he took in the scene. He was followed by Bishoff and the rest of the posse.

"We must do something or that beast will crush him to death!" Stephen shouted.

"It's leg is broken," Ollie commented.

"'Twill be hard to move him with a broken leg, but even harder to move him if we shoot him," added Bishoff.

"Get him off the poor man," Stephen took command. "Shoot him now... later... I care not. Just get him off Arthur and do it now!"

The entire posse worked in unison as they struggled, pushed, and pulled at Arthur's panic stricken horse until they moved it enough to allow them to pull Arthur from beneath it. It was soon painfully clear that the horse was not the only one with a broken leg. Bishoff took advantage of the fact that his master was unconscious and quickly reset the bone in his leg. A piece of it pierced the skin and if they did not get him medical care soon it was almost a certainty an infection would set in. They had no choice but to abandon their rescue mission for Paulette and take Arthur back to the Caldwell plantation.

Stephen was at a loss. His friend most desperately needed attention, yet to abandon their search for Paulette when they were so close to a possible rescue... well... he simply could not. If Arthur had been conscious to assist with the decision making, Stephen would have felt a lot more comfortable. These were, after all, his darkies. Therefore, Arthur would know their strengths and weaknesses far better than he.

Taking a chance on their loyalty to their master, he assigned Bishoff with the task of selecting a few men and seeing Arthur safely back to the Caldwells' plantation. If they traveled hard they would make it there by dark. Hopefully, somewhere along the way Arthur would wake up and take command.

Ollie was assigned the position of lead for the remaining

posse. Since Ollie was with Bishoff when they discovered the village, he was certain that he could get them there quickly. He also recalled a conversation with Arthur where it was mentioned in passing that Ollie was purchased from Indians. It was during his time spent with them that he learned to track so well. Stephen hoped Ollie still held a strong understanding of Indian ways to help them get in and out of the village with Paulette, while keeping their scalps intact.

The discovery of running water perked everyone's spirits up and they dismounted and walked their horses toward it. The distance until they reached the water would allow their horses time to cool down so they could drink their fill from the stream without repercussions.

The ground beneath his feet felt comforting as Stephen led his gelding down a path that was clearly forged by an animal. After looking at its tracks Ollie determined that it was probably a deer. The path led them straight to the water. They did not have much time to spare, but Stephen allowed the men a brief break to take care of business, wash off some of their sweat, nibble on the jerky and hard biscuits they purchased in the village, or simply rest under a shady tree. They were close to the village and it would be better to have the men feeling refreshed with their wits about them when they entered it.

Stephen was no fool. He was fully aware of the temptation a posse full of darkies created for a village that dealt in slavery. The risk of them confiscating his men and killing him was great. No other solution for saving Paulette came forth. He just hoped blonde woman the scouts saw at the river was even her and they weren't walking into danger for nothing.

He could only hope that, if things went wrong, the Indians would let him live long enough to allow them to name their price for Paulette, his darkies, and himself. He already discussed it with Arthur. They were prepared to pay whatever price the Indians named to get Paulette back and keep their darkies from being confiscated. Money was not to be a factor. If the price was so great that Arthur must request assistance from Stephen, then so be it.

The rustling of leaves behind him alerted Stephen and he sat up with a jolt to listen more closely. Within seconds Ollie was at his side with his knife drawn. Noticing the blade reflecting the sunlight, Stephen followed suit and pulled his own.

Paulette was almost blinded by the knife's reflection as she stumbled out of the brush. Losing her footing, she tripped and plunged into Ollie's outstretched arms. Sheathing his knife rather clumsily, Stephen pulled Paulette from Ollie and held her close. She was bleeding from cuts on her face and arms. He could not tell the origin of the cuts, but they looked angry and threatening. Stephen sighed. He found Paulette, but had he found her in time?

"They are after me," Paulette mumbled as she fainted in Stephen's arms.

"Ollie, ready the men. We must leave now," Stephen ordered. When Ollie hesitated, he shouted, "Now!"

The scout kicked his body into motion. Before he could pass the order a Cherokee brave burst from the bushes. Paulette's scream pierced the air as she collapsed in Stephen's arms. Without thinking he dropped her unceremoniously and leapt between Ollie and the brave. He was so close to the half-naked man he could feel his breath against his face. Neither moved. While Stephen seized the opportunity to size up his opponent, it looked as if the brave was assessing the situation in general. Could he be alone?

With lightning speed, the brave pulled his blade and was on the attack. Although not as swift, Stephen managed to have his on the ready in time to thwart the attack. The impact of the brave's assault sent them reeling to the ground. For the first time since he was a young boy, Stephen was called upon to utilize the extensive combat training he was forced to endure to humor his father. His instructor was a weathered old highland warrior with more than one trick up his sleeve. He forced Stephen to learn these combat skills to the point they were embedded in his person. He regularly practiced them in preparation in the event their ship encountered pirates. He never dreamed he would be calling upon these skills to combat an Indian.

The posse looked on in wonder as Stephen's body moved as

if it had a mind of its own. They would have never suspected a plantation owner to possess such fighting skills. When Stephen drove his knife into his opponent's heart with no sign of remorse they took notice. This was not a man to be reckoned with. He earned a new level of respect that was sure to spread through the slave grapevine in no time.

Stephen did not escape unscathed. When he stood up and looked down at his dead opponent, blood from the gash in his arm poured out onto the Indian's face. Ollie was the first to rush forth and offer assistance by way of his shirt. Stephen accepted it gratefully and allowed Ollie to tear it into strips to bind his wound.

They decided not to take any more chances and leave post haste. Stephen positioned Paulette in front of him on his gelding and had one of the men pull her mare behind his horse. When she came out of her faint he would assess her condition and see if she was fit to ride alone. Until then, she would take turns being a passenger on his horse as well as a few of the other men. The horses were tired and he did not want to overtax them with the extra weight she presented. They would have to pass her from one horse to the other at regular intervals until she could ride on her own.

Stephen looked at the men who made up the posse and then back at Paulette. He prayed she awoke soon. He was certain she would not wish to be placed in such a compromising position as in front of a male slave on horseback.

TWENTY-SEVEN

Bishoff got Arthur safely to the Caldwell plantation in record time. The sun was just resting on the horizon when he went ahead of the small group of men and knocked on the front door of the main house.

After giving him a quick reprimand for coming to the front instead of the back, the butler hurried to seek out Sir Caldwell. The house came alive as some rushed to help bring Arthur into the house, some rushed to ready a room for him, some went for the doctor, and some sought out Lady Elizabeth to inform her of the grievous news.

Elizabeth rushed to the top of the stair landing just in time to see Arthur being carried into the small parlor toward the far side of the concourse. Although he was grumbling profusely about the pain he was in, he was coherent and that was a good sign.

She slowly descended the stairs, stopping on each step to pro-long her arrival. It had been a few days since Sir Caldwell laid down the decision that Stephen must be given an opportunity to declare his love before they would support Elizabeth in her mar-riage to Arthur. Since Stephen had not returned with Arthur, but had pressed on with their search for Paulette, she was certain she already knew what he would say. Sir Caldwell emphasized the matter of taking care of all of the legal matters over her marriage to Lord Carlson. For, even if the banns had not been completed, two of the three were read and they had taken their vows in the house of God before his priest and witnesses before consummat-ing that night. This could not be taken lightly.

She held her breath as she stood in the doorway of the parlor and watched the Caldwells' heads bob up and down amongst the sea of servants who swarmed around Arthur in an effort to see to his care. It seemed the only household members missing were herself and Herald.

She looked around the room, but saw no sign of her brother. Where could he be? Surely he was informed of Arthur's arrival as well as his condition. In fact, Elizabeth was quite certain the nearby town had heard of it by now.

Watching the scene before her for just a little longer, she realized that she would not be missed until the chaos subsided. Besides, she did not know what to say to him. Was she to greet him with 'hello my love' or 'I am sorry, but I am not a widow after all so we cannot marry' or ''tis a contest between you and Stephen and may the man who declares his love for me in the most convincing manner to Sir Caldwell win'? What was she supposed to say to this man who claimed he would love her forever, words she had never once heard from her husband's lips.

Elizabeth shook her head and made her way to the atrium Sir Caldwell completed not a few weeks earlier. Located on the southwest wing of the mansion, she sought solace there daily since its completion. Be it morning, noon, or evening; if one was searching for Lady Elizabeth, one was certain to find her in the atrium. She called it her sanctuary, and rightly so.

Sir Caldwell hired the best of the best from his home-land to design and stock this latest addition to his paradise. The designer seemed a pompous fellow with slow wit when it came to table conversation, but his gift of design went unsurpassed. The clever man managed to intertwine plant life from various parts of the world, including Georgia, and have it all cohabit and thrive. Those who were clever with plants and farming found this a truly amazing feat and nearly stepped on each other to get an audience with him so they could question him on his strategies.

Elizabeth listened to the clicking of her one inch heeled slippers on the brilliantly polished Italian marble floor as she made her way to the bench in the bird sanctuary. Because the birds were of an exotic nature, great care was taken to keep their environment as close to natural as possible. This meant the area needed to remain enclosed with large basins filled with water recessed in the floor to resemble ponds running down the middle.

The moon was just trading places with the sun. It provided lighting that left one wondering if one's eyes were playing tricks or if the shadows that seemed to be popping out everywhere were actually real. Visibility within the bird sanctuary was even less because of the condensed foliage and fog that formed every evening.

Several birds squawked in discontent at having had their settled environment disturbed by her presence, but they soon relaxed and sweet silence resumed. Elizabeth sat in focused contemplation for well over thirty minutes before the sound of someone approaching caught her attention.

Not accustomed to sharing the atrium with anyone, she felt almost violated at the thought of another invading her privacy. Her thoughts soon quelled when she realized that the intruder was none other than her brother.

"Where have you been?" Elizabeth asked in a hushed voice.

"Around," Herald's voice was equally hushed.

He was in a mood and thus had no desire be forced into conversation with others of the household.

"Arthur has returned," Elizabeth stated flatly.

"I heard," Herald replied. "So, why do you sit here instead of near his sick bed?"

"I have no answer," she said with a sigh. "I know not what to say or what to do to correct what is happening. I wish to run away and leave both Stephen Carlson and Arthur Moore behind me."

Elizabeth's voice cracked with frustration.

"You do not mean it and you know it," Herald scolded. "I said nothing to you before, but I must say something now." He turned to face her and took her hand and placed it to his chest. "You think I am too young to understand the matters of the heart. My dear sister you are very wrong on that matter. I am already betrothed. Did you know?"

"Why... no, I... I did not know," Elizabeth stammered.

She was dumbfounded. In her mind her brother was always the younger one... the baby. Yet, here he sat before her quite grown up and engaged. It was time she re-evaluated her thoughts on him.

"Yes, and I shall tell you more about it at another time," he said with a sigh. He raised her hand gently to receive a light kiss from his lips before returning it to his chest. "I spent much time in the company of your husband. He suffered many challenges while searching for you." Herald raised his hand when she saw that Elizabeth was preparing to speak. "Nay, nay... I know that you feel he has sought you out for the purpose of divorce or nullification of your marriage. I pledge to you that this is not true. When one spends days upon days with a man, his temperance of voice, his facial expressions, his body language... they grow quite familiar. I am certain that Lord Carlson does indeed love his wife. I am certain Lord Carlson risked his life so that he might once again lay with his wife. Sister dear, I beg you to reconsider your intentions, for I feel that the right man for you is indeed the man to which you are already wed."

Elizabeth gently pulled her hand free from her brother's hold and stood up. After fidgeting with her lace bonnet and smoothing the skirts of her newly made silk gown, she squared her shoulders and lifted her chin a smidgen higher. She dreamt of Stephen Carlson night after night for months and regretted leaving him regularly. It was not simply because of the misfortune that befell her, but because she remembered his touch, his taste, his scent. He haunted her dreams. She wished nothing more than to have the words her brother spoke be true. Try as she may, she could not forget the warm and suggestive letter he wrote to the one woman in the world she hated vehemently. With the exception of his wild uttering while he was atop her, he said nary a word that would hint of his feeling remotely amiable toward her. Of course, she could not say such to the young man seated before her.

"My dear brother, I doubt not that you have my best interest at heart when you speak such things. It was I who was not courted by Lord Carlson before I was locked in my room and forced to marry him and it was I who suffered at his hands those two weeks before I ran away. You are still a romantic, dear Herald, and I pray that never changes." Elizabeth spoke in a tone just above a whisper.

"He spent months courting you," Harold insisted. "Grant it

you may not have realized it as a courtship, but I have it on good authority; not to mention I witnessed it myself when I was home from school. The man spent time getting to know you as best he could under the circumstances. He did not simply take you to his bed!"

Elizabeth clenched her jaw while she watched her brother stand up and leave. Why had she painted such a horrid picture of Stephen to a young man who obviously admired him so; especially when the picture held lies? It was true that her uncle held her prisoner in her room until she was wed, but the reason for her confinement was because of her uncle's concern over her threat to run away. Stephen had no knowledge of its occurrence. Harold was correct in saying Stephen courted her, although she had no idea his clumsy behavior was such at the time. Now that she was more experienced with men, it was easy to look back on her nights with Stephen and see that he had actually been quite gentle. Had she been more willing and knowledgeable, they would have been very wonderful nights indeed. As for Harold's remark about Stephen courting her and not simply taking her to bed... well, she was sure that was in reference to her situation with Arthur, which again was a unique circumstance that had no black and white way to look at it. Her brother may have been correct in his statements, but he was out of line as well. Such matters should not be openly discussed in this way. This was where his youth came into play.

The fact that Stephen never openly courted Elizabeth enough to display even the slightest attraction for her was what weighed heavy on her mind and supported the letter in her impression of his desire for Paulette. For surely, if a man desired to wed a woman he would make some hint of it. Would he not? On the few occasions when she found herself in his company, conversation proved light and limited. The visits were often less than a quarter hour. She assumed it was because he was tortured over having to marry her when his heart was elsewhere. What other explanation could there be?

Lord Stephen Carlson came from a long line of nobility and she was certain the disappearance of his wife almost immediately after their nuptials could prove socially devastating. Combine that fact with his love for Paulette and it was easy to see why he risked his life to find her. Elizabeth made no mistake in allowing herself the illusion that Stephen acted for any other reason.

"Pardon, miss," squeaked a timid black girl who appeared to Elizabeth to be around the age of eleven, "the masta' wishes ya ta come and see ta Mista' Arthur."

Elizabeth looked at the young girl and smiled. After receiving Elizabeth's slight nod to indicate that she understood and would follow shortly, the girl curtsied, giggled, and headed off to report to Sir Caldwell that the Lady Elizabeth was on her way.

"So, are you going to him?" Herald growled from the shadows.

Elizabeth turned with a start. She was so wrapped up in her thoughts that she forgot that her brother was still with her.

"I have been summoned," she said softly. "Therefore, yes, I am going."

"To the man who purchased you and held you in bondage as a sex slave?" Herald continued.

"To the man who purchased me under a falsehood not initiated by him and is eager to make it up to me. He says he loves me and has asked for my hand in marriage," Elizabeth replied. She was rapidly growing annoyed with Herald's refusal to see things for what they were. "Yes, dear brother, 'tis true he purchased me, but he had no knowledge of my true identity and you know that to be true. He has apologized many times over and so the matter shall be dropped."

"You already gave your hand in marriage, unless 'tis now legal to have more than one husband," Herald stated flatly.

"Oh, really!" Elizabeth snapped as she stormed out of the atrium.

When Herald had his mind set a certain way there was no swaying him.

She made her way to the parlor, only to find it empty. Standing in the doorway, bewildered, she heard Sara's tired voice behind her.

"There you are, child. We have been searching for you. He

is in the room at the far end of the guest quarters away from the noise. Sir Caldwell felt it best," Sara sighed.

"You seem vexed," Elizabeth mused.

"Mildly, my dear, mildly," Sara sighed. "In truth I am vexed and confused."

"Truth?" Elizabeth perked her attention. "May I ask why?"

"Please sit with me for a moment before you go to Mr. Moore, my dear," Sara asked in a commanding tone.

Unsure of what to do, Elizabeth decided it was better to risk offending Sir Caldwell by delaying her arrival than to offend her dear friend, Sara, by refusing to sit with her. She followed Sara's lead into a small antechamber toward the south part of the wing into a room Elizabeth had no idea existed.

The décor of the room was thus to satisfy the tastes of a woman. The windows displaying the rich grounds of the plantation were adorned with light and airy coverings that Sara proudly told her were made from cotton harvested from their plantation. The plush divan was covered with the tighter woven cotton in the same red plaid print as the windows and the two upholstered accent chairs of solid red cotton that brought the room together. This was Sara's private room that only she and a few privileged women of her acquaintance would enter. Her husband had been allowed in on the rarest of occasions. This was her sanctuary. Hers and hers alone.

"You would be surprised, my dear, to discover how many plantation homes have rooms as such. Although, I must admit that most of them are reserved for the men in the household. My dear man understood my needs and had this built for me." Sara pointed to a seat for Elizabeth to sit in. "Please sit."

Elizabeth selected the petite chair next to the window. Although it was too dark to look out onto the greens, simply knowing that they were on the other side of the many thick panes was comforting.

"I wish not to upset you or offend you in any way, but I feel that I must speak my thoughts before they tear at my brain and send me addled," Sara said as she reached for the pitcher of spring water her maid always made certain was available and selected two glasses from the six that rested next to the pitcher. She poured a glass two-thirds full and extended it to Elizabeth, who suddenly felt parched and took it graciously. "I have been troubled for some time now on the occurrences I have discovered of late. My shock and surprise when Sir Caldwell admonished you in such a way at dinner quickly quelled as I realized the truth in his words."

Elizabeth could not control the gasp of surprise that escaped her. She had not expected her good friend to not understand her position.

"Now, my dear, please hear me out before you become flustered with my words," Sara purred. It would not do for Elizabeth to become so upset that she was unable to absorb the meaning behind her words. "I would like you to put your feelings away for a moment and look at some facts. Your uncle is a man who honored his duty to his sister by taking in her orphaned children and seeing to their education and care. Although, admittedly, he lacked the warmth and love that one so greatly needs, he never-the-less provided both yourself and your dear brother with a life of privilege that otherwise would never have been. He also took great pains to select a husband for you who would certainly secure your station in society. For even in this land so far from England, his power and influence are recognized and felt."

Elizabeth fidgeted with her glass. Was Sara about to follow Sir Caldwells' example and tell her to remain with Stephen? Surely the woman would do no such thing.

"Now, let us look at the events that have occurred since your uncle pledged your hand to Lord Carlson, shall we?" Sara continued. "You defied him with a plan to run away. Your governess -a woman of sensibility, I believe- saw the folly in your ways and informed your uncle of your plans, resulting in your being confined to your rooms and the wedding being moved ahead so early that the banns were not allowed to be completed. Am I correct so far?"

Elizabeth nodded slowly.

"Fine, then." Sara took a long drink and then continued, "As a woman I can understand that it is every woman's dream to marry for love, but, my dear, those dreams rarely come true. Had you had your mother still with you, I feel certain she would have explained such to you. It is because you did not have the correct female upbringing that both Sir Caldwell and I wish to help you now."

"Thank you," Elizabeth responded, although she was not certain of what she was saying thank you for.

"You are most welcome." Sara said as she sat back, displaying a broad smile of satisfaction. "Now we come to the difficult part. You see, I feel I must point out to you that as a result of your recklessness, your dear husband and brother almost died, not to mention the ordeal you suffered, and the fact that your infant was nearly born a slave."

Elizabeth knew Sara was right. It really was all her fault and no matter whether Stephen was coming to find her for a divorce or out of love as everyone suspected –everyone but her, that is– he and Herald would not have had to look for her and risk their lives had she stayed put.

"Oh, my dear," Sara wailed, fully upset with herself for troubling Elizabeth like she had with such a comment, "if it helps, you are not the only young woman who has acted thoughtlessly. My goodness no. Why, dear Mr. Moore -sweet man that he is- lies broken in our guest room this very moment as a result of chasing after his reckless sister."

Elizabeth's eyes opened wide as she realized that she was being compared to Paulette, the most horrid female she had ever had the misfortune to meet. She would have preferred Sara taken a switch to her bottom than to compare her to Paulette Moore. What upset her even more was the fact that she was right. Elizabeth had acted no better than Paulette, possibly even worse. As a result, she jeopardized the life of her husband, and more so, her dear brother. Just like Paulette jeopardized her brother.

The realization that Stephen was at that very moment risking his life once again to help find Paulette filled Elizabeth with intense jealousy that was so overwhelming she had to fight swooning. Seeing her situation and thinking it was a result of her admonition,

Sara called for help while apologizing to Elizabeth profusely.

TWENTY-EIGHT

Bringing Paulette to the safety of the Caldwell plantation was not as easy as Stephen hoped. Since he worked his horse as much as he dared and she still did not regained consciousness, he settled her in front of one of the other men on her own horse and then later on with another whose horse suffered the stress of their journey favorably and was still strong enough to carry them both in the intense heat of the day. It was shortly after this last transition that she awoke and went into a frightful screaming fit. This caused the horse to rear and for her to fall off.

As if her disorientation was not bad enough, Paulette landed on her arm and it snapped like a dry twig. Stephen seized a flask containing their emergency brandy and took a long drink to steady his nerves. The stress and challenges he endured over the last few months was building within him to such a height he was certain his frustrations would cause him to burst from the inside out.

It took the considerable effort of several men to subdue Paulette enough to allow Ollie, who was the only person with a semblance of medical knowledge, the opportunity to inspect the damage of her fall. Other than the broken forearm and a few bruises, he found no other injuries. Using what he had available to him from the contents of their medical kit, he and Stephen set her arm as best they could and secured it from movement before pressing on with their journey.

Paulette had distanced herself from reality to such a degree that Stephen questioned if she was even aware of his presence. He exchanged horses with the slave, who suffered only minor scratched during the ordeal, and did his best to soothe and reassure her while he held her close to his chest in hopes that the rhythmic beating of his heart would relax her enough to bring her back to the real world. He took in her attire and the disarray of her hair with painful remorse. There was no guessing that she experienced through a life altering ordeal. He just hoped it was not so horrific that she would be unable to heal from it. Now, more than ever, was a test of her strength.

When Paulette was finally coherent enough to ride on her own, Ollie had her mare brought forth and assisted Stephen in helping her onto the saddle.

Positioning her as gently as he could, Stephen scowled as he saw an ever increasing pool of blood staining the saddle. Paulette was obviously starting her female time and he was completely unprepared or even knowledgeable of dealing with it. He looked around to see if anyone else was watching before taking a rag that was used for washing from her portmanteau and quickly stuffing it as far up her rawhide dress as he could without the others looking on. To his surprise and dismay, Paulette did not seem to notice, let alone object to his unseemly behavior.

Their trip was long and tedious as they pressed on without stopping. They reached the Caldwell plantation just as the sun peeked over the horizon. Even in his exhausted state, Stephen could not help admire the beauty of the white washed estate house that was nestled amongst strategically placed chestnut, cotton-wood, and magnolia trees.

Typical to plantation life, much of the household was up and functioning for several hours. Quick to notice their bedraggled party making their way up the long lane that connected their paradise to the rest of the world, they sent word to Sir Caldwell before rushing to be of assistance with Paulette's comfort.

Word spread quickly of the blood stained horse and saddle from the excessive amount of blood that could not be ceased as it pooled from between Paulette's legs. The doctor – who spent the night after attending to Arthur- was summoned from the comfort of the guest room that was set up in the recesses of the ground floor specifically for the occasions when he was required to stay over years ago. He ordered Paulette taken to the treatment room that was adjacent to his own and scurried to the kitchen to order the boiling of plenty of water and some peppermint tea made up for his patient.

It did not take long for his examination to reveal that Paulette was not menstruating. She was miscarrying. Aware that she was unwed, he felt such information was best kept quiet for the moment. When he had a private moment with Sir Caldwell, he would discuss the matter more thoroughly.

Herald placed his energies on seeing to the wellbeing of his brother-by-law. With all the fuss and commotion in the household over the care of Paulette and Arthur, the fact that Stephen did not look well might have gone unnoticed had it not been for Herald's astute and caring attention. Taking it upon himself, Herald guided his friend to the room assigned him and helped him into bed. He saw to the care of his wounded arm and his comfort before requesting that the doctor inspect him as soon as he was free from his duties with Miss Paulette.

Elizabeth stood in the doorway of Stephen's room and watched her brother assist her husband with the removal of his vest and breeches. Her heart twisted at the realization of just how exhausted Stephen was. He always seemed like such a strong, virile man. The concept of him having limitations or human weaknesses never entered her mind. Now, watching her brother so lovingly care for him brought to mind Sara's recent admonitions. Sorrow and regret permeated every inch of her body. She was no different from Paulette and they both deserved whatever fate saw fit to deliver them.

The sound of the doctor's footsteps on the exquisite marble staircase alerted her to his subsequent arrival. Wishing to remain in the background during all the fuss, she slipped away to her room before anyone even realized she had been there.

With her ear against the door, Elizabeth listened to the muffled voices that were floating out of the opened door of Stephen's room just next door. Thankful the doctor had not realized his effort to latch the door was not effective, she opened her own door just a crack to allow for easier listening.

The doctor determined Stephen's gash should heal nicely, but felt he was suffering from exhaustion. It was no wonder after all that he endured these months since he set sail from England. Lord Carlson was young, strong, and of a healthy nature, but even the mightiest of men must rest and nourish themselves in order to maintain such a state. He firmly pointed out that Lord Carlson suffered at the hands of the ferocious waters of the sea and once recovered had not taken time to properly care for his needs. He strongly recommended that the good Lord do nothing, but rest and eat for the next few weeks. He did not even want him leaving his room for at least two days.

Ordering a cup of chamomile tea brought to Stephen immediately, the doctor proclaimed that Herald's stay must be short and that Stephen was to be left to rest for the remainder of the day. Since he had a goodly amount of patients under one roof, he would be residing for a little longer in his rooms on the estate and would make himself available to Stephen later in the afternoon.

Elizabeth closed her door carefully and leaned against it while she allowed herself to cry the tears that threatened to escape for days. She hated herself for her foolishness. If she had not been so childishly impulsive and gone along with Dr. Jameson's scheme, none of this would have happened. She would have never been sold to bondage, Stephen and Herald's lives would never have been compromised at sea, and she would have never had to lay eyes on that evil Paulette Moore.

Paulette! Elizabeth's heart raced when she realized that Stephen had driven himself to the state of exhaustion to rescue Paulette. The memory of her watching him carry the woman's limp body from her horse into the house still burned in her mind. Surely people would understand now that his feelings for Paulette were that of love and it was she and not Elizabeth who he wished to marry. Mr. Caldwell told Elizabeth that she needed to read beyond the words. Well, she had seen enough with her own eyes to know the truth. The truth was that the man she married, the man who occupied her every waking thought and infiltrated her dreams, was in love with another woman. The worst of it was that this woman was the one woman in the world who she despised the most. She was glad that she at least had Arthur's offer of marriage to buffer the blow. She may not love him, but as least she was already familiar with him and his ways and, therefore, knew she would be fine in life.

Remembering Paulette's presence in the house, Elizabeth ran to her mirror to inspect herself. She called for Janet to assist her in making ready for the day. She fully intended to outshine the beauty of the vixen who managed to pour on an excessive amount of fainting drama to overshadow the fact that she behaved like the spoiled chit she was and endangered the lives of more than one man. All thoughts of her own foolish actions were swept away as Elizabeth allowed herself to dwell on her dislike for the woman who occupied the room at the far end of the hall.

Normally Elizabeth enjoyed Janet's incessant chatter, but to-day she found it dull and meaningless. She was just about to ask her for a little silence when the topic of Paulette and her condition came into play. Having no idea what the young woman was speaking of, she pressed her for more information. The speculation of the servants, although it had not been validated by the doctor, was that Paulette lost a child. The blood she lost far exceeded anything their resident midwife had seen during a woman's time. It strongly resembled that of a body flushing life from its womb. In fact, Janet's sister was assigned to clean up the doctor's examination room after they moved Paulette to her room upstairs and she took the linens to the midwife for inspection. The midwife was certain the blood was related to giving birth. Again, it was not confirmed by the doctor or any of the household members.

Elizabeth could not believe her ears. Paulette was with child, or at least had been with child. This was inconceivable-able. How far along was she? Who was the father? She searched the recesses of her mind for a possible beau who could have seduced Paulette, but could come up with no one.

"I wonder how..." Elizabeth muttered, more to herself than to Janet.

"Well, miss, she be wearing the dress of an Indian squaw when they brung her here," Janet volunteered.

"Really... I... I did not know," Elizabeth stammered.

She was beginning to understand what happened.

"Yes, miss. She be bleeding since she fell off the horse and broke her arm," Janet added.

"She broke her arm too?" Elizabeth gasped.

"Yes, miss," Janet replied as she finished adjusting Elizabeth's wig on her head.

Elizabeth thanked Janet for her assistance and bade her leave. She paced the room while she wrestled with her emotions. She should be feeling sorry for Paulette. The poor woman broke her wrist and, from the way it appeared, was raped by an Indian and lost his child. Although the loss of the child was a good thing, since now she could keep her abduction a secret from society and no one need be the wiser, it was still a sad event. No matter who planted his seed inside her womb, the life that tried to take hold was also partly hers and so, in essence, she lost a bit of herself. Elizabeth heard this stated when the head maid at her uncle's estate lost a child and now, after giving birth to James, she was able to understand its meaning.

Try as she may, Elizabeth could muster up only the slightest amount of compassion for Paulette. She knew people would expect more from her than what she was feeling, but they had no idea the cruelty the horrible woman inflicted upon her during her tortuous time in bondage while being forced to do her bidding. She would not wish upon anyone what she sensed Paulette went through, but then again, she would not wish on anyone what she herself endured; with much of it being at Paulette's cruel hand.

Promising to do her best to show warmth to the woman who captured her husband's heart, if only for Arthur's sake, Elizabeth went downstairs to join the others for breakfast.

"My dear girl, you are a ray of sunshine on this gloomy day," bellowed Sir Caldwells as Elizabeth entered the room. "'Tis a joy to see you looking so lovely."

Sara accessed Elizabeth's image and nodded; a smile of satisfaction upon her face.

"Indeed, my dear child you look absolutely marvelous. You are feeling well I take it?" she asked.

"I get better with every day that passes, Lady Caldwell, thank you. My stay here has proved most beneficial," Elizabeth replied.

"Pshaw, what do you mean by stay? This is your home, dear girl. You are no guest. Please remember that," Sir Caldwell said with emphasis.

He burst forth his sentence only seconds before his wife made the same claim. The light hearted conversation that followed picked up everyone's spirits. It was almost forgotten that there were three people above them in need of various medical attention.

The entrance of the good doctor quickly brought that fact back to mind and the mood subdued greatly.

"I must say that Mr. Moore is doing admirably. At the rate he is going, he will be healed within a month," the doctor chuckled as he spooned some scrambled eggs onto his plate. "The young man is already barking that he is bored and wishes to be moved out to the shade of the greens."

"My... already? I would think he would want to lie still for at least another week," Sara chimed.

"Indeed," added Sir Caldwell, "'tis most unusual, is it not?"

"'Tis very unusual, but he is a strong and healthy man. I see no harm in it, providing you have a few strong men who can handle the job," the doctor replied.

Sir Caldwell scratched his chin in thought.

"Well, I will have to think on that. Would they be carrying him alone or will he remain in his bed?" he asked.

"Goodness, no. He can sit in a chaise and they can carry him that way. I have done it in the past, but never this early after setting the break," the distinguished physician stated in a thoughtful voice. "Even so, I believe it will actually do him some good."

"Might I suggest the atrium instead?" Elizabeth offered. "'Tis within the house and not quite as great a journey for everyone."

"It certainly is lovely!" Lady Caldwells added excitedly.

"'Twould be good to see it get some use," Sir Caldwell stated enthusiastically.

Herald, who had been quiet throughout their conversation interjected, "I have to agree, 'tis a good idea."

"I had no idea you even had an atrium, Matthew. you are full of surprises, my good man," the doctor chuckled. "I agree. We shall place him in the atrium."

"I can even order a nice divan set up there for the comfort of his visitors," Lady Caldwell stated as she excused herself to do just that.

The doctor started to call her back to state that he did not wish to cause her an inconvenience, but her husband simply raised his hand and informed their family physician that there was no use trying to dissuade his wife, once and idea took hold. If it made her happy to oversee the selecting and moving of the divan, then let the woman have her pleasure.

Elizabeth sat quietly watching her brother's facial expressions and body language while the doctor and Sir Caldwell discussed the wellbeing of each of his patients. Relief flooded his expression when he was assured that Lord Carlson would be fit and moving about in no time.

TWENTY-NINE

Elizabeth and Arthur's gay conversation could be heard long before Stephen reached the doorway of the atrium. He stopped and listened, uncertain whether he should enter or simply return to his room.

He took much longer than even the doctor expected him to take to recover from his intense state of exhaustion. Herald sat in the room near the window watching him and then watching the world out the window for the majority of the days he lay abed. He was joined by Elizabeth for whatever time her greedy fiancé would allow her away from him.

Elizabeth expressed her concern about Arthur's monopolizing her time during one of her long conversations with her brother. She was torn over who she should be spending her time with. He was awake and alert and requesting her company, but Stephen was weak and still in need of constant watch; not to mention the fact that it was Stephen who had her heart. There were times when her visits with Arthur proved tortuous as she thought of Stephen on the floor just above.

As time passed and she grew more accustomed to splitting her time between both men, she relaxed enough to allow herself to enjoy her visits with Arthur. Now that she was in a position of equality, he opened up to her in light conversation that she found delightfully entertaining. She could certainly see why he was so popular with the ladies as well as much sought after by society in general. His stories were fascinating and captivating. Slowly, ever so slowly, her life as his slave was fading into a distant dream-like memory.

Even though Arthur was confined to his divan, with an occasional amount of time on the crutches the doctor had made for him, he still managed to present her with trinkets and baubles for her amusement. He wanted to present her with something more substantial like an engagement ring, but since Stephen lay upstairs recovering from his ordeal -which included the rescue of his sister- and he felt it would be improper to do such. His conversation with Sir Caldwell made it clear that he was now rivaling his best friend for the hand of the woman they both loved.

Arthur was anxious to discuss Stephen's position where Elizabeth was concerned, but his friend was asleep more than he was awake. The brief times he was alert, he was surrounded with members of the household who were anxious to see to his wellbeing. Arthur wished with all his might that his rival was anyone but Stephen. Under any other situation he would have withdrawn upon the knowledge that his friend had designs on the same woman as he. Not since he realized he loved Paulette had he found a woman who could capture his heart like Elizabeth did. It may not be to the same level of intensity that his love for Paulette reached – he doubted any woman could achieve that- but it was enough for him to not want to release her.

Arthur listened as his men gave him a full report of their search for Paulette after they separated from him right down to the fact that Stephen stuffed a rag up Paulette's dress when he thought no one was looking. He smirked wryly when he heard that part of the tale. As an owner of slaves, he would have thought the man would be aware that nothing, absolutely nothing, could escape the eagle eyes of slaves – especially those who are trained to be alert scouts.

Although he was fully aware that Stephen was doing his best to help his sister, Arthur still could not help a twinge of jealousy over his friend's closeness to her. In the past it was an abstract concept. He and Paulette discussed the fact that Stephen was the perfect candidate for a husband, but Stephen was not privy to this decision, nor had he made a suggestion indicating such. Therefore, Arthur felt no threat by the friendly attention Stephen paid Paulette when he was in her company. After hearing the help's whispering of how romantic Lord Carlson was in rescuing Miss Moore and how he held her in his arms with her head nestled in his neck, Arthur just could not hold back his feelings of frustrated jealousy. Stephen already had claims to Elizabeth and now Paulette. It just did not seem right. If he was not such a good friend, Arthur would have certainly called him on his ways.

Stephen's presence went unnoticed while Arthur did his best to coerce Elizabeth into sitting next to him on the divan when she passed in front of him. She giggled and slapped his hand coyly when he grabbed at her embroidered linen skirt, causing Stephen to turn red with jealous rage.

Stephen engaged in a serious conversation with Sir Caldwell who informed him of his demand that Elizabeth and Arthur not marry until Stephen was given the opportunity to declare his love. He also divulged that he used the time that Stephen was abed to research the laws of England in regards to marriage and discovered that his marriage to Elizabeth was in fact not recognized because the reading of the banns was incomplete. Therefore, Arthur was within his rights to court Elizabeth.

Stephen's heart sank. How could he ever compete with what he was witnessing? He was not as smooth and gay as Arthur. Women never made him work for their attention and he had no idea how to go about it; especially when it came to Elizabeth, who seemed to steal his tongue whenever she was about. He might as well give up now, for it was clear his battle was lost. As he turned to leave, the padding of Janet's soft soled slippers along the cool marble flooring as she rushed in his direction caught his attention.

"What is it, Janet?" Stephen asked.

"Excuse me sir, but I be sent ta speak with Mr. Arthur," Janet was breathless.

"Speak to me then. What is it?" Stephen's tone was firm.

Janet looked at a loss for what to do. Her message was meant for Mr. Arthur, but she couldn't deny Lord Carlson his request. Taking a deep breath and hoping she was doing the right thing she almost spit out the words. "Miss Paulette is in a bad way and the doctor needs help ta calm her."

Stephen looked back into the atrium at the laughing couple.

"Might I ask how the good doctor thinks Arthur is going to

rush to his aid? Has he forgotten the man has a broken leg?" Stephen asked gruffly.

Janet looked as if someone had just slapped her in the face. She was sent with a message. She had not considered how silly the message sounded.

"Well sir," she said shyly, "I don't rightly know. I was just told ta come tell him. The doctor is pretty upset."

"I see," Stephen muttered. "Show me the way, Janet."

The young servant girl's ebony skin went ashen as she looked past Stephen toward Arthur. This was indeed a dilemma. She was told to give the message to Arthur. She could not help worrying about the trouble she might find if she did not fulfill her mission and return with Stephen in his stead.

"Now, Janet," Stephen commanded.

Feeling she had no other choice, Janet gave a slight curtsey and turned to lead Stephen to Paulette's room. By the time he reached the second floor he needed no guidance to her room. He merely need follow the sounds of her wailing and things crashing. When he reached the room, he was horrified by what he saw. Paulette was standing stark naked in the middle of the room holding a knife that was part of the table setting earlier in the day. The doctor was bleeding profusely from his arm while he did his best to coax the knife from her hand.

Paulette's wild eyes were accentuated by her untamed hair that resembled the mane of a lion as it framed her face and fell down about her shoulders, covering her voluptuous breasts with its thick golden tresses. The raging welts from the switch used on her more often than she could recall were still screaming of infection. Stephen had no doubt that her excessive loss of blood, combined with the obvious infection of the gashes across her back, hips and buttocks and whatever other horrific trauma she experienced against her person were the reason for her temporary insanity. At least he hoped it was temporary.

"Help me get that blasted knife from her!" the doctor bellowed as Stephen entered the room.

Stephen was almost upon Paulette when she turned on him

and jabbed the knife wildly in the air, almost grazing his forearm. He jumped back just in time to escape it and looked around for an alternate solution. Noticing the bedding was in total disarray, he bade the doctor to keep her occupied and he raced to the bed and pulled off the top sheet. Without a moment's hesitation he tossed it over Paulette, disorienting her and causing her to fall to the floor.

The doctor quickly dove to the floor near her and slammed the hand that held the knife against the thick carpeting, causing it to flex open and release the lethal weapon. Elizabeth's wails slowly faded to whimpers while Stephen and the doctor helped her back into bed.

"She took me by surprise," the doctor admitted. "I certainly did not expect this." He wheezed as he raised his bleeding arm for Stephen to see. "I am in need of tending. Will you sit with her for a moment?"

Stephen nodded his agreement and the doctor scurried out of the room. Paulette's obvious nakedness showed through the thin linen of her bed sheet, causing him to feel extremely uncomfortable. He moved to the bed and looked down at her. Even in such a state she was a beautiful woman. Although her clothing had always been well tailored to complement her form, they did not do her curves and valleys the justice they deserved. Catching himself staring inappropriately, he pulled the fine tapestry throw up over her slight form, removing her beauty from his sight.

Elizabeth could feel the blood drain from her face as she watched Stephen linger over Paulette's frail looking body longer than need be before covering her with the tapestry coverlet. After escorting Stephen to the room, Janet returned to fulfill the doctor's request and tell Arthur of what was occurring with his sister. Unable to keep up with her on his clumsy crutches, Arthur was only now arriving at Elizabeth's side. He was too late to witness the intimate scene she was unfortunate enough to view.

Arthur hobbled past Elizabeth with little more than a glance and made his way directly to Paulette's side. She was back into a slumbering stupor, but the signs of her struggle with the doctor were still apparent. Arthur looked at the bruises on his sister's shoulders and scowled. This was the first he had been allowed to see her since she was brought back almost two weeks earlier. He did not like what he saw. Had her bruises been superfluous, they would have healed by now.

The doctor placed a solid binding on her broken wrist, but even that was dangling precariously now.

"Where is the doctor?" Arthur's question echoed the tone of a command.

"He was wounded in the battle with Paulette and has gone to tend to it," Stephen replied.

"Wounded? How so?" Arthur asked.

"With this," Stephen volunteered as he raised the knife in the air.

Arthur closed his eyes and shook his head. He had no words to describe the pain he felt in his chest when he looked at the bruises and lashes on his sister's exposed skin. He moved closer and lifted the corner of the coverlet to get a better idea of the extent of her injuries. A loud sucking of air permeated the room, relaying his shock of what he saw.

"May I please be alone with my sister?" Arthur choked.

Stephen bowed to his friend and made his way to the door. He stopped in front of Elizabeth and looked at her briefly before he offered his arm to escort her away.

As Elizabeth rested her hand on Stephen's arm her heart skipped a beat. Memories of him escorting her out of the church after they took their wedding vows floated through her mind. She recalled how dashing he looked while standing next to her. If she had not been pouting so obstinately in her typical immature fashion, she would have also noticed that he was a little nervous.

Her memories moved to his passionate love making. She longed for it again. She wanted nothing more than to pull him nearer and drown in his kisses. Instead, she remained the lady of propriety that the household knew her to be as she allowed him to guide her down the Grecian style hallway toward the stairs.

Elizabeth's mind screamed her agony. Why did he not say something? Did he find her so repulsive that he could not even hold a conversation with her? She wondered if it were Paulette he was guiding, would he be flirting and laughing with her by now?

In actuality, Stephen was in just as much torment as Elizabeth. The moment he felt the light pressure of her petite hand on his arm he went wild with desire. He wanted nothing more than to scoop her up into his arms and tell her how frightened he had been about the possibility of never seeing her again. He wanted to declare his love to her; a love he felt from the moment he saw her rich violet eyes glisten when she smiled. He wanted to tell her that he feared she would leave him again and he was certain that if that happened he would not be able to go on living. He wanted to tell her so many things, but his mouth would not move and his tongue felt thick with fear. He saw with his own eyes and heard with his own ears the joy Arthur brought to her. She never laughed like that when they were together. She never teased and flirted with him. Not once. It was clear to Stephen where Elizabeth's heart lied. He caused her enough pain and anguish. If she had finally found the love she yearned to have when she married, he would not... he could not take that from her. He loved her too much to be that cruel.

The sight of Herald sitting with a cup of tea in the parlor brought relief to them both. Now they had a third person in which to direct their conversation to. Soon Sir Caldwell joined in on their tea party with lively conversation about the latest business amongst the anti-slavery activists. For the first time Elizabeth was able to witness how truly delightful her husband could be. His conversation skills were exceptional and his wit equal to that of Arthur's.

When Lady Caldwell entered the room, he displayed impeccable manners that clearly won Elizabeth's favor. She could easily see why her brother became so attached to him. He was the perfect man... the perfect husband. There was only one problem. He was not her husband, he had never been her husband, and he wished to be someone else's husband.

****

Arthur waited until he was alone in the room. Making certain the door was bolted shut, he moved slowly back to the bed and stood over Paulette's small frame. Ever so slowly he pulled the covers away and stared in horror at his sister's tender, puss riddled, angry flesh.

THIRTY

Margaret Moore stepped out of the carriage in front of the Caldwell plantation house and gaped in awe at its magnificent beauty. She heard whispers of the wealth the Caldwells possessed through conversations at one of the many social parties she attended, but she had not pictured it to be as such. She was told that Sir Caldwell's wealth was surpassed by few. He was even able to work free darkies on his plantation; something that was rare indeed amongst the plantation owners of Georgia who petitioned fervently to have slavery reinstated during its temporary abolishment because their plantations would not survive without it. Sir Caldwell was one of the very few in political societies who did not support such reinstatement.

She heard their mansion was equal to that of a king, sporting thirteen guest rooms and marble flooring adorned with plush carpet with unique designs woven into it. Both were ordered from India. The marble lion's heads on either side of the grand steps leading to an expansive veranda that disappeared around the side of the house spoke of exotic faraway lands. Margaret was certain there was no other place of such magnitude in the colonies. Feeling mildly overwhelmed, she leaned against a pillar to regain her composure.

"Is everything alright, miss?" the livery boy asked as he set her trunk down next to her.

Realizing the sight, she must be presenting, Margaret straightened her back and nodded her head, indicating she was fine.

Sir Caldwell greeted her with genuine warmth as he led her into the parlor where Sara, Arthur, Elizabeth, Stephen, and Herald were waiting. Leaping up to greet their new guest with genuine sincerity, Sara offered Margaret a seat and a cold glass of lemonade; both of which she accepted readily.

Margaret nodded her greeting to each introduction as Sara went around the room.

"Of course, you already know your stepson, Mr. Arthur Moore," Sara stated with bubbly enthusiasm.

"Yes. Hello Arthur. You are looking well," Margaret stated while narrowing her eyes with disdain.

"As are you, dear mother of my lovely sister," Arthur replied.

He had not been able to refer to her as his step-mother since she accused him of such a heinous act as killing his own father; especially since she refused to accept his innocence once he had been vindicated.

"Although it is our greatest pleasure to finally meet you, Mrs. Moore, I regret that it is under such devastating circumstances," Sara continued.

Sara and Margaret traveled on the fringes of the same social circle. Although both had heard of the other, they had never had the opportunity of being introduced. Since Margaret was amongst the pillar of Savannah society, Sara was most eager to seek her acquaintance. She loved her grand plantation home, but there were times when she had to admit that she would have preferred to live in a quaint townhouse in Savannah where she could mingle with society on a daily basis, such as was the case with Margaret Moore.

She reminded herself that she would do well to remember how blessed she was to still have her loving husband by her side. Coveting what others have never does a body good.

Margaret's smile left her face when the gravity of the situation was brought to the forefront.

"How is my daughter?" she asked eagerly.

"We thought it best for you to speak in private with the doctor," Lady Caldwell explained. "He should be joining us shortly. If I understood his message correctly, he was preparing Paulette for your visit."

"Pardon?" Margaret was taken aback by such a comment. "She has no waiting maid?"

"Oh, indeed she does," Sara offered eagerly, "'Tis just that of times the dear girl proves too much for Jane to handle on her own."

The gasp of shock that escaped Margaret's lips permeated the room. Elizabeth looked at Arthur and then lowered her eyes. She was feeling ashamed of herself of late for the hateful feelings she allowed herself to feel toward Paulette. Surely the woman suffered enough to have paid for her sins and possibly the sins of others. Try as she may, she simply could not shake the resentment she felt for the woman. It was not because of the treatment she suffered under her wickedness while a slave in her household -she had actually forgiven her for that- but because she held the heart and affections of the man that she now realized without a shadow of a doubt was the man she loved.

Arthur positioned himself on the divan next to Elizabeth. She could feel his warmth radiate as he found reasons to lean his body nearer to hers than would be considered socially acceptable. Amused by his antics, the Caldwells chose to ignore his wickedly mischievous behavior while Stephen seethed in silently jealousy. Elizabeth, on the other hand, had grown so accustomed to it she hardly noticed anymore.

"You smell as sweet as honeysuckle this day, my dear," Arthur whispered as he leaned past Elizabeth to select a biscuit from the silver tray that rested on the tea cart that was wheeled in for their guests.

"Behave!" Elizabeth whispered in a tone that resembled an amused hiss.

"Arthur!" Margaret snapped. "I fail to see any amusement in your sister's situation."

"Nor do I, my dear lady. Nor do I," Arthur replied, annoyed by the public admonishment he just received. "Which is why I sent for you."

Lady Caldwell cleared her throat and offered more biscuits and lemonade to her guests. Her relief was clearly apparent when the doctor finally entered the room,

Spending only the required amount of time with the group to accommodate the necessities of etiquette, the doctor escorted

Margaret to the small study that occupied part of his suites to discuss her daughter's condition. Margaret could not help question him about the fact that he held a suite in the plantation home, of which he replied in a matter-of- fact matter that it made life easier when he was required to stay on for certain cases. She had heard that such accommodations were quite common amongst those of high noble rank in Europe, but certainly not in the colonies. Margaret Moore was duly impressed.

Born of English settlers who helped to forge and shape Georgia, Margaret Bingley inherited a solid foothold into Savannah's society. As headstrong and foolish young girl, she fell in love with a traveling tinker. Having been brought up on a remote plantation with nary a beau for miles, it took little effort on the young, virile tinker's part to coerce Margaret into his bed in hopes of entrapping her into marriage and bettering his station in life. Discovering their daughter's indiscretions, the influential Bingley's quickly ran the tinker out of Georgia and set out to find Margaret a husband before she was too far along with child. The fact that they would be tricking her new husband into believing that the child was his was not even a factor their consciences considered.

When it reached their ears that one of Georgia's wealthiest plantation owners, the widow Moore, was considering remarrying, they acted on the opportunity immediately. It was not uncommon for a man to remarry prior to the traditional allotted time of mourning, especially in the colonies where family units could make the difference of survival. The fact that the widow James Moore was extremely wealthy and owned more slaves than most of the other plantation owners was a fair assurance that he was not in dire need of a new wife, but never-the-less the eligible ladies of Savannah society began soliciting their wares as early as six months after the death of Arthur's mother. Now, three years later he had finally come to terms with the concept of taking another wife and the Bingley's were prepared to offer him a very attractive dowry if he would consider their daughter.

Mildly surprised by such a substantial offer James sensed there was a strong reason behind the Bingley's offering him such a dowry if he agreed to marry Margaret. Her beauty captured him immediately and he did not hesitate to agree to the marriage. It was love at first sight and whatever hidden motives lay behind their obviously shady deal simply did not matter.

The Moores lived in marital bliss, with no one the wiser that the child Margaret carried in her womb was that of the tinker. No one but James, who was familiar with the body of a woman and suspected the moment she disrobed that she was with child. Of course his discovery of her lost virginity confirmed his suspicions.

The fact that Paulette was not genetically his was never mentioned. James loved her and cared for her as if she was his very own. Seeing the obvious love that Arthur and Paulette had for each other tempted James to speak the truth so that the two could be together as they so desired, but Margaret would have none of it. She had outgrown her silliness and found a solid place in society and would not allow such a scandal to be unveiled, even if it meant her daughter and step-son's misery.

They had argued over it just before James took Arthur on a trumped up mission to check the perimeters of their plantation. There was no threat of Cherokee invasions. James made it up to justify taking his son away from the house for a while to help him ease his obvious suffering over the rift he was having with his sister. It tore at the man's heart to see his son suffer so.

Margaret always contended that if Arthur had not been such a moping fool, James would still be alive to afford her the lifestyle and social status she deserved. As far as she was concerned, even if Arthur did not actually kill his father, he was responsible for his death. For this she would never forgive him.

Arthur harbored similar feelings of hatred for his step-mother. His message requesting her presence was a difficult one to write. He much preferred supplying her trust fund each year and then forgetting her existence in between, but Paulette's situation was a grave one and, after seeing the extent of her infection, he was not convinced she would live much longer. He could not, in good conscience, deny Margaret Moore the right to see her daughter in her final days. Even if she was the most horrid woman he had ever had the misfortune to be forced to deal with. The fact that Arthur was not required to care for her needs, but did so regardless, did not seem to register with Margaret. Paulette mentioned it to her on one occasion, but was quickly put into submission by her mother's cutting tongue. It was bad enough that her daughter chose to live with Arthur rather than accompany her in town, but she would not have her praising him for doing something that his father would have expected him to do. It was his duty to care for her and he knew it. That, at least, was one amiable quality in his favor.

The doctor did his best to explain to Mrs. Moore the events that led up to Paulette's disappearance. He took his limited knowledge of Cherokee life and pieced together what might have occurred while she was held their captive. No one knew how she managed to escape, for she had not been reasonably coherent since her return.

Having the bedside manner of a common doctor and not that of a socialite, he spared her nothing as he went over every detail of Paulette's condition. Margaret's heart flew into her throat and threatened to choke her while her mind whirled as to how she could possibly find a husband for her daughter after being victimized in such a way by the Indians. It was difficult enough to find a man of proper wealth and station, but to find one who was willing to overlook the bride's having had her virginity stolen by a savage, well that was practically impossible. Paulette may as well have slept with one of their darky slaves!

Insisting on seeing her daughter immediately, Margaret followed the doctor to the second floor, making note of the many rooms they passed on their seemingly endless journey to the last room of the wing.

When they entered the room, they found Paulette sitting in a rose colored velvet winged-back chair by the window. Although the curtains were drawn to allow her a clear view of the birds dancing amongst the branches of the magnolia trees, Margaret doubted whether Paulette appreciated it.

Running to her daughter's side, Margaret knelt on the floor

and cupped her daughter's hand to her face. To the surprise and delight of the doctor, his patient responded by looking directly into the eyes of her mother. The two stared silently at each other for a considerable length of time, as if communicating somehow with their eyes.

"Mamma," Paulette whispered as tears flooded her face.

Unable to contain her composure any longer, Margaret pulled her daughter to her breast and released her own heart wrenching tears.

Seeing their need for privacy, the doctor told Jane to listen outside the door for any unusual sounds and to call him if he was needed before returning to the parlor where the rest of the household remained.

Upon hearing that Paulette spoke coherently to her mother, Arthur made way to her room. The doctor and the Caldwells did their best to dissuade him, feeling that mother and daughter should be left alone for a bit longer, but Arthur would hear nothing of it. Stephen stood at Elizabeth's side while they watched Arthur ascend the stairs as quickly as his clumsy crutches would allow.

THIRTY-ONE

Feeling the need for some fresh air, Stephen excused himself and started toward the rear exit. Thinking better of it, he turned and asked Elizabeth to join him. Smiling timidly, she accepted his arm and allowed him to guide her down the cool, dimly lit corridor toward the back of the house.

"I much prefer this part of the house," Stephen said quietly.

"Might I ask why?" Elizabeth responded, hoping her nervousness did not show in her voice.

"'Tis quiet and unpretentious," Stephen replied.

"You find the main part of the house pretentious?" Elizabeth asked with mild surprise.

"Nay, not at all, I just prefer this. I fear I am a simple man who lives amongst splendor," Stephen said.

He cursed himself for his fumbling words. Why was it that he became such a bumbling oaf whenever he was in her company?

Elizabeth smiled sweetly and moved closer as he guided her through the doorway that was much narrower than the one at the main entrance. Although he could have moved out of her way, Stephen stood firm while she did her best to pull her body through the narrow door and still avoid bumping into him. She trembled as she caught his familiar musky scent. Her body tingled from the light touch of his hands around her waist as he helped her through the door. As her foot touched the cool flagstone a few inches below the exterior of the door, her new slipper slid off, causing her to require his assistance with both support and the slipper's retrieval.

"I would have done well to dress more simply today, I fear," Elizabeth stuttered as her hands rested on top of Stephen's.

"'Twould make an easier exit, 'tis true, but I rather like the way you dress, my dear. Your gown brings out the richness of your memorable eyes and these lovely slippers prove an asset to your even lovelier feet. You must have won the milliner over for such finery as this is not common in Georgia," Stephen managed to choke out as he wrestled with his uncooperative tongue. Elizabeth's heart raced with excitement at the complement he just paid her. Could it be that he noticed her after all?

"You are most kind, Stephen," Elizabeth replied. "Oh, I mean Lord Carlson." Her face flushed as she stammered, "forgive me."

"For what?" he asked with a tone that was soft and sultry as he leaned forward so that only she could hear his words. "Damn the laws of England and the reading of their banns, you are my wife and as such you may call me whatever name you wish."

Elizabeth's closed her eyes as the heat of Stephen's breath brushed against her face and his voice caressed her ears. Her knees went weak, forcing her to lean against his solid chest for support. She could hear the beating of his strong heart as he put his arms around her and pulled her so close she thought she might break. She made no move to stop him. She felt as if she were in a dream that she never wanted to awaken from. Was he really claiming her for his wife? After all she had done, after all that had happened, did he still want to be her husband? What about Paulette?

Elizabeth's eyes flew open. What about Paulette? Had she not seen him lingering over her while she slept? Had she not read his letter to her with her own eyes? How could he claim her as his wife when his heart belonged to another?

Elizabeth pushed herself away from Stephen as hard as she could.

"What about Paulette?" she demanded, a little more forcefully than intended.

"I am not certain I comprehend your question," Stephen with genuine confusion.

"I read your letter to her. You proposed to her," she said accusingly.

She blurted the words in such a tone in an effort to contain the tears that threatened to spill.

"So I have heard," Stephen replied flatly.

He wished he had his letter back to read for himself for truly he could not recall making any such proposal to Paulette Moore.

"What do you mean?" Elizabeth asked more gently.

"Arthur made the same claim," Stephen said with a slow shake of his head. "Truly, it was not my intention to have my words read like a proposal to her. I simply was responding to a mention she made in her correspondence to me of the possibility of our marrying. It seemed cruel to send a letter of rejection to her when I knew I would soon be arriving and could gently turn her proposal down. I only stated we needed to talk. I apparently wrote in such haste that I neglected to realize the implications of my words." Stephen reached his hand out to stroke Elizabeth's cheek. "It was my intention to inform her that I was married to the most beautiful woman in England and that this lovely creature captured my heart."

"She proposed to you?" Elizabeth gasped.

She could not believe the gall of the woman. Proposing to a man was simply not done!

Stephen chuckled as he said, "I tell you that I love you and that is all you have to say?"

Elizabeth looked at Stephen with confusion and then embarrassment. She was so consumed by the impropriety of Paulette's actions that the true meaning of his words slipped right past her. What had he said again? She could not even recall.

"You did? You do?" she answered timidly.

Stephen leaned over and kissed her lightly on the lips.

"I did and I do," he cooed. "From the time I first set eyes on you, until now, you have occupied my heart completely. I admit my tongue has been my nemesis by refusing to cooperate. It is most certainly not as smooth and gifted as that of my good friend Arthur in the best of situations, but surely my actions speak of my love. I have risked the ravenous waves of an angry sea and forged through terrain that one would only imagine existed with a body not yet healed, all to find you and tell you that my life without you is empty." He hesitated briefly before continuing, "I am aware that you have pledged yourself to marry Arthur. I am also aware of the circumstances that led up to that pledge. I have no doubt he loves you and would provide for you and your son quite amiably. If you love him, truly love him, and wish to be free of me so you can wed him, then, with a heavy heart I stand aside and cause no problems for you. Arthur is my closest friend. If I am forced to relinquish my claim to you it could be to no better man. I must say that if you have the slightest doubt in your mind about your love for him. If you feel anything for me at all... I beg a chance to prove the depths of my love for you."

Elizabeth stood frozen with joy. Her heart leapt with excitement as Stephen's professed love warmed her from head to toe. This was what she dreamed of all those months of separation. She promised herself that, should she ever be blessed with the chance, she would make up for her foolishness and be the wife he wanted her to be.

"You, you really love me?" she heard herself saying.

Without a moment's hesitation, Stephen bent on one knee before Elizabeth and put her hand to his chest.

"Lady Elizabeth Nottingham-Carlson will you marry me... again?" he asked with a twinkle in his eye.

Elizabeth could not believe her ears. He was actually proposing to her in the most romantic way possible. Could it be that after all her fuss and all the trouble she caused – not just for herself but for others – she was being forgiven? Was she actually being courted by the one man in the world who she longed to be with forever? Had she actually been blessed with the opportunity to marry for love, real love?

Mistaking her tongue tied joy for hesitation, Stephen stood up and continued, "I realize we have not had the time together as you and Arthur have shared. It stands to reason that you would be more comfortable with him. If you have developed a love for him and wish to marry him then I will offer my blessing to you both and walk away a defeated man. But, my darling, if you have even the tiniest reservation where Arthur is concerned I beg you to consider my offer. For truly I know that the love I have inside me for you is enough to carry us both through life." Stephen swallowed hard. His anxiety over convincing her to consider his proposal was beginning to make him breathless. "I believe... I believe that if you would just give me some time... just take a little time to get to know me... well you would..."

Elizabeth's smothering kisses were the most welcomed interruption Stephen could have imagined. He filled with joy as he felt the woman he loved melt in his arms. Their hungry kisses slowly transformed to those of gentle passion. Each savored the softness of the other.

"I love you," Elizabeth murmured. "I did not know that I loved you until it was too late but, I do love you. I never meant..."

"Hush," Stephen said as he placed his finger on her lips to stop her. "It matters no more. Hearing you say those words to me erases all else."

Seemingly oblivious to the world around them, the couple did not notice that Herald had followed them outside and happily witness their reunion. He leaned against the portico column wearing a smile of smug satisfaction. Aware that his sister and brother-by-law were drawing the attention of the servants who were working the grounds, he gently cleared his throat.

Excited to share her joy and not the least bit embarrassed at the realization that they had an audience Elizabeth turned to her brother.

"Herald, we...," she began.

"I heard... As did they," Herald chuckled as he nodded his head in the direction of the onlookers, "and we could not be more pleased."

Stephen kept his arm around Elizabeth's waist as he guided her closer to Herald. Outstretching his arm, he motioned for Herald to join them. With both the woman of his dreams and the young man he had grown to admire in his grasp, he held them close.

"Today is the happiest day of my life," he said in earnest. "Today my family is united as one."

"But," Elizabeth laughed, "what about the ceremony?"

Stephen stood back and scowled.

"Blast," he huffed, "that is a bit of an inconvenience, is it not?"

Herald doubled with laughter as Stephen's obvious sincerity.

"I believe we can get that out of the way rather quickly," he offered.

Elizabeth pulled away from Stephen's embrace and twirled around with her arms spread wide and her gown billowing.

"I am so very happy," she giggled like a school girl.

They were brought back to reality at the sight of Arthur standing in the doorway. The preoccupied scowl on his face made Elizabeth wonder how much he witnessed.

"Forgive me for interrupting. I wish to speak with Stephen of a matter of great importance," he said softly.

Herald scuffed his shoe absent mindedly and gave a slight bow, while Elizabeth curtsied deep. Stephen bade them to excuse him and followed his best friend back into the house. The journey to Sir Caldwell's den was long and tedious as Arthur struggled with his crutches. It was obvious that he longed for more mobility than his body had stamina for. Stephen questioned why he had not sent a servant to summon him, but Arthur only grunted as he continued his journey.

Sir Caldwell waited in his den with two glasses of brandy poured and ready to extend to the new arrivals. He watched as Arthur laboriously positioned himself on the divan and winced every time the injured man winced.

"Lord Carlson, please be seated," Sir Caldwell said in a tone that was a cross between jovial and wary. "I believe we have news that will come as a great shock to you, but as a joy as well."

Having his fears of a confrontation with Arthur over Elizabeth's hand being removed, Stephen sank gratefully into the nearest chair. Its rich, buttery leather felt smooth and inviting to his touch. Arthur's eyes were moist and his hand was shaking as he lifted his glass to his lips. Stephen wondered if his friend's condition was from fatigue or devastation over the loss of Elizabeth. He wondered, once again, how much Arthur heard.

Seeing Arthur's state, Sir Caldwell cleared his throat and then took it upon himself to initiate the conversation with Stephen.

"My dear Mr. Moore, if you do not mind I shall take over?"

he said as he looked to Arthur for permission. When Arthur nodded gratefully he continued. "Lord Carlson...it appears we have a situation about us that I must confess I would never have dreamed would be something that I would have dealt with in my lifetime."

Stephen looked at his friend anxiously. What happened while he was in the room alone with Paulette and Mrs. Moore?

"While Arthur was alone with Mrs. Moore, it seems they had a bit of a... should I say... discussion... over Paulette's welfare," Sir Caldwell continued. When Stephen made move to stand he motioned him to remain seated. "This actually turned out to be a good thing. For during the course of their heated conversation a very important secret came forth. It is one that promises to alter the lives of many for the better." Stephen tossed his brandy down his throat and accepted Sir Caldwell's gesture for a refill while he waited for him to continue. Seeing no tasteful way to present the information, Sir Caldwell blurted it out in blunt fashion. "The fact is, my dear man, that Mrs. Moore married James Moore while carrying the child of another."

Stephen looked at Arthur, bewildered. What was Sir Caldwells saying?

"'Tis a shock, is it not?" Arthur choked out. "All these years... all these damnable years that I have suffered with desire... with a love like no other... for a woman who I thought was my blood. All these years that I have chastised myself for my impure thoughts. All these years when I could have been with the one woman I truly loved... all these years... all these years!"

Stephen rushed over to Arthur's side in time to catch him when he stood in anger only to fall off balance. He could not blame his friend for being angry. It was such a cruel trick to be played on two people who had such obvious love for one another.

"Why did she not tell you?" Stephen asked, still stunned by the news.

"Apparently my father tried several times, but she stopped him," Arthur growled resentfully. "She did not want to taint her good name in Savannah society."

"So, why now?" Stephen asked.

"Because now she is saddled with a daughter that no one of good stature will want. That is why," Arthur roared ferociously.

"I see," Stephen said quietly.

He could not argue such a point, for he knew it to be the truth. Only a man who truly loved a woman would take her in after she lived with a savage and shared his bed, even if it was against her will.

"I will take her and love her, no matter what," Arthur said with a voice that was rich and husky. "I will love her 'til the day I die, no matter what. That poor excuse for a mother knows that. That is why she told me. She wants me to marry Paulette and take her away from here where no one will know her shame. Or should I say Margaret's shame."

Sir Caldwell cleared his throat. He was clearly uncomfortable with the way the conversation was going.

"Where will you go?" Stephen asked.

Knowing how much he loved Paulette, Stephen naturally assumed that Arthur was going to do just what Margaret Moore requested.

"I have no thoughts," Arthur said as he tugged at his wig, "I was born and raised in Georgia. I have only known plantation life. We would have to start over elsewhere... but where? How far away is far enough to spare Paulette the shame of gossip?"

Stephen scratched his chin in earnest contemplation. He wanted nothing more than to help his friend at such a time as this. He contemplated suggesting England, but the gossip ties between the newly emancipated colonies and their former mother country were remarkably thick and he was certain it would not take long for the scandal to follow them, should they choose to settle there. The only factor that spared dear Elizabeth from such talk was that she traveled under an assumed name, with only a very frightened doctor and his scoundrel of a lawyer brother -cowering as they awaited their fate- knowing the truth. Fortunately, they were smart enough to recognize the value of their silence. No, it had to be someplace where Arthur and Paulette could start fresh. Completely fresh.

"Jamaica!" Stephen blurted out, noticeably pleased with his idea. "I will trade my tobacco plantation in Jamaica for your cotton plantation here in Georgia."

Sir Caldwell jumped out of his chair and paced the room.

"By golly, 'tis a bloody amazing idea!" he bellowed with delight.

Arthur looked at his friend in silence. The tears of fear, frustration, relieve and finally joy rolled down his face. He wiped them away shamelessly, verbally making note that he shed more tears these past weeks than he had in his entire life.

Sir Caldwell looked away, feeling mildly embarrassed by such a display of emotion, but Stephen saw fit to hold his friend instead. He knew the emotionally tortured man endured so much more than one man should endure and it was a good thing to allow him the release he needed. It could only do him good.

"You truly are a friend," Arthur choked.

"You truly are my brother," Stephen whispered as he hugged Arthur tightly. Trading his plantation in Jamaica with Arthur served more than one need. Not only was he happy that Arthur was finally able to love Paulette in the manner that he had tortuously desired to do for so long, but the matter of Elizabeth no longer stood between them and their friendship. Admittedly, it would be far easier to remain his friend if he did not have to see him in the company of his wife often and be reminded of the fact that he knew Elizabeth intimately. His friendship was strong, but that would have been a definite test of it.

When the emotion of the room settled enough to discuss the particulars, the men put their heads together to come up with the most efficient way to make the transfer of property in a manner that would be fair and legal. Midway through their planning Arthur stopped to question Stephen about Elizabeth.

After Stephen assured Arthur that he and Elizabeth were reunited and would be discussing the particulars with Sir Caldwell on how to legalize their marriage, he assured him that he held no malice toward him for what occurred while he was under the false impression of Elizabeth's identity. He even teased him about falling for his beautiful wife.

Arthur smiled. Somehow this hellish nightmare they all suffered through finished with a happy ending.

THIRTY-TWO

The church bells echoed across the plantation grounds as they announced the happy reunion of Elizabeth and Stephen. Elizabeth somehow found it in her heart to spend time with Paulette and form some semblance of a friendship with the much changed socialite. This was something that pleased both Stephen and Arthur greatly.

Paulette recovered from her injuries enough to attend the wedding. Although still sore and subdued, she managed to carry herself as efficiently as any lady of Savannah society might in her condition while she held Arthur's arm on her left and her mother's arm on her right.

Arthur and Margaret managed to work out a truce as well as an arrangement for her funds to continue to be sent to her trust from his new plantation in Jamaica. She had no desire to visit such a barbaric island, which suited him just fine.

Now that his sister was settled in her rightful place at her husband's side, Herald was ready to brave the formidable ocean waters and return to England. Not only did he have an estate to claim, but he would need his education to assist him in his duties as Stephen's right hand man with his massive English estates, as well as the plantations in Georgia. If Herald knew his brother-by-law like he felt he did, there would be more properties to come.

Elizabeth requested they have a quiet dinner to celebrate that evening in the Caldwell's formal dining room rather than the traditional formal reception. The last year was a whirlwind of excitement and emotion for her and she looked forward to stability, peace, and tranquility. She left the church on her husband's arm, impishly whispering the suggestion that they sneak off briefly to their rooms.

On their way, they were greeted by Anna and a very bubbly baby James. Stephen held the infant and played with his little hands.

"We shall have to find a way for him to see Arthur on occasion," Stephen offered.

Elizabeth looked confused.

"If you wish, my love," she said. "I suppose it would be nice for him to know the family's best friend. In fact, I was thinking we might baptize him before they set sail and ask them to be his godparents. Do you agree?"

"I am not sure I follow you," Stephen mused. "Why would you ask his father to be his godfather?"

When Stephen expressed his thoughts that James was the name of Arthur's father and since Elizabeth had been with Arthur for so many months he naturally assumed Elizabeth had born Arthur's child, she burst out laughing.

"Look closer, silly man," she said. "Do you not realize you are holding your own flesh and blood?"

After first chastising Stephen for his inability at math, Elizabeth explained that James was also the name of the very kind slave who carried her off in the middle of the night to save her son from being born into slavery.

Elated with the realization that he was a father, Stephen twirled the delighted James high in the air. He remembered meeting the very slave that Elizabeth named his son after. He gave him and his wife bread from their food supply and questioned if he was doing the right thing. Holding his son in his arms now he felt his life was complete. He had done the right thing helping the runaway slaves. In fact, he should have done more.

The following morning Stephen, Arthur, and Herald met with Sir Caldwell behind closed doors. To the old gentleman's delight, they inquired about what part they could play in his mission of mercy.

When you don't find Ailene Frances with her nose buried in a romance novel, you can find her sitting at her computer creating one. An incurable romantic, she loves romance novels of all genre. Be it historical, contemporary, fantasy, paranormal, or true to life, as long as there's a charismatic love situation in the story… she's hooked!

A prolific writer, she authors under multiple pen names in accordance to genre:

Ailene Frances: contemporary and historical romance
Eileen Sheehan: paranormal romance
E. F. Sheehan: alternative romance and drama
Lena Sheehan: self-help and holistic

You can keep abreast of what's happening with her, as well as when new works are being published at:

www.ailenefrances.info.
or
www.sheehan-author.info

A SNEAK PEEK AT PAPER WIDOW
by
Ailene Frances

ONE

The sun rose only an hour earlier, yet it already shone upon the pines with an intensity that denoted the promise of yet another scorching day. Squirrels and chipmunks scurried about in an effort to accomplish their tasks before they were forced to seek shelter from the harshness of the Indian Summer sun.

Elise bent down and carefully relieved her shoulders of the burdensome yoke balancing the water buckets she faithfully hauled from the nearby creek twice a day. Her work worn hands rested on her slender hips as she twisted and bent in different directions to help work out the tightness in her body that was the result of yet another fitful sleep.

For what seemed like the millionth time, she lamented over blindly responding to the advertisement in the Matrimonial News for mail order brides in the west. She was so eager to escape the mundane existence of the Boston Brahmin society that, when the advertisement crossed her path, she rushed to respond with little thought or investigation about who would be waiting for her on the opposite end of the correspondence, what she'd be walking into or what she was leaving behind. She also never questioned just how a copy of the Matrimonial News made it into the Joselyn family parlor.

Now, finding herself alone, penniless, living in a shanty that wouldn't even qualify for an outhouse at home, and ill equipped for the winter that lay ahead, she had plenty of time to ponder this fact; as well as her foolishness.

She understood her foolishness to some degree. She was young; just barely seventeen. Seventeen-year-old women of privilege weren't worldly enough to truly understand the happenings beyond their small social circle.

She'd enjoyed a year of flirtation after her debutante ball before her father announced she'd had an excellent offer for a match with Judd Turnham. Judd was fifteen years her senior, barely reached her height when she wore flat heeled slippers, and had a paunchy middle that spoke of the life of privilege he led. Sure, he was part of the richest family in the Brahmin elite and was due to inherit it all when his ailing father passed, but the thought of his overly soft, stubby fingers touching her the way a man was allowed to touch a wife was more than she could tolerate. It was bad enough when he stole a kiss while escorting her through the gardens and she had to force back the bile that threatened to project up her esophagus. The memory of his acute halitosis and abundant nose hair would probably haunt her forever. So what if the cowboys of the west were notorious for their lack of social etiquette, she'd rather have a tough, virile, and socially inept cowboy than stinky, paunchy Judd any day.

The photograph and description the matchmaker, Eliza Farnham, showed her of Douglas Meacham was so appealing, she made her decision to marry him by proxy that very afternoon. It was done in secrecy, with only the witnesses provided by Eliza to validate its authenticity.

Douglas was a twenty-seven-year-old civil war veteran from Pennsylvania who'd gone west to prospect for gold. He mined long enough to accrue a small financial safety net and acquire a respectable piece of land to ranch in northern Texas. He boasted a small herd of cattle, a solid barn that housed a hearty pig, a milking cow and some chickens, a robust garden, and the beginnings of a house that was strategically placed on the land to allow plenty of room to add on when the children arrived. It lacked only a wife to make it complete.

What started out as a dream adventure quickly turned into a nightmare. Since she'd never had the occasion to ride in the public car of a train before, she wasn't prepared for the grueling, filthy accommodations that were kept hidden from those fortunate to warrant a private car. What little funds she'd managed to squirrel away during her whirlwind departure were stolen from her reticule while she slept. She'd tucked some of her prize jewelry in her travel bag, which went missing after a stop in Oklahoma. By the time she was ready to debark, she had only the clothes on her back and the jewelry on her person. She quickly sold the jewelry to pay for passage on the stagecoach that would take her to the Texas territory of Wichita Falls where Douglas was to meet her.

She spent the entire time on the dusty trek to Wichita Falls fretting about the poor impression she'd make to her new husband because of the unfortunate circumstances. She'd read about husbands having their marriages annulled due to false representation and wondered if the same would happen to her once Douglas took a look at her bedraggled person. There was nothing she could do about it. Her future was in the hands of fate. She just hoped fate would be a little kinder than it'd been so far.

That wasn't to be.

She squatted to reposition the yoke on her shoulders and slowly stood up, being careful not to spill the life sustaining liquid in the interim. Her thighs were much stronger since she arrived three months earlier, making her movements look smooth and easy.

As she crossed what constituted a small courtyard for the humble ranch, she spotted a horse and rider off in the distance. She didn't need to strain to see who it might be. She knew it was Nellie Wilson performing her weekly check.

Elise didn't know where she'd be, had it not been for Nellie's kindness. They'd stumbled upon each other by chance at the station. Elise was searching the streets for Douglas and Nellie was scoping the travelers for her niece, Elizabeth.

Elise met Elizabeth on the train going west. They were about the same age and from similar family backgrounds, but that's where it ended. Elizabeth's father died the year before. Her mother was sending her to live with her mother's sister, Nellie, while she sought a replacement for her late husband. Not only did Elizabeth think finding a husband would be a daunting task amongst the few who survived the war between the states, but the concept of being shoved out of the way in order for her mother to have a better advantage in snaring a man was revolting. She considered her mother far too old for such shenanigans. Since they were financially well off, she couldn't comprehend her mother's neediness.

Reluctant to leave the luxuries and advanced society of the east, Elizabeth monitored her surroundings carefully as the train continued west. By the time they reached Oklahoma, she'd seen enough to make her decide to take matters into her own hands. She bid Elise goodbye, wished her well, and asked her to tell her Aunt Nellie that she was sorry, but she wouldn't be joining her after all before she purchased a ticket back to Boston.

Nellie reciprocated Elise's disappointing news with some devastating news of her own. Douglas was found dead on the road to town just that morning.

Elise was a widow.

"Hello!" shouted Nellie as she reined her mare up next to the hitching post near the front porch.

"I made apple pie," Elise said as she poured the contents of her buckets into a large barrel. "It's still warm."

"What time did you get up to fuss like that?" Nellie asked with a shake of the head.

"I need better bedding," Elise complained as she held the small of her back and motioned for Nellie to follow her inside.

"That Eliza Farnham should be shot for her deceit," Nellie huffed as she scuffed the dirt from the soles of her boots on the edge of the roughhewn porch before following Elise into the cool shack.

"I'd settle for reimbursement of my money so I could buy passage back home," Elise sighed. "I've been looking and looking for any money or gold Douglas might have hidden away, but, so far, no luck."

"Are you sure he had any?" Nellie asked as she helped herself to a slice of pie.

"There's water in the basin to wash your hands with," Elise said in a flat tone.

"You're such a dandy girl, ain't ya?" Nellie chuckled as

she made her way to the basin and immersed both hands into the shallow bowl. Her head twisted and turned, as if she was looking for something. "I thought there was a spring out back."

"He never got around to piping it into the house," Elise said wistfully.

"That would sure make life easier," Nellie said thoughtfully.

"I make two trips a day to the creek," Elise volunteered. "Sometimes three."

"Good heavens, gal," Nellie gasped. "Whatever do ya do with all that water?"

"Make tea, for one thing," Elise said as she reached for the can she kept her tea leaves in and opened the lid. "I found this on the back of the top shelf," she said as she pointed to a wooden shelf placed high enough on the wall over the stove to necessitate a stool to reach the things placed on it. "Douglas had a decent supply of tea and coffee. This smells like home."

"I ain't never developed a taste for tea," Nellie said as she wrinkled her nose and then popped a finger full of pie in her mouth. "It won't keep your belly full in the winter months," Nellie scolded. "What do you plan on doing when the snow falls?"

"The garden is yielding a goodly amount of crops," Elise said as she continued to prepare the tea. "I've also collected a fair amount of apples and nuts. Do you want me to brew some coffee?"

"Do ya have a root cellar?" Nellie asked as she held up her hand and shook her head to indicate 'no' to Elise's offer to make coffee for her.

"There's a large hole dug in the ground that's covered with wooden planks," Elise said. "I think that's what Douglas used for a root cellar because I found some old potatoes, onions, and squash in there."

"Any amount of snowfall on those planks and those skinny arms of yours won't be able to lift them off to get to your food," Nellie mused. "What about heat? Have ya been able to handle the axe and cut yourself some wood for the winter?"

"I need to find the means to leave here before I die," Elise said as she poured hot water from the kettle she kept hot on the stove into the tin pot she used to brew tea in.

"Maybe ya should winter with me and Jake," Nellie offered.

"What about the animals?" Elise asked.

"I thought ya was going to sell them off and use the money as part of your passage home," Nellie said.

"I rode out to see the herd yesterday," Elise said. "It looks like it's shrinking."

"Probably thieves," Nellie offered. "The word's out that you're alone. If ya don't sell those beasts soon, there'll be nothing to round up come time."

Elise pushed a stray hair behind her ear and said, "If I ever get back home, I will never complain about being bored again."

TWO

Nate adjusted his coat collar as he stepped out of the three story, faded red brick building into the crisp fall afternoon air. There was a distinctive skip in his step. He was just given his first big assignment as an employee of the Pinkerton National Detective Agency. His co-workers were Joseph Kennedy and Oliver Sullivan, which suited him just fine.

Joseph and Oliver served with him under the command of Lieutenant Colonel Alexander Biddle at the battle of Gettysburg. Experiences like that bring people together. That along with the fact that they grew up in a small hamlet just south of Philadelphia as friends since early youth practically guaranteed to be an efficient working team. At least, that's what Alan Pinkerton thought.

"Kimble, wait up!" Joseph called as he followed Nate down the stone steps.

"Can you believe the luck of it? I just can't seem to shake your sorry ass," Nate laughed.

"We make the complete package, my good man," Joseph said with a grin.

"Where's Sullivan?" Nate asked as he looked in the direction they just came from.

"He's got a woman to appease," Joseph said. "Damned nuisance, if you ask me. You can't do this job with a woman hanging on your arm."

"Not well, I don't think," Nate said thoughtfully.

"You aren't gonna go get yourself all tied up with one, are you?" Joseph asked in earnest.

"Lilith cured me, but good," Nate grumbled.

"She sure was a sneaky one," Joseph agreed.

"Damned right," Nate nodded.

"I hear he drinks pretty heavily," Joseph said in a hushed tone.

302

"She wanted to money and the prestige of his family," Nate shrugged.

"Yeah, the name," Joseph agreed.

"She deserves what she got," Nate said bitterly.

"I still can't believe she wrote to you after she married that shit head," Joseph said.

"He saved me," Nate pondered aloud. "I should thank him."

"Yeah," Joseph agreed. "I feel a little sorry for him. All I did was witness the deceit and I'm cured of ever wanting a woman."

"At least not for a long time," Nate said thoughtfully.

"Never," Joseph reiterated.

They walked back to their hotel in silence while their minds worked making lists of what needed to be done before they boarded the train headed for Oklahoma the following afternoon.

Since the short notice was an inconvenience for Nate and Joseph, they could only imagine the impact it had on Sullivan. Nate shuddered at the thought of how Alice Smyth would respond to the news. She'd made it perfectly clear that she expected a wedding before the New Year. This assignment was surely going to twist her pantaloons. He wouldn't put it past the spoiled socialite not to confront old Pinkerton himself on the matter.

Yet another reason to be grateful he was single and free.

"This assignment will change our careers. Let's get a drink to celebrate," Joseph suggested.

"I have some things to take care of before I leave. A year is a long time," Nate said. "How about we meet up for dinner and then we can celebrate?"

"That's probably a good idea," Joseph said with clear disappointment. "I have some things to take care of too."

"Did you get fitted for your suit?" Nate asked warily.

"When did you do that?" Joseph asked with surprise.

"Yesterday," Nate replied.

"Hell, you didn't get assigned until today," Joseph complained.

"I keep my ears to the ground," Nate said with a grin.

"Tell Mr. Simon to put it on my bill."

"I can pay for it myself," Joseph said defensively.

"I'll expect to be paid back out of your first paycheck," Nate said firmly.

He really didn't expect to see any money from Joseph, but he didn't mind. Just a month earlier, Nate became the most financially fortunate one of the three friends, with Oliver running second.

Nate was raised in what would be deemed as quality surroundings in the eyes of Philadelphia society. Although he ran in a circle of socialites, he was considered to be on the outskirts of that circle; which was one of the things that goaded Lilith. When he received a visit from the Miller Legal Firm informing him of an inheritance from an uncle on his mother's side, all that changed; or would have, had Nate wanted to make the truth of his inheritance public. Richard Adams was wealthy rancher who never married or had children. Since Nate was the closest relation, the fortune he'd amassed -which included an impressive amount of money along with an equally impressive cattle ranch on the Oklahoma/ Texas border- was all left to him.

Oliver, whose family operated an apothecary and was considered of socially respectable means, had always been considered the privileged one. He also ran on the outskirts of the Philadelphia society circle with Nate, but his family's fortune paled in comparison to the wealth Nate inherited.

After learning of Nate's good fortune, Oliver was quick to point out that, had Lilith only fulfilled her promise of waiting for him to return from war, she could have lived wherever and however she desired. This observation stirred panic in Nate over the potential of being taken in by another deceitful female seeking his fortune under the guise of loving him. Right then and there he swore his friends to secrecy. With the exception of Mr. Miller of the Miller Legal Firm, Joseph and Oliver were the only ones who knew the true value of his inheritance and he intended to keep it that way. Lilith's lies and deceit had truly left their scars.

The reports provided to Nate about his uncle's ranch led

him to believe it was in good hands with the current overseer. This was assuring since, from the way things looked, it would be a few years before he'd be able to inspect the place. Still, believing the old adage, "When the cat's away, the mice will play," Nate decided to have his lawyer plant a ranch hand in the mix who would provide regular reports on the happenings of the ranch.

He and Joseph parted company outside of the tailor shop. Nate reiterated the fact that he expected to be billed for Joseph's suit. After a little more grumbling, Joseph agreed and walked inside.

Nate smiled with satisfaction at the thought of being able to help his life-long friend. The war took its toll on everyone, but none more than the disadvantaged. Joseph's father was killed during the second year of fighting. Less than a year later, his mother died of consumption; leaving Joseph's fourteen-year-old sister and ten-year-old brother to do the best they could to keep their little farm operating enough to support them until Joseph returned from fighting to bring some semblance of normality back into their lives. Caring for his siblings when he was barely able to care for himself was a burden Nate's twenty-two-year-old friend said little about. He didn't need to. Nate had eyes to see and ears to hear. He knew fully the struggles Joseph went through without so much as a complaint.

He reached the office of the Miller Legal Firm and stopped outside long enough to pull his mind into focus on the matter at hand. He wanted to have his affairs in order as best he could before he embarked on an assignment that would demand his full attention. He also had a family depending on him. Although his mother was still alive and well, she also became a widow during the war and both of his two sisters lost their fiancé's. This left three needy women looking to him for comfort and support. His inheritance couldn't have come at a better time. He wanted to arrange for a trust fund to be created for their care, as well as a Last Will and Testament drawn up in the event he didn't make it out of this assignment alive.

THREE

Elise accepted the money Jake received for the sale of her cattle to a nearby rancher with genuine gratitude. He'd managed to round up enough livestock to sell to get her the funds needed to return back east. Now, she just had to make the arrangements. Why she didn't ask him for help when she first arrived, was a mystery.

"So, Mrs. Meacham, we'll be losing ya soon," Jake said as he mounted his horse. "That's a damned shame. I got used to looking at that pretty face of yours with my morning coffee."

"Such teasing," Elise giggled. "I want to go to town and wire my father before I do anything else."

"Wantin' to let him know your comin'?" Jake asked.

"I want to see if I'm welcome back," Elise confessed.

"I can't imagine no pa not lettin' his little girl back into his home," Jake mused.

"My father has strong opinions on things," she explained. "Not only did I go against his wishes when I secretly married Douglas by proxy, but I embarrassed him within our social circle. Judd Turnham comes from the most prominent family in Boston. He was the one my father wanted me to marry, not Douglas."

"Just proves you ain't no fortune hunter," he said with a nod. "Tell the missus I'll be home for supper."

Elise shaded her eyes from the piercing late morning sun as she watched her rugged, yet gentle host ride off to meet with the other riders who waited near the ranch entrance. The intense Texas sun and heat was something she was sure not to miss. Jake told her it was a tradeoff. The Texas heat for the Boston winters. At that point, Elise wasn't sure which was worse.

"So, he's gone?" Nellie asked as she walked and stood next to Elise.

"Just now," Elise replied with a sigh.

"Not to worry gal," Nellie assured her. "My Jake's a tough old buzzard. It'll take more than a few renegade Indians to put him in his grave."

"I'm not used to this," Elise complained.

"You've been out here half a year, gal," Nellie mused. "It would do you to toughen up a bit."

"I have the money to return home," Elise said softly.

"That's a fine thing," Nellie said with a smile. "I'll miss ya."

"I'm not sure what to do," Elise confessed.

"What are ya talking about?" Nellie said with surprise. "You're gonna go to town and purchase the passage back home. That's what you're gonna do."

"What if I'm not welcome?" Elise asked with trepidation.

"I can't imagine a pa not letting his little girl come home. No matter what she did," Nellie said.

"Jake said the same thing," Elise mused.

"We're a lot alike," Nellie chuckled. "Comes with living together so long."

"How long have you been married?" Elise asked.

"Nigh on twenty years," Nellie replied wistfully. "Just me and Jake for nigh on twenty years."

"I'm sorry you never had the children you wanted," Elise said with genuine affection.

"That's nothing for you to be sorry for," Nellie said as she turned back toward the house. "I boiled some water for tea. Now that you're fixin' to leave, I'm finally getting the hang of drinking it. It figures."

"I won't be leaving right away," Elise said as she hastened to catch up with her friend. "I want to send a telegraph to father before I do anything to make sure I'm welcome back."

"That's something I'll never understand," Nellie said as she slowly shook her head.

"It isn't father as much as it is the society we live in," Elise explained. "He arranged for me to marry into the wealthiest family in Boston. It was quite a boon for our family. We're in the top percentile of wealth in Boston. Under normal circumstances it would be difficult to find a match to compare with our status without having to go outside of Boston; maybe even to Europe. The war was unforgiving and cared not whether the soldier was of high society or low. It left the selection of eligible men severely lacking. Father hates to travel long distances. Pairing me up with Judd was, to him, the perfect solution."

"Not to you," Nellie said softly.

"Oh Nellie, I still cringe when I remember that awful kiss he stole in our garden. It makes me want to run to the creek and wash every time. I can't imagine him doing more," Elise said with angst as she sat down at the small wooden table in the center of the large room that served as both the kitchen and the sitting area.

"Do ya even know what that more might be?" Nellie said with a chuckle as she poured hot water from the kettle onto the tea leaves she'd placed in the pot she normally used for brewing coffee. "Ya only have a paper marriage, after all."

"Such things aren't spoken about," Elise gasped.

Nellie tossed her head back and emitted a hearty laugh.

"This ain't polite society, missy," she said jovially. "You'd be surprised what's talked about in these parts."

"I- I guess," Elise stammered.

"Did you mother ever talk to you about it?" Nellie asked with genuine curiosity.

"That's something we do on the eve of our wedding," Elise said.

"Since ya married on the sly and then snuck out of town, ya never had the talk," Nellie continued.

"I don't need it now," Elise said with embarrassment. "I'm fine the way I am."

"I guess ya don't," Nellie said with amusement, "but if ya ever do need it, I'm here to help."

"That's kind of you, Nellie. Truly it is… I think we should change the subject now," Elise said with a voice that showed her frustration.

"Do you plan on going back to your ranch to harvest the rest of those vegetables?" Nellie asked while she slid a tea cup in front of Elise.

Grateful for the reprieve of a topic that made her extremely uncomfortable, Elise nodded. She stood up to relieve Nellie of the makeshift tea pot, secured a small piece of cheesecloth over the spout to catch the loose tea leaves and poured the aromatic liquid into their cups.

When Nellie's gnarled hands lifted the delicate cup to her lips, Elise noticed a chip on its edge. She sighed. Nellie and Jake were born and raised in the Wichita Falls territory of Texas. They knew nothing of the wealth and privileges Elise grew up taking for granted except from the little bit she'd told them. How Elise longed to have them experience it, even just a little. She made a mental note to send a new set of china to them once she was home and settled. She'd also send them some proper furnishings. Just because they lived in a small, two room house with a loft, didn't mean they couldn't furnish it with quality pieces. She smiled when she thought of their reaction to receiving such finery.

"Take the wagon when you go," Nellie said.

"I can't drive it well," Elise admitted.

"It will make it easier to transport the vegetables. I noticed some good sized squash the last time I was there," Nellie said.

"When did you go there?" Elise asked.

"It's become a habit," Nellie said with a shrug as she sipped at her tea. "You'll need to fix those hands of yours before you reenter society."

FOUR

Nate pulled his travel bag from beneath his seat as the conductor announced the upcoming stop to be the settlement of Oklahoma City. It was the end of the line. He'd ridden the railway for the last few months on the lookout for the Jefferson gang with no luck. They were always one step ahead.

The railway extension across Oklahoma was still young with its fair share of perils to contend with. The Pinkertons were there to provide safety against bank robberies, while the army spent its fair share of time riding the rails to protect against Indian uprisings. The Indians were quiet the last few months, but the robberies still occurred now and then; and always when the Pinkertons weren't aboard. Although more dangerous, Nate and his buddies decided to split up so that there would be a Pinkerton on every run.

They'd studied the pattern of the robberies and came to the conclusion that it was the Jefferson gang behind them all. If intel was correct, the gang consisted of six ex-confederates. The two who carried the most influence in the operation were Tom and Daniel Jefferson; hence, the Jefferson Gang.

The next run the Pinkertons were expected to be on required all three of them. It was to carry the month's pay for the workers who diligently struggled to take the railway further west. Prior to that, the hits consisted of relieving unsuspecting passengers of their money and finery. Sometimes it was done by gunpoint with the masked gang frightening the passengers into submission and other times a few of the gang members boarded the train as passengers and carefully stole from prominent looking travelers who were sleeping or had their guard down enough to not notice money or jewels being taken from their bags, reticules, or even their person. There were times when they went so far as to relieve their victims of their entire luggage. This type of thievery was more common, as well as more difficult to spot. The only good thing about it was that the safety of lives wasn't at stake.

This wouldn't be the case on this next run.

Nate stepped off the station platform and headed for the hotel where he knew his two friends waited for him. He had a plan that he was eager to discuss with them.

Joseph leaned against the wall of the newly constructed building while enjoying his cigarette. When he spotted Nate approaching, his slender lips spread into a warm smile as he took one long draw on his poorly rolled cigarette before dropping it onto the dusty ground and snuffing it with the sole of his newly shined boot.

They'd only recently decided to take shifts on the train and he found his time off to be seriously lacking. The people he'd met in the barely settled Oklahoma City were folks who participated in the land run. They came from varied backgrounds, but mainly were southerners who lost their homes or fortunes during the war and sought a new start. Their reception of an ex-union soldier turned Pinkerton was far from welcoming. That, combined with the lack of eastern amenities, was enough to make Joseph long for the companionship of his buddies; as well as his life back east.

"I can't wait to finish this assignment," he said as he fell in step with Nate on their way to the saloon. "I hope the next one is back east."

"What's wrong with the west?" Nate asked with surprise.

"You haven't spent much time off that train," Joseph replied. "Wait 'til you do."

"Why?" Nate asked. "What's wrong?"

"I just don't blend with these folks is all," Joseph replied.

"They seem good enough," Nate said as he pushed through the door of the saloon. He stood a moment while he waited for his eyes to adjust to the new lighting and then moved to the end of the bar.

"They aren't keen on Yankees," Joseph volunteered.

"Why do you tell them?" Nate asked.

"You want me to hide what I am?" Joseph asked with surprise. "Besides, I don't talk like them."

"You were a union solder. Now, you're a Pinkerton," Nate said firmly. "The war is over."

"Soldiers passed through a few days ago," Joseph said as he signaled the bartender to bring him and Nate beer. "They say there's trouble with the Indians just south of here."

"That's going to make what I suggest more difficult," Nate said with a slow shake of his head.

"You got new plans?" Joseph asked.

"Where's Sullivan?" Nate asked as he looked around the empty saloon. "I want him here when I tell about it."

"He managed to find a proper young lady named Annabelle Wilson. She lives back east, but is here visiting. They're on a picnic," Joseph said with a chuckled.

"What about Alice?" Nate asked with surprise.

"His life's too complicated for me," Joseph said firmly.

"When do you expect him back?" Nate asked.

"He knew you were coming in on the train, so I imagine he'll come around any time now," Joseph replied.

"Good," Nate said as he tossed back the remnants of his beer. "I'm going to go freshen up. You and Sullivan meet me for dinner and we'll go over things."

"I hate surprises!" Joseph called out as he watched Nate saunter out onto the street.

***

Dinner consisted of pepper pot soup, fire roasted potatoes, boiled baby onions with a cream sauce, and boiled ham. Nate wasn't a big fan of ham, but it was either that or the roast chicken. He'd had time to observe the look of the chicken coming out of the kitchen while waiting for his buddies to arrive and determined it was more the size of a pigeon than a chicken. Since he was hungry, he settled for the ham. Joseph and Oliver had the same.

Now, his two friends sat sipping on coffee while they patiently waited for Nate to share his idea with them.

"I have it on good authority that the Jefferson gang is hold up about a day's ride from here; maybe two.," Nate began. "I thought we could go check things out. Maybe we can catch these guys outside a robbery and clean up this job once and for all."

"It sure would be nice to get back east," Oliver said.

"I second that," added Joseph.

"When is the shipment coming through?" Joseph asked.

"You don't know?" Nate asked with surprise.

"They're not telling anyone," Oliver said in a hushed tone, "for fear of it leaking out. We'll only be told the day we have to board."

Nate thought about this new bit of information and scowled. "Without knowing the schedule, we can't very well take off for a few days to round these fellas up."

"So, we hold off?" Oliver asked.

"I wonder if we told the sheriff of our plans if we'd be able to get the schedule then," Joseph said.

"We can try," Nate said. "After all, if we get these guys then there's no need for us to even be on that train."

FIVE

Elise hugged Nellie one last time before boarding the stagecoach. Although she wasn't looking forward to the grueling journey back east, she was definitely excited about leaving the hardships of the undeveloped west behind her. Her father, although stern with his words, assured her she would be welcome once again in his home. He'd even gone so far as to send her the funds for her return passage, along with extra for necessities along the way.

Since all she had from the wardrobe she'd brought west with her was the traveling gown on her back when she arrived - and she had no desire to disclose to her family the simple gingham gown she wore daily that Nellie was kind enough to provide for her- she immediately purchased a few well made gowns, a hat, and other items to complete a modest, yet quality wardrobe. Once she was back home, she had no doubt her father would outfit her properly so that she could return to society with her head held high.

She found it difficult to believe that only eight months had passed since she'd secretly become Mrs. Douglas Meacham by proxy and allowed Eliza Farnham to quietly whisk her away. It felt more like eight years.

After waving goodbye to her dear friend until she was no longer in sight, Elise settled back into the seat and closed her eyes while she remembered the comfort and luxuries of her home back east. After being forced to sleep on a thin, straw and corn husk mattress for so long, she vowed to climb into the thick feather mattress on her four-post bed and sleep for a week.

Her fellow passengers were a warm and friendly older couple. They were also headed for the train station in Oklahoma City so she was fairly confident her ride would be easy and safe.

This wasn't always the case with a woman traveling alone on a stagecoach in the west. Passengers of public transit were forced to ride alongside whoever happened to purchase a ticket. She considered herself fortunate that the three of them filled the coach fairly well and there was only room for one or two more passengers for the duration of their journey.

Guilt crept in as she thought about leaving Nellie alone to worry about where Jake might be and when he'd be getting home. Nellie made light of the subject, but, since it was two days since he left on yet another run with the posse to hunt down the renegade Indians and still hadn't returned, Elise knew better than to think Nellie wasn't worried. She offered to postpone her trip until Jake returned, but Nellie wouldn't hear of it. She pointed out that Elise's family was eagerly awaiting her return and would be worried sick if she wasn't on the train as expected. She assured her that, although Jake came home every night for supper no matter who he was with or what he was doing, she still wasn't worried. She assumed they'd gotten a good trail of the Indians and decided to just stick it out and get it over and done with once and for all. Those renegades were rustling far too much of their cattle for anyone to sit quiet and let them continue. It had to be stopped.

The horses were fresh and healthy so the coach made good time. They pulled into the way station at Lawton in time for a late supper of mutton stew and warm biscuits. After a day of dusty, rutted roads -with only an occasional stop to allow them to stretch their legs and relieve themselves- and a small wedge of cheese, bread, and water to stave off the hunger, the stew was well received.

The drivers originally planned on resting a few hours, changing horses, and then continuing on, but when they learned of the Indian trouble just two days earlier, they decided it was safer to wait until daylight to travel the stretch of land that would take them through Indian country. Elise and the other passengers agreed that it was better to be safe than sorry. Even in the daylight, they ran the risk of a raid, but at least they'd be able to see their surroundings, should they have to defend themselves. The word was that the army was in the area. Giving them another night to search for -and hopefully capture- these renegades made sense.

The arrival of three Pinkertons brought excitement into the small way station. When she looked into the handsome face of the very aloof Nate Kimble, Elise immediately regretted her decision to travel in the faded gingham gown and save her new clothes for her arrival in Boston. She smoothed her bodice, skirts, and hair as inconspicuously as she could as the Pinkertons settled in.

Elise sat quietly in the corner of the large room while she observed the newcomers who were deep in conversation with the stage coach drivers and the keeper of the way station. They all looked to be in their early to mid-twenties. They could all claim to be handsome.

The one who was introduced as Joseph Kennedy was the shorter of the three. His sandy hair was cut short and his face clean shaven. Brown eyes twinkled when he spoke, but Elise sensed there was a seriousness about him that ran deep. Oliver Sullivan was as handsome as they came and someone she was sure was popular with the ladies wherever he went. His blonde hair glistened in the firelight in a way that made his pale blue eyes look watery. His thick lips looked as if they wanted to kiss whoever he spoke to. He carried his tall, slender frame with the air of an aristocrat. Elise could easily imagine his commanding presence stealing the hearts of all the women attending one of those tedious balls she missed so much.

She found Nate Kimble to be the most striking of the three. Even after a full day's ride, his dark hair settled nicely along the collar of his Pinkerton coat. It wasn't long enough to pull back into a pique, yet it was still a good length. Perfect brows accentuated his deep set, crystal blue eyes, straight nose, and smooth, thin lips. His jaw looked strong, but not square. She was sure that if she stood next to him he'd tower over her by at least six inches. Of the three, he seemed the least impressed by the fact that she was amongst the company. Where his companions made an effort to make polite conversation with her, he openly ignored her with an attitude that bordered on disdain.

If she lamented once about not wearing her finer traveling outfit, she lamented fifty times while she made polite small talk with the rest of the room.

***

"You're being a little rude to that young widow, don't you think?" Oliver said as he stepped out onto the porch next to Nate and lit a cigarette.

"She's doing fine with the rest of you," Nate replied.

"She's a pretty thing," Oliver said. "Get her out of those rags and I'd bet she'd clean up right nice."

"Don't you have enough women to worry about?" Nate growled.

"Jealous?" Oliver chuckled.

"Fed up is more like it," Nate replied.

"I see her looking at you," Oliver said.

"The last thing I need is a penniless widow to contend with," Nate scowled. "I plan on returning east when this assignment is over."

"What's that got to do with it?" Oliver asked. "She's a widow, not a maiden. Get a good tumble out of her and then go your merry way." When Nate simply chuckled he added, "If you don't, I will."

"As if she'd have your sorry ass," Nate teased.

"She only wants you because you're playing hard to get," Oliver protested. "Women seem to love that sort of thing."

"Is that so?" Nate said as he lit another cigarette, leaned his back against the building, and raised his knee so that the sole of his boot was flat against the wall. "I'm not playing. After Lilith's little game, I have no desire to get myself entangled with a female. If I did, I can guarantee you she'd be a society woman and not some waif traveling alone on a stage coach."

"Oh ho!" Oliver laughed, "Getting a little uppity since your inheritance, eh, Kimble?"

"I did my fair share of mingling with Philadelphia society right alongside you," Nate replied. "It's only right I want my wife to be of fine stock. It's not as if I was raised a waif."

"Like Joseph?" Oliver asked.

"Now who's uppity? His parents were respectable farmers and you know it. He can't help what happened," Nate said.

"At least he still has the farm," Oliver said thoughtfully. "Those poor bastards in the south lost everything."

"Even the high society gals came down a peg," Nate observed.

"You sound so bitter," Oliver said. "It makes me sad."

"I'll get over it," Nate said as he tossed the remains of his cigarette into the night. "The wounds are too fresh, that's all."

"You had a name and money before your inheritance," Oliver said with disgust. "It just wasn't enough for that gold digger."

"Now, I could buy that husband of hers several times over," Nate said with a chuckle.

"If the chit only knew," Oliver said softly.

"She never will," Nate said. "No one will. It only brings gold diggers on your tail. You promised to keep your mouth shut and I expect you to honor that promise."

"I intend to," Oliver said as he raised his hands in the air as if to surrender. "Shit, you're touchy. Go grab that widow and get yourself a piece. It'll relax you."

"A woman shouldn't be traveling alone," Nate said with disgust. "Not a proper woman, anyway."

"She's not with that old couple?" Oliver said with surprise.'

"I didn't think so, but maybe she is," Nate said with a shrug.

"I hope not," Oliver said as he rubbed his hands together with anticipation.

"You're a dog," Nate scowled. "Remember, you're a Pinkerton."

"Easy is as easy does," Oliver said with a light hearted

tone.

"Providing she's easy," Nate said.

"I sure hope so," Oliver said as he adjusted his pants in the crotch. "I could use some relief."

"You only left that girl two days ago," Nate said with surprise.'

"What can I say?" Oliver said with a smirk and a shrug.

PAPER WIDOW IS SCHEDULED TO BE
RELEASED IN THE FALL OF 2017!

www.ingramcontent.com/pod-product-compliance
Lightning Source LLC
Chambersburg PA
CBHW031544240626
47153CB00002B/379